And on the Eighth Day She Rested

And on the Eighth Day

St. Martin's Griffin ⚹ New York

She Rested

J. D. Mason

www.stmartins.com

Library of Congress Cataloging-in-Publication Data

Mason, J. D.
    And on the eighth day she rested / J. D. Mason.—1st ed.
        p. cm.
    ISBN 0-312-30989-9
    1. Abused wives—Fiction.   2. Female friendship—Fiction. 3.   African American women—Fiction.   I. Title: And on the 8th day she rested.   II. Title.

PS3613.A817 A84 2003
813'.6—dc21

2002036892

10 9 8 7 6 5 4 3

Prologue: Truth and Consequences

HER ABUSIVE MARRIAGE WASN'T BORN OVERNIGHT. IT WAS CULtivated slowly, over the course of months and years, seasoned with dashes of insults, and pinches of open-handed slaps, occurring so gradually it was hardly noticeable. All of a sudden, Ruth realized what she'd become: a casualty of a war someone decided to call domestic violence.

Through the years she'd managed to close her eyes to images of herself as a battered woman. She'd shut out voices of experts pointing at her circumstances, calling her a victim, because that was never her posing for cameras with purple-black cheeks and eyes swollen shut by fists. Yes, she and her husband had disagreements, and yes, sometimes he'd hit her, but no, she'd never been abused. And just because Eric had hit her once, didn't mean he'd hit her again. Right? And so what if he had? That didn't mean he'd do it again. And again. And . . .

She loved Eric, more so in the beginning. He'd made it his mission in life to sweep that shy, young girl off her feet, and he did it with ease, putting forth the kind of effort for her that no one ever had before or since. She'd get off the number 42X bus on the corner of 103rd Street and California Avenue Monday through Friday at 6:27 P.M. and he'd be there just so he could walk her home. Back then, she thought it was sweet. Now she knew better. Sweet. Stalking. The line between the two isn't always so clear. Flowers and kind words had been his weapons back then. Holding her hand, taking her to the movies, stroking her hair, all for the privilege, he'd said, of drinking in the rich chocolate color of her eyes, caressing her butter soft skin, and the anticipation of losing himself between the warmth of her pretty brown thighs. Words like that kept her up all night long, replaying themselves over again in her memories like scratched records.

"Aw c'mon now, baby. You mean to tell me a pretty woman like you ain't got no man?" he'd asked sincerely, pressing her hand gently between his.

"No—I haven't met anyone," she'd responded innocently.

Eric's hazel eyes sparkled. "You jus' ain't been payin' attention. I seen the way brothas look at you when you get off that bus. Why you think I'm waitin' on you every day?" In true naive fashion, Ruth shrugged her shoulders. " 'Cause I want them to know I got my sights on you. That's why. These mothafuckas 'round here know not to mess with me"—he hesitated—"or mine." And of course, she blushed.

Eric had been her first everything. Her first boyfriend, first kiss, first lover. He'd convinced her that she was a woman even before she felt like one. What did she have to offer someone like him? He was ten years older than her, had his own credit cards, car, and an ex-wife. Ruth was eighteen, barely out of school and her grandmother's house. She worked for minimum wage as a receptionist at a law firm and lived in an atrocious little studio apartment near downtown Jacksonville. All of her life she'd been too black, too fat, and too ugly to boys, but not to him. He loved her wide hips and believed that heaven lay tucked between her large breasts. Her dark skin made his mouth water and reminded him of the homemade frosting his grandmother used to make when he was a child. To him, she was a desirable woman who needed a real man around to take care of her, and Eric quickly assumed the role of protector, teacher, dictator.

"Sometime it take a while for virgins to like fuckin', Ruthie. But you wait, baby girl. Pretty soon you goin' to like it as much as I do." He'd promised her that the first time they were intimate, and the next and even the time after that. She kept hoping he was right and that she'd come to enjoy the act as much as he seemed to, but she never did. Sex left her feeling stripped of something she could never pronounce, while it left Eric feeling like a superhero.

Her faith in him in the beginning surpassed understanding. Ruth believed that when he called her "baby," he was really saying, "I love you," and that he meant he was sorry every time he said it. There were times she believed he was sorry even when he never said a word.

Growing up was hard and growing up in a loveless, abusive marriage was harder. The conditioning that took place over the years slowly replaced her character and became her personality. Ducking and dodging cuss words and fists and shoes thrown across the room aimed at her head eventually became second nature, and living on the defensive had become a way of life. Gradually, she learned never to let her guard down, because when she did, she paid dearly for it. Every utterance from her mouth, glance in his direction, every movement, was open for interpretation that depended on his mood. "No" meant "yes" and "yes" meant "Whatever the hell you want, Eric. Whatever the hell you say, Eric." Ruth learned quickly never to raise her voice even to make a point and never to raise her eyes even to plead her case.

But for some reason, she'd still managed to find an excuse to believe in him because who else was there for her to believe in? Herself? No. Believing in Eric was easier. He was the decisive one, and knew what he wanted and exactly how he'd wanted it. He had the bigger voice, the bigger attitude, and was a master at getting his way. Every argument they'd ever had, she'd lost. Every point she'd tried to make, every amount of reason she'd ever tried to get him to see, failed and he'd win. Eventually, she stopped trying, hoping he'd feel like a fool arguing by himself. Ruth didn't think he ever did. Feel foolish, that is, because he was too busy relishing in the knowledge that he held her life in the palm of his hand from the first day they met, and that she'd given it to him freely.

But then she fell out of love with him. Ruth couldn't remember when or why it happened. It just did. Had it been the last time he threw his plate at her because he wanted his pork chops fried instead of baked? Or was it the time he'd emptied their checking account without telling her and all the checks she'd written for the bills bounced? Maybe it was the time he crawled on top of her and demanded she scream his name then call him "Daddy." No, that hadn't been it. Then she remembered. It was the last time Eric beat her with a leather belt and chased her around the house screaming obscenities while she crawled around on all fours with snot running out of her nose, trying to hide behind tables, chairs, or underneath the bed, begging him not to hit her anymore. And when he did stop, it was only because his arm was tired or he had somewhere to go. Besides, her ignorant ass wasn't doing nothing but wasting his damn time anyway. Yeah. That's probably when it happened.

Ruth was committed, though. Or maybe she should've *been* committed. Marriage meant something to her, even if it was a bad marriage, because it had been the greatest achievement of her life. She'd grown up watching her mother melt in and out of relationships with men for as long as she could remember. Ruth had adored her mother. She'd fallen in love with her every time the sun rose, but vowed never to be the kind of woman who had more men in her bed than she had fingers and toes. As soon as one catastrophe moved out, another one moved in, usually worse than the one before him, and that's not how Ruth wanted to live her life. No man had ever married Karen, but Ruth had accomplished what her mother had died trying to achieve. She had a husband, and yes, they had issues, but people were supposed to stay together and work through their issues. Love would make it all right and eventually, she and Eric would look each other in the eyes one day and realize that they were in fact soul mates, and destined to live forever in wedded bliss. She lived with that hope for years until she finally came to her senses and realized that she must've been high on crack without even knowing it because shit like that was never going to happen. Here it was, fourteen years later, and she could finally look herself in the eyes and admit that.

It had taken a long time, but ultimately she knew what Eric's role had been in her life. He'd been sent to erase her. To make her disappear, which hadn't been hard for him to do, especially in the beginning. He'd been cunning then, and she'd hardly even noticed that he was doing it. Eric's subtle complaints gradually exposed her inadequacies and his disappointment in her shone heavily on her shame for not being more adept at being his wife. The crescendo of his anger grew with time, and drowned out her weak attempts to defend and explain herself.

"I've been working all day, Eric," she'd tried to tell him. "What the hell have you been doing?" *Whap!*

"If you don't like it, Eric, then don't eat it." *Whap! Whap!*

"But I didn't mean to—I'm sorry!" *Whap! Whap! Kick!*

Eventually, Ruth kept her mouth shut because her silence proved to be golden in their home, unless he just felt like fighting. Then all the silence in the world didn't matter. And still, she stayed.

"Ain't nobody want yo' fat ass, bitch! Ain't no man out there want yo' ass!" he'd laugh. "Look atcha. Black as mothafuckin' tar and big as a elephant!"

Then why are you still here? she questioned in her mind, but never out loud.

He'd laugh, then nuzzle his face in the crook of her neck, and kiss her cheek. "But you my baby, though." Eric's affection always led his hand to her breasts first and he'd cup them, knead them, squeeze them, all the while moaning into her ear, and expecting her to fall submissively into the ecstasy of his arms.

Theirs was a performance choreographed to flow effortlessly. He led, she followed and she'd suffered for it. But fourteen years had taken its toll, and Ruth didn't want to dance anymore. Birthdays have a way of doing that to a woman, forcing her to look at her life, at herself, and sometimes even compel her to make changes in her life whether or not she believes she's ready. Years roll in bringing questions she's forced to ask herself and sometimes even the courage to answer them honestly, once and for all.

He'd taken that insecure girl and built a pedestal for her to stand on, and later on, cursed her every time he knocked her down. As time went on, he didn't bother with the pedestal, because keeping her down was easier—for both of them. And still, in the back of her mind the question lingered: *Why Ruth? Why are you still with him?*

Because he'd kill her if she left. He'd said so himself.

Because her fat ass wasn't shit without him, and where would she go? What would she do?

Because the earth revolved around Eric.

Because most days everything between them was cool and he didn't hit her all the time.

Because she'd provoked him, and if she'd just learn to keep her big ass mouth shut, he wouldn't have to do this.

Because she was his baby—though.

For years she'd accepted that her life was just her life and that's all. She worked, ate, slept, and tried hard not to upset the delicate balance of power in their household, choosing instead to live and die quietly beneath the umbrella of Eric's dictatorship, pissed off at herself for not having the courage to tell him how fucked up she believed the whole situation was. Then suddenly, on the morning of her thirty-third birthday, something inside her clicked. It clicked so loudly, she was surprised he'd slept through it. It sounded like a key opening a lock hidden deep inside her, suddenly opening the door to her own ignorance, fear, hell—even hope—causing her to just sit there for a moment scratching her head, wondering, *What have I done?*

Ruth had been afraid to leave him. She'd been afraid to stay with him. Since they'd been married, she'd been a branch on a tree, bending but never breaking. Maybe breaking would've been easier, but no, her dumb ass had always believed bending was the right thing to do. The only thing to do. Eric had hurt her in every possible way, and short of killing her, she'd lived to remember every one of those ways. Whooping her ass on a whim, or because she'd fallen short of his expectations once again. But what about all the times he'd fallen short of hers?

She stared at him for nearly thirty minutes that morning while he slept, watching him twist and turn in his sleep, scratching and digging, grunting. He was powerless when he slept, but every time he opened his eyes he murdered her. He'd killed her a thousand times with his venomous tongue that lashed out when he suspected she was finally starting to feel a twinge of self esteem. He'd slaughtered her each time he buried his fist in her stomach or slapped her in the back of her head, laughing because he always thought it was funny. She'd become nothing more than an empty shell of a woman because she'd been a naive, eighteen-year-old girl. And Eric had seen that in her the first time he'd laid eyes on her and he'd wanted her because of it, so that he could mold her into exactly what she had become. Nothing.

And on the Eighth Day She Rested

Baby Ruth

BABY RUTH, HER MOTHER USED TO CALL HER. "YOU MY BABY, and you sweet and nutty jus' like the candy bar," Karen would tease. Karen Johnson had moved to Denver from Jacksonville, when she was sixteen, pregnant, and hot on the trail of the man she loved. He'd been in the air force when they'd met in Florida, and was transferred shortly before Karen discovered she was pregnant with Ruth. She'd managed to save up enough money for a one-way bus ticket to Colorado and discovered that he wasn't interested in her or the baby she carried because he was already married, with kids he'd wanted, so she needed to *"Get back on that damn bus, and take your ass home!"* Karen said he'd told her. Only her mother, the Set Aside, Sanctified, Holified Servant of the Lord, Filled with the Holy Ghost (but Cussed like a Sailor) woman, wouldn't let her come back and she ended up staying in Denver.

Soft-spoken Ruth was an immortal teenager and dreamed of being beautiful like her mother and falling in love when she grew up. She listened to music incessantly, had a one-year subscription to *Right On* magazine, and practiced her french kissing on the back of her hand, underneath her covers in her room at night. She'd just finished her homework, and checked on the chicken baking in the oven, when she happened to glance up at the clock on the wall and noticed what time it was: ten minutes to five. Karen would be on her way home by now.

"Fine as wine."

"Built like a brick shit house."

"Mmm . . . mmm . . . baby. What's a man got to do to get in on some of that action?"

Karen Johnson was accustomed to being ushered home by phrases like these, and she didn't mind one bit. "They don't mean no harm, Baby Ruth," she'd say to Ruth who found the comments embarrassing. "Ain't nothin' wrong with a man 'preciatin' a woman. You wait till you get a lil' older. You'll see what I mean. You a shy, pretty girl, dark as molasses, and sweet as honey, got a cute little figure too. I just wish you'd stop coverin' it up with those baggy pants you insist on wearin'."

Ruth watched her mother walking toward their apartment on Champa Street. The sun was starting to set behind the mountains, but it didn't dare set on Karen strutting home in a pair of secondhand Jordache jeans, a pink polo top, and her favorite high-heeled Candies.

"Momma? I know you ain't wearing those shoes," Ruth had argued that morning.

"What's wrong with my shoes?" Karen asked, genuinely perplexed.

"It's cold outside, Mom," Ruth said, sounding mildly irritated.

"It's April, Ruth. Springtime? People do wear sandals in the springtime. So what's yo' point?"

"It's too cold for sandals. That's my point."

Karen rolled her eyes, picked up her purse and keys, and headed for the door. "Well, they my feet, and if I don't mind 'em bein' chilly, why should you?"

Ruth followed after her. "Because I love you and I don't want you to get sick."

"Girl, please. I ain't never sick, and you bein' a lil' melodramatic, if you ask me—as usual." Karen left the apartment, then called out over her shoulder, "And don't forget to put that chicken in the oven when you get home from school."

Ruth shook her head, and then closed the door behind her. "Sometimes," she muttered, "that woman's a mess."

As Karen walked home, the faint melody of Earth, Wind and Fire's "Devotion" could be heard playing in the distance and suddenly she stopped, closed her eyes, then smiled and gently bobbed her head because someone had the good taste to play her favorite song, which was anything by EWF. Ruth covered her mouth with her hand and giggled. Karen was a character, and Ruth always made it a point to be her audience, whether her mother was aware of it or not.

"Hey," Karen said nonchalantly as she entered the apartment and started flipping through the mail.

"Hi. Did we get any bills?"

Karen sighed. "Don't we always." She threw the mail down on the coffee table, slid out of her shoes, plopped down on the couch, and put her feet up.

Ruth picked up the mail and sorted out the bills that needed to be paid. She'd inherited the job of keeping track of them because Karen just hadn't shown any aptitude in that area. Her mother was thirty years old and most of the time they were more like sisters than mother and daughter. But there were times when Ruth wished for Karen to be more like a mother. Mothers did things like pay the electricity bill before the lights were shut off. Mothers brought home real groceries, not just a box of cereal and a carton of milk. Mothers didn't hang out in the clubs until dawn, knowing they had to get up early and go to work the next day. And mothers certainly didn't go without eating for days on end just to make sure they fit into a size five, tripping that the size seven had gotten a little too comfortable. But more than anything, mothers didn't move in new boyfriends every other month, letting them get high or drunk or call everybody in the house names just because they were pissed off about something stupid. Ruth was almost positive that most mothers didn't do things like that, but then, Karen wasn't most mothers.

Different men came in and out of their lives, one dissolving into another, and each time Ruth hoped this one would be *the* one. The one who loved her mother, married her, made babies with her because that's what Karen hoped for. Ruth wished she'd give up, and be content with it just being the two of them. As far as Ruth was concerned, life was perfect when it was just them, but then she'd wake up in the middle of the night to the muffled sounds of Karen's sobs from the other side of the wall in their small apartment. Karen was lonely. She'd said it enough times. She'd cried it plenty of times.

"I'm jus' goin' to keep on prayin' 'cause one day the Lord's goin' to send me someone—send *us* someone to help take care of us, Baby Ruth," she'd say smiling, basking in the glow of her wishful thinking. Maybe as a child Ruth had believed the Lord would send them somebody, but by the time she was twelve she figured maybe the Lord had forgotten, or that he wasn't paying attention, because all the men he did send turned out to be idiots, drunks, or deadbeats. That's when Ruth decided she'd rather find her own husband than trust the Lord to do it. He obviously had too many other things to worry about.

Karen's ritual never changed. A new man in her life meant euphoria. Everything was funny, and the glass was always half full. She'd hold her head up extra high when she walked, made sure she had fresh polish on her fingers and toes, and spent a little more time in the mirror in the mornings, afternoons, evenings, putting on her makeup. Then she'd prepare to tell Ruth about him, whoever *him* was. She'd make Ruth a bowl of ice cream and they'd sit down in the kitchen smiling at each other and giggling like best friends. Karen would prop her elbows up on the table, cradle her lovely face in her hands smiling at Ruth while she inhaled that big bowl of ice cream.

"That good, Baby Ruth?" Ruth's mouth would be so full of french vanilla that all she could do was nod. Karen never ate any herself because she thought it would make her fat, but she enjoyed watching Ruth finish hers, moaning and licking her own lips like she was eating some herself. She stared into Ruth's eyes and gently rubbed her hand down her cheek. "Slow down, baby," she'd laugh. "You don't have to eat so fast, Ruthie. That ice cream ain't goin' nowhere." Karen's southern drawl seemed out of place in Denver, Colorado. As out of place as she did. She'd taken the girl out of the country but there was still plenty of country in the girl.

"You know what?" she'd ask as Ruth guzzled down ice cream.

"Momma's met somebody, Ruthie. Somebody nice." She always thought they were nice, and in the beginning, they always were.

"His name's Walter."

"His name's Glen."

"His name's Bruce."

"His name's Cedric."

Walter ended up being a junkie, stealing what little they had and taking the last of her money to buy whatever it was he was shooting up in his arm. Glen turned out to be married and left Karen to go home to his wife each and every time the woman summoned him back. Eventually, he never came back, so Ruth assumed Mrs. Glen had decided to let him stay. Bruce couldn't keep a job and decided to sit at home, drink all day long, and let Karen be the family bread-winner. One day, she happened to mention that she had a problem with this little arrangement he threw a full can of beer at her and slapped her upside the head a couple of times just in case she didn't get the message. He left but came back, though. He came back quite a few times before she finally got tired of the drama and called it quits.

Then there was Cedric. Good old Cedric. Out of all of them, he seemed to have had the most potential. He had a good job, decent table manners. Sure he smoked a little reefer every now and then, but that was about the extent of his drug dependency problem. Ruth even liked him, but it wasn't perfect. Sometimes he and Karen argued. He'd hit her, but she'd hit back because she swore she'd never let another man treat her like Bruce did and get away with it. Often times they'd fight right in front of Ruth and once, when she tried coming to Karen's rescue, they both yelled at her, to "Get back in that goddamned room and shut the mothafuckin' door!" So that's what she did. They always made up, though. And when they did, peace reigned in the valley, or in this case, their apartment on the Five Points, and they were the epitome of the all-American family on public assistance. Cedric would be in such a good mood he'd take them to the amusement park or out to eat and Karen hugged, squeezed, and kissed all over him and Ruth too, until the next time.

When she told him she was pregnant, they didn't fight, but he gave her an ultimatum, "Get rid of it, Karen! I don't want no more fuckin' kids and if you don't do something about it, I'm gone!" Rather than lose him, she decided to do something about it.

"I got a doctor's appointment this afternoon, Ruth," Karen said. She'd fumbled around all morning, dropping things, muttering to herself, snapping at Ruth.

Ruth had started not to ask, but she was concerned about Karen because she never went to the doctor unless something was seriously wrong. "You sick?"

"Naw," she glanced quickly at Ruth and tried to smile. "It's jus' a checkup." Karen picked up her purse and headed out the door. "I'll see you later."

Ruth had been home from school less than an hour when Karen's key turned in the door. "What are you doing home so early, Karen?"

Karen looked tired. Her eyes were red and swollen like she'd been crying, but before Ruth could ask her about it, she slowly walked toward her bedroom, and then closed the door behind her. Ruth hurried to the kitchen and put a pot of water on the stove to boil for tea. Tea would make Karen feel better. It always did. She made her a cup, just the way she liked it, then took it to Karen sitting on the edge of the bed. Ruth sat down next to her, and pressed her hand against her mother's face. She felt warm.

Ruth handed Karen the cup of tea. "You want some Tylenol?"

Karen shook her head. "I jus' need to rest. That's all." She cradled the cup in both hands and slowly took a sip. Karen lay down and Ruth covered her legs with the blanket folded up at the foot of her bed, and kissed her. "Night, Momma," she whispered. Karen tried to smile, and then let her eyes close.

Hours later, Ruth stared down at her mother lying still in the crimson pool on her bed, knowing that the sound of the ambulance siren wailing in the distance was coming too late. She backed slowly away from the bed, braced herself against the wall, and slid down to the floor. Ruth pulled her knees up to her chest, and watched Karen intently, hoping to see some sign that she was still breathing. The lump in her throat swelled, threatening to strangle her, and Ruth hoped it would. She hurried to wipe the tears filling her eyes, clouding her vision. Someone frantically rang the doorbell and banged repeatedly on the door. And from somewhere else, the sound of someone screaming pierced through the air. Ruth covered her ears, closed her eyes, and prayed that the terrible noise would go away. Had it come from her? she wondered, but she never really knew for sure.

It wasn't until the funeral that she learned the truth about Karen's doctor's appointment. Ruth's grandmother had flown up from Florida and from the moment Ruth laid eyes on her, she wished she'd stayed in Florida.

Grandmother Johnson stood next to a sobbing Ruth, glaring impatiently down at Karen lying cocooned in a pale peach satin lining. "This is what happens when you don't do the Lord's will, girl. Ig'nant! That girl always was ig'nant!"

Ruth couldn't believe what she was hearing. This woman was burying her only daughter. How could she say those things? How could she stand over Karen and call her names like that? "Layin' up with all them men when she shoulda been keepin' her legs closed. Abortion ain't nothin' but killin'. It ain't nothin' but murder, plain and simple. God don't like it one bit." She shot a look at Ruth. "Yo' momma was a fool, child."

In an instant, Ruth had been flipped on her head and tossed into the unfamiliar. She sat silently next to her grandmother on the train they took back to Jacksonville the day after Karen's funeral. Ruth stared out the window watching the open oasis that was Colorado gradually transform into new places lush with huge trees and blossoms. Spring looked different in the east, and especially in Florida where the weight of the heavy, thick air threatened to suffocate her with its oppressive humidity and unnatural heat. Ruth found herself sucking in buckets of air that tasted foreign, just to catch her breath. This was her new home, and she'd share the next four years with a woman that obviously loathed her. All of a sudden, Ruth knew what it was to be truly alone.

————

"How many times I got to tell you to stop slammin' my screen do', girl?" her grandmother yelled from the kitchen. Ruth was late coming home from school. A year had passed since her mother's death and Ruth was a sophomore in high school. She'd stopped off at the library after school because being at the library was better than home.

"Sorry," Ruth answered quietly.

Grandmother Johnson emerged from the kitchen wearing a pink floral housedress that buttoned up the front and her pale pink slippers. She looked so much like Karen sometimes, Ruth thought, watching her. Especially her eyes, except there was no warmth in them. Karen's eyes had been so warm and inviting they made you want to swim in them. Ruth suspected that if her grandmother ever did smile, it was probably like Karen's too. But she'd never seen any evidence that she was even capable of such a thing. The woman's icy stare caused a shiver to run down Ruth's spine as she stopped and stood inches away from the girl.

"I was at the library," Ruth said, nearly whispering. Her eyes quickly dashed to the ground, focusing on those old pink worn-out house shoes.

"I didn't ask you where you been," she said indifferently. "Did I?"

Ruth cleared her throat. "No—ma'am."

"I thought I told you to come straight home from school."

"I know and I—"

The palm of the woman's hand landed hard against Ruth's cheek that stung all the way down to her toes. Ruth choked back her tears and stood motionless at the foot of the stairs. "I'm sorry—Grandmother Johnson," she sobbed.

"Oh yes, Ruth. You certainly are—sorry," she said maliciously. "You one sorry lil' heffa jus' like yo' momma was. She insisted on spreadin' her legs for every Tom, Dick, and Harry that come along, but I ain't havin' that shit with you. You understand me?"

"Yes, ma'am."

"Now," she said, heading back into the kitchen, "you go on upstairs and wash up for supper."

Perhaps that's where she'd learned it. The art of knowing when to keep her mouth shut. That old woman's glares had a way of melting Ruth, making her bleed into walls or floors or into nothing at all. She willed herself invisible in her dreams, even when she was awake, making her lips chapped from biting down on them all the time, holding in her tongue every time she felt compelled to defend herself or Karen's memory.

A week after she graduated from high school, Ruth moved out and never did look back. Two years later, she'd been contacted as the next of kin by the insurance company, telling her that her grandmother had died from kidney failure. Ruth even inherited a little money, which didn't last long with Eric around.

King of Beasts

Even when I was young
I had choices
But I misunderstood them
Got them mixed up with fate
And instead of making my choices
I let them make me
So, here I am

SHE SAT AT THE DINING ROOM TABLE GLANCING BACK AND forth between the door and the clock on the wall that read four A.M. In three hours she'd be getting ready for work and Eric's ass was nowhere to be found. He'd called from work saying he'd be stopping off at one of his boy's crib for a beer then assured her he'd be home in time for dinner.

"Lying bastard," Ruth muttered, finishing two pieces of fried chicken left over from dinner. She wiped her mouth with her napkin and got up to put her plate in the kitchen. Eric was out partying, probably wrapped up in something trifling that smelled cheap. Ruth was twenty-one years old and caught in the trap of being Eric's mother instead of his wife. He'd be home soon, strolling in at sun up, kissing her on the cheek, muttering excuses before heading off to bed to get a little shut-eye, assuring her that he'd be getting up soon to go to work.

"Baby, make sure I'm up before you leave. All right?"

Which she'd do, only to discover him still at home after she came home from work, having just rolled out of the bed and made himself some breakfast. Of course, he'd fuss at her, asking why she didn't wake him up before she left because "he ain't got no more sick time or vacation time" and he wouldn't get paid for missing work which would end up being all her fault.

Ruth was just about to give up and go to bed when she heard his key turn in the door. "Hey baby," he slurred. "You still up? Whatchu doin' up?" Eric stumbled over to where Ruth was standing and kissed her cheek. Ruth frowned at the stench of alcohol, smoke, and Shalimar coming from him. "It's late, girl. You got to get up in the mornin' and go to work. You better go to bed, baby."

"You know what time it is, Eric?" Ruth asked, sternly with her hand poised on her hip.

Eric slowly turned around, unbuttoning his shirt. He sighed, squinted his eyes at her, and smiled. "Naw, Ruthie. What time is it?"

"It's almost time to get up and go to work," she snapped. "Where have you been?"

He shook his head, then turned and headed into the bedroom. "Don't start, Ruthie. I ain't in no mood to fuck with you tonight." He turned on the light in the bedroom, then fell facedown on the bed fully clothed. "Baby, set the alarm for seven, will you? I can't reach it."

Ruth followed him, determined to try and get through to him that she was fed up with his late nights and he needed to get his act together, once and for all. "We've got to talk about this, Eric."

"We'll talk tomorrow," he said, groggily.

"No! Eric, I'm getting sick and tired of this shit!"

Suddenly, Eric found the strength to roll over on his back. "Ruthie! I said I ain't in no mood to be messin' with you tonight. Now, I'm tired and I need to get me some sleep."

She couldn't help it. The sight of him, all crumpled up on that bed talking about how he needed some sleep after partying and drinking all night was funny. Ruth laughed, then folded her arms across her chest and leaned against the doorway. "You should've thought of that before you stopped off at your *boy's crib*," she mocked. "Don't you think?"

Eric glared at her through bloodshot slits. "You think you funny, don't you?"

"No, Eric. You're the one who's funny. I know one thing," she said, going over to the bed and grabbing a pillow, "I'm not sleeping in the bed with your funky ass tonight." Ruth rolled her eyes and went back into the living room to make herself comfortable on the sofa. It was late, and Eric was too drunk to reason with anyway. Trying to talk some sense in him tonight was a waste of time and sleep.

"Ruthie!" he called after her. "Ruthie! Get yo' ass back in here, girl!"

Ruth sighed. "Go to sleep, Eric."

She spread the blanket out over the couch, and crawled beneath it, then fluffed her pillow before closing her eyes.

Eric came into the room wearing a pair of red silk bikini briefs and yanked the blanket off her. "Come on and go to bed, girl. Quit actin' silly."

"I'm not the one acting silly, Eric," she said snatching it back. "So why don't you go to bed and stop playing?"

"I ain't playin', Ruthie." He took her blanket again. "Let's go to bed, baby. It's late and I ain't tryin' to be up all night."

Ruth snatched the blanket back. "Me either."

Suddenly, Eric reached down and grabbed Ruth by the arm. "Get up!"

"Eric?" Ruth said, trying to pull away from him.

"Get yo' ass up!"

"Eric, stop playing! Eric, this isn't funny!"

"Get yo' fat—Damn girl! Get the fuck up!" He struggled to pull her to her feet, lost his balance and fell on top of her.

She yanked her arm from him and pushed him. "If you don't stop!"

Eric gathered himself, stood up and loomed ominously over her. Now, she was afraid. His eyes were glazed over by alcohol. "I'm not playing either, Ruthie," he said matter-of-factly. "Get yo' ass up and come to bed."

Ruth defensively crossed her arms over her chest, refusing to give in to this nonsense. "No."

He'd moved quickly, as drunk as he was, but then Eric was working with instinct. The palm of his hand landed flat against the side of her face, but before she realized it had happened, Eric had grabbed a handful of her hair and pulled her up to her feet. "I said I wasn't playin', bitch!" he spat in her face. "Now bring yo' black ass to bed!"

"I'm calling the . . . I'm calling the police," she gasped, struggling to get free.

He pulled down her head, then raised his knee up to meet her stomach and Ruth crumbled to the floor gasping for air.

Her eyes were filled with tears, but she wasn't crying. At least, not the kind of crying she'd ever known. Eric paced back and forth, mumbling to himself and to her.

"Bullshit! Bullshit! You ain't 'bout nothin' but—Get yo' ass up!" he yelled, reaching down and grabbing her hair again. Ruth struggled to her feet, then Eric dragged her in the direction of the bedroom and pushed her onto the bed. "Move yo' fat ass over!" Eric crawled in next to her and flicked off the lamp on the nightstand. "Piss me off again, Ruthie! I'm gon' knock fire from yo' black ass!"

He muttered under his breath until he finally passed out, but Ruth never closed her eyes.

The next morning, Ruth called in to work and told them she wasn't feeling well, which was the truth. She felt like shit. She drove to nowhere in particular, riding the wave on the slew of emotions racing through her. He'd cussed her out before and once in a while he'd even thrown things at her. A few times he'd threatened to hit her, but never had. Until now. In the back of her mind, Ruth had always believed she'd be ready for him if things ever went this far. She'd hit back. But she hadn't hit back.

She headed south on 95, driving through St. Augustine, Daytona Beach. How much farther was it to Palm Beach? she wondered. And, what would she do once she got there? If she'd had a friend there, maybe she could show up on her doorstep and her friend would pull out a couple of beers and tell her how she needed to leave that sorry bastard because he didn't deserve her.

The sun was starting to set when she pulled up to her house. Eric quickly opened the door and ran out to meet her. "You all right, baby? Where you been, Ruthie? You know you had me worried sick 'bout you, girl. I called yo' job and they said you called in sick. What? You not feelin' good?"

Ruth walked past him as if he were invisible. He followed her.

"We need to talk, Ruthie," he said anxiously. "Now, I got too damn drunk last night and . . ."

Ruth turned to him. "I want a divorce, Eric," she said, quietly.

Eric grimaced, then stood close to her and cradled her face between his hands, kissing her cheeks and eyes. "Naw, baby girl. We don't need no divorce. I'm sorry, Ruthie. You know I'm sorry, baby. I jus' had too much to drink. That's all it was."

"I can't let you get away with that," she sobbed.

"And you shouldn't, darlin'. Ain't no way I should get away with some shit like that. But we don't need no divorce, Ruthie. Please, baby," he pleaded.

Days later, he was still pleading. He reminded her that he'd been drunk, and she'd been partly to blame too. "You know I got a temper, Ruthie. When I get like that, you know you need to back off. That's all you had to do. Back off and none of this would've happened, baby girl."

She'd start to protest, then he'd hold her and kiss her and maybe tell her something about how much she meant to him and promised that it would never happen again. Eric started coming home on time, and got up on his own for work. He called her at the office just to say he was thinking about her, and sent flowers once, in case she hadn't heard him. He caressed her body and her spirit and gave birth to a new kind of tenderness neither of them had ever known he was capable of.

"It won't ever happen again, Ruthie," he'd sworn. And she'd believed.

Beginning of the End

REFLECTIONS SKIRTED OFF THE ST. JOHNS RIVER, CREATING ELU-sive images of a world so much better than her own. Nothing more than illusions floated on top of that river but they were seductive enough to make Ruth wish she could be an illusion too, and not some worn out legal secretary on her way home from another grueling day at the office.

Driving was therapeutic. It relaxed her and alleviated some of the tension she'd been drowning in all day. Ruth sighed, then turned up the volume on the radio, wishing for time to stand still and that the bridge was endless. She wished for a special kind of car that never ran out of gas because it was powered by the sun, moon, air, and sheer willpower. And Ruth would be the only driver on the road, bobbing her head to the music from a jazz station that played nonstop with no annoying commercial interruptions. The night was warm enough to justify using the air conditioner, but that's not what she needed. Fresh air was what she needed, and Ruth drove with the window down, savoring the warm air whipping across her face, filling her lungs every time she inhaled with childish notions of what life might be like if she were free from responsibilities she felt chained to. Responsibilities like her job, bills—marriage.

The city had finally finished construction on the Buckman Bridge and traffic wasn't nearly as bad as it had been. Of course, at this time of night, it wasn't bad anyway because all the smart people were home by now, burping up remnants of dinner and enjoying their favorite television show.

Her working hours were from nine to five, but lately they'd been more like nine to nine. Somewhere along the line, McGreggor, her boss, had decided that the abolition of slavery didn't apply to legal secretaries on a salary. Every time she closed her eyes, contracts and depositions danced behind them, so getting a good night's sleep had been a moot point all week. She hated being a secretary but, unfortunately, she was great at it and had been for almost fifteen years. Working her behind off wouldn't have been so bad if McGreggor had ever felt generous enough to give her one of those rare but much deserved back pats every once in a while. A simple "Thank you, Ruth" or "Great job, Ruth" would've done wonders for her self-esteem. McGreggor wasn't big on gratitude or appreciation, but he was larger than life with his demands and expectations.

Ruth turned down her street, then glanced at the digital green numbers of the clock on her dashboard: 8:30. She sighed. Tonight's agenda included a soak in a hot bath, giving Gerald Albright the privilege of serenading all of her, lush and naked, and a nice cup of plum tea. So maybe it wasn't exactly what some might consider an exciting evening, but after the day she'd had, it would be heaven on earth.

Her hope came crashing to the ground when she spotted Eric's big silver Pontiac parked in the driveway and suddenly all of her quiet plans for the evening slithered down through her stomach, into her intestinal tract and escaped from her behind in the form of gas. She parked her car and turned off the engine, but had lost all motivation for getting out of it. The instinct to cry came to mind, but she quickly shooed it away. If she'd had any money on her debit card, she'd have driven right past the house and gotten her a room somewhere, but that was the problem of living from paycheck to paycheck. It prohibited spontaneity and other dumb things.

She hadn't seen or heard from Eric in nearly two weeks, and had savored every minute of it. This time, it didn't matter where he was or what he was doing or who he was doing it with. She'd refused to trip or allow herself one jealous, insecure thought and even had the nerve to discard the tiniest feelings of inadequacy. No, this time had been different. It had been like a vacation, like spending two weeks on a tropical island in the middle of the Atlantic, casting all her cares to the sea and forgetting all about the issues of her real life. Okay, so maybe not quite that good, but she hadn't missed him and that was the bottom line. In retrospect, she figured that every time Eric had taken off on one of his little hiatuses from their marriage had been a blessing in disguise but it had taken her fourteen years to finally realize it. God had she realized it, though. Years ago she'd cursed him every time Eric left and didn't call or bother coming home. Now she knew better. In all his infinite wisdom, God knew that Ruth had needed him gone even more than Eric needed to be out fucking around. And this separation had served as an example to Ruth of how life could be without Eric—really cool, full of ocean blue peace. The word "bitch" hadn't come up once since he'd been gone, especially directed at her. She hadn't been cussed out for the dry cleaners' putting too much starch in his shirts, and she didn't have to give in to sex or lie that she couldn't have sex because of the persistent period she'd suffered from all these years that her gynecologist couldn't seem to find a reasonable explanation or cure for. If he was smart, he'd know that no woman could bleed as long as she'd been claiming to bleed and still be alive to talk about it, but . . .

She'd just turned thirty-three years old and the fantasies Ruth used to have about her husband had evaporated in the space of time, and now there was nothing left but Eric. The man who had instantly come to his senses and realized how much he loved and cherished her had never shown his face in their house. The one who would get up early in the morning and bring her breakfast in bed, gently kiss her cheeks and hands, then would make love to her in the tender way he never did, had never been more than a figment of her imagination. The man who noticed for the first time how beautiful she was, then apologized profusely for ever hurting her, lived in another house somewhere else. And the Eric who took her out dancing, treated her like a princess and whose sole purpose in life was to protect her and make sure she lived happily ever after, had stood her up years ago.

It had been a gradual awakening, coming with every ugly moment with him. An awakening that usually followed a slap or a barrage of hideous words escaping from his nasty mouth aimed at destroying her spirit. Fourteen years had dripped through her fingers like water and she'd never get any of it back. Ruth sighed, knowing that that had been the real tragedy. It had all been such a waste. She'd lived with his ass coming in and out of her life like it was a revolving door, constantly on guard, anxiously anticipating his temper and unwarranted, undeserved demands on her and her body. For what? To keep the peace and exercise this bruised muscle of her pathetic existence? Basically.

Over the years, his absences from home had left all sorts of ideas running rampant through her mind, though. Perfectly logical ideas, depending on the circumstances or her mood. Divorce. Skipping town. Suicide. Murder. She'd given a lot of thought to killing him. Arsenic had been her first choice, but for it to look like death from natural causes it would take entirely too long. She'd considered shooting him, but worried that she might miss and didn't want to take that chance. Then, she'd entertained the notion of burning the bed with him in it, but Eric was a light sleeper and might wake up before she got a good fire going. So, after mulling it over in her mind, and rehearsing her speech in the mirror, she decided to try a more radical approach: reasoning with him and asking him to leave.

That dirty shirt lying on the floor was the first greeting she got from Eric when she walked into the house. He was home all right and that was how it had always been. With him walking around the house like royalty leaving a trail of shit behind him and Ruth crawling around on her hands and knees picking up after him because he liked a *"clean crib 'case comp'ny comes by."* His grand entrance from the shower, wearing nothing but a towel around his waist, turned her stomach, and Ruth felt so weak in her knees, she knew that if she didn't hurry and sit down, she'd fall. The two of them were literally like night and day. That's how he referred to them whenever he tried to be cute. "You as dark as I am light, Ruthie. You my moon, and I'm yo' sun." He thought that was funny. She never really did. He'd been gone long enough for her to be surprised that he was starting to look his age. Eric looked old to her, and she wondered for a moment if he thought the same thing about her. Gray hairs were sprinkled in with the sandy brown hair he'd worn cut low since getting rid of that Jheri curl a few years back, and the hazel in his eyes wasn't as vivid as it had been a few years ago. The slim, staunch physique he'd once been so proud of had gone soft over the years, especially in his midsection, which dipped over the top of the towel he wore around his low waist. Had his legs always been that skinny? she wondered, staring at what looked like something she'd seen on a bird on the Discovery Channel.

"Hey, baby," he sang out, then walked over to her and kissed the top of her head. "They gotchu workin' late again? I tell you. Them lawyers don't know how good they got it witchu handlin' things over there. Shit. My baby probably runnin' things in that place. Ain't you?" Condescension was never an attractive feature on Eric. Ruth rolled her eyes. She hated him. She hated all of him with all of her and if she could possibly find someplace to put more hate for him, she would. She closed her eyes for a moment and conjured up a mental image of him suddenly filling up with some kind of toxic gas and exploding right there in the living room, which made her feel just a little bit better about him being home.

Call it instinct. Call it been there, done that, but she knew that even before she opened her mouth, she'd regret that night. Ruth knew that she was going to wake the demons and disturb the sensitive molecular structure of this man's universe and set all hell loose up in that house before it was over. She watched him prance around the living room, his mouth moving, always moving, but it didn't matter what he was saying. She'd stopped listening a long time ago, only he'd been too egotistical to notice. He was ugly, and together they were ugly. But while he was gone, this time, that hadn't been ugly. And she craved more of him being gone and never coming back. A knot began forming in the pit of her stomach and she knew exactly what it was. It was fear, but this time she would dismiss it.

"I left you a message at the office. Did you get it?" Eric popped open the can of a beer he'd gotten from the refrigerator.

Ruth stared at him, determined not to back down before she'd managed to stand up. *It's time, Ruth. Do it now, girl, or hold your peace,* she thought to herself. *This time you make him disappear.*

"Where have you been, Eric?" Not that it really mattered, but it seemed to be the logical first question to ask on the HCLCLDU-

HATBGD (How to Confront Lying, Cheating, Low-Down, Unfaithful Husbands After They've Been Gone for Days) list.

Eric grinned, and tried to conjure up a twinkle behind his faded hazel eyes. "Oh, Ruthie"—he took a long gulp on his beer—"you know me."

She didn't blink. She didn't say a word. And she didn't take her eyes off his. Ruth wasn't upset that he'd been gone. She was upset that he'd come back.

Eric cleared his throat. "Well, uh—Leroy had some business he had to take care of in West Palm." She recognized the sound almost immediately and strained to hear the torturous creaking noises coming from his brain and out of his mouth. He called them excuses, but she'd always preferred to call them what they were—lies. "And, uh, he wanted me to ride out with him, you know." Eric shifted his weight back and forth, uncomfortable under the weight of her gaze. "I had to hook him up, 'cause his car ain't workin'. It's in the shop."

"What did you do?" Ruth asked, calmly. "Give Leroy a piggyback ride to West Palm? Because I could've sworn I saw your car parked outside an apartment building on the southside just yesterday, as a matter of fact."

Eric shook his head. "Naw, wasn't my car. Might've looked like mine, but—"

"It was yours, Eric," she said quietly. Her courage was growing. How or why, she didn't really know, but somewhere along the way that seed had taken root and it felt good. Eric was still a mean bastard, but at that moment Ruth was starting to feel a mean bastard well up inside her too. He didn't know it yet, but Ruth knew they'd meet up tonight for the first and last time. It was kismet, fate, destiny, and her finally getting sick and tired enough to make it happen, no matter the cost.

"I know I should've called, baby, but we was runnin' 'round so much I jus' didn't get a chance to."

"Eric—please," Ruth said, exasperated. "Please don't do this anymore." Lord, this is not the kind of mess she wanted to have to deal with tonight. Some jazz, now that would've been nice, and a hot soak in the tub, a cup of tea. Some damn tea!

"Do what, baby? Whatchu talkin' 'bout?" Eric strolled over to her, knelt down in front of her and attempted to wrap his arms around the waist he'd complained was larger than he preferred.

Ruth pushed him away then stood up and stepped over him. "Don't waste your time lying to me, Eric. Who was she? One of your regular hos or a new ho?"

Eric slowly stood to his feet. "Ruthie, now you know—"

"Yes. I do know. I know you should've stayed where you were and not bothered coming back here."

"Baby, I'm tellin' you the truth. I been in West—"

"The truth?" Suddenly, she laughed because Eric and truth were like oil and water; the two just didn't mix. "The truth is, I don't care anymore. I haven't cared in years. Have you?"

Eric shook his head, and rubbed his eyes. "Ruth, now I know we got our problems, but—"

"The only problem we have, Eric, is that we're still married. That's our whole problem!" Ruth's voice was starting to crack. That's not what she wanted because cracks in anything were a sign of weakness and right now, at this moment, she couldn't afford to be weak. Eric was an opportunist and a predator. Predators keyed in on weakness and used it to their advantage to destroy. "It's over, Eric. You and me—we're over and I don't want you here anymore." Eric's image slowly began to blur behind the tears welling up in her eyes. Ruth blinked them away, hoping he hadn't seen them. Damn she was tired. "I can't keep doing this. Too many years—I've been at this for too long, and"—she shrugged—"I'm tired, Eric." There, she'd said it, like she'd sort of said it many times before, but this time was different. She meant it and she believed it. It was real, tangible, something she could reach out and touch. Ruth was finished.

The madness was growing inside him. She could see it in the way he was starting to clench his teeth, and in the way he drew back his shoulders. She heard it in that deep breath he'd just taken. "Ruth— look. I know you pissed off 'bout me bein' gone and all, and I know I shoulda called you but you need to chill the hell out, baby. You need to calm down and listen to what I'm sayin'." Was he talking to her, Ruth Ashton, the epitome of chill and calm? Eric had always been the drama queen, not her. "I'm home, baby and I've said I'm sorry." He took a step toward her with his arms outstretched. "C'mon and give me some sugah and get over it. All right?"

Ruth stepped back, but she wasn't about to back down. "I am calm, Eric. I've been calm the whole time you've been gone." Tea would've been nice, but wine was what she needed now. She opened up the china cabinet and pulled out a glass and the bottle that had been sitting there for God knows how long. She turned her back to Eric so he wouldn't see her hands trembling, blew dust off the glass then filled it to the brim with the warm, bloodred concoction, then gulped down half the glass before coming up for air. Being drunk right now wasn't such a bad idea.

"I got some scotch in the kitchen if you want a drink, Ruthie. That mess is ancient. Probably gon' make you sick or somethin'."

Ruth turned abruptly to him, and then filled her glass again. "If you want to fuck around, I can't stop you."

Eric laughed. "Who said I was fuckin' 'round? What the hell—"

"I've never been able to make you be faithful to me, Eric, but I can stop you from running back to my bed while you wait for some other heffa to change the sheets and fluff your mothafuckin' pillow!" *Whew! What the hell was in that wine?* "I don't need you here, Eric." Ruth swallowed another gulp, then drew back her shoulders. "I never have."

That's when it happened. The condescending Eric decided to leave the house, and in his place the real Eric appeared. The mean one. Fire blazed behind those aged hazel eyes, turning them a vivid shade of green. *Oh yeah*, she thought to herself. *There he is. I was wondering when he'd show up.*

"Oh you need me, bitch! You definitely need my ass!"

There'd been a time in her life when being called a bitch would've hurt her feelings, but lately, that hadn't been the case. Between all that wine she was guzzling and her new found attitude, Ruth was starting to feel brave, or was it stupidity she was feeling? When you're high on old wine, and mad as hell, it's kind of hard to tell the difference.

She laughed at him. "For what? What the hell do I need you for, Eric? I've got to hear this because I can't seem to come up with one good reason on my own. Why don't you help me with this one? Come on. I'm listening." Ruth turned up her glass and finished off the last of her wine. Then she filled it again. She looked at Eric and smiled. The callousness of her argument had pierced his heart and hurt his feelings, though he'd never admit it. Fat ass, black ass, Ruth Ashton had the nerve to stand up with a few insults of her own to Eric, player-dawg extraordinaire. She'd hit a nerve and it made her proud.

"You don't know either?" she asked sarcastically. He was off balance. She saw it in his face and Ruth felt mean. Real mean. Eric mean. "Look, it's not a big deal, Eric. You don't want me and I don't want you. So, what's the issue?"

Eric looked like she'd just asked him to explain the theory of relativity. "The issue?"

"The issue, Eric! What's the damn point? You haven't wanted me in years! And I haven't wanted you either! So what are we doing?"

"You pushin', Ruth, and I ain't in no mood for this shit," he said in a low growl.

"So?" Ruth shrugged. "Leave. Get o-u-t *out*, Eric. Why make it hard on yourself? Why the hell do you feel the need to keep coming back here when there's obviously someone or some*thing* out there you'd rather be dealing with?"

"Oh, so you gon' try and make me leave my own mothafuckin' house. Is that it? I live here too, bitch! And—"

"And?" Ruth interrupted. "Since you live here, then tell me something. When was the last time you contributed anything to this household, Eric? When was the last time you got up some money for the mortgage?" *Enough Ruth.* "When have you bought furniture, paid a bill or even bought a bag of groceries?" *Stop it, Ruth. Enough.* "The only contribution you have ever made to this house is sucking up any excess oxygen and space not being utilized by anything important!" *Too late.*

Eric's green eyes threw daggers in her direction, but she was protected by her impenetrable armor of anger and they bounced right off her. Hell, she'd moved beyond the threshold of her greatest fear and Ruth wasn't even afraid of the inevitable anymore.

He lowered his chin. "Who the fuck you think you talkin' to?"

Ruth swallowed hard. "The only other person in this room. I'm talking to you, Eric. Finally—I'm talking to you and you are listening to me. I'm telling you what I think—about you—about us! I'm finally getting this shit off my chest because I'm tired of holding it in. It ain't doing me one bit of good in here." She pointed to her chest. "But you need to hear it, as much as I need to say it, and I don't regret one single word coming out of my mouth!"

He stepped toward her. "Oh, and yo' black ass is gon' get it all out now, huh?"

"Yes! My black ass is! And I'm going to keep on talking until you finally get it through your thick head that I don't want you in my life anymore! I don't want you in my house! I want you gone!"

"You keep on talkin', bitch. You keep on and while that smart ass mouth of yours is workin', I'm gon' be workin' on yo'—"

Ruth rolled her eyes. "Here we go. Threats Eric? We can't talk about this like grown people? You gotta come back with threats?"

"More like promises, Ruth," Eric said coldly. "You know better than to piss me off. You know better. But I know you're pissed off because I been gone so long. And yeah, I been fuckin' 'round. You know I have. Damn right I have!"

"I know you have. I'm not stupid!"

"No, baby girl. You ain't stupid, but you sure as hell can't fuck worth a damn!" He laughed.

"Thank you, Eric."

"If you could," he said, trying to turn the tables on her, "I wouldn't have to step out. I wouldn't have to get my satisfaction from those so-called hos as you put it."

"Like I care where you get your *satisfaction*. You can have all the satisfaction you want, Eric, as long as you keep going. I'm tired!"

"You said that already."

"I'm through watching my husband waltz in and out like he's a single man, fucking everything remotely female and bringing shit you get from them home to me! I'm through with you bringing your sorry ass home whenever one of your little girlfriends discovers how much of a son-of-a-bitch you really are and kicks you to the curb! I'm tired of you coming in here, using up my electricity, eating up my food, and putting your hands on me!" Ruth picked up the dirty shirt he'd left on the floor and threw it at him. "Now get your shit and get the hell out!"

Eric caught it, and then threw it back. "I said I ain't goin' no goddamned where, bitch! Now you back the fuck off before I . . ."

Out of the corner of her eye, she saw his fingers curl into a fist, but even that wasn't enough to thwart this mission she'd embarked on. "Before you what, Eric?" But she already knew. In the pit of her stomach she knew what he was about to do. And she knew it was too late to back down now. She'd said too much and he'd been pushed farther than she'd ever pushed him before. Even if she were to apologize, it wouldn't have been enough. Crying wouldn't have been enough, or pleading, or groveling. Nothing else she said now would make one bit of difference and Ruth committed herself to the idea that she was giving in to suicide.

Veins in his arms protruded from his forearms. "Yo' ass done gone too far, Ruth! Too far." Eric began taking steps in her direction.

Ruth backed up toward the bedroom. Her heart pounded like a fist on the inside of her chest and she knew he could hear it. "I'll tell you what. You don't even have to pack." She rushed over to the bed and knelt down to pull a piece of luggage from underneath it. "I'll do it for you, Eric. That make it easier for you? Huh? I'll pack all your shit for you, and all you got to do is get your clothes on and leave." Ruth grabbed his clothes hanging in the closet and began throwing them in the suitcase.

"Leave my shit alone, Ruth!" Eric snatched the suitcase from the bed then hurled it across the room into the wall, barely missing her head.

"You will get out of my house, Eric! I want you gone!"

Eric's fist came out of nowhere fast, like a missile, two quick punches to her face.

Ruth screamed, but not from the pain of his blows. She screamed because she was tired of this, of him. And it had to stop. She had to stop it. Gathering up every ounce of her strength, she lunged at him, digging her nails into his face. "You bastard! You goddamned . . ."

Eric pushed her off him, and into the wall. Ruth picked up the empty suitcase by the handle, struggled to her feet, then swung it at him, hitting him in the arm. "Get out! Get out!" she screamed at the top of her lungs.

Eric grabbed the suitcase from her, then turned her own weapon against her. "You fuckin' bitch!" She stumbled and fell at the impact to the side of her head. Ruth crumbled at his feet, knowing he wouldn't let her get up again. His attack was brutal, inundated with cuss words that melted into kicks that melted into pain that melted into her. "I don't hear yo' fat ass mouth now! Who the fuck you gon' put out now? Huh, bitch? You puttin' my ass—"

"Umph! No . . . umph! Stop . . . Eric . . . umph! Please . . . Oh God! No . . ."

"I told you . . . shut yo' big ass mouth! Ruthie . . . I told you . . . I don't see yo' ass tryin' to put me out now!"

Casualties of War

SHE DROVE SLOWLY DOWN EVERY SIDE STREET SHE COULD FIND on her way to the hospital, fighting against the kind of pain that was too excruciating to wrap in an Ace bandage, put ice on, or take a couple of aspirin for. Ruth took quick short, quick, breaths, praying she didn't pass out before she made it to her destination. Her right eye was swollen shut, and her left hand lay throbbing in her lap. She'd tried to bend her stiff fingers around the steering wheel then accepted the very real fact that they were probably broken, leaving her one good hand to drive with. Everything about her at that moment was broken. Eric had walked out in a way he never had before. He'd made the effort to pack this time, swearing under his breath that he was through with *"her dumb ass, once and for all." Did he mean it this time?* she wondered. *Lord, please let him stay gone,* she repeated over and over again in her mind.

"Was it worth it, Ruth?" she muttered, gasping for every breath. "Was it worth—all this?" She pulled over to the side of the road, fighting back tears. The last thing she wanted was to be discovered looking like this by some decent, upstanding citizen who wouldn't understand the bargain she'd made with the devil. Yes, he could beat her ass, as long as he left and never came back. As long as he packed up his shit and fell off the face of the earth. Then yes, it had been worth it. And yes, she'd do it all over again if she had to. Ruth eased up off the brake, then slowly maneuvered her way onto the road until she made it to the emergency room.

They'd given her some potent sedatives, but not potent enough to keep her from dreaming. She dreamed about her mother, Karen. She was young and pretty just like she had been before she died, and she sat on the edge of Ruth's bed smoothing down her hair, promising her, "It's gon' be all right, Baby Ruth. Jus' you wait a minute. You'll see." Her smile was better than any medicine and she felt the warmth of her mother's breath against her cheek as she leaned down to kiss her. Ruth forced open her eyes, hoping it wasn't a dream, and hoping the soft hand covering hers really was Karen's. But it wasn't. It belonged to a woman named Clara, who was a counselor in the hospital. She was an older woman with a pretty face, soft and round, the color of cinnamon. Except for touches of gray around her hairline, she looked youthful.

"Hello there," she whispered, smiling tenderly at Ruth. "I guess they must've drugged you up pretty good, huh?"

"Not enough," Ruth muttered through swollen lips.

"Well . . . I think they're going to let you leave in a day or two. Anyway, you'll get more rest at home than you would in this old hospital. You do have a safe place to stay, don't you?" Genuine concern showed on Clara's face, and Ruth would've smiled, but knew Clara would understand if she didn't. "I can get you a place if you—"

"No . . . thank you."

Clara patted Ruth's hand. "There's a policeman down the hall. I'll go get him and you can tell him everything. They'll pick him up and arrest him immediately if—"

"No," Ruth whispered.

"I think you should press charges, dear. In the long run—"

Ruth shook her head no. She didn't want to file charges or talk about what had happened in her marriage to any policeman or even sweet Clara. She had what she wanted. Eric was gone. That's all that mattered. And if she had anything to do with it, he'd stay gone even if it meant ending up here in this hospital again, or better yet, maybe next time, he'd be the one here. Besides, pressing charges wouldn't change what he'd done. Talking about it wouldn't change it. Her body ached, but she was used to that. It was as much a part of her life as washing the dishes or brushing her teeth. The physical wounds always healed quickly, but it was the mess inside that a doctor, counselor, or policeman couldn't fix. Ruth expected Clara to put up more of an argument, but was thankful when she didn't.

Clara smiled on her way out the door. "If you feel like talking later on, just ask the nurse to find me. They always know how to reach me."

"Thank you," Ruth said quietly.

"Clara." The nurse at the station recognized that look on Clara Robins's face as soon as she'd come from the new woman's room. "Don't you dare do this to yourself again."

Clara leaned over the counter and whispered. "What's her phone number?"

Noreen crossed her arms defiantly and shook her head. "If she didn't give it to you, then I'm not giving it to you."

"I just want to check on her after she leaves, Noreen. Make sure she's all right."

"Then ask her for her number."

"It would be easier if you gave it to me. You know I can make you give it to me."

"You don't need it, Clara. I take it she didn't want to file charges against the bastard." Clara didn't answer. "Well, if she doesn't want to help herself, why should you bend over backwards to help her?"

Clara sighed. "Because she doesn't have anybody else."

"How do you know? She might have a whole host of relatives who knows that bastard was beating on her and got sick of trying to talk her into leaving him only to hear some lame excuse about how much she *loves* him. I'm sorry, Clara. But I've seen it too many times, and you have too. You get yourself all wrapped up in these women's lives, giving up your sleep and peace of mind, all for them to go back to some fool, and you never hear from them again."

"Not all of them go back, Noreen. I've helped some of them."

"Yes, you have, honey. But those were the ones who wanted to be helped. Some women"—Noreen glanced at Ruth's door—"don't want your help. So why waste your time or your energy worrying about them?"

"You going to give me her number?" Clara asked wearily. She sure appreciated Noreen's concern, but sometimes it sounded too much like nagging and she wished the woman would mind her own business. Clara had been doing this for over twenty years and she wasn't the one who needed help right now. She was fine, but the young woman in that hospital bed, she wasn't so fine. Ruth lay in that bed looking like she didn't have a friend in the world. She lay there looking like she didn't need one either, but Clara knew better. Whether Ruth Ashton knew it or not, whether she wanted to admit it or not, she needed somebody. Maybe not now, but eventually Clara knew she would.

It was the look on their faces that drew her in, even more than what they said or, as in Ruth's case, didn't say. Women like her had been pummeled into believing this was the best they deserved and that's what Clara would not, could not, stand for. Even if this woman did have family and friends who'd given up on her, Clara knew that sometimes all a woman needed was another chance to make the right decision, someone to listen to her. Not judge her or criticize her or tell her what she needed to do, but just listen to her. Lending a good ear could make all the difference in the world. Clara would never forgive herself if she gave up on this Ruth, even if she had given up on herself. She'd wait a couple of days, and then give her a call. Maybe she'd hang up in her face, and that would be her prerogative. Then Clara would leave her alone. But if she did need to talk, or even needed to not talk and just sit with someone, then Clara felt an obligation to be there.

Out of the Dark

RUTH CALLED THE OFFICE AS SOON AS SHE GOT HOME TO LET them know about the terrible car accident she'd been in, and yes, she was fine. No, it wasn't her fault and her car, though badly damaged, wasn't totaled and would be fixed in a couple of days. And, oh yeah, she bumped her face on the steering wheel, which is why she looked like Apollo Creed after he'd gone a few rounds with Rocky, and no, she doesn't have airbags.

She'd been lying on the couch since she'd gotten home, watching slivers of sunlight that managed to slip in from behind her closed blinds slowly creep across the room, until, hours later, they'd disappear altogether and set with the sun. She'd pushed Eric to do this, but then, didn't she always. Funny how she'd generously given him credit for being the driving force in their marriage, when in fact, it had been her. Ruth had designed their relationship without even knowing it until now. She'd created that monster of a marriage, and put all the responsibility on Eric who never really had a clue as to what was really going on. But she knew the buttons and how they worked to set him off. She knew which tone in her voice soothed him and the kinds of words that endeared him to her, even temporarily. She knew how to smile at him when she didn't feel like smiling and even though she couldn't remember the last time she really looked into his eyes, she knew how to make him think she was looking into his soul. He hadn't manipulated her, she'd manipulated him, only she'd been too stupid to realize what she was doing and it ended up backfiring on her.

Ruth wrapped her arms tightly around herself and coughed. People with healthy ribs tended to take two things for granted, she thought to herself. Inhaling and exhaling. She sat up slowly, and then picked up her cup of tea off the table. The steam rose up and caressed her bruised, swollen face. Karen had loved tea. She believed every ailment known to woman could be cured by a cup of hot tea. Headaches, cramps, colds, botched abortions, miscarriages, broken ribs, crushed noses, fourteen years of hell with the likes of Eric. But tea didn't heal, it just felt good going down.

Ruth slowly sipped from her cup, then leaned back and closed her eyes. She'd made Karen a cup of lemon tea sweetened with two teaspoons of honey the day she'd died. It had been her favorite. She missed her mother sometimes; there'd been no one in her life who knew her the way Karen had known her. There'd definitely been no one who'd loved her the way she had. She was the kind of woman you wanted to put in a glass jar like preserves and maybe spread a little of her on a slice of warm buttered toast. Ruth wondered what Karen would say to her now, if she were here. What would she think of her Baby Ruth, who'd had her ass kicked for the umpteenth time by her husband? Ruth sat up slowly, took another sip from her cup, and then placed it on the table wondering why she even gave a damn about what Karen might've thought of her when the woman never even thought much of herself. Ruth wasn't fourteen years old anymore and Karen had had issues despite Ruth's best efforts to remember otherwise.

The day after the beating was always worse than the beating itself. The adrenaline was gone, the drugs had worn off, and the pain refused to let her forget what had happened despite her best efforts to do just that. Eric had stopped trying to hide the revulsion he felt for her a long time ago. She'd seen it in his eyes, tasted it in his venomous tongue, and absorbed the sting of his words through her pores. With everything he'd done to her, the words had cut the deepest. They'd been branded into her soul because they'd always been his most accessible weapons and the hardest for her to dodge. He'd kicked her hard enough to leave an imprint of his shoe on her thigh

and called her "stupid." He'd busted her lip a hundred times and
called her a lousy bitch (as opposed to a good bitch?). He'd broken
all of her fingers at least once and called her a "good-for-nothing
piece of shit." The bruises would eventually go away, the bones would
mend, and the swelling go down. But the words lingered, piling up
inside her like garbage, and when he wasn't around to pile on some
more, she could usually regurgitate them to remind herself of who
she really was. A stupid, lousy bitch who's a good-for-nothing piece
of shit. That pretty much explained how she felt at the moment.

Bernie stood in Ruth's doorway, looking stunning as usual, wearing
a burgundy business suit with a straight knee-length skirt, a belted
jacket cinched tightly around her waist, and matching pumps with
black tips on the toes. Her luxurious bone-straight mane cascaded
down past her shoulders. This was her "public assistance hair," she'd
explained. Meaning that someone from the public had assisted her
by putting in every track to her specifications and she'd paid them
dearly to do it. And of course, her makeup was flawless.

Bernie stood there for a moment, shaking her head in disgust.
"Car accident, huh?" Ruth wore a baggy T-shirt that had frayed at
the hem from years of use, and a pair of old sweats with holes in the
knees. She'd managed to gather up the tangled mass on her head
into some kind of ball, and tied it together with an old elastic head-
band.

"Bernie . . ." Ruth said, walking away, regretting having even answered the door.

"Looks more like you been hit upside the head with a dump truck.
Or maybe a husband with a bad attitude?"

Ruth rolled her eyes. Being hospitable wasn't a priority for her at
the moment. Besides, Bernie hadn't been invited and people who
weren't invited didn't deserve hospitality as far as Ruth was concerned. She made her way over to the sofa and carefully eased herself
down. "Thank you, Bernie. And yes. I'm fine," she said dryly.

Bernie found a place to sit, then looked around the house. "He
gone?"

"Who?" Ruth asked, absently.

"Attila the Hun. Who the hell you think I'm talking about?" she said smartly.

"I had an accident, Bernie. That's all it was. I was driving and—"

"And bullshit, Ruth!" she snapped. "And I'm a dummy and he's a saint and you a fool for letting him do this shit to you!"

Ruth stared at this woman, who was more of an acquaintance from the office than a friend. "You have no idea what you're talking about, Bernie. I had an accident."

"Who you think you're fooling, girlfriend? We been working together for how long, and you think I don't know? Hell, you think everybody in that office doesn't know?" Bernie sat back and angrily crossed her legs.

Tears clouded her eyes, and Ruth barely heard herself ask the question. "Everybody?"

"How many damn accidents can a woman have in a year, Ruth? A month? A week? Of course we all know."

Hearing that hurt almost as badly as the bruises and broken bones. Of course they all knew, Ruth thought to herself. How stupid could she have been thinking that a little makeup could cover up a black eye or busted lip? How many times had she tried to explain away Ace bandages? She'd been an idiot who'd fooled herself into believing she was smart. Only, no one else had been fooled at all. What a fucking joke.

"Have you eaten?" Bernie asked, sounding almost sympathetic.

Ruth shook her head then cleared her throat. "I'm not hungry."

Bernie was already rummaging around in the kitchen cabinets before Ruth had finished answering her question.

They'd met at the law firm three years ago when Bernie was hired on as a paralegal for one of Jacksonville's more high-profile litigation attorneys. Folks around the office called them the odd couple because they seemed as opposite as two people could be, and yet were inseparable. Mitch Taylor, the attorney, was a blond-haired, blue-eyed, health nut, while Bernie was an in-yo-face, neck twirling, sistah girl who could hold her own in the hood or at a dinner party. But when it came to business, Bernie shone like a cast member on one of those law shows. Mitch trusted her, he respected her, and some say, they'd even slept together. It was a known fact that they were often seen at the same social functions after working hours. Bernie would some-times visit Ruth in her cubicle and casually mention that Mitch had gotten her an invite to an exclusive party, or that *they'd* had dinner with a client. But she never insinuated that there was more going on between them, and Ruth, though curious, thought it impolite to ask.

Bernie found a can of chicken noodle soup, poured the contents in a bowl and warmed it up in the microwave. She propped her hand on her hip, then turned to Ruth, still sitting like a big lump on a log of sofa. "He is gone, right?"

"Yes," Ruth whispered.

The microwave beeped, and Bernie sat the bowl of soup down on the table, then searched the kitchen until she found a spoon. "Come on over here and eat." Ruth hesitated, but did as she was told. Bernie sat across from her at the table. "You got grits?"

Ruth stared down at her soup. "No."

"Every woman needs to keep herself some grits around the house, Ruth. Don't you know about grits?" Bernie smiled. Ruth shook her head. "Where you from, girl? Grits are the cure all for ignorant ass men, especially husbands. See"—Bernie leaned forward like she was about to tell Ruth a secret—"you wait until he's asleep, get him drunk or give him some pussy if you have to, but just get his ass to sleep. Then, you ease out of bed, go into the kitchen and boil you a pot of hot, sticky grits, then pour them scalding grits all over his shit."

Ruth chuckled, then instinctively clutched at her sore ribs to help ease the pain. "You're a trip."

"Damn right I am. Every man who knows me knows what kind of trip I am, which is why none of them gives me any trouble."

"No, I'll bet none of them do," Ruth responded quietly.

"You've been living with this for a long time, haven't you?" Bernie asked sincerely. "I kept hoping you'd talk to me about it."

"I couldn't. You'd think I was an idiot."

Bernie patted Ruth's hand. "And so what if I did? You still could have come to me. I know how to be tactful when I need to be, and I wouldn't have told you to your face that I thought you were an idiot for marrying that man. Not at first."

Ruth smiled, and tried to hold in her laughter. "Don't make me laugh, Bernie. It hurts."

"I don't know what it is about you, girl, but I've liked you since day one. And you ought to feel honored, because I don't get along with females all that well. Never have. But I like you."

"Well I like you too."

"No, you might think you like me, but you really ain't sure what to make of me. Which is fine. I understand, believe me. If I were you, I wouldn't know what to make of me either. But"—Bernie winked, and then smiled—"we might just end up being buddies before it's all said and done. What do you think?"

Ruth tried to smile, but her swollen lip made it nearly impossible. "I think I'd like us to be friends."

"Good. Now eat your soup."

"I'm really not very hungry, Bernie."

Bernie glared at her. "Girl, if you don't eat that damn soup!"

"I don't want the damn soup!"

"I didn't ask you if you wanted it. I just told you to eat it."

"And if I don't?" Ruth asked defiantly.

Bernie sat back and sighed. "You know, I don't ever have to leave. I ain't got nowhere to go. So you and me, we can sit at this table all night long waiting on you to finish that soup, if that's what you want. And I can talk, girlfriend. I can hold a conversation with you, myself, the walls, all night long if I want to and you don't want to hear all the mess I got to say. I can talk in my sleep, until I lose my voice, hell, I can whisper you to death. Now eat the damn soup or show me where the bathroom is so I can brush my teeth and pee before I get comfortable!" Bernie's argument won the battle and, reluctantly, Ruth ate the damn soup.

The worst thing about throwing a pity party for herself was that no one she invited ever showed up. Not even God.

Bernice

"THE LORD TAKES CARE OF FOOLS AND CHILDREN," BERNIE MUTtered to herself, pulling into the garage of her townhouse. And Ruth was no child. She'd sat with Ruth for hours until the evening news came on, and Ruth dozed off on the sofa. Bernie didn't bother to wake her. She turned off the television, covered Ruth with a light blanket, and quietly let herself out. Bernie had done most of the talking, biting down on her tongue every time the urge to fuss and cuss Ruth out eased up on her. The last thing that woman needed was to be bombarded with shouldas, wouldas, or couldas. Bernie at least had sense enough to know that. But once she was feeling better, oh, she was going to definitely come at girlfriend like a ton of bricks.

"How the hell you gonna let that mothafucka get away with this?" she rehearsed in her mind, along with, "I don't blame him. I blame yo' ass for letting him do it!" It was definitely coming and Ruth had better be ready when it did, because Bernie had never been one to hold her tongue for too long. It just wasn't in her nature.

Good taste. She was guilty of having plenty of it, in the way she dressed and in her home. Bernie's elegant apartment represented her views on how she saw herself. Classy, elegant, yet comfortable and welcoming. Okay, so the word "welcoming" wasn't necessarily an accurate description of her persona, but that didn't mean her home couldn't be. It welcomed her with a loving embrace each and every time she entered it. She'd had the nerve to put white carpet in when she bought the place. As was customary, Bernie immediately stepped out of her shoes as soon as she entered and slid into her baby blue slippers waiting for her by the door. Limited editions and prints from the likes of Charles Bibbs and Frank Morrison decorated her oyster white walls. Her eggshell leather sofa and loveseat were tastefully adorned with colorful mud and kente cloth pillows and throws. Her oldest son, Sean, always marveled at her place whenever he came by, and he'd never failed to ask "Momma? How you affording all this?" He'd wink with a sly grin. "You got a sugah daddy?"

Bernie always laughed, then snapped back at him that it was really none of his business. But no, she didn't have a sugah daddy.

"Oh, paralegals make a ton of money, I suppose?" he'd ask sarcastically.

"Not necessarily. But some paralegals got some damn good credit and know when to hit up a good garage sale or flea market sometimes. Now, take them shoes off before you stain my carpet!"

Bernie eased herself down onto the sanctity of her loveseat, closed her eyes, and finally took that deep breath she'd needed all evening. Sympathy, empathy, compassion, and understanding all had a way of leaving her feeling drained, which was why she usually tried to avoid them at all costs, if possible. Ruth had needed them, though. Funny how she had come to like that woman even though they'd never spent a whole lot of time together. Before today they'd eaten lunch together a few times, but nothing more than that. Ruth was just easy to like, that's all. And she'd always been one hell of a great listener, soaking in every ridiculous escapade Bernie had chosen to share with her like she was watching one of those daytime talk shows. She had a quiet elegance to her, despite the mess she was living in. Bernie could see it, even if Ruth never could. And Bernie appreciated that quality in her, because she wasn't pretentious with it. Bernie sometimes had a problem with pretentious people. They reminded her a lot of herself and that just wasn't cool. Ruth's problem was she was too nice. Bernie had seen signs of it at the office, when folks didn't seem to mind dumping all their work on her desk, because she never protested. Not openly anyway. But Bernie had seen her roll her eyes and utter things under her breath behind their backs, and from the looks of things, it had been Ruth's niceness that had gotten her wrapped up in the mess of a marriage she was in too. *Too bad*, Bernie thought. She never understood being nice like that, because she never had been. She'd been the only girl in a family full of boys, and had gone on to have a houseful of her own boys to take care of so, no, nice had no place in her world. Nice could get a woman killed if she wasn't careful, which it obviously had come close to doing to Ruth. But Bernie would take care of that. Once Ruth was up to it, she'd let her hang out with her sometimes and teach her how to raise a little hell. Folks respected a woman who could raise some hell more than they could a woman who never did. Bernie knew one thing: If Ruth's husband—what was his name? Eric?—if Eric had been her man, that fight would still be going on. Either that or her ass would be behind bars for murder, because she'd have beaten the shit out of him. Plain and simple. If she couldn't do it to him while he was awake, she'd get his ass while he was sleeping, and she'd wake him up just in time for him to see that cast-iron skillet coming down on his head.

The phone rang and Bernie glanced at her caller ID before answering it.

"Hello Miles." She sighed, knowing that she didn't have the energy to deal with him. If she were a different kind of woman, she'd have given some thought to making up an excuse as to why she couldn't see him tonight, and let him down easy without hurting his feelings. But it just wasn't in her blood. Poor man. Miles could be a little sensitive sometimes, a little emotional. She blamed it on his youth.

"I wish you'd get rid of that thing," his baritone voice crooned into her ear.

"Then how would I know it was you?" she teased.

"That's my point. Sometimes a man likes to surprise his woman." She could tell he was smiling.

Bernie let out an obvious sigh. "How many times do we have to have this conversation, Miles? I am not your woman, baby. You know better."

"Wishful thinking, Bernie. That's all it is." He was trying to hide the twinge of disappointment in his voice. Bernie could tell and decided that maybe she did need to rescue him after all.

"I keep telling you that I'm too old for you." She rolled her eyes at her own self for falling into that sympathy trap again. First Ruth had dragged her there, and now Miles was coming through to try and finish her off.

"And I keep telling you that age don't mean nothing to me. Especially where you and I are concerned."

Miles was trying to fall in love and Bernie regretted ever laying eyes on his ass. But he was addictive to her ego, which happened to have an insatiable appetite for the kind of attention he gave. She quickly decided it was time to change the subject. "It's late. What's up?"

He chuckled. "Hopefully you and me. I called earlier, but you weren't home. I left a message, though. Did you get it?"

"No. I haven't even checked my messages yet."

"Well?"

Bernie smiled. "Well, what?"

"Well, where you been?"

Bernie stopped smiling. "I beg your pardon?"

"I'm teasing, Bernie," he lied. "I know better than to try and check you like that."

"I certainly hope so, Miles. And I'm a little testy tonight, so be careful how you decide to play with a sistah."

There was no humor in her tone, and Miles decided to find an escape route as quickly as possible, before Bernie decided to throw some of her irritable wrath in his direction. He decided that maybe it was best to forego the comment he'd thought about making regarding PMS. "I'd love to play with a sistah," he said thoughtfully. "How about some company?"

"I'm tired and I've had a long day."

"A back rub might help. You know I'm damn good at rubbing backs. Especially tired ones."

That did sound nice, she thought. Miles had great hands, and a way with tired, worn out muscles too. But one thing would lead to another and—Miles had a way with a whole lot of things, she concluded. He liked to pamper and worked hard to impress. Images of him materialized into her mind. Images of tall, lean, handsome, dark chocolate Miles, hovering over her, his bald head, shiny with perspiration from his efforts, and all nine and a half inches of—"Bernie? You there?"

"Yeah," she said, sounding dazed. "Come on over, Miles."

"I'll be there in twenty minutes," he said, before hanging up.

Bernie closed her eyes and threw back her head, taking her time and concentrating on the issue of the moment. "Aw, yeah, baby," Miles moaned. "That's it, Bernie. That's it, girl."

Miles's hands kneaded her breasts, then pulled her down to him and wrapped his lips around her erect nipple.

"Oh . . . mmmm."

Bernie's hips moved slowly, backward and forward and Miles rose up, matching his thrusts with hers.

"Damn, Miles," she gasped.

"Is it good, Bernie? Is my shit good to you?"

"Yes! Oh, yes!"

As tired as she was, Bernie still couldn't sleep. The clock on the nightstand read 2:17 A.M. She stared at Miles, snoring quietly next to her, worn out from the magic he'd worked. Miles didn't know what it was to disappoint her, at least not sexually. Sleeping, he looked even younger than his thirty-two years, and a sense of the outlandish began to creep up inside her. The two of them were so silly together. Miles and his weird fetish for stretch marks. His eyes lit up like lightbulbs the first time he caught sight of hers.

"You're so beautiful," his voice quivered, as he stared at the golden trails on her lower belly. It made her a bit uncomfortable in the beginning, but now she was used to him. He loved to run his fingers lightly over them, and then his tongue, imagining that they tasted like something, but she couldn't think what. She'd asked him why he was so into stretch marks, but he couldn't seem to come up with a reason. Bernie figured that he'd had some kind of trauma as a child. Like maybe he'd seen his momma naked, and thought her stretch marks were candy or something crazy like that. She just left it alone, though. He loved her stretch marks and she loved the way he loved them, and they both came to that understanding and that's all there was to it. Miles was fun. Dramatic, but plenty of fun.

This wasn't how she'd planned on her life being at this stage in her life. Bernie was forty-three years old and had no business messing around with men not much older than her sons. Forty-three. Where did the time go? she wondered. Sometimes it amazed her that her circumstances had changed so drastically. Her life had been predictable and well thought out. It had been designed just the way she'd wanted it, and she'd just taken for granted that Monty, her ex-husband, had wanted it that way too. They'd met in high school when she was a sophomore and he was a senior. After he graduated, everybody thought they'd break up, but they didn't. He was crazy about her back then. Things happened fast and out of order. Bernie got pregnant, they got married, and nobody believed it would last, but it did. It lasted over twenty years, and then suddenly, it was over. Or maybe it hadn't been so suddenly. Years later, she knew there'd been nothing sudden about it at all. He'd stopped making love to her. He'd stopped coming home on time from work. They'd stopped talking to each other. Monty could be so stupid sometimes, but she figured he couldn't help it. He had no idea how to hide an affair, coming in smelling like he'd just showered. Fumbling through lies and getting all mixed up in them when she pressed him for details. Believing he was smart enough to make her think she was exaggerating or overreacting or imagining things, so hell yeah! She lost her cool and she lost it all over him.

"Who is she, mothafucka!" she'd screamed in his face, stabbing him in his chest with her two-inch, crimson acrylic nail. "Who's the bitch you're fuckin', Monty? Who's the skank?"

He'd never been good under pressure, at least, not her kind of pressure, and like Bernie knew he would, Monty cracked right before her eyes, and told her everything, including the six-year-old daughter he was helping to raise.

All Bernie remembered was going upside his head, and him leaving, vowing, "It's over, Bernie! I'm gone! I'm gone for good!"

Monty kept his promise. And they divorced and he married the heffa.

Monty had known Bernie for twenty-two years and he knew better than to think she'd curl up, die, and fade away in the wind just because his weak ass was gone. Shiiit! To hell with him and the bitch he'd ripped off her momma's titty! Bernie hurried up and got her paralegal certificate, got her hair done, maxed out all his credit cards before the divorce was final, and hadn't looked back. If he didn't want her, somebody would and somebody always did too. Men younger than Monty, and finer than Monty. Creative, innovative men, who knew better than to protest one bit when she threw a condom at them, demanding they put it on or leave because she wanted to get her groove on but that's all she wanted from them.

Call it temporary insanity, or revenge, or some kind of middle-age crisis. Hell, maybe she had developed a mental disorder after her marriage ended. But she was happy, wasn't she? That was the question she couldn't seem to find an answer to. In the beginning, her own sexual revolution had made her happy—at least she believed it had. She'd finally been able to release all her frustration and pent up passions with reckless abandon and believed she felt better afterward. Sometimes, however, she wasn't so sure. Miles's handsome ass turned over on his side, and he mumbled something in his sleep. He seriously wanted to believe he was falling in love, and all she could do was tell him how ridiculous he was. But she admired him for it sometimes, because he still had faith in love and shit like that. Bernie remembered being that way once, but in all honesty she'd fallen out of love with Monty long before they'd split up. She just hadn't seen any reason to admit it. At least Monty did something about it, and found in somebody else what they'd lost years ago. Bernie would've stuck it out. She'd have probably stayed married until death, and been pissed off and miserable about it.

Loving and being loved required a whole lot of energy, and Bernie figured she'd used up all hers in her marriage. Now she had enough energy for herself, but that was it.

Miles muttered again, then draped his arm across Bernie's waist. "What's for breakfast?"

Bernie rolled her eyes, then turned over to finally try and get some sleep. "Whatever you decide to pick up on your way home, I suppose. Now, hush. I'm trying to get some sleep."

Today

❧

THE FIRST TIME CLARA CALLED, RUTH ABRUPTLY ENDED THEIR conversation in less than sixty seconds, and politely asked her not to call back. The second time she called, Clara managed to get Ruth to tell her how she was feeling, they discussed the weather, the Jaguars and even the possibility of Ruth filing charges before she suddenly had to go. Ruth ended their conversation again, but this time, Clara clocked it at sixteen minutes. The third time she called, she'd actually convinced Ruth to get out of the house that she'd been imprisoned in for two weeks since she'd left the hospital and have lunch with her.

Clara had insisted that they eat outside, on the balcony of an Italian restaurant overlooking the river. "You need some sun, dear. Sitting up in that dark house all the time ain't doing a thing for your spirit."

Ruth closed her eyes, and let the rays soak into her skin like lotion, too immersed in the warmth to argue or protest. She swallowed a couple of painkillers before the waiter brought their food.

Clara noticed Ruth occasionally picking at her plate of spaghetti, and nibbling on her salad. "It's not good taking all those pills on an empty stomach." Ruth took a small bite of salad, and then sipped on her iced tea. "That prescription ought to be about out now, isn't it?"

"Did you bring me out here to lecture me, Clara? Because if you did, we should probably leave," Ruth snapped.

"A good lecture wouldn't hurt." Clara smiled.

Ruth rolled her eyes. "It wouldn't help either."

"Then I won't bother. But please eat something. Lunch is on me and I hate seeing good food go to waste."

"I've got money. I'll pay for my own lunch," Ruth said dryly.

"Why you acting like this?" Clara asked, finally letting her frustration come through. "I'm concerned about you, Ruth. Let me be concerned about you."

"Why *are* you so concerned? You don't know me. You don't know anything about me, Clara. And honestly, I don't appreciate being one of your bleeding heart causes. I'm sure there are plenty of other women out there who want, maybe even need, your time. I'm not one of them." Ruth angrily threw her napkin on to the table.

"Only because you're too stubborn to be one of them." Clara laughed at the expression Ruth shot in her direction. "That's right. I called you stubborn because that's exactly what you are, Ruth Ashton. A stubborn, silly woman with some far-fetched idea that she doesn't need anyone or anything."

"Maybe I don't."

"Or maybe you don't want to admit it."

Ruth pushed back from the table, picked up her wallet, and threw money on the table. "Thanks for lunch, Clara. I'll catch the bus home."

"You sit your hardheaded behind down this instant," Clara demanded. "I'll knock you down before I let you leave here. Now sit still."

Ruth glanced around, embarrassed at the scene Clara was causing, and then sat back down. "Say whatever it is you've got to say, so we can leave."

"I ain't saying nothing. I'm just going to eat, and we ain't leaving until you eat too, so"—Clara nodded her head at Ruth's plate—"get busy, dear. And what you don't finish up, you can take home for later."

After lunch, Clara had insisted on walking it off and she and Ruth strolled the shops of the Jacksonville Landing Mall. Clara talked incessantly. Ruth hardly said a word. "I've had quite a few husbands. My first husband, Anthony." Clara shook her head and moaned.

"Mmm. Now he was my first love. I adored the ground that man walked on. I sure did. We met in college and fell in love. Shortly after that, I ended up pregnant, and we were happy about it, but we hadn't expected it and weren't prepared for it either. It was hard sometimes, with us being so young and all, and with a baby, but we didn't do too bad. He worked at the paper mill while I went to college. My momma and his momma took care of Carolyn, that's my daughter. Anyway, we'd been married four years when he was diagnosed with lung cancer. A year later, he passed away." Clara saw a pair of shoes in a display window, and stopped. "You think the heels are too high on these shoes?"

Ruth shrugged. "They're too high for me, but—I suppose if you like high heels . . ."

"Child, I'd fall and break my neck in them shoes." Ruth surprised Clara by laughing. "After Anthony died, I met Harry. Now he was a good man too. I've been blessed to have had good men in my life. Harry came right in and after he courted me for a little while, asked me to marry him. And I said yes, because he was so good to me and Carolyn. The thing is, I married him on the, what do you call it, rebound?" She looked to Ruth for confirmation, who nodded her head and smiled. "He was smart enough to figure it out, but not me. I cried like a baby when he left, until I realized he'd done the right thing for both of us. He stayed long enough for me to finish school, though, and get my degree. Then there was Mark. Me and Mark stayed together for nearly sixteen years before I got tired of his ass."

"I thought you'd said that they'd all been good men."

"They had been. Mark was a good man, he was just a lousy husband, that's all. Didn't know what it was to come home at a decent hour. Always stopping off somewhere or spending money we didn't have. Turned out we made better friends after the divorce, though. We still friends and every now and then he stops by, and I'll make him some dinner, or we'll go out to eat. Of course, his wife ain't all that happy about it, but Mark doesn't care. We're friends, and he's always been better to his friends than he ever was to any of his wives."

Clara talked all afternoon about everything and nothing and anything to keep silence from filtering in. Silence might allow space for Ruth to interject her desire to go home and be left alone. She'd had enough of that, as far as Clara was concerned. Shoot, this woman needed to see that time hadn't stood still no matter how hard she'd wanted it too. In that house she'd closed herself up in, maybe it had. But outside, no. And Ruth needed to see that, and if it took getting her out of that house every day for her to realize it, Clara was prepared to drag her out kicking and screaming if necessary.

Clara slowly pulled her car up into Ruth's driveway. Surprisingly, Ruth didn't make a run for it like Clara thought she would. "Thank you for coming out with me, Ruth. I hope it made you feel better."

Ruth stared at her house, or rather, her dungeon, not as anxious to get back inside as she'd been when they'd left. She twisted the strap of her purse between her fingers. "Thanks for inviting me, Clara. And—I think I do feel better."

"Have you heard from him, since . . . ?"

Ruth quickly shook her head. "No. Thank goodness." Tears welled up in her eyes, and she wiped them away before they had a chance to fall. "I think he's got someone else."

Concern shone on Clara's face. "And what if he didn't? What if he didn't have someone else, Ruth? And what if he wanted to come home? Would you let him?"

"I'm finished, Clara. No. No, I'll never take him back."

Clara reached over and put her arms around Ruth, while she cried quietly on her shoulder. "Shhh . . . baby. It's all right. You ain't so alone, Ruth. I'm here if you need me. I'm always here if you need me. Getting rid of him was the best thing you could've done, baby. And I know it's hard now, but time will make it easier. It always does."

Ruth stood in her doorway and waved to Clara as she drove away. Clara had a way of talking too much, and eating too fast, and spending way too much money on shoes. She'd had too many husbands, wasn't as close to her only daughter as she'd have liked to have been, and lacked the good judgment to know when to leave well enough alone. But she smelled like roses, Ruth thought, inhaling the faint scent of Clara's cologne on her shirt. She had a way of laughing that came from deep down inside and sounded warm when it met her ears, and her hugs were infectious. All in all, it had been a pretty good day.

A Thousand Steps

As much as she hated to admit it, being back to work had been the best thing for her. Ruth hadn't seen or heard from Eric in over a month, and each day that passed without word from him sealed her fate more and more that maybe it was finally over.

"Wishful thinking, girlfriend," Bernie had told her. "Get you a restraining order. Fools like that don't know the meaning of the word 'over.'"

Ruth later mentioned the idea to Clara and she agreed it would be the best thing to do. She sat at her desk reading over the court order. According to that piece of paper, Eric had to stay at least one thousand feet from her at all times, or else. Or else she'd call the police and they'd come rushing in to rescue her, arrest Eric on the spot, and throw away the key. It was a simple enough concept, so why wasn't she convinced it would work? Because it seemed too simple, that's why. And if it really were so easy, then why the hell hadn't she done it before?

Bernie strutted over to Ruth's cubicle wearing a lime green linen suit, with matching shoes and fingernails and two cups of coffee. She handed one to Ruth, then sat down in the chair next to her desk and took a sip from her own cup.

"Dang, Bernie. You think that suit's bright enough?" Ruth asked sarcastically.

Bernie casually pretended to brush lint from her thigh. "Oh? I see we're feeling good enough to dish out a little sarcasm these days."

"I'm teasing," Ruth said apologetically.

"Tease all you want my sistah. This suit looks damn good on me"—Bernie smiled—"and that's all that matters."

Ruth laughed, then picked up her cup of coffee. "You're a mind reader, Bernice. I've been trying to get me a cup of coffee all morning."

"Is that it?" Bernie asked, leaning over Ruth's desk to get a glimpse of the restraining order she'd convinced her to get. Ruth handed it to her. "You know, your life might've been a whole lot easier if you'd done this before."

"I should've done a lot of things—before, Bernie. Like run screaming in the opposite direction the first time he said 'hello' to me."

Bernie smiled. "Well, our parents teach us not to talk to strangers for a reason. Some folks are stranger than others and they're the ones they try to protect us from. The crazy ones."

Ruth sighed. "But he didn't look so crazy in the beginning."

"Sure he did, Ruth. But you were young, and, I'm sure like most young women, you saw what you wanted to see."

"Hindsight is . . ." she muttered to herself.

"Always crystal clear."

She stared at Bernie for a moment. Ruth had no idea how it had happened, but they'd become friends. That's something she'd never had a lot of and now, all of a sudden, she had two—Bernie and Clara. Having friends meant having someone to talk to or listen to. It was nice.

"Begging and pleading works wonders on a twenty-year-old." Ruth laughed, then mocked Eric's desperate pleas for forgiveness, "Baby . . . I . . . I . . . I'm sorry, baby. Please, here—lemme see. Oh, it ain't that bad, Ruthie. It'll be fine. Lemme . . . lemme put a Band-Aid on it for you. Lemme get you a wet towel."

Bernie grinned, and then mocked Ruth's closer to accurate response than Ruth was comfortable with. "But Eric," Bernie said in an exaggerated high pitched tone, "it's broken."

Both women laughed hysterically, trying to keep from disturbing the whole office. "You are so wrong for that, Bernie."

Bernie composed herself, then looked at Ruth. "I'm just playing, girl. You know I am."

"Yeah, but you pretty much nailed it. Sad . . . but true." Sadness welled up inside her. Bernie hadn't missed it, even though Ruth had tried to hide it. It showed in her eyes. "I used to believe I needed that man. I believed he'd change or I'd change, or hell, somebody would change."

"If everybody came correct to relationships in the first place, nobody would have to change."

"Ain't that the truth," Ruth said, taking a sip from her cup. "Did I ever tell you, I was pregnant once?"

Bernie shook her head. "When was that?"

"Years ago. I thought, this is it. This is going to be what's going to fix this marriage. We're going to have this baby, and that's what's going to settle him down. Because ain't no way he's going to want to act ignorant knowing he's got a kid looking up to him." She'd never told anyone this story before. Ruth glanced nervously at Bernie, surprised that she was telling it to her.

"What happened?" Bernie whispered.

"He didn't want no goddamned baby, Bernie. His words, not mine." She swallowed hard, and then took a deep breath. "He took off, like he always did, and I didn't hear from him for a few days. Then some woman called my house saying that he'd been with her and that I was a sorry ass excuse for a woman because I couldn't keep him." Bernie handed her a tissue, but Ruth waved it away. "When he finally came home, we got into it. And—I told him I was leaving him. I'd packed and started to leave." She leaned in close to Bernie and whispered the rest of her story to her. "He grabbed me by my hair and threw me on the floor. Then, he pulled off his belt, and—"

Bernie couldn't believe what she was hearing. "Oh no . . . Ruth."

Embarrassment washed over her, and shame. She decided not to tell Bernie about how he dragged her into the bedroom, and ripped into her from behind until the burning turned into numbness and a bloody mess. She didn't go into detail about how, after he'd finished, he'd bathed her, then gently dried her off, helped her on with her nightgown and tucked her into bed. Or about how he'd kissed her goodnight, then warned her, *"Don't make me do this again, Ruthie. You know I don't like actin' like this."*

She picked up the restraining order and looked at it. "You really think this is going to help?"

"It'll help if he wants to act a fool," she said. *Dammit, Ruth!* Bernie said to herself. *Why'd she have to go and hit a sistah's nerve like that?*

"By the time the police get to me, he'll have plenty of time to act plenty of fool, Bernie."

Bernie stood up to leave and straightened her skirt. "Well, even if he does," she winked, "you just make sure you get a few good licks in before they come get him."

Ruth's phone had been ringing off the hook since she'd been home. It was late, and she knew it was Eric, and she knew he was pissed. Ruth sat up in bed, staring at the phone, debating over whether she should finally answer it or not.

"Hello?" she said hesitantly.

"What the hell is this shit, Ruth?" Eric roared into the receiver.

Ruth's heart beat hard in her chest. "Eric, you're not supposed to be calling here."

"Bitch! That's still my mothafuckin' house and my mothafuckin' phone and I'll call when I damn well—"

"You're violating the restraining order by calling me. You're—"

"Fuck yo' goddamned restrain' order, Ruth! It don't mean shit to you and can't do a thing to stop me from puttin' my foot up yo' black ass either! Why the hell you fuckin' with me?"

Ruth's voice quivered. "If you come near me, Eric, I'll—"

"You'll what? What the fuck you gon' do, Ruth? Huh? Whatchu think yo' sorry ass is gon' do to me?" Ruth's mouth moved, but nothing came out. "What? I'm askin', Ruthie! What the hell you gon' do?"

How many times has he used this trick? she wondered. Intimidation. Even over the phone and with a restraining order hanging over his head, Eric had pulled a sure thing out of his arsenal expecting her to fall for it. But she couldn't afford to do that this time because if she did, he'd have the upper hand, and if she gave it to him this time, he'd never let it go, and Ruth had grown weary of Eric's advantage.

"I'll call the police," she said more sternly. "If you come near me I'll call the police, Eric, and have them arrest your ass!"

Eric was unusually quiet for a moment, gathering himself. The calm before the storm? "Before or after I kick yo' ass, Ruth?" he asked matter-of-factly.

"Just make sure you get a few good licks in before they come get him."

He sighed heavily into the phone. "I'm tired of yo' fat ass, Ruthie. You don't need no restrainin' order 'cause I'm through. I'm the one who left you, girl. I'm the one that got sick of you, bitch! I still got shit up in that house, and I'll be by tomorrow to get it. And ain't nobody's restrain' order goin' to keep me from gettin' my shit, Ruth! You jus' make sho' you ass ain't around." Eric slammed the phone down in her ear.

He kept his promise and by the time she got home from work, all of his things, and some of hers were gone. A few days later she had all the locks changed, got a new phone number, and took the gun Bernie had given her and put it in the drawer of her nightstand by the bed. Not that she ever figured she'd use it, but it seemed to make Bernie feel better knowing she had it.

Chasing Good Intentions

IT WAS LATE, AND SHE WAS EXHAUSTED. BILLS AND RECEIPTS were strewn across her desk, covering up the old calculator she'd been chained to all day, trying to balance the books. But no matter what she did, the numbers kept coming up the same, and Clara had to face the fact that the center was running out of money with no prospects for any new funds to come through. She picked up a faded newspaper clipping and stared at the headline blaring back at her, "SAFE HOUSE OR BROTHEL?" The story beneath it detailed the account of one woman's accusations of Clara and her facility, corroborated by some low-life private detective hired by this woman to locate her daughter-in-law who was living in the shelter at the time. That Anderson woman's lies and money had turned the shelter upside down and inside out. There was a time when Clara had thought justice would come riding in on its white horse and save the day. But even after she'd been cleared of the charges, the damage had been done.

Eight months ago, Earline Anderson had come skidding up in a long black limousine, with six police cars behind her, lights and sirens blaring, bursting through the door, claiming that Clara was some kind of madam, running a prostitution ring.

"What the hell is going on?" had been the first words out of Clara's mouth, as the police stormed in and arrested every woman living in the house at the time. The children were taken away by social services, and Clara had to undergo a grueling investigation and endure public humiliation for the authorities to find out what she already knew. The woman had lied. All charges were eventually dropped but things were never the same. Donations ceased to come in, and requests for grants were repeatedly denied.

"Lord," she said exasperated, "the Bahamas are looking mighty good right about now. I wonder how much a one-way ticket would cost?" Visions of a crystal clear ocean, something cool and blue in a frosted glass, adorned with a tiny orange-and-yellow umbrella, and a dark skinned young man named Samuel rubbing her back and shoulders filtered into her thoughts between bills that needed to be paid and next quarter's budget requirements.

The knock at her door interrupted her fantasy. "Come in."

One of the women living at the shelter timidly peeked in. "Hi Clara." She smiled.

"Hello Marie. Everything all right?"

"Yeah. I've just finished up the dishes and was on my way to bed. You need anything?"

Clara smiled, touched by the woman's kindness and consideration. "No, sweetheart. I'm fine. You go on to bed now."

"Well, don't be up all night, Clara. You need your rest too."

Marie softly closed the door and Clara took a deep breath. Yes. She did need some rest. She needed some help too, but finding it was easier said than done. No one ever stayed for long, especially after the scandal. Not that she could blame them. Even Clara was running out of steam. Trying to save this place was like running up a sand dune, and lately she'd felt like she was getting absolutely nowhere very fast. The truth was, she'd never been any good at handling the administrative tasks of running the shelter. That had been Ruby's job.

"You just save the souls, Clara," Ruby had told her time and time again. "I'll do the paperwork." Ruby balanced the books, raised the money, paid the bills, and built relationships with sponsors. They'd worked together like a machine back then, and between the two of them, there was nothing they couldn't accomplish. Now Clara was buried in a mess she didn't know how to clean up, and she wondered if maybe this wasn't God's way of telling her it was time to move on.

A lump formed in her throat at the thought of Ruby Higgins.

She'd been the glue that had held this place together, and without her Clara saw it falling apart right in front of her eyes. It should have been the other way around, she'd always thought. And if it hadn't been for one minor change in plans, it would've been.

Had it really been four years? Clara wondered. Asha Barlow had been getting ready to move out of the shelter and into her new apartment, but the landlord had insisted on painting it first. The girl had gone through such a horrendous ordeal, having spent a month in the hospital after being beaten nearly to death by her boyfriend. She'd been seven months pregnant and lost the baby. It was that loss that had sent her to the shelter. "He's taken everything from me, Clara," the girl sobbed. "And there ain't no way I'm going back to him."

She'd been in the shelter for three months before getting a job and the new apartment. The last thing she'd wanted was to spend even one more night in the shelter, so Clara offered to let her stay with her for a few days until her apartment was ready. But at the last minute, Clara had some unexpected guests come in from out of town, and Ruby agreed to let Asha stay with her. A phone call in the middle of the night delivered the news to Clara. Asha's boyfriend had broken into Ruby's house and shot and killed them both, and then turned the gun on himself. Clara crumbled. Everyone kept telling her that there was nothing she could've done. For some reason, she could never accept that.

The phone rang and Clara's pulse raced. This time of night a ringing phone could mean anything, usually something terrible. "Hello?" she asked anxiously.

"Clara?" Ruth asked. "I figured you'd be there."

"Is everything all right?" she asked instinctively.

Ruth laughed. "Yes. Everything's fine. Look, I'm sorry to be calling so late, but I've left a few messages on your home phone, and—"

Clara breathed a sigh of relief. "I'm sorry, Ruth. I've been so busy."

"That's fine. I just hadn't seen you in a while and wanted to know if you'd like to go to lunch or something later this week."

Clara laughed. "Yes. That would be nice. How about Sunday? We could go to brunch."

"Sunday's good. Ever been to Eden's Garden? I hear they do a fabulous spread."

"That sounds wonderful, dear. About eleven?"

"I'll be there," Ruth said assuredly.

After she hung up the phone, Clara turned off the calculator and stacked the papers up in one corner of her desk. The clock on her desk read 10:30, which was much too late to be looking for a miracle. Clara rubbed her tired eyes. She was looking forward to having brunch with Miss Ruth who was fast becoming one of her favorite people. Over the years, Clara had come to see a woman's problems and her personality as being one in the same. It was hard to separate the two most times. But Ruth seemed to make it her mission to try and separate them in herself. She seemed to be intent on keeping her past out of their conversations, choosing instead to talk about other things. Things that friends talked about, like clothes, current events, talk shows. Clara hadn't made a new friend in years, but Ruth had become her friend. One that still refused to accept rescuing because she insisted on saving herself, but had allowed Clara the honor of coming along for the ride.

Suddenly Clara wondered who was really saving who. She'd been so wrapped up in the politics and business of this job that Clara had nearly forgotten what it was to have a friend. Ruby had been her friend, and Lord, she missed the mess out of Ruby Higgins. Clara stood up, stretched her arms over her head, then grimaced at the sounds of her fifty-four-year-old joints cracking, sounding like brittle wood. Clara gathered her purse, turned off the lights, and closed the door behind her on her way out. There was a nice brandy waiting for her at home and she would almost swear she heard it calling her name.

Peace

"RUTH?" MR. MCGREGGOR CALLED FROM THE INTERCOM ON Ruth's desk.

Ruth sighed, then rolled her eyes dramatically before responding, "Yes, Mr. McGreggor?"

"I still haven't seen that partnership agreement for Lewis and Haverty? I thought you told me you'd have that finished today," he snapped.

"I finished it yesterday, Mr. McGreggor."

"Well, why isn't it on my desk?"

"It is on your desk. I put it there this morning." The man was notorious for misplacing things in that black hole he called his office, and Ruth usually ended up being blamed for it, or responsible for finding it. She'd put the file on his desk that morning before he'd come in and laid it in his chair so that he'd be sure to see it. It had probably gotten sucked up his ass or something, she thought, smiling.

"I don't see it," he said irritatingly.

Ruth took a deep breath and spoke slowly, "I put it with the industrial lease and the LLC operating agreement, Mr. McGreggor."

"The industrial . . . Oh yes. Here it is." He abruptly hung up without so much as a "Sorry Ruth" or "Oops, my bad."

"Ruth?" he buzzed through again.

"Yes."

"Do you have Shelton's guarantee agreement ready?"

"No. You told me you didn't need it until tomorrow's meeting."

"I told you we moved the meeting up a day."

"No, Mr. McGreggor. I don't think you did. I'd have written it on my calendar if—"

"Never mind. The meeting's today, Ruth, at two and I'll need that agreement on my desk in an hour."

"An hour? But what about—"

"An hour, Ruth." Ruth was so mad she could spit. She hadn't even started on that damn agreement because she'd been so busy with all the other crap he'd piled on her desk at the last minute. Most of the time, she felt like a circus animal trained to jump through hoops, because that seemed to be her specialty at the office. Hoop jumper! And bonehead, her boss, was the ring master. Ruth glanced at his calendar she maintained for him on her computer. He'd be out of town the following week, which meant she'd practically be on vacation.

Ruth had just turned off her computer to go home for the evening and looked up in time to see Bernie making her way over to her cubicle for her customary end of the day how-you-doing visit. "What's up for tonight, girlfriend?"

"I thought you'd be gone by now. Ain't it a little late for divas?" Ruth teased.

"Yeah, but some of us divas still have to work for a living, girl. I've got my fingers crossed for that trust fund, though, which ought to be coming through any second now. But shhh. Don't tell Mitch. He'd have a heart attack if he ever thought he'd lose me."

Ruth's eyes grew wide at the sight of an opportunity dropping dead at her feet. "Can I ask you something about Mitch?"

"What do you want to ask me about Mitch?" Bernie asked coyly, knowing full well where this was leading.

"Are the two of you—you know—intimate?"

"Not lately!" Bernie smiled slyly. "But he and I have reached an unspoken agreement on the subject."

"Meaning?" Ruth asked, trying to hide her shock at Bernie's confession.

"Meaning, we make better friends than lovers. Besides, I've never had much of a penchant for white men anyway. Mitch and I experimented. He'd never been with a black woman and I'd never been with a white man." Bernie shrugged. "Now, we can both say we've been there."

"So, it's never gotten in the way of your working relationship?"

"Mitch is my friend, and he always will be. Besides, fucking him could mess up a good thing. Mitch hangs tough with Jacksonville's elite, and sometimes he lets me tag along. Never know when one of those might come in handy—an elitist. It's not what you know, but—you know the rest."

Ruth giggled. "You're amazing."

"Girl, I am, and thank you for having the nerve to say so."

"You're welcome."

"And if you ever want to tag along on one of those fancy social functions Mitch is always going to, let me know. He likes you anyway and I'm sure he wouldn't mind having you around. He's got a lot of single, handsome friends," Bernie said slyly. "Handsome lawyers, black, white, just choose your flavor, momma."

"I'm not even divorced yet, Bernice. Why would you tell me something like that?" Ruth propped her hand on her hip, and waited for something resembling a decent response to come out of Bernie's mouth.

"Divorce? You waiting on that?"

Ruth laughed. "Some of us do."

"Saints?"

Ruth rolled her eyes. "No. Just people who aren't in a hurry, that's all. Besides—" Ruth started to say something, but decided against it. "Never mind."

"Never mind what? What were you going to say oh saintly, unhurried one?" Bernie teased.

"Look at me, Bernie. I don't exactly have men standing in line, sweating me."

"Yeah, that outfit ain't cute, honey."

Ruth sucked her teeth. "I'm not talking about the outfit. I'm talking about the fact that I weigh a hundred and ninety pounds. I'm huge and I'm not about to lie to myself and think there might be someone out there looking at me. Don't nobody want this."

Bernie crossed her arms. "Eric tell you that?"

"It's got nothing to do with Eric."

"Damn near everything about you has to do with Eric, Ruth. Like it or not."

"He didn't make me sit up and eat junk all night."

"Well he kept you from having a life. What the hell else was there for you to do, but eat?"

Ruth shook her head. "You don't get it, Bernie. You've never had a weight problem, so you have no idea where I'm coming from."

"A weight problem? Child, you took care of your weight problem when you changed the locks on the door. Eric was your weight problem. Now that he's gone, the rest is gravy."

Ruth laughed. "Gravy's been part of my problem. But I am trying. I started a diet a few weeks ago so wish me luck. All right?"

"Good luck. So, what we going to do tonight?" she asked, quickly changing the subject.

Ruth sighed. "After the day I've had, *we* ain't doing nothing. I'm going home to sit in my favorite chair, sip on a glass of wine, and listen to Anita Baker sing all that nonsense about lovin' and apologizin' and baby this, baby that. You know how she is."

"Yeah. Got some crazy ass notions about love. That's for damn sure."

Ruth laughed. "I'm not convinced either, but she sure sounds good."

"I've got a better idea. Let's go to Jim's Place and get a drink. It's ladies' night. Two for one and all the hot wings you can eat."

"Didn't I jus say I was on a diet? Besides, I'm not into clubbing, and I wouldn't be very good company anyway. I'm exhausted."

"Since when has anyone ever accused you of being good company? I just wanted you to come along to be the designated driver," Bernie said teasingly.

"Ha. Ha. Ha," Ruth said dryly. "You think you're funny."

"I have my moments."

"Well, you go and have fun for both of us, Bernie. I'm wiped out."

"Oh girl, you know me. Fun is my middle name and don't nobody know how to have fun like I know how to have fun. But you just wait. By the time I'm through with you, you're going to know how to have a good time your damn self."

"Reading a book. Now that's a good time. You ought to try it. A good book, a quiet evening alone—"

"Some warm milk and crackers, then a nap. Sounds thrilling, dear. You scare me sometimes."

"Well, I don't do it on purpose."

Bernie's expression softened and she asked, genuinely concerned. "How you doing, though? Seriously."

"I'm all right, Bernie. Just trying to get myself together. That's not easy you know. I've got an awful lot of baggage." Ruth laughed. "And it weighs a ton sometimes."

"Sure it does and it can take a while to unpack all of it and put it away. But you be patient with yourself." Bernie winked.

"I cry all the damn time, but—it feels good. Like I'm purging myself. Let's see"—Ruth held up her hand, and then counted on her fingers—"Anger, guilt, shame, confusion, lack of both self-esteem and confidence. Did I forget anything?"

"Lord, I hope so!" Bernie laughed. "That's plenty."

"Well, I'm working on getting rid of them. I certainly don't want them, but they've been mine for so long, I'm not sure how to let them go."

"You can let them go, Ruth. The thing is, you've got a bad habit of hanging on to them, but that's all it is. A habit. In time you won't have any trouble getting rid of them. No woman in her right mind wants to carry around no mess like that."

"Well, there you go. Who said I was in my right mind?"

"I do. Believe it or not, you are more in your right mind now than you've been the whole time I've known you."

"That's good to hear." Ruth smiled. "Blame it on prayer, some good books, and no drama. That's all I need right now."

"Well." Bernie turned to leave. "You just promise me one thing."

"Anything."

"When you're finished unloading all that junk, mending those wounds, and piecing together that broken spirit of yours, we're going to get together and go to Jim's Place for some margaritas and hot wings."

"Definitely, girl."

"Your treat?"

"Absolutely. I owe you."

Bernie smiled. "No, Ruth. You owe yourself."

———

Ruth kept her promise to herself and curled up in her favorite chair as soon as she got home. Peace and quiet was addictive. Most evenings she'd come home to this chair and not bother to turn on anything—the television, stereo, even the lights. She'd been indulging herself since Eric had been gone, settling into a calm that had been foreign to her most of her life. She knew she'd never willingly give this up again. Not without a fight, anyway.

Ruth cradled her wine in her hands, immersed in the kind of vibe that made the rest of the world seem far enough away not to be an issue anymore, wondering how she could've ever lived for thirty-three years without this. Even when Eric was gone, the anticipation of him coming back was enough to keep her in hell and she didn't dare get used to her solitude. She'd constantly check the refrigerator, making sure it was filled with everything he liked. Or she'd check and double-check his laundry to make sure it was folded the way he preferred and put away just the way he wanted it. Her mind had constantly been filled with the challenge of keeping everything perfect and not giving him a reason to get angry. There was no peace or quiet in living like that.

Bernie was always telling her to relax and finally Ruth realized she was learning how to do that. Sometimes it wasn't easy, though, because she'd become conditioned over the years to always being prepared for a fight, and there were moments where she still expected him to come blazing a trail through the front door, mad as hell and ready to wage war all over her ass. What had surprised her most was that he hadn't. Whoever she was, this other woman was doing one hell of a job holding his interest, keeping him so wrapped up in her that Ruth really was of no consequence to him anymore. In retrospect, she knew she never had been.

She smiled, wishing she could bottle up peace and quiet and spray a little on her wrists, behind her knees, between her breasts like perfume, and inhale the sweet aroma of the undramatic all the time.

"What have you done to me? I can't eat. I cannot sleep. And I'm not the same anymore—no, no."

There she goes again, Ruth thought, smiling. Anita Baker hitting the proverbial nail on the head, singing exactly what Ruth was feeling. No, she wasn't the same anymore either.

Free Bird

RUTH WALKED TENTATIVELY THROUGH THE HALLWAYS OF THE
Duval County Courthouse. The place where she and Eric were married and the tomb that imprisoned her joy nearly fifteen years ago
when she condemned herself with two little words, "I do." But today,
she was here to get back what she'd been tricked out of when she
was that naive eighteen-year-old girl. Freedom.

Ruth walked into the courtroom to the sight of Eric, who she
hadn't seen in eight months, and his new love interest, Sheila. *Go
on with yo' bad self!* Ruth tried not to stare at the girl. Bless her heart,
Sheila had come dressed to the hilt for the occasion, wearing a red
leather miniskirt, white ruffled blouse, accessorized with red panty-
hose and three-inch high-heeled white shoes. A gold-plated chain
belt held her together while at least a foot of hair molded into
mounds of loops, curls, and waves added to her very short stature.
Ruth caught a glimpse of her smile, and nearly passed out at the
flash of silver in her front teeth, completing this girl's fashion statement.

The girl looked young enough to be his daughter. Hell, maybe she
was his daughter. Lord knew Eric was capable of just about anything,
the least of which was incest. Ruth guessed her age to have been
around eighteen, maybe nineteen. All in all, she was an attractive
young woman. For the life of her, Ruth couldn't figure out what the
girl could possibly see in an old man like Eric. For that matter, what
had she ever seen in him? She could ponder that question for an

eternity and still not come up with an answer that made any sense. Sheila was the girl he'd been seeing when they'd broken up. Ruth shifted in her seat at the sight of them, thinking how tacky it was for Eric to bring his new girlfriend to his divorce proceedings, but then, what he did was no longer any of her business, which was fine with her. She was just glad he'd showed up.

They glanced back at her, giggling like children, and whispering loud enough for her to hear. "That her, Eric?"

"Yeah, baby. That's her."

Sheila turned and gave Ruth a thorough assessment before rolling her eyes and turning back to him. "Damn! She is big. Whatchu do with a big old woman like that?"

Eric shrugged. "Shiiit! I made sure I got on top." Sheila laughed.

There he goes again, Ruth thought to herself. Reminding her of how insignificant her feelings have always been in his world. But none of that mattered to her now because this day belonged to her. Not to Eric and not to his little valentine on two legs either.

She sat behind them, wondering how she should feel. The man she'd spent almost half her life with, her husband, was sitting in front of her with his new woman at their divorce proceedings and very soon her marriage to him would be over. As if it never happened? Hardly. Remnants of him would likely always be a part of her. No matter how hard she tried, she'd never be able to wash away the scent of her past with this man, and she'd definitely tried. After a while, she just figured that the best she could hope for was that time would gradually fade the pungent odor of her marriage and that soon, the memories would become so faint, she'd have to wonder if maybe she hadn't dreamed the whole thing.

All of a sudden, Eric didn't look so intimidating anymore. Watching him, Ruth saw him magically transform into exactly what he was: a forty-four-year-old man desperately needing to feel important. Sitting next to that child, his arrogance screamed for her attention because if she didn't give it to him, no one else would give a shit about him. Lord, how come she hadn't seen it before? He wasn't even good looking, and the man was as dumb as a peanut, which is why he had to meet all of his girlfriends on their way home from grade school. No grown woman, no mature, adult woman who knew anything about something would give his sorry ass the time of day. Suddenly Ruth realized the truth of why she'd grown tired of him and the truth of why his pathetic ploys of manipulating her, winning her back, or threatening her into submission had failed to work. She'd grown up.

They waited nearly an hour for their names to be called to go before the judge. Of course that seemed like an eternity to Ruth, but it would be over soon. Any ties to Eric would be severed completely, including giving him back his last name.

Ruth had spent all night praying and begging God to make Eric show up here today. "Heavenly Father," she'd said, kneeling down by the side of her bed, sipping occasionally from a sour apple martini, "I know I brought this shit on myself. I know I made a mistake by marrying this asshole, but I was stupid and I was young and young stupid people have a terrible sense of judgment. Please . . . please! Don't make me have to pay for this one forever. Get Eric's ass to the courthouse, Lord. Whatever it takes—thunder, lightning, floods, plagues—please! Whatever you've got to do, God, I don't mind." Ruth had tears in her eyes, knowing that yes, God did sometimes answer prayers, and even a little bit of faith could move mountains, or in her case, get Eric to show up at their divorce.

Standing in front of the judge, she waited patiently while he decreed the divorce final. She didn't contest and crossed her fingers, closed her eyes and prayed some more that he wouldn't either. Then, it was over. Her marriage was finally over, and Ruth stood numb for a moment trying to gather her thoughts and sort out the ramifications of the impact of it all.

"Thank God!" Both the judge and Eric stared at her. *Oops!* She hadn't meant to say that out loud.

On her way out of the courtroom, Eric's friend Sheila, the naive, little idiot that she was, glared at her as if she were the enemy. Ruth almost felt sorry for her and wanted to tell her that the enemy was the man standing next to her, but she didn't. Let the little heffa figure it out on her own.

"Ruthie," Eric called out as she passed him on the way out of the courtroom. Ruth turned and looked in his eyes for what she'd hoped would be the last time. He wasn't her husband anymore and Ruth felt relieved, regretful, remorseful, oh, and did she say relieved?

"Goodbye, Eric," she said to him, before leaving the courtroom.

Once out of the building, Ruth gazed out over the river and realized how beautiful it looked for what seemed like the first time. "Free at last! Free at last! Thank God Almighty! I'm free at last!"

A man going into the building stopped and smiled at her. "Divorce?"

Ruth grinned and nodded her head. "Yep!"

"Congratulations!" He smiled back.

She skipped down the stairs toward the parking lot. Maybe this would be a good day to meet Bernie at Jim's Place for those margaritas and hot wings, she thought to herself. To hell with the diet!

Brand New

SHE LOVED MORNINGS, ESPECIALLY THESE DAYS. RUTH LAY IN bed, stretching like a cat, relishing tranquility that greeted her with a kiss. Daylight crept through the window blinds and etched shadows and sunshine onto her skin. Feeling good was becoming a common occurrence for her these days because she'd started over. Ruth had finally escaped from the confines of those dingy, beige walls saturated with Eric's cussing and fussing, and that dirty brown carpet that had soaked up her blood, sweat, and tears like a thirsty sponge. It had been nearly six months since her divorce. She'd sold the place and moved into a condo so small that she had to go outside to change her mind, but she loved it. There was just enough room for her and not an inch more. The couple who bought the house moved down from Georgia to be closer to their family, and they were ecstatic to get a place. Ruth didn't want to throw rocks at their elation to reveal the kinds of secrets held prisoner inside those walls. She just hoped they'd be happier there than she'd been. She fell in love with the condo the first time she saw it, and decided on the spot that it was meant for her. It probably held secrets too, but she didn't know what they were and she didn't care to know. All that mattered was that a fresh coat of paint and shiny hardwood floors greeted her when she walked in and any secrets lurking around this place were really none of her business.

Naturally, Eric had given her a hard time when she told him she was selling the house. After all, it was, his *"goddamned house too!"*

Yeah, his name was on it, but he'd never done shit for it. She'd been the one to clean it, keep the lawn mowed, fix whatever was broken. He just ruled it, and she concluded that in his mind, that had been an invaluable contribution. Instead of buying him out, she promised him half of what she got from the sale minus any repairs she was responsible for fixing. He was cool with that. They'd paid $36,000 for the house, and it sold for $115,000. Ruth sent Eric a check for $15,000. Math had never been one of Eric's strong suits, and the diluted explanation she'd given him seemed to suffice. She never bothered to tell him, though, that there hadn't been any repairs needed on the house.

Ruth took her part of the money and used it for the down payment on her condo, and bought all new furniture. She managed to find a luxurious butter-soft suede loveseat the color of sand and an antique ivory armchair on sale at a discount furniture store on the southside of town. Both had big, fluffy pillows that cradled her like a baby every time she sat down on them. Then, some dummy at a yard sale practically gave away a beautiful antique oak coffee table that Ruth was smart enough to snatch right up without appearing too eager, of course. It all matched perfectly—the condo, the furniture, her contentment.

She stared out the window, watching Jacksonville, Florida, wake up on this beautiful Saturday morning. Ruth sipped gingerly on her cup of tea, listening to Rachelle Ferrell humming a delicious melody from her stereo, trying to decide if she felt like leaving the house, or if she'd prefer to stay in, and lounge around in her pajamas all day. Maybe she'd do her nails. She smiled. Or maybe, she'd just pack her bags, say to hell with it, leave everything behind—her condo, new furniture, Florida—fill her car with some extra panties, tampons, and Oreos and drive off into the sunset. The truth was, just moving out of the house had been a huge step for her, so she knew better than to think she had the guts to really run away. But she wished she did have that kind of courage. She'd throw caution to the wind and let the road take her to wherever it wanted her to go. And when she got there, she'd stop long enough to pee, then get back in the car and drive off toward some other sunset in some other town, until she'd hit every last one of them. After that, she'd start all over. "One of these days," she muttered, then laughed and took another sip of tea. Maybe one day she'd take herself up on that dream, but until that time came, this place would do just fine. Ruth felt renewed here because her new home was filled with her energy and no one else's. It had become her haven and sanctuary. Everything in it belonged to her and her spirit ruled this small, two-bedroom world, which was cool with her because her spirit was pleasant and easy to get along with.

Ruth discovered the little park a few blocks from her building early one morning when sleep ended a little too early and her mind was flooded with the dreaded disease of thought. Too much of it, like anything, can be hazardous to a woman's health and she needed to get away from it, so she decided to take a walk to clear her head and stumbled onto this place. The first time she showed up, the ducks in the pond looked at her like she was crazy. How dare she come here, sit on their park bench, and not bring breakfast? Of course, she quickly learned her lesson and Pinky, Stinky, Dinky, and Jamal ate well whenever she came around—popcorn, bread, leftover pizza. She'd tried sharing her low fat menus with them, but figured by their reactions that they weren't on no damn diets and she'd better get them some real food—or else! Eventually, she found herself shopping for a family of five—herself and the ducks.

She'd never admit it out loud, of course, but she marveled at the woman she'd seen on her visits to the park, darting around the lake, walking at a pace that defied all reason. Ruth had no idea how many times the sistah had been around the lake before she got there, but she counted at least five or six more laps before she'd finish, get in her car, and leave Ruth to the solace of nature and ducks. She looked good, Ruth thought, trying not to stare. She was obviously in very good shape, and thin. Ruth shifted uncomfortably, knowing that all the salads and yogurt in the world would never make her look like that. She'd lost some weight. Not a lot. Not enough for most folks to notice, but a few pounds. The woman walking around the track was probably a size eight, Ruth surmised. Of course, from looking at the woman, Ruth figured she'd probably never been that big in the first place. Skinny people obsessed over being skinny and those were the people who had gym memberships and walked twenty laps around lakes filled with greedy ducks. They were pretty close in height, Ruth noticed, pretending not to stare. About 5'3", maybe 5'4". She would never want to be that skinny, though. Ruth turned up her lip and peered over the rim of her shades at Miss Super Walker propelling her petite little self around the lake. All that exercising couldn't be healthy, she concluded. That woman walked like she was obsessed and no kind of obsession was good. She'd learned that from her marriage.

"Mornin'," the woman said, smiling as she passed Ruth again.

"Mornin'," Ruth mumbled, wondering if her ass had ever been that tight. Maybe years ago, when she was younger. Girlfriend couldn't have been more than twenty-five, maybe twenty-six. No. Ruth sighed. Her behind had never looked like that. As a matter of fact, it had gone out in search of adventure long before she'd hit twenty-five. Where did the time go?

The peck on her leg startled her. "Damn ducks!" Inky, or was that Stinky? One of them had suddenly contracted rabies or something and had started attacking her shin. She looked down at her bag and realized she was out of food, which explained it. Besides, it was time for her to go anyway. These ducks knew that if she were to sit here much longer, she'd be late for work so they instinctively got her up and moving before she'd have to face the wrath of McGreggor the Merciless. Damn, she thought, looking back at them fondly. How come nobody ever told her that having pets was this cool?

Two weeks later, Ruth sat in her usual place while her ducks finished off the last of the corn flakes. She was just about ready to leave when Miss Super Walker appeared out of nowhere. "Mornin'," she said, but instead of whisking past Ruth at the speed of light, she surprised her and actually sat down.

"Mornin'," Ruth replied hesitantly, wondering what in the world this woman wanted.

"I'm May," she said, extending her hand for Ruth to shake.

"Hi . . . May. I'm Ruth."

After a few seconds of uncomfortable silence, May decided to break even more of the ice between them. "You doin' all right?"

Ruth cleared her throat, hoping she didn't look as uncomfortable as she felt. "Um . . . Yes. I'm fine. And you?"

May smiled. "I'm feelin' pretty good. I been seein' you out here jus' 'bout every mornin'."

Ruth quickly discovered that May's southern accent was as thick as molasses and listening to her was going to take a lot of patience. "Well, I only live a few blocks from here and sometimes I just like taking a little walk before I go off to work."

"You work on Saturdays?"

Ruth looked confused, and then it suddenly dawned on her. "Saturday . . . Oh! No, I mean . . . it is Saturday, isn't it? No. I don't. But, I just like coming out here. That's all."

"You ever thought about walkin'?"

"Walking? Like you?"

"Yeah." She smiled. "I try and do it every mornin' if I can, and I love it."

You would, Ruth wanted to say, but decided against it. *And no, I don't go for walks that threaten to break the sound barrier, but thanks for asking.* She wanted to say that too, but—"Well I've . . . I don't think I'd have enough time, you know . . . with having to get to work so early and all."

"Well, what time do you have to be at work?"

"Nine," Ruth said quickly.

May laughed. "Oh, girl, you got plenty of time to get a good workout in. I have to be at my job by eight-thirty and I work downtown. Where do you work?"

Ruth hesitated before answering. "Downtown."

"You got sneakers?"

Ruth looked down at her feet. "I've got these."

"Those the only ones you got?" May asked, crinkling up her nose.

"Well . . ." Ruth tried not to sound offended.

"You'll need somethin' with more support than those. Otherwise you could hurt yo'self. There's a discount store on Wells Road called Sports Way Shoes. You can get a good pair of walkin' sneakers there for less than fifty dollars."

Ruth stared speechless at this presumptuous woman, wondering what in the world she was implying. And why would she need to spend fifty dollars on a pair of shoes to sit out here and feed ducks? "Thanks. I'll keep that in mind."

"Good," May said, getting up. "Then I'll see you here on Monday, but you've got to be here at 6:30 if we're goin' to get to work on time. Okay?" May smiled, then set out on her daily trek around the lake.

"Yeah . . . Monday." Ruth chuckled. That woman was out of her mind if she thought Ruth was showing up at 6:30 Monday morning in new shoes to walk around the park with her skinny ass. Some folks were just rude like that, though, and she figured that maybe it would be best for her to just find herself a new park and stay out of this woman's line of fire altogether.

"Hey, girl!" May beamed walking in Ruth's direction. "I see you got some new sneaks."

Of course Ruth had only decided to do this because she'd contemplated doing something to help get rid of the weight and dieting alone hadn't really helped a whole lot. Besides, she liked walking and having a partner would be nice and maybe even give her the encouragement she needed to stay motivated. That's all.

"How they feel?"

Ruth nodded and smiled. "Pretty good."

"Good. You stretch yet?"

"Sure," she lied. She was out of shape, but not that out of shape. After all, they were only going to walk, not run a marathon.

"Then let's go."

Halfway into the first lap, Ruth knew she'd made a terrible mistake. It seemed a simple enough concept, walking off the fat, but she might as well have been climbing Mt. Evans.

"C'mon girl!" May called over her shoulder. "You can do it!"

For two full laps Ruth huffed and puffed behind May's little perky behind, until her legs felt like steel beams and tears filled the brim of her eyes. All she could think of was how she could manage to crawl home and still maintain some shred of dignity. After the second lap, Ruth had no choice but to sit down, and watch May finish all ten laps without hardly breaking a sweat.

"You did good, Ruth."

"Please." Ruth rolled her eyes. "It was all I could do to finish that second lap."

"But you finished it and that's what counts. It'll get easier over time." May smiled. "Do you know I used to weigh almost two hundred and twenty pounds?"

Ruth was shocked. "You?"

"Yep. It's taken 'bout a year for me to get it off, and it's been hard. I do this nearly every day because I have to or I'd blow up like the blimp. I cut out all the fried chicken, mashed potatoes, and sweet potato pies too, and Lord knows I love me some sweet potato pie." May looked at Ruth as if to say she should consider watching what she ate too. Ruth looked out over the lake, debating on whether or not she needed to argue with this woman about things she knew nothing about. Like the fact that Ruth had given up all that stuff over a year ago. And that everything she ate was low-fat this, or fat-free that. Sure, she indulged sometimes, but only in moderation. Of course, she'd consumed half a fat-free carrot cake she'd made over the weekend, but hell, it was fat-free, kinda. And it had carrots in it! That had to count for something.

"I'm tellin' you, Ruth. Exercise and eatin' right—make you feel a whole lot betta 'bout yo'self."

Ruth folded her arms defensively across her chest. "I don't feel bad about myself, May."

"I'm jus' sayin' carryin' 'round all that extra weight ain't good fo' you. You and me, we 'bout the same height, don't you think? And I know what kinds of problems bein' overweight can cause, especially as you get older. We probably 'round the same age too. How old are you, Ruth? If you don't mind me askin'?"

"Thirty-four."

"I'm thirty-six."

Ruth's chin dropped and rested on top of her weak thighs. Thirty-six! That heffa didn't look a day over twenty-six. How the hell could she sit there and be thirty-six? "I'd have never guessed you were— You don't look your age at all, May."

"You say that like bein' thirty-six is old, girl."

"I'm sorry. I . . ."

"Don't worry 'bout it. I believe that if a woman feels good, she's automatically goin' to look good. I don't mind folks knowin' how old I am, 'cause I know I look good. And I ain't tryin' to be conceited neither. But I take care of myself and that makes me feel good. It's all 'bout takin' care of you on the inside, Ruth. I know we don't know each other well enough for me to be sayin' all this to you, but I think I've been where you've been, or at least, close to it. I know you probably thinkin' you don't have control over most things in yo' life, but you have control over this and you should do somethin' 'bout it, if for no other reason than yo' health." May stood up to leave. "Now . . . I betta get goin' or I'm goin' to be late. See you in the mornin', same time?"

"Sure, May. I'll be here."

May waved as she walked away. *Damn*, Ruth thought. Was that woman psychic or did Ruth have "My life has been hell since the day I was born" tattooed on her forehead?

May Flowers

MAY HAD TAKEN HER NEW FRIENDSHIP WITH RUTH AND RUN with it. Ruth agreed to meet May for their morning walks every other day and May had welcomed the company. Of course, Ruth's stamina wasn't what May's was, and since she wanted someone to talk to, May knew Ruth was a captive audience for one, maybe two, good laps around the lake, so she had to talk fast.

"Actually, Jeff is my second husband. My first husband, Frank, was killed in a car accident."

"Oh," was the best response Ruth could come up with between huffing and puffing like a whale. "I'm—sorry."

"Yeah, I was sorry too. So sorry, in fact, that I nearly gave up on life completely. Girl, I was a mess 'cause he was my everything like the song says." She smiled. "Of course, we had our share of problems like most couples. Money mostly. But I loved me some Frank. He was my first love and as far as I was concerned . . . the only man in the world for me. You ever felt like that 'bout anybody?"

"No."

"Well, when you do"—May glanced quickly at Ruth—"and I know you will 'cause God never meant for any of us to be alone." She couldn't put her finger on it, but she didn't need to. It was obvious that Ruth was a lonely woman. May had made out the faint outline of a ring on her finger. She'd lost someone. That much was obvious. "Anyway, after Frank died, I felt like he'd taken me with him. You know how hard it is to be alive on the outside, but dead on the inside?"

Ruth knew. "What about—your—kids?" she managed to say.

"What about 'em? If it wasn't for my momma, I don't know what I would've done, Ruth. My poor babies lost both their daddy and their momma at the same time, only they didn't understand it 'cause I was still here. But I might as well have been dead too. My world had been wrapped up in that man and I didn't even know it till he was gone. All of a sudden I realized I didn't have a damn thing. Oh, I had the insurance money and my kids, but I didn't have anything 'bout me that knew how to make a life without him. You know how that feels?"

Ruth swallowed hard. "Yes."

"It ain't easy for a woman to admit that 'bout herself. Thinkin' she ain't nothin' without a man, but I found myself sinkin' down deep into a big, black hole, and you know what scared me?"

"What?"

"Not bein' able to climb up out."

May had become a recluse in her small house, feeling more afraid than she'd ever felt in her life. Afraid because she'd had no idea how to save herself. At the end of every day, she made a promise to herself that tomorrow she'd get up out of that bed, put on some clothes, and get out of the house. But then tomorrow would come and the best she could do was muster up another promise for another day.

"Yo' chil'ren need they momma, May," her mother had fussed. *"You want me to send the po'lice in there afta ya? Lawd, whatchu doin' to yo'self, gal? He gone, but you ain't."*

"All I did was sleep, and when I wasn't sleepin', I was eatin'. I had enough money where I didn't have to work. My kids stayed at Momma's all the time and no matter what anybody said to me or how much folks fussed at me 'bout gettin' myself together . . . I wasn't even tryin' to hear 'em, girlfriend. I was pit-i-ful."

"So—what—happened?" Ruth asked, gasping for air, trying to ignore the pain of her flesh falling off her calves.

"God," May said, matter-of-factly. "I mean, it wasn't like some kind of beautiful spiritual revelation like you see in the movies or

read in books. But girl, if you ever want to know the truth 'bout
yo'self, ask God. If you ever need to know the truth 'bout yo'self, He
goin' to tell you whether you want Him to or not. God put His big,
ol' foot smack dab in my ass and said, 'May! What the hell you think
you doin'?' That's what He asked me."

"God—didn't—say that," Ruth said, still gasping for air.

May rolled her eyes. "If I'm lyin', I'm dyin'."

Ruth grinned. "God—cusses?"

"Girl, He God. He can cuss if He want to and I was bein' hardheaded. He had to cuss me 'cause nothin' else was gettin' my attention."

"How do you know—it was—God?"

" 'Cause it got my attention, that's how I know. What the hell
did I think I was doin'? Folks had been askin' me that same question
but I jus' ignored 'em. But let God ask you somethin' like that. How
you goin' to ignore God? Even if you try to He jus' gon' t' keep on
askin' till you finally answer 'cause you goin' to get tired 'fo He does."

"So—what—happened?" Ruth asked intently. In some aspects
May's story was a lot like Ruth's. Not that she would've mourned
Eric's death, but she'd mourned her own for years.

"I started seein' what I was doin' to myself. Child, I blew up like
a balloon and couldn't fit into any of my clothes or shoes. And my
po' children—You know what happened?"

"What?"

"I got even more depressed than I already was." She laughed. "And
I ate more and slept more—"

Ruth looked perplexed. "But—I thought you said—God told you
He'd fix it?"

"Girl, God didn't say He was fixin' nothin'. He jus' asked me what
the hell I was doin' 'cause it wasn't up to Him to fix it. It was up to
me."

"Well—what made you want—to fix it." Ruth was getting light-
headed, and she willed each step with all the mental and spiritual
energy she could muster.

"I'd been thinkin' all along that with Frank gone, I didn't have a
damn thing to live fo'."

"But your—kids?"

"Exactly," May said easily. Her whole conversation had been effortless and Ruth was starting to resent her for it. "My kids. My babies. And me. Frank wasn't a perfect man, but he was a good man, he knew how to live. Whatever he chose to do, he worked real hard at it. Always talkin' 'bout, 'Don't do nothin' half-assed, May. And don't let them kids do nothin' half-assed either.' Frank never did nothin' half-assed whether he was workin' or playin' or takin' care of us. The last thing he'd want was for me to be sittin' 'round like I was, doin' nothin' but gettin' big as that house I was locked up in. He'd always taken a lot of pride in us," she said fondly. "Always thought I was so pretty and his kids were so well-behaved and I'd managed to let it all fall apart. Everything he and I'd worked so hard for was fallin' apart. So, what the hell was I doin'?"

"And you—got over it?" Ruth winced. "Just like—that?" If she weren't so anxious to find out how this story ended, Ruth would've sat her behind down a long time ago. But nosiness can be a strong motivator.

"Hell no!" May snapped, glancing at Ruth. "It took a while. When God asks you a question like that you can't get away with bullshittin' Him. He wants an answer, and I danced around one for months, tryin' to blame everybody else but me. 'It was all Frank's fault, Lord. He was the one who made me need him so.' Then I tried blamin' God. 'Why'd You have to take him from me when You knew how much I needed that man?' "

"What did He say?"

"He didn't say a word, 'cause He knew I knew better. Wasn't nobody to blame but me. Not Frank, not God. May was the one layin' sprawled out on that bed eatin' them pork chops and mashed potatoes. Not Frank. Not God. May was lettin' another woman raise her children. Not Frank. Not God. May was the one feelin' sorry for herself all the damn time. Not Frank—"

"Not God?" Ruth finished the statement for her.

" 'Course not. Eventually, I got my fat ass up and out of that house and discovered that the world hadn't stopped turnin' simply 'cause I wanted it to. Life goes on, Ruth."

Ruth glanced at May. "And on—and on."

"You can't stop 'cause it ain't goin' to stop. So why not make the most of it?"

"May." Ruth's eyes were starting to water. "I'm cramping. How many laps is this?"

"Four. We comin' up on yo' bench. You did good, girl. Why don't you rest?"

"I'm going to go one more, then I'll rest."

May smiled. "Good for you."

Shave and a Haircut

BERNIE STOOD IN RUTH'S DOORWAY, STARING AT HER FROWNING. "What the hell? Girl, what did you do to all that beautiful hair?"

Ruth rubbed her hand over her head, and smiled sheepishly. "Bernie?"

"You had beautiful hair! A head full of thick, curly hair. The kind people like me pay good money for."

"It's not that bad, Bernie."

"Not that bad?" Bernie sighed, slowly entering Ruth's apartment, staring intently at her curly and very short hair. "Why in the world would you let a razor get anywhere close to that head, when folks like me dream of running barefoot through shit like that?"

Ruth couldn't help but laugh. "It wasn't a razor, Bernie. It was a clipper with a number two guard and an edge up. And stop looking so disgusted. It's only hair. My hair, and it will grow back."

Growing up, Ruth's long, thick mane had been her crowning glory. She'd inherited it from her mother, who relished how much of a fuss men often made of her own hair. *"They like to run they fingers through it, and feel how soft it is. Men jus' like long hair on a woman, Ruthie. Jus' 'bout all of 'em do."* Karen's hair was always perfectly coifed, bouncing and behaving like she'd just stepped out of a salon. When Ruth was younger, Karen had insisted on doing her daughter's hair too, which was always perfectly in place, decorated in a rainbow of bows and barrettes. For a while after her mother died, Ruth worked hard at making sure her hair looked nice. But as the years passed, she'd spent less time on doing hair, and more time, working, cooking, cleaning, taking care of Eric, being miserable with Eric, getting rid of Eric, and now—coming to terms with who she was, without Eric. So, who had time for hair? May wore her hair short, and bragged all the time about how little she had to do with it, and how good it felt when it was hot, and how sexy her husband thought she was. Ruth's hair had become a whole lot of things over the years. It had become a place to hide her insecurity and bruises, beneath bangs and curls. It had become a weapon for Eric, who insisted on pulling it every time he decided he needed her undivided attention, and it had become a burden and another thing she didn't want to be bothered with anymore, at least for the time being. Bernie might've thought she was silly, but Ruth had started a cleansing process that began with Eric, and ended with herself, and included a new home, new furniture, exercise, and a haircut. The minute all that shit hit the floor, Ruth felt light as a feather and nearly floated up out of that barber's chair, finally liberated from deep conditioners, relaxers, and residue from Eric's filthy grip.

Bernie sat her purse down on the coffee table, crossed her arms, and grimaced at Ruth, feeling absolutely betrayed. "How come you didn't call me? I could've talked you out of it. I could've told you, Ruth, 'Don't do it, girl. It'll be fine, and I'll be there in a minute.' I could've saved all that lovely hair and kept you from letting that barber go buck wild on your hard head!"

Ruth rolled her eyes, then headed into the kitchen to check on dinner. "You're being ridiculous."

"I'm being ridiculous?"

"Bernie," Ruth said, looking right into Bernie's eyes. "I've been a slave most of my life to my marriage and my hair. Now I'm liberated from both of them, and I feel good." She crossed her arms defiantly over her chest.

"You could've got some cornrows, Ruth."

"I didn't want cornrows, Bernie," Ruth snapped.

Bernie blinked back her frustration. "Cornrows are cute, and you wouldn't have had to cut—"

"Didn't you promise to make us some daiquiris?" Ruth said, changing the subject.

"Yes." Bernie exaggerated a quivering lip to go along with her pitiful expression. "I did."

Ruth shook her head and laughed. "Strawberries are in the fridge, sweetie."

Nearly a year had passed since her divorce and she was Ruth Johnson again. Ruth had finally gotten around to getting her maiden name back, and it had been like being born all over again. Ruth Ashton had been a basket case and a drag to be around. She cried all the time, looked ten years older than she actually was, and dieted in between late-night fast-food and ice cream binges. She'd even been dumb enough to believe that a diet soda really could reverse the horrendous caloric effects of a double-cheese supreme pizza (hold the onions) and a brownie fudge sundae.

In the six months that Ruth had been exercising with May, she'd lost nearly twenty-five pounds and felt like a million bucks. May had casually mentioned that the weight had seemed to melt right off, but that was too idealistic a statement for Ruth. She'd worked her butt off to lose that weight, and that's all there was to it. Of course, she still had a zillion or so more pounds to go before she'd reached her goal, for which she'd planned the shopping spree to end all shopping sprees.

Ruth and Bernie sat down to dinner that included grilled jerk salmon, seasoned brown rice, steamed broccoli, and a light strawberry shortcake for dessert. The food was absolutely delicious and even Crab Eating, Send Me to the Grave with a Babyback Rib in One Hand and a Bucket of Fried Chicken in the Other Bernie enjoyed it.

Ruth was busy in the kitchen, loading dishes into the dishwasher, while Bernie made herself at home in the living room, curled up on the loveseat, gingerly sipping on her daiquiri. "I signed up for some classes at JU the other day," Ruth said over her shoulder. "Some business classes. I start in two months."

"Sounds like a good idea to me. What's your major?"

Ruth shrugged. "I don't know yet. I think I'll take a few different classes here and there until I find something I like."

"Ain't nothing wrong with that."

Ruth came into the living room, drying her hands, then sat in the loveseat across from Bernie. She groaned and wrinkled her nose. "It's going to take forever for me to get a degree, though, working full time and taking classes part time."

"Well, what's wrong with taking classes full time?"

"I thought about it, but—I don't know."

Bernie sipped on what was left of her daiquiri, then looked at Ruth. "Why not? It's just you, Ruth. It ain't like you've got a house full of hungry kids to feed."

Ruth nodded. "That's true, but that's a lot to take on, Bernie. Working full time and tackling a full load at school."

"Who said anything about working?"

Ruth stared back at Bernie like she'd lost her mind. "Uh, excuse me Miss Thang, but some of us need a job."

"And some of us," Bernie said, peering at Ruth through narrow eyes, "can get by without a job for a little while. At least long enough to get a degree in four years instead of forty. But then," Bernie said nonchalantly, "that's totally up to you."

"I really don't think I could afford to—" Bernie stared indifferently into space, plucking something from between her teeth with her pinky nail. "You really think something like that is feasible, Bernie? I mean—really? You don't think it would be crazy?"

Bernie leaned forward, and rested her elbows on her thighs. "And so what if it is, Ruth? Who the hell cares?"

"I don't want to do anything rash, Bernie."

"Look at your head, Ruth." Bernie grinned. "You've cut off ten feet of hair, girl. If that ain't rash then I don't know what is."

Ruth laughed and ran her hand over her head again. She'd been doing that a lot lately. "You've got a point."

Damn! Bernie thought sitting back on the couch. Who was this woman sitting across from her looking as if she were on top of the world? Ruth was a far cry from the woman she'd been when Bernie had first met her. She'd blossomed right in front of her eyes, into something that had a backbone and a will to do more than just exist. Ruth had been resurrected and Bernie had been privileged to watch the whole thing. It was downright inspiring, she thought, smiling. "By the way. I like your hair."

Ruth grinned. "Really? I mean . . . you really do?"

Bernie nodded. "I really do. Looks good, girl. You've got a pretty face."

Ruth's smile disappeared. "Don't say that."

"Why not?"

"People always tell a big woman she's got a pretty face, like that's going to make her feel better about being heavy. I hate that."

"Oooh, see there you go," Bernie said, pretending to be frustrated. "I give you a compliment and you act a fool over it. I ain't saying nothing else nice about you."

"I ain't acting a fool, Bernie. I'm just saying—"

"You're not a big woman, Ruth. Who do you think you're trying to fool? Like I don't have eyes. Like I don't see you sitting over there trying to get skinny."

Ruth laughed. "I ain't *trying* to get skinny," she said smartly. "I *am* getting skinny."

Bernie nearly choked on her drink. "You still walking with what's-her-name?"

"Her name's May, and yes. We're still walking in the mornings."

"You know I can't stand her."

"You don't even know her!" Ruth nearly shrieked.

"I don't have to know her to know I don't like her." Bernie burped. "Excuse me."

"Why don't you like her, Bernie?"

"She sounds a little too good to be true, if you ask me," Bernie said, waving her hand in the air. "Got a perfect figure, perfect husband . . . kids. Can't nobody be that damn perfect. I think she lying about something."

Ruth rolled her eyes and sucked her teeth. "I never said she was perfect, Bernie."

"Damn near."

"May's nice. Okay, so she goes a little overboard with this fitness thing, but she's cool, and I think you'd like her. I told her all about you, and she seems to think you sound fascinating."

"Oh no you didn't!" Bernie snapped. "I know you ain't telling my business to that heffa."

"Bernie, if I didn't know better, I'd think you were jealous."

"Damn right I am!" Bernie retorted. "I've invested a lot more time and effort into you and our friendship, and I'll be damned if some other heffa comes up in here and moves in on *my* best friend."

Ruth was shocked. Bernie had come right out and said it, and Ruth sat speechless for a moment.

"What?" Bernie asked, looking a little embarrassed.

Ruth grinned. "Your best friend?"

Bernie sat back and defensively crossed her arms in front of her. "That's what I said, ain't it?"

Ruth got up from where she was sitting and sat next to Bernie on the couch, bumping shoulders, trying to keep from laughing. "You're my best friend too, Bernice."

"I know," Bernie said indifferently.

"And, if it's any consequence, nobody can hold a candle to you, so you can stop feeling insecure. You and I are like sisters, and nobody can ever come close to replacing you in my life." She smiled.

Bernie pressed her lips together to keep from smiling back. "You remember that."

"How can I forget with you hanging around all the time reminding me?"

Before leaving, Bernie finally got around to giving Ruth the housewarming gift she'd been promising since Ruth had moved into her apartment, only so much time had passed it had become a housewarming, Memorial Day, Fourth of July, Labor Day, birthday, thinking about you gift all wrapped into one.

"What's this?" Ruth asked holding the device up in the air, staring curiously at it, suspecting she knew what it was and fearing she might be right.

Bernie grinned. "Haven't you ever seen one of those before?" Ruth looked confused and shrugged. Bernie carefully took it from Ruth's hand. "It's a vibrator, Ruth."

Ruth's chin dropped and her face turned a deep shade of purple. "A sex toy?"

Bernie beamed, knowing she'd caught Ruth off guard. She put it back in the box and handed it to Ruth. "Don't worry, girl. You'll figure it out." With that, she turned and left, laughing all the way to her car.

After Bernie left, Ruth quickly put the box away on the top shelf of her closet, wondering what in the world she was supposed to do with it. Of course, she'd never even think of using it. Bernie had another thing coming if she thought Ruth was going to get her freak on with a piece of electronic equipment. After all, she couldn't even wipe her ass without feeling embarrassed. So what the heck would she do with a—

Thank God Mother Nature knows when and how to take control of a situation. There are urges, forces on the planet that are powerful enough to compel a woman to examine aspects of herself she wouldn't otherwise consider exploring. Some of these urges are so potent they force a woman to look deep inside herself and dare her to be honest about her own desires, her needs. That's when curiosity becomes her playmate and suddenly, her vibrator becomes her best friend. Masturbation became some of the best sex Ruth had ever had. She named her new friend Maxwell, and Maxwell was a hell of a lot more pleasant to deal with than Eric ever was. Whoever thought earthshaking orgasms could come with a set of instructions and a warning label?

Dream Walking

I'm tripping all over myself
Trying to get to him
Hoping not to fall too hard
Or too much in love
Praying I won't break my own heart
But to be happy
Just this once

OCTOBER IN JACKSONVILLE, FLORIDA, FOR RUTH MEANT THAT she wasn't going to melt like butter in a hot skillet if she wasn't attached to an air conditioner before noon, and that the jazz festival was in town. Sprawled out on a blanket beneath an enormous oak tree, Ruth was caught up in the moment as the melodies danced on the air, and a light-skinned sistah scatted something cosmic into the microphone. All the while the sweet, fall breeze lightly licked against her skin as if to say, "Ruth Johnson, girl, you are absolutely delicious!" Her eyes were closed, but her ears were wide open, letting the music soak deep into her soul.

This was a moment indicative of the life she'd come to know and love and even take for granted. Ruth's divorce had been final for two years. She'd just started a new semester at the university and had been seriously contemplating taking Bernie's suggestion and quitting that dead-end job of hers to become a full-time student. Money wasn't the issue, but security was. She'd worked since she was sixteen, and as much as she despised working at the law firm, it was a sure thing—with benefits. But the idea of spending the next ten years getting a degree wasn't all that appealing either, and Ruth was anxious to obtain her next goal, which was to get a degree in something that made her "boss" material. She still hadn't decided what that could be, though.

She'd taken a psychology course and actually enjoyed it. Her motivation for taking the class in the first place was to hopefully try and figure herself out. Every time she turned a page in her text book, Ruth kept expecting to see a picture of herself in it, smiling and waving and looking like a perfect clinical example of paranoia, schizophrenia, post-traumatic stress syndrome, manic depression, or something-or-other. She'd also taken an introduction to business management course, which she surprisingly enjoyed, and more and more, she was leaning toward getting her BA. What surprised her more than anything was the fact that she was actually pretty good at school, and homework was a hell of a lot easier than struggling through a regular nine-to-five day in and day out.

Ruth was so caught up in the music, she hadn't even noticed him standing in front of her.

"Excuse me," the luscious voice said to her. She slowly opened her eyes and stared up at the most handsome man she'd ever seen. She must've fallen asleep, she decided, and died and gone to heaven and this glorious creature is simply a character in a dream, or perhaps, he was an angel.

He smiled at her, then suddenly raised a camera to his face, pointed at her and snapped her picture.

"Oh yeah," he said, grinning from ear to ear. "That was nice."

"Who are you?" she asked, startled, and quickly sat up. "And why did you just take my picture?"

Adrian shrugged. "Beautiful woman enjoying some beautiful music on a beautiful day . . . of course I had to take it."

Ruth eyed him suspiciously, then made a quick but thorough assessment. He was the color of milk chocolate, with coal black eyes tucked beneath heavy, sculptured brows. His full lips were framed nicely by a perfectly manicured goatee, and he was as tall as the tree she was sitting under with shoulders broad enough to rival the wingspan of a 747.

He slowly knelt down in front of her and without even so much as a warning, gazed hypnotically into her eyes, then extended his hand for her to shake. "I saw you when you came in." Ruth raised her hand to his, mesmerized as she watched his long fingers wrap themselves around her hand, nearly covering it completely. "My name's Adrian."

Of course you are, she wanted to say, but thought better of it. But any man who looked that good had no choice but to be named Adrian, or Donovan, or Sean, or Denzel. Ruth made a mental note to close her mouth and stop staring at the man. She nervously cleared her throat. "I'm Ruth." Adrian hadn't let go of her hand yet. *Shouldn't he have let go by now?* she wondered, hoping he never would. "Are you a photographer?"

Finally he let go and toyed with his camera. "Strictly amateur. It's a hobby."

Get a hold of yourself, man, Adrian said to himself, gazing into the most beautiful brown eyes he'd ever seen in his life. Lashes like that could definitely whip a brotha into submission if he wasn't careful, but at the moment, being careful wasn't his priority. Ruth sat cross-legged on a blanket, wearing jeans that were faded in all the right places and obviously custom made just to fit her. And that smoke gray sweater she wore dared him not to stare at anything below the neckline, teasing him with a hint of cleavage peeking out over the top. Over the years, he'd managed to convince himself that he preferred long hair on a woman, but not on this woman. She was lovely, and the fact that her hair wasn't much longer than his enhanced the fact.

While he toyed around with the camera, Ruth had a chance to take a couple of deep breaths when he wasn't looking to hopefully pull herself together before he had a chance to notice her melting into a puddle at his feet.

"So do you usually go around taking pictures of strange women whenever the mood strikes you?" she said, trying to sound annoyed, but from the smile on his face, it was obvious that she hadn't done a very good job.

"You don't look so strange to me. And no, I usually don't make a habit of it. But you looked like you were holding on to something real special there for a moment, and I was just hoping to immortalize it. That's all."

Ruth started to tell him he could immortalize just about anything she had, but thought better of it. She'd never been one to believe in love at first sight—until now, that is.

Adrian motioned toward the main stage, "The lineup's pretty good this year. This your first time at the festival?"

"No, I um . . . I come every year." Ruth hoped she was the only one to notice the quiver in her voice and the fact that she was fumbling around with the cup to her thermos like an idiot. "Would you like some hot chocolate?"

Adrian shook his head. "No. Thanks."

She couldn't believe how handsome this man was, and how much she wished he'd leave, but more important, how pleased she was that he hadn't.

"Mind if I sit down?" he asked, stretching out his long legs, next to her on the blanket. Ruth moved over a bit to make room for him, trying not to hyperventilate at the fact that he was just inches away, which alone was enough to threaten to make her cum. "It's okay— isn't it?"

"Sure. It's fine. You sure you don't want any hot chocolate?" she asked again, for lack of anything better to say.

Adrian laughed. "I'm all right. You're here alone, aren't you?"

Ruth stared at him, unsure as to why he'd ask a question like that. "Why?" she asked, sounding defensive.

"Just asking," he quickly said. "I just don't want some big, muscle-bound brotha coming over here kicking sand in my face."

"Oh, no. No there's . . . I mean, yes. I'm—You don't have to worry about that."

"Is it my imagination or are you shy?" Adrian smiled again, and Ruth wanted to tell him to stop doing that, but again, thought better of it.

She shifted uncomfortably, and pretended to adjust her bookmark in the book she hadn't even started reading. "Shy? Me?"

"Yes," he replied softly. "You."

"Well, it's just that I don't know you and—"

"I'm being forward," he said apologetically. "I'm sorry. It's just that, when I saw you come into the park, well, I find you very attractive, and I wanted to take advantage of the opportunity to let you know that." Ruth sat dumbfounded and at a total loss of words. "You um . . ." Adrian glanced at her hands. "You're not married?"

"Thank you," Ruth said quietly.

Adrian looked confused. "I beg your pardon?"

"About the—me being attractive," she nearly whispered. "But no. I'm not married. I'm divorced. Are you? Married?"

"No. If I were married, I wouldn't be sitting here trying to talk to you."

"Is that what you're doing?" She smiled. "Trying to talk to me?"

Adrian laughed. "Do you mind?"

Did she mind? How would he know to ask her that? she wondered. All of a sudden, or maybe not so suddenly, the dynamics of life were changing on her again, and she hadn't been prepared for it, but looking at him, it was hard as hell not to welcome it. She'd spent an afternoon intoxicated on hot chocolate, jazz, fresh air. Maybe adding a little Adrian, whatever his name was, to the mix couldn't hurt. Ruth had been running from this, swearing she'd never even so much as give another man the time of day if she could help it, because Eric's spirit still haunted her even when she wasn't paying attention. After all this time, she still had to remind herself that he wasn't going to come storming into her apartment making demands on her life, but the possibility lurked in dark corners of her memories. Adrian was definitely fine, and maybe, just maybe, he was as nice as he seemed. Maybe he wasn't the animal Eric had been, and maybe it was time for her to give a man a chance. Only she knew that this time around, a brotha would have to work at impressing her, and not the other way around.

Ruth smiled, shyly, then put her book away. "No. I don't mind."

Adrian flashed that movie star smile of his, then began bobbing his head up and down to the contagious melody coming from center stage. "That's nice."

"Do you have a favorite musician, Adrian?"

He shrugged. "Hard to say. I like the contemporary sound well enough, but nobody moves me like Trane."

"You like Monk?" Ruth asked, starting to feel more relaxed.

"Yes, and Davis, and most of the classic stuff."

"Me too!" Ruth put her hand to her chest. "But, I have to admit,

I'm a huge Earl Klugh fan. And Benson." She blushed. "I've got a crush on Benson."

Adrian stared into her eyes. "He's a lucky man. You have a beautiful smile, Ruth."

Had she been smiling? she wondered. "Thank you. I like yours too."

There was definitely magic mixed into the music and the afternoon, and as far as Ruth was concerned, Adrian had some magic of his own. He was gorgeous, intelligent, funny, loved jazz and didn't seem to mind at all whenever Ruth finished his sentences. He was originally from Ohio, but moved to Jacksonville several years ago to take advantage of a career opportunity as a network engineer. He graciously answered every question she threw at him: no he had never been married, had no children, and was surprised that after fourteen years of marriage, she didn't have any either. They shared sandwiches, jazz, and a lovely afternoon in the park, and Ruth wondered if things in her life had ever been this good, or if they could ever get any better. She came up with a resounding "no" to both questions, and savored the afternoon she and Adrian spent together.

Adrian insisted on walking her to her car when it was time to leave, despite her very weak, half-hearted protests. "You really don't have to do this, Adrian. It's a long walk back to the park."

"Not a problem, Ms. Johnson. It's the least I can do."

Ruth pressed her lips together to hold in the massive grin threatening to escape from them. "Well," she said, stopping at her car. "I appreciate it, and this was fun. I had a great time."

"Enough of a great time to give me your number?" Adrian's hands were buried deep in his pockets and he rocked back and forth on his heels and toes like a teenage boy asking out his first date.

Ruth was at a loss. She honestly hadn't prepared herself for the possibility that this man would want to call her or even see her again. Spending the afternoon together had been cool, but what in the world would she do with him beyond that? The whole time they were together, Ruth had allowed herself to be whisked away on a carpet ride of Adrian's pleasant company and personality, but wasn't that enough? After all, the last thing she wanted was to catapult herself into something as foreign to her as a relationship. What she and Eric had had hadn't been a relationship. It had been a catastrophic occurrence. As much as she wanted to give Adrian her number, her old buddy apprehension rushed her like an entire defensive line, made her panic and throw a critical interception. "I don't think so, Adrian."

Disappointment quickly washed over his face, but Adrian composed himself in the hopes of maintaining some shred of his dignity. "But I thought you said you had a good time?"

"I did have a good time." Ruth tried to smile. "But—" *My ass needs to go home and choke on a bone,* she wanted to say but didn't.

"Oh, I see. I'm not your type. Is that it? What? I'm too short? Too tall? Ugly?"

Ruth curled her lip, knowing this man did not believe he could possibly be ugly. "Don't even go there, Adrian. You're every woman's type, and you know it."

"Obviously not yours," he said humbly. "So, why don't you let me call you, Ruth?"

"So, call me Ruth," she teased, feeling silly as soon as she'd said it.

Adrian didn't seem to find her little joke the least bit amusing. "I'm serious. I had a good time too, and well, I'd like to see you again. Maybe we could go to dinner or something."

"Adrian." She sighed. "Look, I haven't dated anybody in years, and honestly, I'm really not sure I'd even remember how."

"Years?"

"Literally. Not since my divorce. Scratch that. Since before my divorce. Before my marriage."

"Damn!" Adrian frowned. "That long?"

"Yeah, so—"

"So that means you're not going to give me your number?" She nodded again. "Then, I won't push it," Adrian said reluctantly.

"I did have a nice time with you, Adrian," Ruth said, putting her things into the backseat of her car. "You're a nice guy."

"Yeah. I'm a nice guy. One who can take rejection, and take it pretty well too, believe it or not. And for the record, I had a good time too."

Ruth got inside her car and started up the engine. "Take care." She waved as she pulled out of the parking lot, watching him from her rearview mirror. She wasn't going to be too hard on herself; after all, this was a first step to allowing the hint of a relationship to come into her life. Before spending this afternoon with Adrian, she hadn't even thought about it. Thanks to him, she could safely say maybe it was time to start thinking about it.

He hadn't been the first man to come on to her since her divorce. More and more, she'd been getting a taste of what that was like. She'd told Clara that it was probably due to the fact that she'd lost close to fifty pounds, which had only proven her point that men didn't like big women.

"Child, that's the most ridiculous thing I've ever heard," Clara had argued. "It's not the size of a woman that turns a man on. Look at me," she said, balancing her fists on her very wide hips, and sticking out her chest. "I am not a skinny woman, and I don't have to be. But you best believe that if I want a man, I can get a man. And it's always been that way. The thing is, I've got it going on in here"— Clara tapped herself lightly on the chest—"which is where true beauty lives. The only reason men are saying anything to you now is because you feel better about you, and they can see that."

As much as she'd enjoyed her day with Adrian, Ruth knew that she wasn't ready for anything serious right now, and more important, that Adrian didn't deserve to have to deal with the kind of garbage she was still carrying. Maybe one of these days, another Adrian would come along and give her another chance, but for now she was more comfortable without one.

A Way Out of No Way

❧

RUTH IMMEDIATELY CALLED CLARA AFTER READING THE ARTICLE in the Saturday morning paper and rushed right over to the shelter. Clara had mentioned that there'd been a few problems but had obviously downplayed the seriousness of the situation. Ruth held the paper out in front of her, with Clara's picture on it, and thrust it at Clara as soon as she opened the door.

"How come you didn't tell me things were this bad, Clara?" Ruth asked, concerned.

Clara took the paper, then put on her reading glasses. "I should've known they'd put the worst picture they could find of me in here." She gestured to Ruth to come in, and led her to the small office down the hall. The house was an old, renovated Victorian and very different from what Ruth had expected. The pastel yellow walls were decorated with rose patterned wallpaper at the borders, and cherry wood accented the baseboards and stairwell.

Clara closed the door behind them. "Have a seat," she said, without looking up from the paper. Then Clara found her own seat behind the desk. Rows of pictures were mounted on her wall. Pictures of women and children, all with Clara draping her arms over each and every one of them. "Why didn't you ever tell me I looked this old?" Clara asked, frowning.

"Because you don't."

Clara smiled and held out the newspaper to Ruth pointing at her picture. "You see all those gray hairs? That means I look old, and you should have told me, seeing as how you're my friend and all."

Ruth couldn't help but smile. "But I never noticed because I don't see gray hair when I look at you, Clara. Which is why I never said anything. Now why don't you tell me what's going on."

"The article says we're out of money." She shrugged. "So, we're out of money." Suddenly, Ruth saw something she hadn't ever seen in Clara before. She saw a weariness creep across her face, and for a moment, she did look old. Or maybe just tired.

"Has everyone moved out already?"

"Some of them have. Others are getting ready to. All of them are scared, including me, but it wouldn't do any good for them to see me sweat. So, I don't." She smiled. "These ladies aren't strangers to me, Ruth. I care about them as if they were my own children, which is what Carolyn has always resented me for. 'You care more about total strangers than you do me!' she used to tell me, and sometimes, I almost believed she was right about that."

"I'm sure that's not true, Clara."

"Sure it is, and I'm not apologizing for it. I love my daughter, adore her, but she's always been well taken care of. There was always someone there for her, to look after her, and protect her. Despite it all, that girl has never known what it is to be afraid for her life, and I thank God for that. She's married to a wonderful man who'd give her the world if he could. Her father doted on her, even her step-fathers, aunts, uncles, grandparents. I always thought that if I were to fall off the face of the earth, there'd be a hundred women waiting to mother my child, and I was right. But the women who come through here, most don't even know what it's like to have someone care about them. Oh, they've got plenty of folks criticizing them, pulling at them, lecturing them, but most of them don't know what it is to have someone just listen to them without judging or complaining." Clara leaned back in her chair. "That's been my job all these years. That's what I'm good at."

"I'm so sorry, Clara."

"Me too, but hell, maybe it's time for me to move on anyway. I've been thinking about going back to work for Social Services. I can't stand the system, but at least it comes with a paycheck and I can still help some people."

"Well, maybe you can get a lawyer, and—"

Clara shook her head. "No money and no time for all that, baby. Besides, what would he do? Make these organizations give me money? Legal battles can go on forever, and I just don't have forever anymore, Ruth."

"And all this is because of that Anderson woman they mentioned in the paper? The one who made all those terrible accusations?"

"Accusations plus money equals incriminating evidence and yes, dear. That was the beginning of the end of this place. Or maybe, it was Ruby's death," Clara said introspectively. "Hard to tell. All I know is, I've been trying to run this place on my own for years and I'm tired. Tired of scraping and begging just to keep the lights on another month."

"I've got some money, Clara," Ruth said anxiously. "Maybe I could give you something, just to help out for a month or even two. Long enough for you to figure out what—"

Clara chuckled. "Oh, Ruth Johnson. You have come such a long way since the first time we met. You remember that night?"

"I remember. I didn't want to talk about it."

"You still don't, but that's fine. A huge change has come over you, baby. A good one, and I am so damn proud of you."

"I could've ended up here."

"No. Not you. You were too stubborn to end up in a place like this."

"But this place needs to stay open, Clara. So many people need it, and if it's gone, where are they going to go?"

"This isn't the only shelter in town, Ruth. They've got a ton of places for people to go. The city doesn't even need me here, which is why they don't mind seeing this house close down."

"So, you're just going to let them do that? You're just going to let them close it down?"

"I don't have much choice."

"You always have a choice. We can figure out something, Clara. I'm sure if we put our heads together, we can figure out a way to get some money so that this place can stay open."

"We?" Clara asked inquisitively. "Well now, if you've got some ideas, baby girl, I'd love to hear them. But you'd better talk fast because I've got to be out of this place by next spring."

"I don't know. I mean, I can't think of anything right now, but— Just give me some time. Maybe I can come up with something."

Clara smiled. "Excuse me, then Miss Johnson. I'm not feeling as optimistic as you are, but I can definitely appreciate your passion for the cause and all. Like I said, we've got less than a year before we have to be out of here, so—"

Ruth couldn't even explain to herself why keeping this place open was so important to her. Maybe because it was important to Clara. She'd worked so hard helping people. People like Ruth and to see all her efforts go down the drain over someone else's vindictiveness just didn't seem fair. In the back of her mind, she also realized that perhaps somewhere in all this she'd be able to find some retribution of her own. Yes, Eric was out of her life. Yes, she'd managed to pick up the pieces and move on, but there was still something deep inside, nagging at her. Ruth hadn't been able to put her finger on this un-discovered and unresolved issue.

Fate had brought Clara into Ruth's life for a reason. Without even trying, Clara had filled a void and also, without trying, Ruth had let her. Had it been the void left behind by her mother? Or, had it been one that even Karen hadn't been capable of filling? Whatever the case, Ruth found herself welcoming it and pushing it away all at the same time.

The small rooms held entire families crowded into each of them, but Ruth concluded that living in a crowded room, a safe room, had to have been better than the alternative. There were several children there, sullen and withdrawn with eyes who'd seen more of life than they should have. Clara introduced Ruth to Sharon, a tall, tailored brunette who looked a lot like a young Elizabeth Taylor. She'd rushed in, carrying a briefcase in one hand and a little girl, with big blue eyes like her mother's, in the other. Sharon had just found a new apartment and would be moving out soon.

Sharon and Ruth sat on the side of a twin bed in the small room she shared with her daughter, talking like they were old friends. Kindred spirits.

"I just started my own business," she announced proudly. "Catering. Started it about four months ago." She handed Ruth her business card.

Four-year-old Megan sat on Ruth's lap holding on tight to a doll that was apparently her best friend. The little girl was soft and sweet, which her mother assured Ruth was a temporary condition. There was a time when Ruth had dreamed of having a little girl of her own, but the possibility of that ever happening was becoming more unlikely by the second and that biological clock of hers ticked so loudly, sometimes it kept her up at night.

"How long were you married, Sharon?"

"Five years. He's a doctor. A neurologist. We'd been married about six months before he . . ." She smiled at her daughter, careful not to say too much about her husband in front of Megan. "What about you?"

"Fourteen years. No children."

"How'd you manage that?" she asked, genuinely surprised.

"He didn't want any," was all she said. It was all she needed to say because Ruth could see in Sharon's eyes that she understood.

"You ever feel like all that stuff happened to somebody else? Like you were watching a movie?" Sharon asked, staring out the window.

"Yeah. A terrible movie. With some bad actors." The two women laughed.

"He controlled everything, Ruth. He used to tell me how to dress, when to sleep. It even got to the point that if I wasn't home when he called me from work, he'd take the car keys away from me as punishment. How do you let somebody get that kind of control over you like that?"

"Gradually? I don't know. Maybe we put too much faith in them." Ruth shrugged. Sharon was looking to her for answers, but Ruth still didn't have any, even after all this time.

"Well, if a woman can't have faith in her husband . . ."

"Right. Who can she have faith in?"

"The thing is, everybody blamed me. Even now, my family, his—'You brought it on yourself, Sharon.' They tell me that all the time."

"Well, nobody had to tell me a thing, because I told myself that all the time. I've been divorced for two years and I still blame myself for what he did to me," Ruth said, regretfully.

"I hate feeling like that." Frustration welled up in her voice. "I listened to him blaming me for everything, and my family and my friends. All saying that what happened was because of me. I don't know, Ruth. Something about it just isn't right."

"No, it's not right. Because it lets men like them completely off the hook. Takes all the responsibility away from them, and drops it on our hard heads. That's the problem. Maybe we're the ones who need to change, Sharon," she said, decisively. "Maybe you and me should make a pinky pact right here and now."

Sharon giggled. "What kind of pinky pact?"

Ruth lifted her hand and extended her pinky. Sharon did the same, and the two hooked their little fingers together. "Let's put the blame where it belongs for a change."

She looked at Ruth and smiled. "On them?"

"Yes! I'm tired of carrying the load of his mess. And what's wrong with saying it was Eric's fault my life was hell?"

"And it was Darren's fault my life was hell!"

"You got that right!"

"Whew!" Sharon sighed. "I feel better already."

Ruth laughed. "All we need now are some eight-by-tens with their faces on them and some darts."

"Talk about your cheap therapy."

Ruth and Sharon had an understanding between them that transcended their cultural differences. Their histories were so similar that they had no choice but to become friends.

Ruth said her goodbyes to Sharon and Clara, with a million ideas running through her head. Clara had been so immersed in the problem that maybe she needed someone to look at it from another perspective. What harm could it do?

Ruth had been promising to treat Bernie to lunch for ages, so she figured she'd kill two birds with one stone. Feed her and pick her brain for ideas at the same time. "I don't know, Bernie. I need to do something. And I can't explain why, but I can't just walk away without trying."

"Sounds like she's already tried everything, Ruth. I understand that you feel you need to come to her rescue, but sometimes the system's bigger and badder than we are and ain't nothing you can do about it."

Ruth had offered to take the woman to a nice little Caribbean restaurant downtown that she'd heard so much about, but Bernie insisted on Tyrone's Fish and Grits. As long as she had lived in Jacksonville the fish and grits combination just never appealed to Ruth. So instead, she settled for a fish sandwich and coleslaw.

"There's got to be something she hasn't thought about. She said she'd found a few people who were willing to give donations, but not enough. What we need to do is figure out how to get more."

"Too bad she couldn't have a fund-raiser or banquet," Bernie mentioned casually.

"A what?"

"Folks have them all the time. Big banquets with two-hundred-dollar plates of rubber chicken and plastic mashed potatoes. Raise a lot of money if you plan it right. People like dressing up and rubbing elbows, especially if the 'right' people show up."

Ruth laughed so hard she nearly fell out of her seat. "Bernie, girl! You are a genius! A fund-raiser! Why can't we do that? Why couldn't we just throw a big ass party?"

Bernie stopped eating and all of sudden looked scared to death. "Ruth . . . honey. I don't think it's that simple. I'm sure there are all kinds of legal issues to deal with, not to mention the planning. What do you know about putting together something like that? And you could never do it by yourself. All that work, and . . ."

Ruth smiled brilliantly at this woman, her best friend in all the world. "Do you have any plans for the next couple of months?"

Bernie licked the last of the fish crumbs from her long, manicured nails, wiped her mouth, then threw the napkin on her nearly empty plate. "No! Ruth, don't you even—"

"C'mon, Bernice. Please? I've never asked you for much the whole time we've been friends. You know I haven't. And I wouldn't ask you for this except it's a lot for one person to handle and you're so good at things like this. Much better than I am. I wouldn't even know where to start. You know you're such a social butterfly." Ruth fluttered her eyelashes pleading for Bernie to help her.

"Look, I sympathize with the cause and all, but I am not going to commit myself to something like this, Ruth. It's huge and I've got a life."

"I understand that, honey. I do. But think about those women, Bernie. Look at me. I'm your best friend and I'm one of those women. You helped me when I needed it more than you'll ever know."

Bernie sighed. "I helped you because I love you, Ruth."

"Then if you love me, help me do this. Please?" She put on her best pitiful expression in the hopes that Bernie would be moved to do the right thing and stand tall for sisterhood and women all over the planet. Surprisingly, it worked.

Bernie rolled her eyes. "Okay. I'll look into some things."

"Yes! Oh bless you, girl!"

"But that's all I'm doing, Ruth," Bernie said, holding up her hand.

Ruth grinned so hard her face went numb. "Thank you, Bernie. And you know I appreciate anything you can do."

"You're a pain in my ass sometimes. You do know this?"

"Yes, but I love you." Ruth beamed.

"Whatever."

Ruth called Clara as soon as she got home to tell her about Bernie's idea, and Clara suddenly found a burst of energy to express some of her own excitement.

"I'd thought about a fund-raiser, but . . . You really think something like this can work?"

"I have no idea, Clara. But it can't hurt to look into it and that's all we're doing right now. I mean, who knows?"

"All the news I've been getting lately has been bad news, Ruth. Maybe my luck's about to change."

"Well, it may turn out that we can't do it after all, Clara. It's a great idea, and I think we might be able to pull it off. But I don't want you to get your hopes up, in case this thing doesn't pan out."

Ruth could tell Clara was smiling. "No, darling. Let's get our hopes up, Ruth. Just for a minute. Let's get our hopes way, way up."

Light My Fire

BERNIE SAT AT THE DINING ROOM TABLE IN MILES'S APARTMENT, sipping on a glass of merlot, trying not to look impressed by the skills he had displayed in the kitchen. She had no idea what possessed her to accept his dinner invitation this evening. The line with Miles had been clearly drawn in the sand as far as Bernie was concerned. Sex, pure and simple. Nothing more and nothing less. But gradually Bernie noticed Miles taking liberties more and more, coming dangerously close to infringing on the idea she had of the ideal relationship with a man ten years her junior.

Miles set a basket of sesame rolls and a fresh garden salad on the table next to the lasagna he'd made, then he took his seat across from her.

"All right now," he said, placing his napkin in his lap. "Time to get this party started right, girl."

Bernie laughed, then shook her head. "If your intention was to impress a sistah"—she bowed her head graciously—"I must say, baby boy, I'm thoroughly impressed."

Miles sat back, genuinely surprised by the compliment. "Oh, so this is what a man's got to do to impress yo' ass, Bernie? Slave over a hot stove all day?"

Bernie sucked her teeth, then unfolded her napkin in her lap. "Pretty much," she said casually. "Can you fry chicken?"

Miles laughed. "You're a trip."

"Yeah, but that's what you like most about me," she teased.

"No, I like other things more. Believe that."

The faint sound of "Pieces of a Dream" played in the background. Miles had definitely set the stage for the evening. He'd turned the lights down throughout the apartment and lit candles. He'd even gone so far as to buy fresh oriental lilies for the occasion. All that was left was to convince Bernie to show up, which had taken some serious begging and pleading on his part, but it had worked. Bernie's usual argument of being too tired had grown weak, and he knew, even if she didn't want to admit it, that she wanted to see him as much as he'd wanted to see her.

After dinner, Bernie helped him with the dishes, then the two of them went into the living room and slow danced to Will Downing.

"You know better than this," she said, just before he dipped her.

"What?" Miles asked, gazing deep into her eyes before he kissed the tip of her nose.

"You know better than to act like we're a couple, Miles."

Miles smiled. "We ain't a couple, Bernie?"

"No. We fuck, and that's about the extent of it."

"You fuck, baby," he said, with a sly grin. "I make love."

Bernie laughed, then rolled her eyes. "If I didn't know better, I'd think you were leading me on. Trying to make me think you care."

Miles stopped dancing, then sat down on the sofa and pulled Bernie down next to him. "And what if I do care?"

She thought he was teasing, but suddenly the look on his face told her otherwise. "Don't mess this up, Miles. You know where I'm coming from. I haven't led you to believe anything else, and I'm not interested in anything else," she said firmly.

"Why? Because of my age?"

"Partly because of your age."

"Oh, so it's cool to fuck a younger man, but it's not cool to fall in love with one?" he asked, sounding slightly offended.

"We've had this conversation before. Don't sit there looking like this is a revelation to you, because it's not. Ain't nobody ever said anything about love, and we're not going there, Miles." Bernie's own frustration was starting to come through, which Miles had hoped could be avoided, but he'd been preparing himself for this conversation for a long time now. Bernie was stubborn and had dictated the nature of their relationship from the beginning. He'd gone along with it, because in the beginning it had been cool. Miles hadn't expected any more than she had, but somewhere along the line, things had changed. At least for him.

"Yes, Bernie. We are going there. Tonight, we're finally going there. I'm falling hard for you, baby," he said seriously. "And I'm tired of this just being a fuckfest to you, because that's not what it is to me."

"Miles? What the hell are you talking about? How can you call yourself falling for me, when you don't even know me?"

Miles laughed. "I don't know you? Hell, Bernie! I know you better than you know you."

Bernie glared at him. "You've lost your damn mind. You don't know a thing about me outside of the bedroom, Miles, because if you did, then you'd also know that this whole conversation is futile. I'm not trying to fall in love with anybody, especially with someone barely old enough to drive."

"I'm thirty-two, Bernie, not twenty-two. I'm a younger man, yes, but I'm not a child. Hell, I make more money than you, I've traveled more than you. I've been married too, Bernie. And I've got kids. So why the hell you insist on making me sound like I've just graduated high school?"

Bernie sat back and angrily crossed her arms over her chest. "You're not listening to me, boy. You never—"

"And you can keep that *boy* shit to yourself, woman. Whenever you get pissed off at me, I'm your *boy*, but when my ass has got your legs all spread up in the air then I'm a man," he said sarcastically. Bernie shot him an icy stare. "That's right. I'm a man, Bernie. A grown man, who knows what I want, and I know how to work hard to get it."

Miles had grown tired of dropping subtle hints. He was tired of beating around the bush, and more than anything else, he was tired of being patient, hoping that Bernie would come to her senses and want to take this relationship to the next level the way he did. They'd been seeing each other for months now and all he knew was that he wanted more. Bernie conveniently played the age card whenever it suited her. And when that didn't work, she threw her failed marriage up in his face. In the beginning, he'd understood and even empathized, but as time went on her excuses had played out. Hell, his marriage had failed too, but he'd be damned if he'd let that keep him from making the most of his life. Miles knew what he wanted, and Bernie was it. She was a strong and beautiful woman. Stubborn as hell, bossy as all get out, but he'd seen a softer side of her. Moments when she'd forget and let her guard down, like when they'd made love. Call him crazy, but he knew he was nuts about her, and he also knew that if she stopped trying to be such a hard-ass for a minute, she might just be crazy about him too.

Bernie sighed and rolled her eyes in frustration. "Why do you insist on making this hard? We were doing fine five minutes ago. Our relationship—"

"Has been on your terms from day one, Bernie, and that's not cool anymore."

"They've been on my terms for the last six months and you've gone along with it just fine. Now all of a sudden you want to flip the switch?" she asked, angrily.

"And what if I do? What if I want to turn this whole relationship upside down and see where it leads? What's wrong with that?"

"What's wrong with it, is that that's not what I want, Miles."

Miles stared into her eyes at a coldness he'd never really seen before in her. "That's the bottom line, Bernie? What you want and to hell with everybody else?"

"That's the bottom line. Take it or—you know the rest." Now she was being cruel, and she knew it. From the look on his face, Miles knew it too. He had a fantasy going on inside his head, and insisted on dragging her into it. He wanted a commitment, and Bernie just didn't have it in her. She'd been committed for over twenty years to something she'd put all her faith in, that had backfired in her face and she'd convinced herself that she was better off without all that nonsense again.

He hadn't expected this to be easy, but all of a sudden he was starting to feel like he'd made a fool of himself. "Is the idea of being with one man so terrible, Bernie? Is being my woman, or anybody's woman, what turns you off?"

Bernie sighed. "I like my life the way it is. There are no complications. I do what I want to do, the way I want to do it, Miles. I know what it is to be committed. I know how to do that, if that's something I have to do, but I'm not willing to go there anymore."

"Because your ex left you for someone else?"

"Because it didn't work out."

"Did it ever occur to you, Bernie, that he might not have left if you'd given him reason to stay?"

Bernie felt her chest tighten. "What the hell is that supposed to mean?"

Miles had the advantage now and he decided to make the most of it. "It means that you're a control freak."

"Miles—"

"No, let me finish. You say I don't even know you. I know you and I know that all twenty years of your marriage were probably run on your terms to your specifications and after twenty years of being henpecked I'd think a man would get sick of it after a while. Maybe she didn't take him from you, baby. Maybe you drove him to her," he said unemotionally.

Bernie glared at him. "Fuck you, Miles!" she spat.

Miles slowly got up and walked over to the door, then held it open for her to leave. "I guess I'm not the man for you after all, Bernie."

Bernie picked up her purse to leave. "I tried to tell you that," she said on her way out.

Bernie drove home, pissed off enough to cry. *Damn. When was the last time that had happened? Who the hell did his ass think he was?* She'd never led Miles on. Not once since they'd been seeing each other had she ever given him the impression that she wanted more from him than what they had. It had been easy, convenient, and all the fulfillment she'd needed. So now he blamed her for not wanting more.

To hell with Miles. "He can kiss my ass," Bernie muttered pulling into her garage.

Fancy This

❧

As far as Ruth was concerned, Cinderella was alive and well and living in Jacksonville, Florida. She was also a black woman who'd changed her name to May Edwards. May answered the door wearing a crimson angora, cowl-neck sweater and winter white rayon slacks, looking positively stunning. She'd wrapped up the outfit nicely with a pair of red, sling-back pumps.

"Hey, girl." She beamed as Ruth walked in. "Welcome, welcome. Here, let me take your coat." Ruth hadn't really dressed up, but after looking at May, she wished she had. "You look great, Ruth. Love that outfit."

Ruth wore a simple black, knee-length skirt, a royal blue, long-sleeve sweater, and black flats. Sure she was comfortable, but May looked like she'd stepped right out of a spread from a fashion magazine.

"Your house is gorgeous, May," Ruth said, marveling at the huge cathedral ceilings and immaculate decor.

"You think so, girl? Thank you. I told you, we jus' put it on the market. Know anybody who might be interested?" She winked and smiled at Ruth. Yeah right, Ruth thought. Like she could really afford what they were probably asking for a place like this. Even if she could, it was way too much house for her.

"I'll ask around and get back to you." Ruth smiled.

May's taste could best be described as elegant. She'd obviously avoided the whole made-to-order, living room-in-a-box concept, and had painstakingly taken her time to search for and buy each individual piece of furniture, wall hanging, vase, and pillow. Then, she managed to put it all together to make it look like something a professional spent months designing. Mahogany wood accented the place, complemented by a heather gray decor, seasoned with splashes of subtle color here and there.

"By the way, where're the kids? I was hoping to see them."

May had been bugging Ruth for weeks to come by for dinner and meet her family. Allan, thirteen, was her oldest and a music prodigy who managed to get first seat in the school orchestra for violin and was supposedly the Michael Jordan of the new millennium. Her daughter, Shannon, was nine, an aspiring ballerina, and had made the honor roll every year since kindergarten. They sounded like wonderful kids. Perfect kids. Ruth figured that when the time was right, she needed to sit May down and give her a firm warning. Perfect children, the kind who never gave their parents any grief at all, usually harbored closet suicidal tendencies, suffered from low self-esteem, eating disorders, and were likely to end up in abusive relationships. She'd learned that in her psych class, and also from personal experience.

"Allan's spendin' the night with a friend and Shannon's at my momma's. Tonight's jus' for us grown folk," May said, leading Ruth into the kitchen. "Can I get you somethin' to drink? The wine is delicious and perfectly chilled." She poured Ruth a glass before she had a chance to answer.

"Dinner smells delicious. What's on the menu?"

"Mmmm." May stepped over to the oven, and pulled out a silver pan covered in foil. "My momma's secret recipe for baked chicken, fresh, steamed vegetables, wild rice, and for dessert, I thought we'd indulge a little." She smiled mischievously at Ruth. "Homemade cheesecake."

Ruth's heart jumped up into her throat. She hadn't had cheesecake in ages, and the very thought made her head spin. "May!" she gasped.

"Child, we work hard out there. And ain't nothin' wrong with a lil' self-indulgence every now and then. Shoot." She propped her hand on her hip. "I need some incentive every now and again, and knowing I can splurge on a lil' slice of heaven every once in a while, is what keeps me walkin' 'round in circles like a fool."

Speaking of heaven, Ruth nearly fell on her behind when May's husband, Jefferson, joined them in the kitchen. His grand entrance was breathtaking, to say the least, and the man wasn't even trying to be breathtaking. Jefferson's penetrating hazel eyes were stunning in contrast to his ebony complexion. He was dark. Even darker than Ruth, with a physique to rival that of a professional bodybuilder, which was obvious even beneath the cream colored sweater and black slacks he wore. He was completely bald, and Ruth thought it suited him perfectly. Having hair would've been a distraction, though minor, to his obvious good looks. Perfectly straight, flawless white teeth beamed in Ruth's direction as he walked toward her, extending his hand to shake hers.

"Hello," he said graciously. "I'm Jeff. You must be Ruth."

Jeff was the epitome of male physical beauty, if there were such a thing. However, Ruth couldn't help but notice one thing. He was short. Way short. Like-no-taller-than-her short. Really. He stood next to her and Ruth found herself staring back at him, eye to eye. If she'd had on socks, she'd have towered over the brotha. In her high heels, May did tower over him, but neither of them seemed to have a problem with it.

"Hello, Jeff. It's nice to finally meet you." Ruth grinned.

"You too. May talks about you incessantly." That was scary.

"Oh, Jefferson. I do not." She gave him a playful, painless slap on the arm, then cut her eyes at him.

"It's all good though," he reassured Ruth. Only she wasn't so re-assured. Ruth still hadn't told May everything about her marriage. Mainly because whenever she and May were together, May usually did all the talking. But she couldn't blame it all on May. There'd certainly been opportunities, she just hadn't taken advantage of them to give May all the details. Ruth had incorporated her friendship with May into her "fresh start," so to speak, and it never seemed necessary to tell her everything that had happened before they met.

"You don't need to tell everybody all yo' business, Baby Ruth," Karen had taught her. And she'd been right. There were some aspects of

her life she didn't feel comfortable exposing, not even to her friends. There were exceptions, of course, like Bernie, who'd had a bird's-eye view of the transformation. Bernie had known Ruth almost from the beginning. She'd suspected all along that there'd been trouble in the paradise of Ruth's world, and in time all her suspicions had come to light. And Clara had met Ruth at the crux of her transition, and had adopted the task of helping her to heal. May had come to know this new Ruth. The old Ruth had no part in this friendship as far as she was concerned, and Ruth made it her mission to keep the dirtier aspects of her past right where they belonged—behind her.

Jefferson poured himself a glass of wine and the three of them talked while May finished preparing dinner, which she insisted she needed no help with.

Jeff was an architect. He and May met at their sons' basketball game several years after May's first husband died. Jeff's son, from a previous relationship, was a year younger than Allan and he was playing on the other team. According to Jeff, it had been love at first sight.

"How'd you know she wasn't already married?" Ruth asked, listening to Jeff tell the story.

"That's the same thing I asked him, Ruth. This man jus' walks up to me and asks me for my phone number. For all he knew, my husband could've been sittin' right there."

"She'd come in by herself and she wasn't wearing a ring so I just figured it was worth the risk and decided to take my chances." He grinned and kissed May on the side of her neck. "It paid off."

Suddenly, the doorbell rang and May smiled devilishly at Ruth. That was enough to immediately let Ruth know something was up. How long had May been insisting that Ruth get out more, find herself a man and settle down?

"Girl, you need to hurry up and get you somebody. Have some babies 'fo yo' eggs get too old and yo' children run the risk of bein' born with two heads or somethin'."

May had been pleading with Ruth for months to let her introduce her to a few nice eligible bachelors, and Ruth realized that the woman had taken it upon herself to do just that.

"Adrian, you've already met my wife, May."

"Yes. Hello, May. Nice to see you again."

Ruth turned just in time to see Jeff standing in the doorway of the kitchen with her "date" for the evening and she could hardly believe her eyes.

May recognized a miracle when one had the nerve to slap her upside the head, and this one had done exactly that. Ruth mentioned meeting a nice man at the jazz festival a few weeks back, and the name sounded familiar. For the life of her, she couldn't remember where she knew it from, and decided to mention it to Jefferson. An Adrian Carter worked at the same company he did, and the two would get together sometimes and play racquetball. What a small world and God would've never forgiven her if she'd let this opportunity pass her by. Ruth might not forgive her either, she speculated, ignoring the glare in the woman's eyes. But what the hell? Having Ruth pissed off at her was nothing compared to having the Lord pissed off at her. Besides, Ruth couldn't be mad for too long. The man was gorgeous!

Close your mouth, Ruth! she told herself. *How many times do I have to tell you that?* "And this is a friend of ours . . . Ruth. Ruth Johnson. Ruth . . . Adrian Carter." Jeff smiled, looking as cheesy as his wife, and all Ruth could do was fight the urge to look as idiotic as she felt. Adrian smiled, and nodded. "Ruth."

"Hi." *Damn girl! Is that all you can say?* she wondered if he'd remembered her. From the looks of it, no. The man didn't seem to have a clue as to who she was. *Whatever.*

Adrian turned back to Jeff and handed him a bottle of wine. "Zinfandel okay?"

May stepped in like Joan Cleaver. "Zinfandel's perfect," she said, breezing past Ruth, taking the bottle from him. She gave Ruth the "follow me into the dining room" look on the sly and Ruth excused herself from a very uncomfortable situation.

Safely in the confines of her hallway bathroom, May began justifying herself before Ruth could cuss her out like she kept trying to do, but May wouldn't let her get a word in edgewise. "Ruth, now I know you're mad at me."

"May—"

"But if I told you he was goin' to be here, you wouldn't have come over," May whined and pouted.

Ruth folded her arms across her chest. "No. I wouldn't have."

"He's such a sweet man, Ruth, and ain't he fine? If I wasn't already married—"

"May, I don't care," Ruth said through clenched teeth.

"Look, it's jus' dinner, girl. It's jus' a few hours of yo' time and if you don't like him, you never have to see him again, Ruth. That's a good-lookin' man out there."

Hell yes, he was good looking. Ruth wasn't blind, but she'd told the man she wasn't interested in seeing him again. Thank goodness he didn't have the slightest idea of who she was or he'd have thought she was a fool and had set this whole thing up herself. "I just wished you'd have warned me," Ruth argued, trying to keep her voice down.

"I would've, but you so shy sometimes and I mentioned him to Jeff the other night because I knew that name sounded familiar and—"

"I'm not shy, May. I'm just not interested in dating right now. I'm not ready to—"

"And you'll never be ready if you don't come out from behind that wall you got built up, honey. I think he might be wonderful for you. Jus' give tonight a chance. Please?"

Ruth stood there, staring at May, wondering when was her ass going to get a backbone and learn how to just say no?

May's dinner was absolutely delicious and Ruth decided to use it as her excuse not to say much during the conversation while everyone is eating. Not once did Adrian ever let on that he recognized Ruth. Initially, that memory lapse in him had proven to be exactly what she'd wanted, but as the evening wore on, she found herself offended by it. How could he not remember? They'd spent an afternoon together, talking and laughing. He'd looked deep into her eyes for crying out loud, going on and on about how pretty they were and now he had the nerve not to—

After dinner, they took the party into the living room, sipped on cognacs and listened to the tale of Jeff and May's wedding day.

Ruth silently counted down the minutes, anticipating the small window of opportunity that would provide the perfect excuse for her to take her behind home. May and Jeff sat kissing and cuddling on the loveseat. Adrian was on one end of the sofa and Ruth sat safely in the armchair by herself.

Ruth quickly glanced in Adrian's direction to see if he was as uncomfortable with their display of love and affection as she was. He politely smiled back. Yep. That was an affirmative.

"I love you, baby," she whispered.

"I love you too, darling. You know I do." *Earth to Jefferson. Earth to Jefferson. Hello. There is life outside of that woman's eyes*, Ruth wanted to scream. He must've read her mind because all of a sudden his spirit was back in the room and he remembered he had guests. "Have you seen the model of the new house, Adrian?"

"No. I've heard a lot about it, though."

Jeff led the way to his office and sitting on a big table in the middle of the room was a scaled down model of a palace. "It's bein' built in Ponte Vedra as we speak." May beamed.

"This is impressive," Adrian said, leaning over it. "You design this, Jeff?"

"Every inch," he said proudly. "I promised May I'd build her the house of her dreams, when we were married, and . . . Well, barring any major setbacks we should be moving in by next summer."

May looped her arm around Ruth's. "Didn't I tell you it was beautiful, Ruth?"

"You certainly did, and it is beautiful, May."

"When it's finished, we're havin' a housewarmin' party. I know you comin', girl."

"Wouldn't miss it."

May had told Ruth once that all she had to do to get her way with Jeff was to pout, or in extreme circumstances, do a little crying. Which sounded kind of childish to Ruth, but she imagined May being the kind of woman who could get away with something like that. Ruth never could, though. Of course, she'd never tried pouting with Eric. Crying, yes. Begging, sure. Pleading, definitely. But never pouting.

Ruth offered to help May with the dishes but Jeff insisted that she was a guest and it was his duty to help her. Ruth interpreted this as being their way of leaving her and Adrian alone together since they'd hardly said more than five words to each other all evening, but she had made up her mind that she was not playing along with this game or giving in to these people's wicked schemes. Besides, Adrian obviously wasn't interested anyway, so when no one was looking, she stepped out onto the patio and practiced her goodnight speech. *Ummm . . . I've had a nice time. Wonderful dinner, May, and yes, next time we'll do it at my place.*

May and Jeff had a huge backyard and the full moon illuminated it like a stage. As perfect as those two were, Ruth figured it probably wasn't shining on anyone else's backyard but theirs right now. The sound of Adrian's voice abruptly invaded her quest for solitude and set about a million little butterflies free inside her stomach.

"It's a nice night."

Ruth started to turn around, but thought better of it. "Yeah . . . it is."

Adrian sauntered over, stood next to her and whispered, "Are they getting on your nerves too?"

Ruth laughed. "Yes, they are."

"Good. Then it's not just me. How've you been?"

Ruth stared at him, surprised he was even talking to her. "So, you do remember me? I'd thought you'd forgotten."

He smiled. "Of course, I remember. Brothas always remember the women that diss them."

"I didn't diss you," she gasped.

Adrian shrugged. "You dissed me, Ruth."

"No, I just didn't give you my number," she said, trying to defend herself. Of course she hadn't dissed him. Women didn't diss men like Adrian. He'd just caught her at a bad time, that's all. Like, after her marriage.

"Exactly."

She chuckled. "But that's not diss'n you."

"My feelings were hurt." Adrian placed his hand flat against his chest and desperately tried to appear wounded.

"They were not."

"Sure they were."

"Well, I'm sorry. That wasn't my intention."

"I accept your apology," he said casually.

"Thank you." Ruth glanced quickly inside the house. "Did you know about this tonight?"

"I knew that they wanted me to meet someone. I just didn't know it was you."

"So, why'd you go through with it?"

He smiled. "Because she was giving him a hard time and I empathized with the man. Besides, he begged me to come, and I figured, what could it hurt? Did you know?"

"I didn't have a clue."

"If you'd known, would you have shown up?"

Ruth giggled. "Probably not."

"That's right." Adrian nodded. "You're not ready for a relationship right now. Isn't that what you told me?"

She sighed. "Yes, that's what I told you. I also told you it wasn't personal either."

"Of course it's personal, Ruth. Rejection from a woman for a man is always personal."

"I told you at the park. I think you're a very nice man."

"I'm nice, but you don't want to have anything to do with me. Makes sense."

Ruth crossed her arms in front of her. "Are you always this sarcastic?"

"Not usually, but, like I said, I'm hurt. You're real good at giving a brotha a complex, Ruth."

"Then you shouldn't want my number, Adrian," she said matter-of-factly.

He grinned. "I can't help it. I think you've got it going on."

Ruth blushed. "You're funny."

"I'm not trying to be funny. I'm being honest."

"Well, I'm flattered." She smiled. "Coming from someone like you, that's quite a compliment."

"What's that mean? Someone like me?"

"You already know, Adrian. I don't think I have to say it."

"I wish you would."

"Someone like you? Handsome. Pretty darn special," Ruth said, trying to make it sound like she was teasing.

"Thank you. Now I'm the one flattered. And so, I can call you . . . when?"

"You're welcome. And it's getting late."

"And?"

"And I'd better be leaving."

"In the nick of time, right?"

"Excuse me?"

"If I ask you for your number now, can I expect a different answer this time? Or are you going to shoot me down again?"

Ruth sighed. "Why won't you just give up on me? I'm a hopeless cause."

"Because I like you," Adrian said, staring into those big, brown eyes of hers.

"You barely know me."

"So?"

"So, how can you be so sure you like me?"

Adrian suddenly eased his arms around her waist and before Ruth knew what was happening, his warm soft lips were locked onto hers. Ruth's legs turned into limp noodles and it was all she could do to keep from fainting. His mouth was absolutely precious and she savored the delicious taste of this man. Oh God, she thought. *If this is heaven, just let me die right here, right now.* Adrian kissed away all her inhibitions, doubts, fears, issues, regrets, mistakes, pain, tears, bad memories, and disappointments. He kissed in hope, desire, longing, intimacy, passion, and wishes.

He pulled back and gazed down at her. "I'm sure."

"I don't have a pen," Ruth said breathlessly.

"Just tell me. I'll remember."

Yours Truly

JEFFERSON EASED HIMSELF DOWN BETWEEN HIS WIFE'S FIRM
thighs knowing full well, he didn't need to rush. He pushed himself
inside her, as far as he could go, then gently lowered his weight on
top of her. May instinctively locked her legs around him at the an-
kles, held his face between her hands, and slowly probed his mouth
with her tongue.

"Take yo' time, baby," she whispered between kisses. "You jus' take
yo' time with me."

With Jefferson, the missionary position was making love. May
loved being able to stare into his rich, hazel eyes, suck on his full,
tender lips, and pull him farther inside her with her hips. Together,
they moved like dancers in perfect unison, in sync, rhythmically
blending from two bodies to one. Tears slid down the sides of her
face, as her mind filled with thoughts of just how much she loved
this man. How much she needed him. Even with Frank, it hadn't
been this good. Jeff filled every nook, cranny, crevice of her body
and her soul, and yes, she'd give her life for him if he'd asked her
to.

"You can't possibly love me the way I love you, Jefferson." She'd
told him that time and time again, desperate to make him understand
the depth of what she was confessing.

He'd smile back at her, kiss her hand, and assure her. "Oh, yes I
can."

But May knew better. Her love for him bordered on obsession.

One that she fought daily to control. If she could've kept him in her pocket for the rest of his life, she would. Other women knew what she had. They could see it in him when he walked down the street. He was fine inside and out, up and down, and she'd fight tooth and nail to keep him.

"You act like you can't get on without a man, May," her mother had fussed. "You was the same way with Frank, and here you go again with Jefferson. Gon' drive him away if you ain't careful. Men don't like women that's too possessive. Gon' drive him away."

"Talk to me, baby," Jeff moaned in her ear. "Tell me how good this is."

May wrapped her arms tightly around him, and squeezed her thighs close. She nibbled on his earlobe. "I love you, Jefferson Edwards. My baby," May whispered. "I love you so much. Jus'—Don't stop, darlin'. Don't ever stop."

Eventually, Jeff shuddered and then let out a long, slow moan into the pillow beneath her head. Then his body relaxed on top of hers, and soon May heard him drift off to sleep. She held him in her arms all night, because he was exactly where he belonged.

Was she possessive? May was in love, and yes, as far as she was concerned love had better be possessive, or else some other woman would step up and try to take away the best thing that ever happened to her. Men were weak like that, and women were conniving. Frank had been weak, but she'd never told anyone. Naturally, he'd denied ever fooling around on her, but May knew better. Frank was flirtatious and handsome. He loved the attention he got from women, which is why she worked so hard to give him so much attention from her, so he'd ignore those other women. But she suspected there was no such thing as enough for Frank. Pieces of paper with phone numbers scrawled on them fell from his pockets.

"Business prospects, May," he'd argue. "That's all it is, baby. Stop tripping." He'd get angry with her sometimes, accusing her of being jealous and insecure. "You're the woman I love, May! I married you! Why the hell do you insist on believing I'm out there messing around with somebody else?"

Sometimes, she wondered if Jeff could be weak like Frank. Even her daddy had been weak for women, taking her along with him when he stopped off at one of his girlfriends' house when they were supposed to be running errands.

"Sit right here, May Baby," he'd say, smiling down at her. "Daddy be out in a minute."

Then he'd disappear into a back room with the woman, and come out thirty minutes later, buttoning up his shirt.

"Don't tell yo' momma we stopped off, May Baby." He'd rub her hair. "You understand, Daddy jus' had to take care of some business, that's all. But don't say nothin' to yo' momma 'cause she don't need to know."

May never said a word, and eventually he stopped taking her, but she always knew he'd never stopped cheating.

No, she thought hugging Jeff tighter to her. He wasn't like any man she'd ever known before. He was her reward and her blessing, and nothing or no one would ever take him away from her.

Well, I'll Be

THE DAY AFTER DINNER AT MAY'S, ADRIAN'S KISS STILL HAD Ruth reeling and riding high on cloud number nine as she headed over to Bernie's house to tell her about it. The two sat out on the patio, sipping iced tea, and listening to Aretha Franklin, "You make me feel like a natural woman." How appropriate, Ruth thought, smiling.

"Let me get this straight," Bernie said, leaning forward looking intently at Ruth. "*You* had a date?"

"Don't get your panties in a bunch, Bernie. It was just dinner, that's all. And it wasn't a date . . . exactly." Ruth fought hard to maintain some semblance of composure, which hadn't been easy since she'd left May's house the night before.

"Dinner." Bernie leaned back in her seat, studying Ruth for signs of everything she probably wasn't telling her. "Dinner's good. It's a beginning."

"A beginning to what?"

"A beginning to cleaning that old dusty pussy of yours."

Ruth laughed. "It's not dusty, Bernie. I prefer to use the term 'preserved.'"

"Preserved is good. Old and dusty is more accurate, but hey, it's your pussy. So, is he fine?"

"He's incredibly fine, if you must know."

"I wouldn't be asking if I didn't want to know, sweetie." Bernie smiled. "What's his name? Maybe I know him."

"It was the guy I met at the jazz festival. Remember? I told you about him."

"It was him?" Bernie asked, surprised. "How'd that happen?"

"May and I were out exercising and I mentioned him to her. As it turns out, he works at the same company her husband works for."

"Damn! Talk about kismet. And what's his name again? You sure I don't know this dude?"

"I hope not," Ruth said pitifully.

"What's that supposed to mean?" Bernie asked defensively.

Without meaning to, Ruth had offended her friend and she quickly tried to recover, hoping Bernie hadn't noticed the little Freudian slip. "Nothing."

"No, now come on out with it, Ruth. What do you mean you hope I don't know him?"

"I'm sorry, Bernie. I didn't mean anything. It's just that—"

Bernie crossed her arms over her chest. "It's just that if you think I might know him, then you think I might've done him?" Ruth shrugged. "Contrary to what you might want to believe Ruth Johnson, I have not slept with every man in Jacksonville and we need to get that clear right here and now."

"I know, Bernie. And I'm sorry. Really. I didn't mean to imply that you had."

Bernie was offended, but not as offended as Ruth believed she was. Hell, she had slept with a lot of men after her divorce. But not lately. She really couldn't blame Ruth for what she thought, though. Bernie talked a good game, but in reality, her game had dwindled down a whole lot to the likes of Miles, which surprised her more than probably anybody. She'd insisted on practicing safe sex with all her lovers, but gradually the idea crept into her mind that even so-called safe sex might not be safe enough, and the last thing she wanted was to become a statistic of the AIDS epidemic or hepatitis count. So for the last six months it had just been Miles. The thing is, that kind of monogamous behavior definitely had its drawbacks, which had come to light the other night. She hadn't heard from him since.

Bernie sat across from Ruth, damn near blinded by the glow emanating from this woman since her encounter with that dude she'd met at May's.

"So, what's he like?"

"He's very nice." Ruth blushed.

Blushing annoyed Bernie. "Nice? What the hell is nice?"

"Nice, Bernie. Nice is just . . . nice."

"And what else?"

"Is your period coming?"

"My period?"

"Somebody's a little cranky today. If you ask me," Ruth teased.

"I'm not cranky or PMSing, Ruth. I'm just trying to get some answers from a sistah. That's all."

"And I'm giving you answers."

"You're giving me—'nice.' I can't do nothing with that."

Ruth laughed so hard, she sprayed iced tea across the patio. "See what you made me do?"

Bernie smiled. "No, that *nice* brotha made you do that. Not me. So what did you say his name was?"

"His name is Adrian Carter," Ruth said, composing herself.

"And he's all that?"

"He's more than all that." Ruth blushed again and Bernie rolled her eyes.

"Would you do him?" Bernie teased.

Ruth shrugged. "I hadn't thought about it."

"Figures."

"What's that supposed to mean?"

"You don't ever think about doing anybody. I swear. Your ass is some kind of secret experiment engineered by the government to implement the extinction of the black race. How can a woman go without fucking for two years, Ruth? It just ain't natural."

"I can't help it if I've got self control. I can't just screw anybody, Bernice. I'm sorry, but I just can't. There are too many diseases going around. Too many freaks."

"Ever heard of condoms? Ever heard of mace?"

"Ever heard of abstinence?"

"Not since I was in the seventh grade."

"Not every woman is as free-spirited as you are, Bernie. Some of us want to wait for the right man."

"Ain't nothing wrong with that. But until the right man comes along, a little extracurricular activity never hurt. Just buy you a box of condoms, carry some in your purse, and make him slip it on before he slips it in. It ain't hard. I mean, you ain't had none in a long time, Ruth. Wouldn't nobody blame you for getting your groove on, even if it was just a little bit. I know you think about it. I know you miss it."

"Nope," Ruth said casually.

"Nope?" Bernie stared at her in disbelief. "Yeah right. You don't miss having sex?"

"No, Bernie. I don't."

"Stop lying, Ruth. I know Eric was an asshole but . . ." The expression on Ruth's face was starting to make Bernie uncomfortable. "You serious? How can you not miss it? How can any woman in her right mind, with even a semihealthy libido not miss sex?"

"I don't miss sex. What's the big deal?" Of course, Bernie had no idea how endeared Ruth was to Maxwell.

"Sex is the big deal," Bernie reiterated.

"Sex is overrated," Ruth said, waving her hand in the air.

Suddenly she noticed the vein over Bernie's left temple start to swell and pulsate madly, which usually happened every time something upset her. Ruth sometimes worried that if Bernie wasn't careful one of these days her head was going to explode. "Overrated! How the hell can you say sex is . . ."

Ruth frowned. "Damn, Bernie. Did I hit a nerve?"

"Girl! I know what it is," Bernie said, taking deep breaths to try and calm herself down. She pulled her address book from her purse and started fumbling around in it, letting the business cards and pieces of paper fall as they may. "I've got the number to a good gynecologist. Now, I'm sure this is something he can fix, baby. Maybe prescribe you some pills or something. Where did I put . . ."

Ruth gently put her hand on Bernie's and smiled tenderly. "Bernie, I don't need to see a doctor. There's nothing wrong with me. I just don't happen to be one of those women who thinks sex is all that. It happens, and there's nothing wrong with me."

"Ruth, something's wrong, honey. But don't you worry. We're going to get you some help, and . . . Here it is." Bernie held out a white business card to Ruth, then quickly pulled it back. "You want me to call and make the appointment for you? I can go with you if you like. You're not in this alone, Ruth. I'm here for you, girl. You know I am."

Ruth couldn't believe it. Bernie sat there looking as if she was about to cry. "Bernie, I'm not sick. I just do not like sex. Pay attention. I'm fine and I don't need to see a doctor."

Bernie stopped and stared at Ruth with so much pity in her eyes that Ruth was starting to feel guilty.

"You really don't like—"

"Sex. And no," she said, shaking her head. "I don't. I never have."

"But why not, Ruth?"

"Dammit, Bernie! It's not like I've just told you I have a fatal disease. Why are you taking this so hard? It just doesn't feel good. That's it."

"Ruth—"

"It doesn't, girl. I've never gotten anything out of it. Well, except for a few yeast infections and some other stuff Eric brought home. Anyway, it's not a big deal. Besides, thanks to you, I've got Maxwell now." Ruth smiled. Bernie looked confused, not knowing that Ruth had named the gift Bernie had given her. Ruth winked and it dawned on Bernie what she was talking about.

"Maxwell? Oh . . . *Maxwell.*"

"Girl, I like me some Maxwell." She grinned.

"Ruth, Maxwell's not meant to be a substitute for the rest of your life. I just gave you that to tide you over until—"

"Until what?"

"Until you meet a nice man, honey."

Suddenly, Ruth burst out laughing and immediately knew from the look on Bernie's face that she'd hurt her feelings. "You're sweet, Bernice Watson," she said apologetically. "And thank you for caring about me and thank you for Maxwell. But right now he and I are fine."

"I know what it is now," Bernie sighed. "You've never been with anybody but Eric."

"And Maxwell."

"Stop playing, girl. This is serious," Bernie scolded.

"For who?"

"Ruth, Eric was all wrong for you."

"Maxwell's perfect."

"And your body knew that, which is why it didn't respond the way it's supposed to."

"I don't know about all that, Bernie," Ruth said skeptically.

"Listen. I know what I'm talking about. You find yourself someone nice, baby. Someone who cares about you . . . I guarantee you won't think sex is bad at all."

"Bernie, why can't you just accept the fact that I might be frigid? I have."

"No. You're not frigid, Ruth. Not the way you and Maxwell probably go through batteries." Ruth laughed. "Every man isn't Eric. There are some out there who are gentle and caring and loving. Maybe this Adrian is one of them."

"I don't know. I don't want to think that far ahead. One day at a time is about all I can handle. Know what I mean?"

"I know, girl."

No, she had no idea. How could she? For a woman like Bernie the world was her playground and the men she met were her playmates, as far as Ruth was concerned. Sure, Bernie had gone through some disappointments of her own, but she'd never let bitterness hold her prisoner, or regrets bury her deep inside her past like Ruth had. Bernie bragged constantly about her sexual exploits and Ruth listened, trying to fathom how she could enjoy herself so much while someone else pounded himself inside her body just so he could "get his." That was something Ruth didn't think she could ever understand. But the flavor of Adrian, the warmth of his lips, the sweetness of his tongue, those things she understood perfectly.

"Did I tell you he kissed me?" Ruth said quietly.

Bernie smiled. "No, you didn't. How was it?"

Ruth smiled too. "It was wonderful, Bernie. Best kiss I ever had."

"Like I said, Ruth . . . it's a beginning and the best kiss you've ever had is a fine place to start."

Meeting of Minds

⚜

THE WEEK FOLLOWING DINNER AT MAY'S, ADRIAN HAD LEFT SEV-
eral messages. By Wednesday, Ruth still hadn't gathered up enough
courage to return any of his calls. She'd tried but halfway through
dialing his number she'd lose her nerve, hang up, and curse herself
out for being too chicken to go through with it. It should've been
easy enough, she reasoned. All she had to do was dial his number,
wait for him to answer and then say what? Hello? That made sense.
Hello: universally simple and straight to the point. "Hello, Adrian."
Even better. Interactive and yet personable. How hard could it be?
"Hello Adrian," she'd say simply, and the rest would flow naturally.
Or, maybe she'd say it slowly, seductively: "Hel-lo A-dri-an." For
some reason, Ruth had the dismal feeling that she was about to blow
this whole thing and all of a sudden it dawned on her that she was
a complete and total moron when it came to men.

Ruth sat curled up in the chair in her living room, lost in space
with Adrian Carter. Everything about him was right, from the way
he moved to the way he walked. His smile was mesmerizing and his
eyes hypnotic. It was as if someone had peeked inside her mind,
taken a sharp pencil and drawn her idea of perfect on a man. Then
listed his perfect man attributes in a column next to his picture.
Classy, intelligent, handsome, romantic, great kisser, all around wonderful human being. Hell, who was she trying to fool? She wasn't his
type. She must've had an aneurysm or something without realizing

it, which was why she'd forgotten that there was no way a man like that could genuinely be interested in her. Ruth rubbed her temples, awed by the realization of just how powerful insecurity could be. It had a way of tearing away a woman's self-esteem like a ferocious animal, leaving behind shreds of despair dangling off the bones of her raw and bloody pride. Melodramatic? Sure, but from her experience Ruth surmised it wasn't far from the truth. Of course, there was only one thing for her to do whenever she felt like this. Ruth went into the kitchen and searched frantically for the pint of french vanilla ice cream she'd hidden in the back of her freezer.

Adrian could have any woman he wanted, she thought, stuffing huge spoonfuls of ice cream into her mouth and he probably did. At this very moment, women were probably lined up outside his home pining over him, sweating him, throwing panties at him, and if he were like most men, he was probably lapping up the attention, taking full advantage of the situation and savoring every drop of womanness he could get his greedy little hands on. Shame on him for trying to pull the wool over her eyes. Suddenly, it dawned on her that Adrian Carter was nothing more than a mega-mack-daddy-player-pimp-I'm-gonna-hit-it-and-run-'cause-I-ain't-got-time-for-you brotha. He was smooth with it, though. She had to give him credit for that. The more she thought about it, the angrier she became, because this man was trying to run a game on her, and to think she'd almost let him get away with it. Ruth angrily shoved the spoon deep into the quart of ice cream, then back into her mouth. He almost had her fooled, pretending he was a nice guy with a personality that wouldn't quit, pretty, white teeth, and only the best, most honorable intentions. But if he thought he was going to get over on somebody, she was not the one. He could take his pathetic-ass rap and good-looking self somewhere else and play on some other unsuspecting female's heart strings because there was no way she'd ever let him pull on hers!

Fifteen minutes later Ruth scraped out the last spoonful of ice cream, and was immediately overwhelmed by guilt. So much guilt, in fact, that she rushed into the bathroom, stuck her fingers down her throat and threw it all up. She'd worked hard over the years, sticking to her diet and the common sense, nutritious eating habits she'd developed, and there was no reason to let issues with some man she hardly even knew ruin her life.

The clock next to her bed read 9:47 P.M. As hard as she'd tried, sleep just wouldn't come. Okay, so it wasn't that late. But she'd tried everything to get her mind off him. Watching television hadn't worked, listening to music definitely didn't help because all she owned was jazz and slow songs and it all reminded her of him. She made a promise to herself to stop off at the music store on the way home from work and buy some gangsta rap or something. Snoop Doggy Dogg, Master P, Ice T or Cube or anybody.

The sound of the phone ringing startled her and, without thinking, Ruth answered it. "Hello?"

"Ruth? It's Adrian."

Ruth's heart jumped up into her throat, but somehow she managed to find the strength to speak anyway. "Hello—Adrian."

"Did I wake you?"

"No . . . no. I just got in," she lied. "How are you?"

"I'm good. Just uh . . . been hoping to catch up with you. I've left a few messages in case you hadn't noticed." He laughed, nervously.

"Yeah, I got them. I've been meaning to call, but I've been so busy."

"No problem. I understand. It's late and I'm not going to keep you. I just wanted to let you know I was thinking about you."

Ruth sat straight up in bed. Her heart beat so fast, she thought it might jump out of her chest. "You were?" she asked, trying not to sound excited.

"Yes. I had a good time the other night, and I was hoping you did too."

"Yes, Adrian," she said, smiling. "I had a terrific time. And I've been thinking about you as well."

"Oh yeah? What were you thinking?"

That you're a mega-mack-daddy-player . . . "That I'm glad May and Jeff had us over for dinner."

"Me too." He chuckled. "I wasn't all that hyped about that blind-date thing, but when I saw you . . . Well, let's just say it turned out to be a good night after all. I think you are one beautiful woman and . . . you taste good too."

"Like baked chicken and wild rice?" *Ruth, you idiot!* Why in the world did she feel so compelled to make a joke out of everything? The man had just told her she was beautiful and she had to trivialize it with a joke. Ruth wanted to kick herself, but she didn't want to run the risk of Adrian hearing it.

He laughed. "No. Like a sweet black woman with a pretty mouth."

"That's about the nicest thing anyone's said to me in a long time. Thank you," she said blushing, choking back another cocky response. Damn, she was a grown woman. How come it was so hard for her to act like one? "You're very sweet, Adrian."

"Thank you. I'm trying to make a good impression."

Ruth bit down on her bottom lip. Her nerves were trying to get the best of her, but she was determined not to let them. "I told you, I'm out of practice."

"Yeah, I remember you telling me that it's been a while. Right?"

"It's been forever and I'm definitely going to need a refresher course in dating one-oh-one."

"Don't we all?"

"I'm serious."

"So am I," he said.

Say what's on your mind, Ruth, she told herself. *This time, just lay all your cards on the table and if he doesn't want to play, well, at least you know where you stand, girl.* "Can we just keep this real? No games, just—all cards on the table."

"Do you think I'm playing games, Ruth?"

"No. No, that's not what I'm saying. I just hope we can both be honest with each other. That's all," Ruth said quickly. "I don't want to have to guess where you're coming from. Know what I mean?" Had she said too much? Maybe she'd implied too much or gone too far. Adrian was quiet for a moment, and Ruth suspected she'd probably blown it with him already. She'd come on like gangbusters and the man had just called to say hello.

"I know exactly what you mean. And if it's any consequence, I don't want any games either, Ruth. I don't have time for them."

Ruth sighed. "That's a relief." Adrian laughed. "One day at a time? Sound like a good idea?"

"Can't ask for better than that. And I'm looking forward to every one of those days. Can we start with dinner on Friday?"

"Dinner on Friday would be lovely."

"All right, then. I'm going to jump in the shower and go to bed, and let you get some sleep too. But I'll give you a call again tomorrow."

"I'll look forward to it."

"Goodnight," he whispered before hanging up.

Ruth smiled from ear to ear, then gathered up her pillow, wrapped her arms around it, pretended it was Adrian and slept like a baby.

Landing

ADRIAN KNEW HOW TO BE COOL. HE WAS NEARLY THIRTY-FIVE years old, and yes, he had mastered the art of cool and composure and very seldom ever lost either. But it took all the will power he had not to reach out and touch something on that woman. Ruth answered the door wearing a red knit dress that clung to every damn curve on her body. He gulped, but not so that she would notice. God help him. He wasn't sure if it was his imagination or if her skin was indeed shimmering. It was definitely possible. Women knew little tricks like that, and he'd learned it was best for a man to just admire them, and keep his mouth shut.

"Hi, Adrian," Ruth said nervously, wondering if Adrian could tell her knees were knocking.

He looked breathtaking in his smoke gray suit and black turtle-neck sweater. "Hey. I'm a little early," he said apologetically.

"Oh, that's okay. I'll be ready in a few minutes." She closed the door behind him and hurried toward her bedroom. "Just a few last minute touches, and—we can go."

Adrian had been looking forward to this since he and Ruth had met at the jazz festival. Obviously she was shy, and possibly even a bit insecure, but she'd definitely had an impact on him. The thing is, insecurity usually came with issues, and from the conversations they'd had, Ruth no doubt came with issues. He'd reached that con-clusion more from what she hadn't told him, then from what she had told him. The last thing he'd wanted was a woman with baggage, but damn she was cute.

"Nice place," he said, surveying her apartment.

"Thanks," Ruth answered from the bedroom. "It's small, but—"

"No, it's cool. Plenty of room for you, right?"

"Plenty. Have a seat. I'll be out in a few minutes."

With the bedroom door closed securely between them, Ruth grabbed a pillow from her bed, hurried into her closet, shut the door and whimpered into the pillow. "He is so fine! Oh my goodness! Lord have mercy! Goodness gracious!" She finally stopped tripping long enough to come out and check her makeup and hair. Ruth took a few deep breaths in an effort to help calm her nerves. *C'mon, Ruth. It's just dinner, girl. What's the big deal?* Adrian was the big deal. Probably the biggest deal to happen to her in her whole life and he had no idea. There was no way she'd tell him what tonight meant to her. It meant a second chance. Ruth stood in the mirror, staring at her reflection. She'd never figured on it happening, and until now she'd never given much thought to starting over with someone. Now she knew better. She not only wanted a second chance. She needed it. Before tonight, the only thing that had motivated her had been distancing herself from the past. Tonight was a new kind of beginning for Ruth, one where she would take the chance to step out in a different direction and maybe even put herself back on the line.

"If he only knew," Ruth muttered to herself. God, she didn't want him to know. Let him think she had her shit together. Let him think she was all that. Please. Just for tonight. Let him think she was the woman he'd always dreamed of.

Dinner was nearly painless. Naturally, she said some things she wished she hadn't, accidentally dropped a piece of chicken in her lap and used the salad fork when she should've used the dinner fork, but Adrian was gracious enough to pretend not to notice. After dinner, they both agreed that they needed to work off that meal and decided to take a stroll along the riverwalk. The lights from the Jacksonville Landing reflected off the St. Johns River, and danced on the small waves, while the gentle breeze encouraged Adrian to do the polite thing and put his jacket over her shoulders. Being with Adrian was easy. Ruth was amazed that she didn't have to spend time or energy second-guessing herself, or reading his moods, looking for what he really meant in the midst of what he'd said or hadn't said. Instead, she was free to enjoy his company and conversation. This was all so new to her and it was lovely.

"So, Jacksonville isn't your home either?"

"No. I'm originally from Denver."

"Denver?" Adrian said, raising his eyebrows. "They got black folks in Denver?"

"Ha. Ha. Ha," Ruth answered dryly. "You're funny. Anybody ever tell you how funny you are?"

He shook his head. "No. Nobody ever has. So, what brought you out here?"

"My mother died when I was fourteen and I was sent here to live with my grandmother."

"I'm sorry. That had to be rough." He sounded genuinely concerned. "How'd she die? Or am I getting too personal?"

"Complications from surgery," she said, not feeling the need to elaborate.

"That's a hard thing to deal with at fourteen. Hell, it would be a hard thing to deal with at any age."

"It was hard then and sometimes it still is." Ruth stared out onto the river, hoping to cast any sad feelings out into the water, instead of letting them interfere with the evening. "Karen was my world, and as far as I was concerned, we were going to be together forever. All my friends were in a hurry to grow up and get as far away from their parents as possible. But not me." She laughed. "My plan was to kidnap Momma so we could spend the rest of our lives together on some deserted island. Just the two of us."

"What about your father?"

"Nope. No room for him. He'd have to get his own island. Actually"—she shrugged—"I never knew him."

Adrian leaned over and said softly in her ear, "His loss."

She smiled. "It was. Momma was beautiful."

"You must look a lot like her, then?"

Ruth looked up at him, flattered once again by his generosity with compliments. "Anybody ever tell you how charming you can be?"

"Sometimes, I am charming. Other times, like now, I'm pretty straightforward, which gets me into trouble every now and then." Adrian winked.

"Uh-oh. Then I'd better be careful. Never know what you might say."

"As far as you're concerned"—Adrian took hold of her hand— "nothing bad. I'm sure."

Neither of them said anything for a while. The slight chill in the air seemed to draw them closer together as they walked, and eventually, Adrian put his arm around her shoulder. Ruth nuzzled into the warmth of his arms, relishing in how comfortable she felt.

"All your family here in Florida?" he asked.

"No, the only family I had was my grandmother, but she died years ago. What about you? Do you have a big family up there in Cincinnati?"

"Cincinnati. Cleveland. Alabama. Maryland. I've got a big family. Period." He laughed.

"What's it like, having a big family?"

"It definitely makes for interesting family reunions, weddings, things like that. Other times it can be a pain in the ass."

"Why?"

"I don't know. Everybody expects you to remember birthdays, anniversaries, graduations, baptisms." Ruth laughed. "Then they all expect you to send something. Mainly money."

"Well, there are pros and cons to everything, I suppose."

"Absolutely everything."

Suddenly Adrian stopped, leaned back against the wall of the boardwalk, and gently pulled Ruth into his arms. He'd been trying to do this all night, gaze deep into her eyes, but she'd been avoiding it, until now. This time he had her in a position where avoiding him was impossible, and Ruth was hypnotized like the proverbial deer in the headlights.

"Did your mother have big, beautiful brown eyes like you?"

She smiled nervously and tried to make light of the situation. "The biggest and the beautifulest."

Adrian chuckled. "Then your daddy must've had some ugly eyes."

"He probably did." Ruth quickly tried to change the subject. "Who do you look like? Mom or Dad?"

"The mailman," he said, smiling.

"Oooh! If I ever meet your mother—"

"Now, you know I'm kidding."

"Is your dad handsome?"

Adrian shrugged. "He thinks so. Mom thinks so."

"Then he probably is."

Everything about this woman seemed inviting, Adrian thought. Ruth had a sweetness about her that drew him in, compelling him to get close. Not to mention, that beautiful figure of hers was pretty compelling in its own right. Adrian couldn't help himself. He knew he'd end up making a move, but he also knew that he'd have to take it slow and easy.

Without warning, Adrian leaned toward her and started kissing her lightly on the neck. "You know I'm trying to behave myself?" he mumbled in between kisses.

"Oh . . . are you?" She could hardly breathe. The sensation of this man's lips on her skin had caught her off guard in the best way, and it was all she could do to contain herself.

"I promised I wouldn't rush things with you. I think I've kept my promise. Don't you?" Adrian's lips had moved up her neck to her ear, and he pressed her earlobe tenderly between two very sensuous lips. "I promised I wouldn't make any sudden moves," he whispered lushly.

Ruth swallowed hard, and fought to catch her breath. "This isn't a move?"

Adrian slowly ran his fingers across her lower back, and held her so close Ruth wasn't sure where she ended and he began.

"It's not sudden." He grinned, planting small kisses on her neck. "I've been contemplating this all evening, but if you want me to stop, then you just say the word, and I'll back off."

Back off? *Don't you even think about it*, she said to herself. "No. No, this is nice."

"Mmmm. You smell good," he moaned.

The warmth of his breath against her neck was absolutely lethal and what was left of Ruth's little composure evaporated into thin air. "Thank you. It's new. I just got it today as a matter of fact and it's called . . . Oh shoot! I don't . . . remember what it's . . . called, but . . . I just bought it today and—"

"You said that already," he whispered.

"Did I? I'm sorry. I don't usually repeat myself but—"

Adrian interrupted her mindless rambling, and caressed her lips with his, then slowly eased his warm tongue into her mouth. Ruth closed her eyes, cherishing the moment and the very real fact that time, for them, stood completely still. When he'd finished, Adrian held her against him. Ruth rested her chin on his shoulders, inhaling him, melting into him, memorizing him, hoping this night never ended, and praying silently that he'd hold on to her like this until his arms fell off. It was Adrian who finally broke the spell.

"I'd better get you home," he said, letting go of her.

"No, Adrian. Can't we stay here a little longer, just like this?"

Was that a pout she felt coming on? No way. It couldn't be. Women like May pouted. Women like Ruth didn't know how.

Adrian laughed. "I promised I'd take my time with you, Ruth. And if I don't get you home, I can't guarantee I'll keep my promise."

As good as he felt and as wonderful as this evening had been, Ruth knew he was right. She wasn't ready for more than this, but it had the affection that she'd been starved for for so long. The human touch has been known to revive, cure, revitalize, but Eric's touches possessed no such hidden powers. She and Adrian walked back to his car holding hands. It amazed her how rehabilitating a good hand-hold could be.

Adrian parked in front of Ruth's apartment building and walked her to her front door. He bent down and kissed her again. "I'll call you tomorrow. Maybe we can get together sometime this weekend."

"I don't have any plans," Ruth said, entirely too anxiously. She made a mental note right then and there to learn to play harder to get.

"I've got to go out of town on Monday and I'd like to see you before I leave."

"How long are you going to be gone?" she asked, eagerly.

"A few days. My company is flying me off to San Francisco."

"I hear it's nice there."

"It's all right." He shrugged. "I'm usually in meetings and hotels all day, so I don't get to see much of it."

"What a waste," Ruth said, frowning. "Haven't you been to Nob Hill? What about the Golden Gate Bridge? I've always wanted to see Haite—" Adrian interrupted her again with another kiss, which she didn't mind one bit.

"The Black Arts Festival is here this weekend at the convention center. I was thinking about going on Sunday. You free?"

"Sure," Ruth said excitedly, then quickly composed herself. "I mean—yeah. I'd love to go."

"All right. Then I'll call you tomorrow about a time."

"Yeah, that's fine. I'll be home, so Sunday's good for me."

"All right, baby." He kissed her one last time. "You get on inside, now. And goodnight."

Ruth closed the door behind him, then braced herself against it once she was safely inside and took a much needed deep breath. It had been a very good night and if she weren't careful, she'd trip all over herself for Mr. Carter. This was perfectly understandable. The man was fine and incredible and every other adjective in the dictionary that meant out of this world. If he had any ulterior motives, he'd been really good at hiding them. But whatever his motives were, his methods were the bomb!

Adrian sat in his car for a moment before leaving. The scent of Ruth's perfume lingered on his jacket and he smiled. He'd never considered himself a player, but for years he'd definitely valued his bachelor status. In the back of his mind, he'd always known that ultimately he'd settle down to one woman to grow old with, like his parents had done. Family was important, and more and more, he could see that. He was getting older, and the time to start thinking about settling down was long overdue.

"This one could be special, man," he murmured to himself. "Take your time."

Adrian turned the key in the ignition and headed home.

Back Stepping

"IT'S UGLY, RUTH," ADRIAN FINALLY SAID, AFTER MUCH DELIB-erating. "You really like that?"

Ruth's zealous grin quickly disappeared. Damn. It wasn't that ugly. It was eclectic, perhaps, but not ugly.

"Well—yes. It's different."

Adrian laughed. "That's an understatement."

Ruth wasn't about to let Adrian's conservative views on art deter her from something she thought was beautiful. So, she immediately went on a mild-mannered offensive. "I just thought it would look nice on my coffee table. It's unique, and I can appreciate that."

"Let's keep looking," he said, gently taking her hand. "Maybe we can find something else for your coffee table."

"Maybe if you try to use your imagination a little, you could see that sometimes there's something special in unique things," she hinted.

"What about something like this?" He pointed to a ceramic sculpture of a man and woman whose bodies wrapped around each other like two snakes in mating season.

"It's nice. I've seen that somewhere before, though." *Probably Wal-Mart or someplace like that near the checkout counter. Generic.* That's the word that came to mind, and that's where Ruth kept it. "You like it?"

"Don't you?"

"Sure," she lied. "It's beautiful."

She might have tried to hide it, but he'd caught it, that unenthusiastic tone of voice that bordered on condescending. "You don't like it."

"What? I do. No, it's nice. Really."

Adrian smiled, then took her by the hand and led her to the next display. "You don't like it." Ruth smiled.

Suddenly, he stopped. "Now this—you can't tell me you don't like this."

Ruth frowned at the painting in front of them. It was an abstract of an African warrior. At least, that's what it looked like from that particular angle. She tilted her head just a bit to the left, and it looked like something else altogether. Ruth was just about to comment when they were interrupted.

"Hello, Adrian." She was a goddess, tall and beautiful with a flawless honey gold complexion, long sandy brown hair cascading down her shoulders and eyes big enough to swim in. The woman kissed Adrian seductively on the cheek, then glanced briefly in Ruth's direction as if she were nothing more than a fly on the wall. Ruth immediately stared up at Adrian. If he were the least bit uncomfortable by this woman's obvious show of affection, he didn't show it. "Ashley. How've you been?"

Adrian fought to maintain his composure on the outside, but inside he was shaking in his shoes. This was one of those tricks of fate life sometimes likes to play on a man, and instinctively he suspected there was no way he'd come out of this unscathed. He hadn't seen Ashley in months, and now here she was going overboard as usual on that whole seductress act of hers. Ashley was full enough of herself so that no one else ever needed to make the effort. She'd dumped him before he'd ever had the chance to dump her, but he'd been leading up to it. That's for sure. Yeah. The sex had been off the hook. Actually, the sex was what had held them together. Ashley was game for just about anything, but between the ears, it was empty, except for the fact that it was all centered on her.

Ashley smiled and took a step closer to him. "I haven't seen much of you lately. Where've you been hiding?"

"Not hiding," he said casually. "Just busy."

Ruth stood by impatiently feeling as though she'd disappeared and neither one of them seemed to notice or even care. Old flame? she wondered looking at Ashley. Of course she was. Girlfriend was making it all too obvious that she and Mr. Carter had spent quality time together. She was standing close enough to bump heads with the man. Ashley ran her hand down Adrian's arm, expertly slipped his hand out of Ruth's, and sandwiched it between her own.

This kind of scene was entirely too awkward to her, and Ruth decided it was time to make an exit, and leave Adrian alone with this heffa he couldn't seem to take his eyes off of. She started to walk away, but Adrian quickly managed to grab her by the elbow before she could make her indiscreet getaway.

"By the way, this is my—" Ruth put her hand on her hip, and glared at him anxiously, waiting to hear what he had to say. His—*what* exactly? "This is Ruth. Ruth . . . Ashley."

Neither woman said a word. Ashley glanced quickly at the space above Ruth's head, then made her vanish again and cast her gaze back into Adrian's eyes.

"Adrian." She pulled a business card from her purse, then wrote something down on the back of it. "Here's my number in case you've lost it. Call me? Maybe we can get together sometime and catch up on . . . things." She smiled sensuously and sashayed away.

He tried not to smile as she walked away, and he tried real hard not to watch her ass sway to the rhythmic beat only heard by canines and men, but his effort was futile.

"She was . . . cute," Ruth said, in an effort to regain even an ounce of her composure. Of course she felt like an idiot for saying it. The man wasn't blind and certainly he could already see that. The woman was drop-dead gorgeous.

"What? Oh . . . yes. She is," he said, pretending to turn his attention back to the painting.

"She's tall."

"You never told me if you liked this or not."

"Can we go now?" Ruth asked, bitterly. Miss America's little appearance had definitely put things back in perspective for her. Ruth had no business being here with Adrian.

"Now? But we haven't been here that long, Ruth."

"I know. I'm . . . I've got a headache."

Adrian knew better. "A headache? That was sudden."

Ruth spotted the exit and headed in that direction. "It happens like that sometimes and I'd really like to go," she snapped.

Adrian followed her. "This is about Ashley, isn't it?" he asked, trying to keep from making a scene.

"Of course not," she said abruptly. "I'm not feeling well and I just need to go home, Adrian."

"Ruth . . . baby, look," he said, wadding up the business card she'd given him, and dropping it to the ground. "It's not what you think. I'm not interested in her."

Not interested in her? How dumb did he think Ruth was? What man in his right mind wouldn't be interested in a woman like that, especially if she was in heat for him the way this Ashley vixen was obviously in heat for Adrian.

Ruth picked up the pace, and hurried outside into the parking lot. "I'm really not feeling well, Adrian. That's all." She didn't even bother to look behind her to make sure he was coming. As far as Ruth was concerned, it didn't matter one way or another if he gave her a ride home or if she took the bus. All she knew was that this date was over.

Neither of them said a word on the drive back to Ruth's apartment. She stared out the window, feeling pretty silly, and not just about her reaction to Ashley, but because this afternoon had confirmed what she'd suspected was true all along. Ruth wasn't ready for this. She wasn't ready for the Adrians of the world, or their ex-girlfriends either. Ever since her divorce, she'd devoted herself to keeping a low profile, wading through each day in stealth mode. The less drama in her world, the better, and relationships always seemed to come attached at the hip to drama. That's not what she was looking for. Ruth still had issues and rather than drag someone else into them, unwillingly and unknowingly, the best thing she could do was to come to terms with them on her own first.

"Thanks, Adrian," Ruth said quietly, and she quickly opened the door to the car. "I had a nice time."

Adrian reached across her, and closed the door. "You know you're making a whole lot out of nothing."

Ruth inhaled deeply, staring out the window, because if she'd looked at him, she'd have probably broken down in tears. "Maybe I am."

Adrian fought to hide his own frustration. His relationship with Ruth was just getting started, and the last thing he wanted was for it to end over something stupid.

"She and I used to see each other, Ruth. It was a long time ago, and there was never anything serious between us," he said, hoping to reassure her.

"You don't have to explain anything to me, Adrian. It's not you. It's me," Ruth said, annoyed.

"Don't give me that. It's bullshit and you know it. If you've got a problem with me, then you need to tell me what it is, Ruth. And none of that 'it's not you, it's me' shit."

Ruth quickly blinked away tears forming in her eyes. "You know what? Maybe it's best if we—"

"If we what?"

"There's a lot going on with me, Adrian," she said softly. "I've got some things I need to work out here"—she pointed to her chest—"and until I do that, then . . ."

The expression on his face clearly indicated that he knew where this was going. "Is that what you want? You want to leave this alone?"

Ruth nodded. "I think it would be best."

"No. What would be best is for you to talk to me. If you need to get something off your chest, baby"—he shrugged—"I can't think of a better time or place than to do it right now."

"You wouldn't understand," Ruth said simply.

"Try me."

"It's complicated."

"It usually is." Adrian leaned close to her. "But I'm listening."

Ruth sat still for a moment, realizing that this was her opportunity to come clean, and recite her whole life story. He'd laid himself out on a silver platter, ready to succumb to the tale of all the ridiculous escapades of her life, and all she had to do was open her mouth and tell him. For the life of her, Ruth couldn't bring herself to do it. She had no idea where to start, and even if she could begin telling the story, where would she end it, if in her mind, it still hadn't come to an end?

"I've got to go. You take care of yourself." Ruth hurried out of the car and inside her apartment building.

A cup of hot chamomile tea was tucking her in to bed. Ruth couldn't sleep, not after the way she'd acted with Adrian. It had been for the best though. Sometimes she would forget, but days like the one she'd had with him reminded her that all was not well in the psyche of Ruth Johnson, because no woman in her right mind would've let a man like that get away. She'd come a long way, but still had a hell of a journey ahead of her. *Damn!* Ruth said to herself. *Healing is hard work.* She smiled, remembering how she'd insisted to Bernie that sex was overrated. But overrated or not, with Adrian she'd have just suffered through it the best way she could. Talk about torture. The phone rang, startling Ruth from her moment of self-revelation.

"Hello?"

"Hello," he said. Adrian sounded tired. "Were you sleeping?"

"No, not yet." The sound of his voice calmed her. Or maybe it was the effects from her tea. No, Ruth knew the tea had nothing to do with it.

"I've um . . . I've got a couple of tickets to the Luther concert next week and was wondering if you'd like to go with me?"

Ruth closed her eyes tight, then mouthed the words "Thank you" to God and to any other spirit out there who'd come to her rescue and give her just one more chance to right her wrongs. She'd gotten out of his car today prepared to cut her losses, wallow in a little self pity, then pick up the pieces and boldly go forth on her next adventure. But maybe she needed to stand her ground and devote some effort to this one. That could be a good thing, but she definitely had to gird her loins to do it. Running would be easy. Staying, and seeing where this could lead, that would take guts.

"I'd love to go with you, Adrian," she said, letting the smile spread across her face.

"I was hoping you'd say that. I had a hell of a time getting tickets this late in the game." He laughed.

"I didn't think you'd call me again."

"I didn't think you wanted me to."

"I'm glad you did."

"Me too. Goodnight, baby."

"Goodnight, Adrian."

Best Friends

Best friends are where you bury your secrets and plant your hopes for safekeeping. Ruth had learned that lesson from her friendship with Bernie. They didn't always get along or see eye to eye on things, but it was all part of the magic of their relationship. Neither of them had ever had a sister, so they had adopted each other.

They spent the afternoon in the mall, shopping until Ruth was finally able to convince Bernie that her poor feet just couldn't take it anymore.

"If you don't get me to someplace where I can take off my shoes and put my feet up, I'm going to cry, Bernie. I mean it. I'm going to stand here and cry and embarrass the mess out of you."

She'd made her point, and Bernie rushed her back to her place, fixed Ruth a white wine spritzer while she poured herself into Bernie's sofa and sighed at the sensation of blood flowing back into her toes.

"Your hang time ain't like mine," Bernie teased. "All that damn walking you're doing with what's-her-name, and you can't do the mall? You ought to be ashamed of yourself."

Ruth laughed. "Mall walking is different from park walking, Bernie. I have to spend money in the mall, and that's what makes me tired."

Bernie had been uncharacteristically quiet all afternoon. At first Ruth thought she might just be tired from all the overtime she'd been putting in lately, but sitting in her living room, looking at her, she could tell it was more than that.

"You going to tell me what's on your mind?" Ruth asked.

"What?" Bernie asked, seeming preoccupied. "Oh . . . I'm just tired, girl. Been busting my ass getting ready for this case, and . . . I'll be glad when it's over."

"When's the court date?"

"We start next week, but I have a feeling it could drag on for a while."

"And that's all that's bothering you?"

"That's enough."

"The boys okay?"

"They're fine."

"Everything all right with your boyfriend?" Ruth knew this would shake her up.

Bernie peered at Ruth over the rim of her wineglass. "My boyfriend?"

Ruth smiled reticently. "Miles."

"I'm not even going to justify that absurd question with an answer. You know better than that," she snapped back.

Bernie had mentioned Miles to Ruth occasionally, but never felt it necessary to elaborate on her relationship with him. However, Ruth had put two and two together and soon realized that Bernie had been seeing Miles exclusively for quite some time.

"Miles and I went to dinner."

"Miles left his tie at my house."

"Miles is on the other line. Can I call you back?"

"You two have a spat?" she asked playfully.

That vein on Bernie's head was starting to protrude again. Ruth had definitely hit a nerve. "I'm going to spat you, if you don't talk about something else."

"Bernie? What's wrong with admitting you've got a thing for the man? C'mon, I think he's good for you."

Bernie glared at Ruth. "And what the hell do you mean by that?"

"It means that having a nice man isn't the worst thing in the world."

"Is that right? And where did this revelation come from, Ruth? You go out on one date and all of a sudden you're ready to write an advice column on love?" she asked sarcastically. "When I need your advice, I'll ask for it. Until then, you're more than welcome to keep your little opinion on the subject to yourself."

"I'm just saying, Bernie. You go out of your way sometimes to pretend you don't—"

"Pretend? Who's pretending, Ruth? Not me," Bernie said. "Miles was a booty call. That's all he ever has been to me, that's all he ever will be. I don't have to justify that to you or anybody else for that matter. And if he doesn't like it, he can get the hell on!"

Suddenly it dawned on Ruth that Bernie wasn't kidding. Ruth had pissed her off without trying, and Bernie was using all the strength she had left to keep from going completely off on her ass. Damn! Ruth thought. *What the hell had happened between Miles and Bernie?* It was clear from Bernie's reaction that he'd been more than a booty call, whether she wanted to admit it or not. Ruth might be naive sometimes, but some things were as clear as day. She wondered who Bernie was trying to convince that Miles had meant nothing to her. Ruth or herself?

Neither of them said anything for a while. It was Ruth who finally broke the silence. "I've um . . . been calling around town for possible venues to host the fund-raiser." She and Bernie hadn't discussed the idea since in ages. With everything going on, Ruth suspected Bernie was no longer in the frame of mind to take on the project.

Bernie leaned back and closed her eyes. "Is that right?" she asked casually.

"Renting a place can be pretty expensive, even for one night. Hotels charge a fortune for banquet rooms and food."

"Yes, they do. I've got a friend over at the Hilton. He's a manager there and he owes me a big favor."

"Woman, is there anybody in this town who doesn't owe you a favor?" Ruth teased.

"We've got a room if we want one, big enough to feed and entertain about three hundred of our closest friends." Bernie smiled.

Ruth sat straight up. "Bernie, girl! Are you serious?"

"Don't I look serious?" she asked calmly. "You know I don't play when it comes to business."

Ruth stared at Bernie with genuine concern. "Bernie, you know you don't have to do this. I understand if—"

"Would you stop? I told you I'd help, and I'm helping," Bernie said. "Don't get on my nerves, Ruth. I ain't in the mood," Bernie fussed.

Ruth laughed. "Well, that's one major obstacle out of the way. That's wonderful, girl! And to think, you got us a room without even trying."

"There's only one problem, though. We have to use it before the end of February, or he can't let us have it. He's leaving, moving back to Louisiana."

"February? That soon?" February was less than three months away and for the life of her, Ruth had no idea how they'd pull this thing off in that amount of time. "That doesn't give us much time."

"Aw, but we can do this, Ruth." Bernie smiled. "We're going to have to kick it into overdrive, but we can definitely do it."

"We?" Ruth beamed. "I thought you were just going to look into a few things? When did this officially become a *we* operation?"

"Since I know how much this means to you," Bernie said sincerely. "You've come such a long way from where you started out, and I am so proud of you. Of course we have to do this. Clara needs our help, so we're going to help her."

Bernie hadn't actually met Clara, but from the way Ruth spoke about her, she knew she had to be pretty special.

Ruth suddenly felt like Bernie's faithful sidekick. "Well then . . . I guess we'd better get down to business."

Bernie waved her hand in the air. "Girl, please. I've already started." She went into her bedroom and came back with an action list as long as her arm. "So, we've got the location," Bernie said, scratching that off her pad. "And I've started the guest list." She handed it to Ruth, who knew Bernie had connections, but she had no idea Bernie had contacts like the names on that list.

"Girl, you know all of these people?" Ruth gasped.

"Of course I do," Bernie said casually.

"You know Councilwoman Douglas? Councilwoman Susan Douglas?"

"Yes, I know the woman, Ruth. What's the big deal?"

"How'd you meet her?"

"We've got the same beautician," Bernie said dryly.

"Connie? But Connie specializes in—"

"Weaves."

Ruth's chin dropped to the floor. "Councilwoman Douglas wears a weave?"

"Now I know you didn't think that was that woman's real hair."

"I did."

"Ruth, I've got more hair on my eyebrows than she's got on her head. Don't be so naive, girl."

"You know Carl Johnson. Channel Five's Carl Johnson?"

Bernie smiled, remembering Carl with his freaky self. She hadn't seen him in over a year. His last words to her were "call me," but for some reason . . . "Oh, I know him all right."

"Bernie!" Ruth laughed.

"Don't ask," Bernie said firmly.

"You didn't. Did you?"

"Didn't I say not to ask? I promised I wouldn't kiss and tell, so—"

"You've never kept that promise before," Ruth argued. "What's he like in person?"

Bernie rolled her eyes and ignored Ruth's inquiring mind. "Anyway, we've got the location, a partial guest list. If you or Clara know anyone else we need to send an invitation to let me know. We'll need to get them out as soon as possible."

"Well, what do you want me to do?"

"You work on the menu. My friend at the Hilton insisted on us using the hotel caterer, but you know those folks don't know how to cook. Besides, they charge too damn much. I told him we already had a caterer."

Sharon from the shelter immediately came to Ruth's mind. "I think I've got a good caterer already lined up."

"Good. Just make sure they can cook. I know most of these people personally, courtesy of Mitch the Man, and the last thing I need is for them to go around talking behind my back about how bad the food was at my fund-raiser."

Ruth looked at Bernie. "My? What happened to *we?*"

"That's what I said. We'll need some entertainment too. You can take care of that. Somebody or something impressive, please. Keyword: *professionals,*" Bernie emphasized. "If you need some help with this, let me know."

Bernie went on and on with her ideas and Ruth sat next to her, in awe that she'd managed to get so much work done on her own. She put her arm over Bernie's shoulder and hugged her. "This is going to be great, Bernie. I can't wait to call Clara and tell her about it."

Bernie smiled. "Why don't you call her now?"

Two and Two

❧

IN THE YEAR THEY'D BEEN EXERCISING TOGETHER, RUTH HAD NO problem keeping up with May on their ten lap trek to good health. May still obsessed over keeping up with her workout, making sure to pass on some of that motivation to Ruth, which was cool. Ruth knew in her heart of hearts that it wouldn't have been hard for her to lock all the doors and windows, curl up with a box of doughnuts, a diet soda, and lose herself in cable television. So she appreciated her friend's dedication to the cause and all. Besides, Ruth felt better than she had in years. She'd gone from a size twenty to twelve, and relished her new found energy and confidence.

"I got the invitation to yo' banquet the other day," May huffed.

"Good," Ruth puffed. "You and Jeff coming?"

"Wouldn't miss it."

"I'm glad. It's going to be really nice. You won't be disappointed."

"Well, for two hundred bucks a plate we better not be," she teased.

"It's for a good cause."

"A battered women's shelter?"

"A shelter for victims of domestic violence," Ruth corrected her.

"Same thing," May said matter-of-factly.

Neither of them said anything for a few minutes, until May finally asked the question. "You ever live there?"

Ruth wasn't surprised. As a matter of fact, she'd expected the invitation to stir May's curiosity, and she was relieved that it had. "No."

"He was abusive, though? Yo' ex-husband?"

"He was."

"I had a feelin' it was somethin' like that."

"Why?"

" 'Cause you weren't pissed enough for it to have been another woman and you seemed unsure of yo'self, 'specially when we first met. I don't know. You jus' seemed tired and a little scared. When I first saw you, you looked like a woman tryin' to erase her past, maybe even herself. I saw it in yo' eyes."

"My eyes?"

"The eyes are the windows to the soul. Haven't you ever heard that? It's true. Sometimes you can look into a person's eyes and piece together a whole history of where they been, who they are, without them ever tellin' you a thing."

"You saw my history in my eyes?"

"I saw a history that wasn't very pretty."

"No, it never was."

"You ain't the same woman, though."

"Well duh!" Ruth said sarcastically. "I've only lost forty pounds, May."

"That ain't what I mean and you know it. You got more respect for yo'self and it shows. I don't care if you hadn't lost forty pounds."

"It's hard sometimes, though. I spent so many years disrespecting myself and letting him do it, it's hard to remember not to live like that anymore."

" 'Course it is. But it was probably harder living with that mind-set. Wasn't it?"

"Much harder."

"How come you never told me?"

"I was embarrassed. That's not the kind of thing I want to share with my new friends. 'Hello, my name is Ruth and I'm a battered woman. Wanna do lunch?' "

"That the only reason?"

"I didn't want you to judge me. It's easy for a woman to say she'd never let a man hit her and get away with it. But it's a whole different story when you've got a mad man standing over you breathing fire through his nostrils with his fists balled up, cussing and calling you names you never even heard of. Screaming about how fucked up you are and how sorry your dumb ass is. It's never the actual fight that scares you. It's everything leading up to that. Waiting for the bomb to drop is more terrifying than when it actually hits the ground."

"I wouldn't know, sweetie. I hope I never do."

"With a man like Jefferson, I don't think you'll ever have to know, May."

"Did you love him?"

"Thought I did in the beginning. Now I know I just didn't know any better."

"He ever love you?"

"No."

"Doesn't it hurt knowin' that?"

"It used to, but I think it would've hurt more if he had loved me and treated me like that."

"Well, if you didn't love him and he didn't love you . . ."

"Why stay married?"

"Yeah."

"I think I depended on him. I depended on him to keep me from being totally alone, even if it meant being miserable. I even depended on his lies, I suppose. There were moments when he made me feel important, even wanted. Unfortunately, it was usually after he'd finished beating my ass over something stupid."

"Does Adrian know?"

Ruth glanced at May. "No. I haven't figured out how to tell him, or even if I need to tell him. Things are so new between us right now . . ."

"I understand." May smiled. "Was Eric as pretty as Adrian?"

"No man on the planet is as pretty as Adrian."

"I beg to differ," May protested. "Jefferson is just as pretty, if not prettier."

"That's because Jefferson is your man and you're supposed to think he's prettier."

"Is Adrian yo' man, Ruth?"

"No, he's my friend."

"But he's workin' on bein' yo' man?"

"Will you stop? He and I are just friends and that's all."

"For now," she said smugly. "Bernie goin' to be at this banquet?"

"Yep. She's helping put the whole thing together."

"She sounds like a good friend."

"The best."

"I'm lookin' forward to meetin' her."

"She's lookin' forward to meeting you too," Ruth lied.

Suspicious Minds

❧

"Hey, baby," Jeff sang into the answering machine. "I'm going to be late coming home tonight. One of our VIP clients flew in this afternoon, and a few of us are taking her out for dinner and cocktails to discuss the project. I think I told you about it. The new business complex we've been working our asses off to get? Well we got it, and now the real work begins. Anyway, I'm turning off the ringer on my cell, but I'll have it on vibrate. If I don't get back to you right away, leave a message and I'll call. Hopefully, I won't be out that late, but—you know how these things can go. Love you, baby doll."

May ordered out pizza for the kids and spent the evening alone in her bedroom. He'd said "her," hadn't he? He was having dinner with a client and that client happened to have been a woman. Her good sense spent the better part of the evening trying to convince herself that it was harmless and Jeff was doing exactly what he'd said he was doing. He was having dinner with colleagues and a client. Which colleagues? she wondered. He hadn't said.

May flipped through channels on the television, seeing but not hearing, unable to focus on any of the shows. The phone rang and May glanced at the caller ID. It wasn't Jeff, and she decided to ignore it. She wasn't in the mood to talk to anybody but him, and he wasn't answering his phone.

"Momma?" her daughter called from the other side of the door. "Momma? Telephone."

"Tell 'em I'm asleep, baby," May said dispassionately.

May glanced at the clock. It was nearly ten. "Y'all go to bed!" she called out to her daughter at the sound of her footsteps going down the stairs. "You hear me?"

"Yes, ma'am," Shannon called back.

She called him several times, just to check on when he might be coming home and to see if she should wait up for him.

"If I don't get back to you right away, leave a message and I'll call."

May bit down on her lip, wondering why he hadn't called. She turned off the television, then crawled into bed. As usual, she was overreacting, suspecting things that couldn't possibly be true. Jeff had never done anything to raise her suspicions. He was faithful and honest. Not like Frank, who'd insisted on bringing her worst suspicions to light. She'd caught him with another woman, sitting at a bar once. The woman was whispering in his ear, and Frank's arm was around her shoulder.

"We was just having drinks, May. Nothing else happened."

"Like that ought to pacify me, Frank? And what if I hadn't come in when I did? Would you have fucked her then?" May was livid, and rightfully so. It hadn't been the first time she'd caught him with another woman. But she'd never threatened to leave him over it, because that's not how marriages worked. Her momma and daddy fell out all the time over his affairs, but they stayed together. As a matter of fact, they were still together, after forty years of marriage, and they'd be together until one of them died. Right or wrong, May believed in that kind of devotion and it wasn't easy.

"In order fo' yo' marriage to survive the things me and yo' daddy went through, you got to let it go, May Baby," her mother told her, time and time again. "None of them other women meant anything to yo' daddy, but his family—his family meant the world to him, which is why we still together."

Jeff was becoming a company man, more and more this past year. He was moving up and away from the actual day-to-day duties of an architect, and was being groomed for management. He had a staff of designers working under him now, and he spent most of his time catering to high-profile clients. Which meant dinners and cocktails, trips out of town, weekend meetings. In a nutshell, it meant less time at home, and more away from her.

May lay staring up into the darkness, knowing she needed to get a handle on her jealousy. "He ain't done nothin' to make you feel like this, May," she whispered. "You lettin' yo'self go crazy over nothin' and it ain't right. Jeff's a good man. A damn good man. He's a damn . . . good—"

Headlights lit up the front of the house, and May heard the garage door open. She held her breath. He was home. May swallowed hard, not sure of how to feel. Relieved? Or should she brace herself? She knew exactly what she'd do. She'd watch. Would he shower before she had a chance to get close to him? Would he smell like the bitch he was with tonight? Would she find traces of lipstick on his collar? His underwear? Would he have his watch on, his wedding ring, or would he have some pathetic explanation for losing them?

May heard him coming up the stairs, and as soon as he opened the door, instinctively she shut her eyes, and pretended to be asleep. She heard him undress, then go into the bathroom and turn on the shower. May clenched her jaws tight, and her eyes tighter. *Come over here, Jeff,* she pleaded silently. *Come over here and kiss my cheek. Please!*

He quietly closed the door behind him and stepped into the shower.

Fallin'

GOODNESS GRACIOUS! RUTH THOUGHT, STARTLED AWAKE BY THE phone. She glanced at the clock telling her it was one-thirty in the morning, and immediately reached the conclusion that somebody was sick or dead or worse.

"Hello?" she anxiously asked into the receiver.

"Ruth? Hey, baby. It's Adrian. I know it's late, but I've been in meetings all day, then dinner with business associates tonight. But I told you I'd call."

Ruth fell back onto her pillow, relieved that the news wasn't bad, and that it was Adrian's voice on the other end of that phone. "Adrian, are you back?"

"No, I'm still in San Francisco, and you were on my mind and I wanted to say hello."

A wide grin spread across her face. "You've been on my mind too."

"Oh, yeah?"

"Oh, yeah. I have to admit, I've missed you."

"You miss me enough to come see me?"

"Yeah, right." She giggled.

"I'm serious. I can have a ticket waiting for you at the airport. You keep fussing at me about not seeing more of San Francisco, so why don't you come out and see it with me?"

Ruth sat up in bed. "Are you serious?"

"Of course I'm serious," he said, leaving her speechless. Adrian listened to silence on the other end of the phone, which to him meant she was either thinking about accepting his offer or looking for a way out.

"Can I call you back?"

"No, you can't," he said firmly. "You can tell me you're coming, though."

"Adrian, this is such short notice and I know you don't expect me to just hop on a plane to California just like that."

"We're talking a weekend, Ruth. One weekend." He sighed. "C'mon, sweetheart. Let's do this."

"I don't know what to say. The invitation is definitely tempting."

"I'll have the ticket waiting for you at the airport," he promised quickly. "The plane leaves Florida at nine and I'll see you when you get here, baby."

Ruth hung up and lay staring up at the ceiling, knowing sleep was a lost cause tonight. Was she really going to get on a plane in the morning, fly all the way across the country to spend the weekend with him, and what exactly was he expecting to happen after she arrived? Maybe his intentions were innocent enough: little sightseeing, a few meals, some harmless kissing, perhaps a little fondling, and then . . .

Ruth turned on the light and immediately started dialing Bernie's number.

"Ruth?" Bernie answered groggily.

"Bernie, guess what?" she blurted out. "Adrian just called me. He wants me to fly to California to spend the weekend with him. He's going to have a ticket waiting for me at the airport in the morning."

"Ruth?" Bernie asked again.

Ruth rattled on without hesitation. "I don't know what I should do. I mean . . . I hardly know this man."

"Ruth?" Bernie finally managed to get her eyes to focus and shook her head at the ungodly hour on her clock.

"Yes, it's me, Bernie. It's Ruth," she said, mildly irritated. "Bernie, what do you think? You think I should go? I don't know. That's a lot of money he's talking about spending and I'd hate for him to pay for the ticket and I don't show up," Ruth rambled on. "Most of these airlines are really stingy about refunds. He'd be out of hundreds of dollars. How much do you think it costs to fly from here to California? I should call and find out, huh? I'll have to pay him back. You know how I am. I couldn't take his money like that. Yeah, maybe I'll pay him in installments. Something every month until I've paid him back, because I don't want to owe anybody anything. You know what I mean? Bernie? You there?"

"Ruth," Bernie finally said.

"I don't know what to do, Bernie. I'd like to go, but . . . I'm scared."

"Of what?"

"What do you mean of what? Of . . . of . . . I don't know. I just am."

"Ruth Johnson, you're a grown woman and if you want to go to California then go to California, but don't call me and wake me up in the middle of the night to ask my permission ever again, or I'm going to have to cuss you out," Bernie spat and then abruptly hung up the phone.

"Damn," Ruth muttered. "She didn't have to be so rude about it. Of course I'm a grown woman. I know that, but it's not about me being a grown woman. It's about doing the right thing. I've been so good lately at doing the right thing. I can't remember the last time I messed up or made a stupid decision. Ever since I left Eric, doing the right thing is the only thing that matters. Because with him, I did the wrong thing for a long time and I paid dearly for it. And if I keep on doing the right thing, maybe I won't end up in a mess like that ever again." That's what it was about. Not about being a grown woman who desperately wanted to go to California and spend the weekend with tall, dark, and handsome Adrian and take some chances with her life, maybe even have the time of her life.

"Don't even go there, Ruth. Now's not the time to be impetuous," she said out loud. "I mean, Adrian is a wonderful man and you like him a lot. But even though you really don't have any plans this weekend, flying all the way to the other side of the country just doesn't make sense. And if it doesn't make sense, then it's not for you. It's not what you need." Besides, she thought, continuing her conversation with herself in her head, Adrian would have her alone in a hotel room for two days and Ruth knew exactly what that could lead to. Sex, and sex had a way of messing everything up. She and Adrian had had a good thing going on, and the last thing she wanted to do was ruin it by complicating it with sex. All of a sudden, Ruth decided she wasn't going.

She turned off the light, laid back down and closed her eyes, daring them to open again before morning. Two seconds later Ruth stared up at the ceiling and a big grin spread across her face.

"Okay . . . okay," she said excitedly, sitting up in bed. "I'm going to San Francisco?" Was she? "Yes!" she said decidedly. "I'm going to San Francisco! I am going to San Fran-cis-co!"

Suddenly, Ruth threw back the covers and started jumping up and down on her bed like a five-year-old. "I'm going to San Francisco! I'm going to San Francisco!" Forget right or wrong. Her grown ass was going to throw caution to the wind and tomorrow she would be on a plane headed west to spend the weekend alone with Adrian!

What the hell was she doing in San Francisco? Ruth suddenly felt stupid standing there in the airport looking like she should've kept her ass in Florida. She prayed silently that he hadn't forgotten about her, but hoped like crazy that maybe he had so that she could turn around, go back home, and spend the rest of her life pissed off at him.

"Hey, baby," he whispered over her shoulder. Ruth turned around and stared up into Adrian's eyes, standing there in all his fine-ass glory. "Damn, I'm glad you're here." He bent down to kiss her and just that quick, she was glad she was here too.

Adrian took her by the hand, slid her bag off her shoulder and onto his, and loaded her into the car. The top was down and the two of them speeded down the coast. Suddenly, Ruth's jet lag was cured. She'd never seen a more beautiful stretch of highway in her whole life and Ruth knew that if it were up to her, they'd spend the whole weekend driving up and down the entire West Coast. Adrian took a detour off Highway 1 to Panoramic so that they could do a little sightseeing. The giant redwood trees of Muir Woods were out of this world and Adrian graciously posed for about a dozen pictures. Ruth looked up into forever, straining to see the top of those trees, realizing just how much of a trip God could be. Where did He come up with this stuff? she wondered to herself. Eventually, they drove back to Panoramic and onto Highway 1, until they reached their final destination, Stinson Beach where Adrian had reserved a cabin for the weekend.

He pulled her into his arms as soon as they were inside and nuzzled his face in the crook of her neck, creating a winding trail of tiny kisses from her earlobe to the top of her shoulder. Ruth shuddered, loving the way he felt against her, then tensed up at the sensation of Adrian's hands slipping down below the sanctity of her waist, cupping her ass like a basketball, and pulling her even closer into him. And yes. That was his dick pressed up against her, obviously armed and dangerous and eager to move much more quickly than Ruth had prepared herself for. She managed to ease herself away from him coolly enough for him not to notice just how much she was tripping.

Ruth nervously cleared her throat. "I'd better put my things away. Where's my room?"

He smiled and pointed to a door behind her. "The bedroom is right behind you."

"The bedroom?" Ruth looked quizzically at him. "Where's the other one?"

"What other one?"

"Aren't there two bedrooms?"

"One's plenty," he said, pulling her close to him again.

"Is it?"

Before she'd flown all the way out there, she'd thought so. While driving across the Golden Gate Bridge, she'd thought so. Standing there in his arms, in that little cabin, with only one bedroom, suddenly, Ruth didn't think so. She'd wanted to do this. Ruth had desperately wanted to trade in Maxwell for the real thing, for Adrian, but now the knots swelling up in her stomach had convinced her otherwise.

Adrian took one look at the expression on her face and the smile he'd worn all afternoon faded away into obvious disappointment. "You take the room. I'll sleep on the couch."

"No, Adrian," Ruth said apologetically. "I couldn't ask you to do that. I can sleep on the couch. Really, I'd rather."

"No," he said dryly, picking up her luggage. "I insist." Adrian carried her things into the bedroom, leaving Ruth standing in the middle of the room, feeling awful.

Later, Ruth and Adrian shared a romantic dinner on the beach while watching the sun settle down for the night. Adrian had ordered in a picnic basket filled with white wine, fresh strawberries and green grapes, cream cheese, a fresh sourdough loaf, sliced roast beef, turkey, and spiced mustard. After dinner, they held hands and strolled leisurely down the white sandy beach. Adrian started feeling playful, and decided to splash a little water at Ruth. Of course, she couldn't let him get away with it, so she splashed him back. Before she realized what was happening, Adrian surprised Ruth and, Lord have mercy, scooped her up in his arms!

"Adrian! Adrian!" she screamed, hanging onto him for dear life, convinced that if he dropped her, she'd surely die. "Please! Adrian! Put me down! Adrian! I'm too heavy!"

Adrian grimaced. "Oh, baby! My back! My back! Oh . . . Ruth! You're breaking my back, Ruth!"

"I'm serious!"

"Oh! Ow! Damn, baby! How much you weigh? You don't look like you that big!"

"Will you please put me down?" she insisted.

"All right. All right," he said putting her back on the ground, clutching at his back like he was in agony. "Damn! I think I might need some traction."

"Nobody told you to play weight lifter," she said, sounding irritated. "Serves you right."

Adrian quickly straightened up. "You're not heavy."

"I've been heavy my whole life, Adrian," she said tersely. "I know I'm heavy."

"No, baby." He smirked. "You're really not heavy. You're thick."

Ruth propped her hand up on her hip and cocked her head. "What's the difference?"

"About fifty pounds," he said playfully. "You got a two-second head start, and then I'm coming after you." Ruth giggled, and ran as fast as she could back to the cabin, with Adrian hot on her heels.

Adrian emerged from the bathroom wearing nothing but the bottom half of his pajamas. Ruth stared mesmerized at the sight of the broadest chest she'd ever seen. And where the hell did he get all those biceps and triceps? she wondered.

"The shower's all yours," Adrian said, pecking Ruth on the cheek as he passed her in the doorway. And who told him he had to smell that good just to go to sleep? she asked herself, resentfully watching him pour himself a glass of wine.

Ruth showered quickly and then slipped into an old worn football jersey she'd packed just in case she couldn't work up the nerve to wear the chiffon nightie and matching thong outfit she'd bought a few weeks earlier. The nightie stayed safely tucked in the bottom of her suitcase, and regretfully she knew it would probably never see the light of day.

Adrian had taken a pillow and blanket from the bedroom. "Are you sure you don't want the bedroom, Adrian? It doesn't seem fair for me to sleep in here, after all you paid for the place."

He smiled, then kissed her on her cheek. "No, love. I'm cool. Sweet dreams."

"Goodnight," she whispered.

The last thing he'd expected was that he'd end up sleeping on the couch. Adrian lay still, staring up into the darkness, willing back his frustration and disappointment, thinking he should've known better. He'd actually managed to hold on to his optimism up until the point where Ruth emerged from the bathroom wearing an old worn-out football jersey three sizes too big. That's when he accepted that she'd turned out the lights and this party was definitely over. It was definitely going to be a long weekend.

Ruth couldn't sleep. How could she, knowing he was on the other side of the door? Opportunity had presented him to her on a silver platter, and yet she'd still managed to screw it up. Ruth couldn't bring herself to make love to Adrian, but she'd endured sex with Eric for more than a decade and handled it like a pro. How many times had she lay there letting Eric fuck her, faking orgasms, and pretending it felt good when it didn't? Ruth wandered back through her memories, and cringed at the sight, sound, and smell of them.

"Who's pussy is this, baby?" he'd grunt from behind her.

"Doggy-style, doggy-style," he'd laugh. "Ain't nothin' like hittin' it from behind," he'd tell her. Ruth balanced on all fours on the bed, while Eric stood behind her, pounding unsympathetically, commanding her to respond. "Answer me, bitch! Who's goddamned pussy is this?"

Ruth bit down on her lip, grimacing with each thrust. "It's your pussy, Eric. All yours." Her body was there, but her mind would be somewhere else, memorizing details of anything, from a shirt draped over the back of a chair across the room, to ingredients needed to make gumbo she'd been craving.

"Tell me it's good, baby," Eric would moan. "Tell me how good it is."

"It's good, Eric. It's so damn—good."

Eventually, he'd come, pull out and go to the bathroom to pee. Then he'd usually go into the kitchen, get a beer, and sit down in front of the television, flipping through channels with the remote, leaving her sitting there, without so much as a kiss, a thank you, or a pat on the ass for a job well done. Bernie thought she was strange for not missing sex. For the life of her, Ruth couldn't see what there was to miss.

She glanced thoughtfully at the door to the bedroom. Adrian wasn't Eric, though, and wishful thinking had compelled her to weave together scenarios in her mind of what it might be like to make love to him, but they were unraveling right before her eyes. Ever since they'd met, Ruth found herself masturbating like crazy with poor Maxwell, who, out of nowhere, would grow arms, legs, and Adrian's beautiful face, hovering over her whispering over and over again, "I love you, Ruth." Fantasies of Adrian licking, fondling, and tasting every inch of her, burying himself as deep inside as possible without giving her an aneurysm, constantly invaded her thoughts. And Ruth would gaze back into his eyes, waiting and watching for the climax of their union until finally, she'd have no choice but to cum all over him harder than she'd ever cum in her life. When it was over, she'd open her eyes, and Adrian would be gone, leaving behind the mechanical sound of Maxwell droning on and on lifeless and rigid until Ruth would push the off switch. Why couldn't she get over it, whatever it is? Ruth wondered. What was it? What was it she was so afraid of?

Adrian tapped lightly on the door and peeked in. "You all right?"

Ruth quickly sat up in bed, and wiped away tears, hoping he couldn't see that she'd been crying. "Yes, I'm fine."

Adrian shrugged his shoulders, then turned to leave. "No," she called out to him.

He walked into the room, sat down on the bed next to her and placed his hand tenderly against her cheek. "What's wrong, baby?"

Absolutely nothing is wrong, she wanted to tell him. Not anymore. Not with him sitting there. The vulnerability in her eyes embraced him. He could tell she'd been crying, and at the same time, Adrian saw that she needed him. He couldn't explain why or how he knew it, and doubted she could explain her need for him either. But at the moment, it really didn't matter. Adrian leaned in to Ruth and gently kissed her eyelids, her nose, and lips.

Is this it, God? Is this my chance? Ruth prayed, silently. Adrian pulled down the sheet covering her legs, placed his hand lightly on her knee then slowly slid it up her thigh to the hem of her shirt. Instinctively, Ruth raised her arms, letting him raise her jersey over her head. She shivered, embarrassed at being naked, drew her knees up to her chest, and wrapped her arms around them, desperately holding herself together. Adrian stood up and slipped off his pants, then crawled over Ruth to the other side of the bed and pulled her into his arms, and planted soft kisses on her face. Ruth wrapped her arms around him, then pressed her ear to his chest relishing the rhythm of his heartbeat letting it lull her into calm, knowing that even if it was only for one night, this was where she belonged. In his arms, in this bed, in San Francisco.

"That better?"

"Yes," she whispered.

Adrian put his hand under her chin, raised her face to his, and filled her mouth with languid kisses. He gently took hold of her hand, guided it down his torso and gently wrapped her fingers around his erect penis, knowing that her introduction to this part of him needed to take place before they made love. Without warning, Adrian rolled

Ruth onto her back, raised himself above her and stared down at her.

"You're a beautiful woman, Ruth," he whispered earnestly.

Ruth choked back tears. "I don't think so, Adrian."

"But I do."

His lips left a trail of kisses down her shoulders to her breasts, and he carefully cradled each of them in his hands, giving each of them his undivided attention, savoring her breasts like they were precious fruit.

"Mmmm . . ." she moaned as he grazed his warm moist tongue across her nipples that instantly erupted into tiny peaks. Ruth's legs spread to accommodate him and the sensation of his penis tickling between them was so exciting, she could hardly control herself. "Put it in," Ruth begged. "Please, Adrian. Put it in." Her hips rose up to meet his, hoping to catch him and pull him inside her, but Adrian wasn't having it and made it clear that he was in control.

"Not yet," he whispered. "We've got all night, Ruth. All weekend."

Adrian eased out of bed and went into the other room. When he came back, he dropped condoms on the nightstand and smiled at Ruth.

"Thank you," she mouthed, and smiled.

He quickly slipped one on and crawled back into bed, then took her hand in his and softly kissed her palm. Adrian made love to her mouth with his, and darted his tongue in and out, in and out, in and . . . He gradually eased himself inside her, while Ruth instinctively raised her knees to welcome him.

"Damn . . . Ruth. This is good, baby. So—"

Adrian didn't pound himself inside her or demand she say things she didn't feel. He was smooth, sensual, and most of all, considerate. Ruth's fingers traced a path down his back to the base of his spine, where she savored the slow rise and fall of his ass against her palms. Adrian moaned when her hips met his. Nothing had ever felt this good to Ruth. Not even Maxwell.

"Oooooo . . . Adrian."

Suddenly, he surprised her and pulled out, and licked a wet path down to her naval and planted a kiss there. The sensation sent chills through her.

Ruth giggled. "That tickles."

Adrian continued exploring her with his mouth, kissing and sucking down her thighs to her knees, to her shins until he found . . . her feet. Lord! Who knew? Never in all her years of living would Ruth have guessed that having her toes sucked would feel so good.

"Oh my goodness, Adrian!" she gasped.

He laughed. "Mmmm . . . You like this, baby?"

"Yes!" she said breathlessly. "Oh . . . yes . . . yes . . ."

"Me too." Adrian finished with one set of toes then immediately started on the others.

"No . . . Adrian!" It felt incredible. Too incredible, and unbearable.

"I thought you liked it?"

"I do . . . no . . . I mean, I do . . . but . . . no." Ruth pulled her feet from his hands, concluding that nobody should have that kind of power over another person and that toe sucking should be illegal.

"You want some more of me?" He smiled, leisurely raising himself back over her.

"Oh . . . yes. Yes." Ruth pleaded, pulling him close, hungrily devouring his neck, earlobes and shoulders, like she was starving and he was the buffet.

She closed her eyes, and held her breath at the sensation of him slowly easing himself inside her. Ruth couldn't remember a time when she'd wanted anything as much as she'd wanted him. Adrian rocked slowly at first, savoring the warmth of her, the wetness of her, fighting to keep his cool, and not lose his mind in the exquisiteness of this woman.

Instinctively, Ruth began to match her rhythm to his, raising her hips in time to meet Adrian's, forcing him as far inside her as possible.

"Oh . . . Adrian!" she gasped, over and over again. Ruth held him close to her, with all her strength, until she'd dissolved into him, and in her mind, they were no longer separate.

Adrian lay on top of her long after they'd finished, still inside her, kissing her eyelids, nose, lips. "You know how long I've been wanting to do that?"

Ruth smiled. "Do you know how long I've wanted you to do that?"

"Why were you crying?" he asked, tenderly.

"I don't know," she said.

He smiled. "Yes, you do. Tell me?"

"It's silly."

"Can't be that silly if it made you cry."

Ruth stared intently into his eyes. "I wanted to be with you."

"That is silly. All you had to do was peek your head outside that door. I'd have come running."

"Is that all I had to do?" she asked, softly.

"That's all you ever have to do, Ruth. When are you going to figure that out?"

"I don't think I'll ever understand what you see in me."

Adrian kissed the tip of her nose. "I see everything in you, Ruth Johnson. Absolutely everything, but that's all."

They didn't do much sightseeing and neither of them complained. Ruth and Adrian spent most of the weekend naked in the cabin, occasionally taking long walks on the beach and a trip here and there into town, mainly to pick up fresh crabmeat and sourdough bread for sandwiches and white wine to wash them down with.

On their final night at the cabin, Ruth remembered her new nightie tucked in the bottom of her suitcase and decided she was ready to wear it. Adrian's eyes lit up at the sight of her. "Damn, baby girl," he exclaimed, welcoming her into his arms.

She beamed. "If you'd prefer, I can put my football jersey back on."

"Don't you dare. As a matter of fact, I say we have a bonfire with that jersey as the guest of honor."

"That jersey is sacred, Adrian. And if you harm one thread on that shirt, I'm throwing you in the ocean," she teased.

"We've got to get up early if we're going to catch that flight out in the morning. From the looks of things, you're going to keep me up all night," he said, grazing his fingers down her back.

"Why don't we go AWOL and not go back to Jacksonville? We can stay right here and live off crabmeat sandwiches."

"And each other?" he asked, knowing for certain Ruth wouldn't argue the point.

"I like the idea."

"It's not bad, but I'm starting to get sick of crabmeat sandwiches."

"We can find something else to eat. Know how to fish? We can really live off the land and catch fish right out of our ocean."

"Our ocean?" He smiled.

"Yes. That little part right outside the front door."

"I wish."

"So, we have to go back?" Ruth pouted.

"Yeah, but we're going back together."

Together. That was a concept Ruth hadn't entertained in a long time, and not surprisingly, she was looking forward to it. This weekend had been like a dream, and any moment, she'd expected to wake up, but prayed she never would. Thankfully, Adrian had seen to it that the dream lasted all weekend. "How come you've never been married, Adrian?"

"What's the politically correct thing to say? I never found the right woman?"

"That's hard to believe. I would think you'd have found lots of right women. Have you ever been in love?"

"Sure I have."

"Have you broken any hearts?"

"Yes."

"I knew it."

"But I've had mine broken too."

"By what's her name? Ashley?"

"No, not by Ashley."

"Was it just a sex thing?"

"Pretty much."

"Was she good in bed?"

"How many hearts have you broken, Ruth?" Adrian asked, quickly changing the subject.

"Me? None."

"C'mon."

"None. Really. I told you. I was married forever, so . . ."

"You didn't break his heart?"

"Eric's? No."

"Who left who?"

"I don't know. We sort of left each other."

"After all those years? There had to be more to it than that?"

"There is. There's a lot more to it, but I didn't break his heart."

"Did he break yours?"

"Lots of times."

"You ever going to tell me what really happened between you two?"

"I don't know. Maybe. I don't know. There are a lot of things about my marriage, myself, that I'm still trying to sort out. I'd like to be able to lay it all out on the table for you, but how can I, when I'm not even sure what *it* is?" To tell him that her husband physically abused her would be like telling him only half the story, in her mind. That explanation put all the blame on Eric and Ruth still wasn't convinced it all belonged on him. Something inside her still longed for answers to questions she didn't even know to ask, and in those answers was healing that would allow her to come to terms with her role in her marriage. Besides, Adrian was the present and Adrian could possibly be a future. Eric was the past, and the idea of bringing her memory of him into this relationship seemed sacrilegious.

"Secrets aren't good, love."

"And I'm not keeping secrets, Adrian. I'm just being careful, right now. That's all."

"That's fine, but you just keep in mind that if we're going to be together, we're going to have to be open with each other. I want you to know me, and I want to know you."

"There's not much to know, Adrian. Besides, you're probably more interesting," she said, kissing his neck.

"Well, I'm not full of secrets like some folks 'round here," Adrian said sarcastically. "You want to know something about me, all you've got to do is ask."

"So I'm asking. Why do we have to go back to Florida? Why can't we sell all our stuff, invest in some loincloths and fishing poles, pay up the rent on this place for another five years and forget about the real world altogether?"

"And then what? Since you're trying to change the subject."

"And then . . . we can have sex in our spare time. And I'm not trying to change the subject. I'm just trying to talk about something else."

He laughed. "It's a nice dream."

"We can make it real."

"You've almost got me sold on the idea, baby. Keep talking." Adrian slipped his hand between her thighs, and gently eased his long finger inside her, then pulled it out, and put it to his lips.

A brilliant smile spread across her face. *Wow!* Ruth said to herself. *That's intriguing.*

Miles Between

BERNIE LOOKED STUNNING IN HER ANKLE-LENGTH BLACK SILK dress and stiletto knee-high boots. Heads turned as the hostess escorted her to the table, but she was used to that. Her long hair was pulled back into a ponytail that hung down past her shoulders, and the low scooped collar of her dress revealed just a hint of cleavage.

A waiter quickly arrived at her table. "My name is Andrew and I'll be your waiter this afternoon," he said pleasantly. "May I get you something to drink?"

"I'll have an iced tea with lemon, please." That's why she liked this place. The service was prompt, the food delicious, and it was conveniently right across the street from the office.

The waiter returned quickly with her drink. "Will you be needing a few more minutes to decide what you want?"

"No," Bernie said, still reading the menu. "Give me the plantain-crusted mahi mahi with mango salsa."

"Soup or salad?"

"Salad with Vinaigrette dressing, please."

"No problem," he said, taking the menu. "I'll be back shortly with your salad."

Bernie took a sip from her tea, and skimmed the room expecting to see someone she knew from work. Instead, she saw Miles, sitting at a table near the window, with his arm draped over the back of the chair of the woman he was with. The two were obviously immersed in an intimate conversation, which occasionally included quick pecks on the lips from time to time.

It came without warning, and at first she had no idea what to make of it. But eventually it came into view, and Bernie immediately recognized it. Jealousy welling up inside her like lava in a volcano threatening to blow up the mothafuckin' restaurant and everybody in it. The girl was petite, dark, and had a head full of braids that she kept pushing out of her face, and when she didn't do it, he did. Cute? Hardly. But young, probably no more than twenty-five.

"Ma'am?" the waiter said for the third time.

"What?" Bernie snapped. The sound of her own voice brought her back to reality, and she apologetically looked at young Andrew, staring down at her like she was about to go postal. "I mean . . . Yes?"

"Would you like wheat rolls or sesame with your meal?"

Her mind went blank, and all of a sudden she had no idea what wheat or sesame rolls were.

"I could bring them both out, and if you don't want them—" The unmistakable quiver in Andrew's voice told Bernie that she must've looked like a wild animal to the boy, and she quickly tried to compose herself.

"That's fine. Yes." She swallowed hard. He'd turned to walk away, but Bernie stopped him. "And, can you bring me a vodka collins, please? A big one."

"Sure. No problem." The boy hurried away and returned a few minutes later with her drink, which Bernie quickly gulped down.

She thrust the glass back at him. "Another one," she demanded.

Miles whispered something in the girl's ear that made her giggle like a schoolgirl. Bernie sat in awe, watching them, wondering what the hell was her problem. She hadn't wanted Miles and had told him so in no uncertain terms a month ago. And now, here she was, about to lose her damn mind at the sight of him with another woman.

"I don't want a relationship, Miles," she'd told him time and time again. "We're friends who fuck, and that's it." And that had been it, exactly. But watching the couple across the room it was all she could do not to jump her ass up, leap over a few tables, pull out every last one of those goddamned braids on that child's head and slap him across the face with them.

The waiter returned with another vodka collins and Bernie's meal. Suddenly, she didn't have an appetite, but she sucked down her cocktail like it was Kool-Aid, glaring at Miles and his date. When the girl got up and headed in the direction of the ladies' room, that's when Miles saw her. He stared at Bernie for a moment, then smiled slightly, and raised his glass in her direction. Son-of-a-bitch! she wanted to scream, but instead Bernie started choking on her drink. Miles chuckled.

Aw, hell no, girlfriend! she screamed in her head. The last thing that bastard needed was to see her sweat him and his little playmate. Bernie sat up straight, then leisurely started eating her lunch. She knew better than to think he'd gotten over her that quickly. Miles had been sniffing around her for months, begging, panting, pleading, and begging some more. Of course he'd seen her. He'd caught the scent of her sweet ass pussy, hypnotized by the shit calling his name. She glanced up at him, and yes, Miles was watching her. And he had wiped that silly ass grin off his face too. Bernie noticed his girlfriend bounce back into the room, take her seat next to him, grinning from ear to ear. But Miles wasn't grinning. He quickly paid the bill and they left.

He might be able to fool his girlfriend, Bernie concluded, and he was maybe even capable of fooling himself, but there was no way he could've ever fooled Bernie. The man had it bad for her, and as long as she walked this earth, he always would.

The real question was, why the hell did she give a damn?

Peas in a Pod

SHARON AND RUTH SAT ON THE FLOOR OF SHARON'S APARTMENT thumbing through magazines and card files looking for recipes. Winona Judd's rich melodies soothed them on the outside while the bottle of red wine they'd just about finished soothed them on the inside. They were like little girls playing with dolls with a stamina that long outlasted Megan, sleeping soundly in her room.

"What about a nice marinated filet of beef?" Sharon asked, pulling the card from her recipe box. "Sound good?"

"What is it?"

"Marinated filet of . . . beef?" she answered, like it was a trick question.

Ruth frowned. "Is it cooked?"

Sharon laughed and shook her head. "You're so silly."

"Is it?"

"You like escargot?"

"No. And I know that ain't cooked," Ruth said.

"Have you ever even tried escargot, Ruth?"

"Sharon, I don't need to try it to know I don't like it."

"Maybe our guests will."

"I don't think so."

"Ruth, these people are paying two hundred dollars a plate. Don't you think we should give them their money's worth?"

"Absolutely not. The budget calls for chicken, Sharon. How many times do I have to tell you that? We serve anything other than chicken, we don't make any money."

"Chicken's so predictable."

"Predictable or not, that's what we're having. Now look for chicken recipes and stay away from anything expensive, exotic, or raw."

"Cordon bleu?" Sharon asked dispassionately, holding up another recipe card.

"Now you're talking."

"It doesn't get any more predictable than that."

"Good. We're keeping with tradition, then. You're not going to cook three hundred meals by yourself are you?"

"Oh, no. I'm going to get me some help and stop worrying. I keep telling you I've got this covered. You just do your part."

Ruth suddenly looked very concerned. "I don't know, Sharon. You've got me worried, girl. If I left it all up to you, these people would be eating lobster and escargot and we can't afford that."

Sharon sighed. "I know. I know."

"Do you? I mean, I hope you do because—"

"Let's not argue, Ruth."

"I'm not arguing."

"Let's not go there."

"I'm not going. I'm just saying—"

"And I hear you. Believe me, honey. I want this to work as much as you do. Maybe more. I used to live there. Remember?" Sharon explained.

"I know. I'm just saying—"

"And I know how important this is to you, Clara, everybody."

"I know. I'm just saying—"

"You want chicken? Chicken it is."

"Thank you. That's all I'm saying." The wine had obviously gone to her head, because Sharon rolled over on her side and laughed so hard Ruth thought she'd pee on herself. Just then, Ruth noticed that the bottle was empty and got up to get another one from the kitchen. "There are going to be a lot of big shots at this thing," Ruth said, pulling the chilled bottle from the refrigerator. "Politicians, business executives, local celebrities. Rich folks."

Sharon quickly sat up and composed herself. "I know. And I'm going to take full advantage of this opportunity too, which is why this meal has to be perfect."

Ruth plopped back down on the floor and filled their glasses. "Your business could really take off after this, Sharon."

"Oh, Ruth, wouldn't that be something? I could be catering to big shots—"

"Ballers," Ruth interrupted. Sharon stared at her with a confused look on her face. "Nobody calls big shots, 'big shots' anymore, Sharon. They're called 'ballers' now."

"Ballers?" Sharon carefully repeated. Ruth nodded. "So, I could be catering to big shots, or ballers, or whoever, but somebody's going to want my escargot," she said, rolling her eyes.

Ruth was stunned. She had no idea white women knew how to do that.

"Knock yourself out on those raw snails, girlfriend, and more power to you or anyone else who'd let one of those things slither down the back of their throat."

"Don't knock it until you've tried it. You'd be surprised how pleasant some things can feel in the back of your throat." She giggled and gulped down a glass full of wine.

"You drink too much."

"Oh right!" Sharon snapped. "Like you've only sucked down half a dozen glasses of this stuff, or have you had so many you can't keep count?"

"I sip. I don't guzzle. You guzzle. A related attribute to deep-throating, Sharon?" Ruth said sarcastically.

"Have you ever tried it?"

"Not willingly, because it's disgusting."

"Oh, it is not."

"Not to you. You're a white woman. Everybody knows white women get off on that kind of mess," Ruth said indifferently.

Sharon stared at her in disbelief. "Black women do too."

"Girl, please. Not anybody I know."

"Then you are all missing out and I feel sorry for you."

"Tell me this. What's so great about having a dick down your throat?" Ruth asked, sounding indignant.

Sharon winked. "Depends on the dick."

"Dick is dick." As soon as she said it, she knew better. Ruth smiled, knowing Adrian's dick wasn't anything like Eric's dick. But she was trying to make a point.

"No, dick isn't dick, Ruth."

"What are you? A dick connoisseur?"

"No, but I know a good dick when I taste one."

"Ugh!" Ruth grimaced. "That is so gross, Sharon!"

"You're such a prude. I can't believe . . . how old are you?"

"Old enough to know I don't like giving head. So there."

"You don't know what you're missing."

"You keep saying that."

Sharon sighed, then ran her tongue seductively over her lips. "Mmmmm . . . sure would be nice to have one right now."

"Sharon?" All of a sudden, Ruth was starting to feel uncomfortable and wondered if she should leave the room.

She closed her eyes and held her hand up in front of her face, pretending there was a penis in it. "I like to lick the sides first, up and down like it's a lollipop. Mmmm . . . men like that." Sharon giggled. "Then I take my tongue and graze it over the tip, around and over and around—"

Ruth was appalled, watching this woman sitting there showing her the proper technique of giving head. What was even more appalling was the fact that Ruth was truly mesmerized by it.

Sharon opened one of her eyes. "Know what really drives them crazy?"

"No. What?" Ruth asked intently.

"Wrapping your warm, moist lips around the head and kissing it like you'd kiss his mouth. I tell you, Ruth. You don't know what you're missing, girl."

Ruth quickly inhaled the wine in her glass and all of a sudden realized how much she missed Adrian.

Sharon still had pictures of Darren, and Ruth admitted that she had a few of Eric too. Darren was handsome and didn't look like he'd hurt a fly, but no one had ever accused him of hurting flies, just his wife. Deep inside, Sharon still loved him, though. Ruth could see glimmers of it in her eyes as she stared at the photos. What an awful feeling that must be, Ruth decided, to love the man who tormented you.

"He thinks I'm going to fall on my ass and come running back to him," Sharon slurred. "It's been nearly a year and he still thinks that, Ruth."

"How often do you see him?"

"Every other weekend. He comes to pick up Megan."

Ruth was shocked. "He gets visitation?"

"As long as he continues getting counseling, yes. He's a good father and she's crazy about him. He'd never hurt her. It's just me he had the problem with." Sharon reflected quietly for a moment. To everyone else, he was a wonderful man, kind and generous. But when she was alone with him, the Darren everyone else knew and loved changed into Sharon's own private monster.

Sharon swallowed another sip of wine. "Know what I want?"

"A dick?" Ruth teased.

Sharon smiled. "Besides that. I want to be successful. I want this catering business to take off and make me a ton of money. I want to show Darren and everybody else who thought I was crazy for leaving him that I can do this. That I can be something more than just his wife. As long as that's all I was, Ruth, as long as I paid more attention to that than I did to making a better me, it was easy for him to disrespect me. I should've fought harder for that. Respect."

"You can never have enough of that. Can you?" Ruth asked thoughtfully.

Sharon looked at her with tears in her eyes. "No. I guess not. I won't ever go back to him. I can't."

Ruth knew that they'd both had too much to drink, but filled their glasses one last time before either of them passed out. "Can never have enough I-told-you-so's under your belt. Here's to redemption." The two women lifted their glasses and toasted whatever victories they'd earned, now and in the future.

"Can we talk about something else?" Sharon asked.

"Of course we can."

"How's Adrian?"

"He's wonderful," Ruth said, blushing. Adrian had that effect on her. Just the mention of his name, or a fleeting thought of him, or . . . shit just about anything having to do with him made her blush. "He's coming over tomorrow night for dinner and we might watch a few movies."

"Yeah, watch movies," Sharon teased, casting an exaggerated wink in Ruth's direction. "You never did tell me about San Francisco?"

Ruth stared out into space, wondering what there was to tell, since she'd hardly even seen San Francisco, but she quickly cleared her throat, and prepared to give Sharon the lowdown on what little she did see outside Adrian's naked booty. "Let's see . . . we drove up the coast to Muir Woods. I've got pictures and I'll bring them over next time I come. Ummm . . . we did manage to catch some good jazz at this club on Nob Hill and I saw Alcatraz from a distance, but I don't know. A prison as a tourist attraction just doesn't work for me. Then we—"

"Ruth?" Sharon interrupted. "How was it with Adrian in San Francisco?"

Ruth shrugged. "Oh . . . well. He was cool, you know. He played tour guide as best he could, considering he doesn't know much about the place either. Very accommodating. Very considerate. Very . . ."

"Did you two make love?" she blurted out.

"Yes." Ruth smiled. "We did. Quite a few times, as a matter of fact."

Sharon squealed and clapped her hands together. "I knew it! I've been dying to ask you that all night. C'mon. Tell me all about it."

"Oh Sharon . . . it was . . . He was . . . I had no idea sex could be that good."

"With the right person, it is good."

Ruth sat her glass on the table, then rolled over onto the floor on her back and gazed dreamily up at the ceiling. "He must be right then, because it was all good all the time."

"I take it you didn't give him a blow job though," Sharon said sarcastically.

"Not this time. But after tonight I'll definitely give it some thought."

"I'm telling you. You don't know—"

"I know. What I'm missing."

"Guess what?" Sharon asked, anxious to share some good news of her own.

"What?"

"I met somebody too."

Ruth quickly sat up. "Sharon . . . who?"

"His name is Wayne and I met him at the produce market on Lee Highway last weekend."

"You give him your number?"

"I did and he called me the other day and asked me out." Sharon's divorce wouldn't be final for another two months and she'd made a promise to herself not to get involved with another man at least for the remainder of this life. But Wayne had approached her on a day when she was wading knee-deep in loneliness, bringing a warm smile and the reddest hair she'd ever seen on a man. Of course, her intent was to make a new friend. He could be someone to see a movie with or share dinner with every once in a while, and for now, that was plenty.

"I don't know, Ruth. You think it's too soon? I mean, I'm not even officially divorced yet."

"You're asking the wrong person, girl. I have no idea what I'm doing. Adrian's wonderful and I love being with him, but I don't have a clue about where this is going. Or why. Or when." Ruth laughed.

"You still got your guard up too?"

"Couldn't put it down if I wanted to."

"He sounds wonderful."

"He is, but that's not enough," Ruth said reflectively. "It's not him. It's me. I can't just throw away fourteen years like they never happened. Be nice if I could, but I'm still that woman. Bernie says I'm not, but I know I am and I scare myself more than any man ever could."

"What are you afraid of, Ruth?"

"Of not paying attention, not listening to myself. I'm afraid of not speaking up when I should. I'm afraid of forgetting about me again. I haven't changed, I've just started paying attention to who I am and I don't want to forget Ruth. Does that make sense?"

"Tons."

Pride Cometh

Bernie, clara, and ruth agreed to meet at higgin's house for planning the fund-raiser. Bernie's list of contacts had already proved to be invaluable and donations had begun pouring in from women's groups, churches, and anonymous donors from all over the state.

"It's not what you know, but who you know. That's my motto," Bernie bragged.

When they arrived, Clara was busy getting a woman and her children who'd arrived late the night before settled in to the house, and she asked Bernie and Ruth to wait in her office. Bernie had never been there before and was amazed by all the photographs of Clara on the wall. "Why does she have all these pictures taken?"

"So she won't forget," Ruth said warmly. "All of those women have been through here. Some of them have started over and are doing pretty good for themselves, some have gone back and some . . . some have died."

Bernie glanced at Ruth. "Your picture up here?"

"Yeah." Ruth smiled, and pointed out her picture with Clara. "We took it last week." Minutes later, Clara opened the door. "Why don't we take this meeting in to the kitchen, ladies? I've got some coffee on and one of the ladies has made some cookies for us."

The three of them sat around the small kitchen table discussing budgets, menus, and seating arrangements.

"The invitations are out and the RSVPs are in. Sharon's got a handle on the menu . . . I think we're just about ready," Ruth announced proudly.

"Not so fast, missy," Bernie said abruptly.

Ruth glared at her like she'd lost her damn mind, wondering when the hell she had become "missy"? "What now?"

"Entertainment? I believe that's your area."

"Yes, it is."

"And?"

"And? I'm working on some things."

"Like what?" Clara asked, smiling. "You say that every time we ask you about it, but you never tell us specifics. What are you working on, darlin'?"

"Don't just sit there grinning. What? Who?" demanded Bernie.

In dramatic fashion, Ruth rolled her eyes. She'd been hoping to surprise them, but from the looks on their faces, realized that they weren't having it. "Well . . . for openers, Sonny Micelles."

"*The* Sonny Micelles?" Bernie asked skeptically.

"The one and only," Ruth replied smugly.

"How in the world did you get Sonny Micelles to do this?"

"You're not the only one who knows important people, Bernie."

"Like I said, how did you get Sonny Micelles to agree to do this?"

"How do you think?"

"Begging?" Clara asked.

"Exactly. And it worked too." Bernie and Clara burst out laughing. "What?" Ruth asked, slightly offended. "Look, he's coming and that's all that matters. So . . . laugh. Laugh all you want." She shrugged.

Sonny Micelles was big, and Ruth owned every CD he'd ever recorded. A few months back, she'd seen him on the Grammy Awards. That's when she decided to find a way to contact him.

"He put on a bomb performance at the jazz festival and so I managed to get in touch with him through the promoters whose names were listed on the back of the schedule I'd saved," Ruth explained. She pulled out a copy of the letter she'd written from her organizer and laid it on the table in front of them.

Dear Mr. Micelles,

My name is Ruth Johnson and I'm a survivor of domestic violence. I've been a fan of yours for years and I'm writing to solicit your help for a very worthy cause. Needless to say, Higgin's House has proven to be a lifesaver for many women, and I mean that literally. Your presence at our event would be phenomenal and would represent a strong show of support that the residents of Higgin's House would remember for the rest of their lives.

Clara smiled affectionately at Ruth. "That's wonderful, Baby Ruth." Ruth's eyes widened and she couldn't believe it. No one but Karen had ever called her by that name. "Thank you, Clara," she said softly.

Clara had no idea of what had just happened between them, but she sensed that it had been special, even if it had happened in an instant.

"Ruth, how were you going to keep something like this to yourself? You know we talk every day about the fund-raiser and you've got the nerve to keep Sonny Micelles all to yourself? You ought to be ashamed of yourself," Bernie fussed. Ruth and Clara both laughed at her antics. "What else you got going on besides Sonny Micelles?" Bernie asked, eyeing Ruth suspiciously.

"Well, Miss Watson, if you must know," Ruth said, twisting her neck in true sistah-girl-with-an-attitude fashion. "Have you ever heard of the Mona Harris Dance Company?"

"You didn't?" Bernie's eyes grew as wide as saucers in anticipation of what Ruth was about to tell them.

Ruth sat up proudly. "I did."

"Ruth! Mona Harris is bringing her dancers all the way up here from Miami to dance at our little fund-raiser? How the hell did you—"

"Begging," Clara said, simply.

"Not only begging, Clara, but also discovering that I was sitting next to the woman's niece in my English class last semester," Ruth exclaimed. "The girl's in her freshman year at JU and has absolutely no aptitude for the English language. So I offered to tutor her on the weekends at the library on campus. She's sweet as pie, but let's just say she's not all that bright. Anyway, I happened to mention one day what we were planning and that's when she told me who her aunt was, and that Ms. Harris might be willing to have her company perform for us at the fund-raiser because she does things like that all the time. To make a long story short, the girl spoke to her aunt, who called me, and after going back and forth on the details for a while, she agreed to bring her company up to perform."

This time, Bernie was the one grinning. "I'm through. I ain't asking you nothing else."

"And," Ruth continued, "Miss Cleo Walker will be our finale."

Clara clutched at her chest and collapsed back in her chair. "Lord have mercy! Child . . . Cleo Walker? You managed to get her to come too?"

"Yeah, which was really hard, because her publicist is a hard-ass and Cleo's on tour so she'd have to make a special trip out here, which Ms. Publicist didn't think was a good idea and told me that every time I called, which had to have been at least fifty times," Ruth rambled on, hardly stopping long enough to catch her breath. "Then one day I got lucky and Ms. Walker was in her publicist's office, for some reason or another. She overheard the conversation and asked to speak to me, so the publicist handed her the phone and we talked and talked. She's really down to earth. I mean, we talked like old friends. Did you know she was from Texas? Anyway, I told her what was up and do you know . . . she told me she'd been abused, but not by a husband or anything, but when she was a little girl . . . anyway . . . I told her I wouldn't tell anybody because she doesn't want it to get out because she's famous and all, but she said . . . yeah. She'd do it."

Bernie and Clara stared at Ruth with their mouths hanging open and she couldn't help but to feel magnificent. Ruth had never worked so hard on anything in her whole life, but this, *this* meant something to her. It was the most important thing she'd ever been a part of and she'd been determined to work her ass off for it. After all, her friends were depending on her for a change. In the past, it had always been the other way around, but now it was her turn to come to somebody's rescue and Ruth relished it.

They finished their meeting and on their way out, Ruth spotted her sitting on the side of the bed in one of the small rooms of the shelter, brushing her oldest son's hair.

"Dang, boy. You need a haircut already." Ruth stopped dead in her tracks and stared at her. Her face was bruised and swollen and the elegant mound she'd once worn so proudly on her head was gone. The woman stopped brushing the boy's hair and stared back at her. "Yes?" she asked politely.

Ruth had no idea what she was going to say, but she walked into her room, sat down next to her, and put her hand underneath the woman's chin. Ruth examined her bruised face. "You all right?" she asked, genuinely concerned.

Tears filled the rim of her eyes and the young woman quickly turned away. "I'm cool. I just—" She shrugged. "I got tired of it . . . that's all."

"I did too."

She looked into Ruth's eyes. "Do I know you?"

"No," she lied.

"You look familiar to me. Do you live here too?"

"No. I'm here for a business meeting."

The girl shifted uncomfortably next to Ruth. "I'm just staying here till I get on my feet. Shouldn't be long . . . I hope. I need to find a job and a place to live." She smiled at her children. "He wasn't their daddy, but he was better than nothing."

"No, he wasn't," Ruth said sternly. "You're better than nothing, baby. Remember that."

She tried to smile, but her swollen lip wouldn't allow it. "I like that outfit you got on. You get that from the mall?" Ruth smiled, but didn't answer. The woman cast her gaze to the floor. Ruth could see in her the shame that she obviously felt. She'd felt it too. "I used to look good too. All the time, before I hooked up with him. Then he kept thinking I was messing around on him, but I wasn't. I even stopped fixing myself up so nobody would look at me. Then he just fussed about how bad I looked all the time. I don't think it mattered one way or another, really."

She smiled back and held her hand. "It never does."

Ruth quietly closed the door behind her on her way out, leaving the woman alone with her children.

"Who was that?" Bernie asked.

Ruth swallowed hard before answering. "That was the woman Eric left me for."

Giving In

ADRIAN'S HOME WAS EVERY BIT THE BACHELOR PAD, DECORATED with black leather furniture, gold accents, a big screen television and a CD rack that stretched up to the ceiling. A shelving unit in the corner of the living room displayed pictures of Adrian's family and of him during his days of playing defensive end at the University of Ohio. He'd played there the entire time he was in college, and even managed to get drafted into the NFL by the Atlanta Falcons, where he played a season before an injury ended his career.

"Football was never a life or death matter for me," he'd told her earlier. "It was a game. A game that paid extremely well, but I didn't major in football in college. My pops made sure of that. He'd say, 'Boy. I ain't paying for you to go to school to play games,'" he said mocking his father's voice. "'Hell, you can always play games. I'm paying for you to get an education. So, stop bullshittin' and get one.'" Adrian laughed at the memory.

They'd ordered in pizza and Ruth and Adrian spent the better part of the evening watching movies, tickling, and drowning each other in kisses. Adrian referred to the evening as foreplay, and she savored every minute of it.

They'd been seeing each other for several months now, and she still hadn't been able to tell him about her marriage to Eric. Sometimes he'd bring up the subject, but as time went on, his inquisitions lessened, and Adrian figured when she was ready she'd tell him everything. He just hoped that when she did reveal her past to him, that it would help him to fill in some gaps. Ruth had a tendency to be guarded sometimes, emotionally, even physically. Like she was afraid he'd hurt her. Maybe her husband had hurt her.

"How can you watch this?" Ruth said, covering her eyes to keep from seeing the horror movie's gory scenes.

Adrian stretched out on the sofa with his head at one end, and Ruth at the opposite end with her feet propped up on his chest. He rubbed them gingerly, while watching the movie. Yes, he had a foot fetish. He knew it and didn't give a damn who else knew. A woman's feet were sexy. Ruth's feet were sexy.

"Check it out. He's about to cut him open. Baby? You watching?"

"No," Ruth said, still covering her eyes. "I'm not watching, Adrian. It's disgusting."

"Is that the liver or the pancreas?" he asked. "Ruth? Aw! You missed it."

"Thank goodness."

Ruth spent the rest of the movie watching Adrian watch the movie. Resisting him was hard work, which is why she'd given up trying. Ruth knew she was putty in his hands, but Adrian had been too sweet to take advantage of it. She'd been building up to tonight, knowing she'd have to tell him sooner or later about her marriage. The fund-raiser was a month away, and he needed to know before then. He'd gotten his invitation and asked what her connection was to this whole thing, and Ruth quickly explained that she and Clara had been good friends for years. But she'd never told him how they'd met. He needed to know before the event next month. Gathering up courage to tell him hadn't been easy. When she was with Adrian, it was like Eric never happened. There were moments when he materialized in her mind, but she'd learn to quickly push them aside, and get back to the business of being happy, rather than to dwell on the past.

"When this is over, we can watch part two. I got it here some-where," he muttered, rummaging through the stack of DVDs he had strewn on the coffee table.

Ruth smiled. "Do we have to?"

"Baby, we can't watch part one without watching part two. The serial killer comes back to life, and stalks the police chief."

"Sounds riveting," Ruth said dryly.

"And after that, we can watch that chick flick you wanted to check out," he said, sighing heavily.

"It's a good movie, Adrian. Even has something called a 'plot' in it. You might like it."

"Yeah, yeah."

Suddenly, without warning, Ruth knew that now was the time to tell Adrian about her marriage. If she didn't say it now, she might not ever tell him the truth.

"We fought a lot." Ruth heard herself speaking, but it didn't sound like her voice at all. She felt like a spectator, watching a movie, and the woman was someone else. Sadness threatened to overwhelm her all of a sudden, but she didn't understand why.

"What was that?" Adrian asked absentmindedly, still fumbling through DVDs.

"Eric. My ex-husband and I." Ruth's voice was so soft, she could barely hear herself. "We fought a lot."

Adrian stopped what he was doing, then pushed the mute button on the remote control. Ruth's eyes were glazed over with tears, and he wanted to scoop her up in his arms, but decided to just let her talk.

"You two argued?" he asked carefully.

Ruth slowly shook her head. "No, we fought. Or rather, he did." She smiled nervously. "I just sort of . . . let him . . . fight."

"He was abusive." It was a statement, not a question.

She nodded. "It was his way of getting his point across, whatever that happened to have been at the moment."

Adrian sat quietly, taking it all in. He'd suspected abuse had been the issue, but until now he hadn't been willing to jump to that conclusion and accept it as gospel.

"It was pretty bad sometimes," she continued. "You'll forgive me if I don't go into details?"

"I'll forgive you," he said thoughtfully.

What did Adrian think of her now that he knew? Did he think she'd been a fool, a glutton for punishment? Or worse, did he feel sorry for her? Ruth stared at him desperately trying to read the expression on his face, but there were no answers hidden there that she was able to discern.

"It explains a lot." Ruth looked at him, confused. "Why you tend to jump when I come at you suddenly. And why you watch me so closely when you think I'm not looking." He smiled.

"I do those things?"

"Yes, sweetheart. You do."

A tear escaped down her cheek. "I didn't know."

"Well." He shrugged. "Now we both know, don't we?"

Ruth sat up and drew her knees up to her chest. Relief set in that she'd finally told him, followed by doubt as to how he'd respond. The thought of never seeing him again set into her mind. She tried pushing away the notion, but it sat there like a brick. Adrian wasn't down for drama. He'd said that enough times since they'd been see-ing each other.

"Life is complicated enough without adding unnecessary drama to it," he'd told her. Ruth wanted to jump up and down and scream *But it's over now, Adrian! Eric is gone and that old me is gone! And all that's left in the world is you and me.* Maybe telling him had been a mistake.

"Come here," he said, reaching out his hand to her. "And hurry."

Ruth quickly sat up and crawled on top of him. Adrian pulled her securely into his arms. "You'll watch part two with me?" he said, teasing.

Ruth sniffed. "Do I have to?"

"God, I hope so." Adrian put his hand under her chin and lifted her mouth to his, then kissed her languidly.

"Part two should be pretty good," she said, smiling. "I'd love to watch it with you."

Leaps and Bounds

MAY QUICKLY MADE HERSELF AT HOME IN RUTH'S CONDO, TAK-
ing off her shoes and socks, and sitting sprawled out on the living
room floor, stretching her legs to keep them from cramping. If Ruth
didn't already have a best friend in Bernie she'd definitely see if May
wanted the job. Of course, there was nothing that said a woman
couldn't have more than one buddy for life.

"Bernie said planning this fund-raiser would be a lot of work, but
that was the understatement of the decade," Ruth said, coming out
of the kitchen with two cups of coffee. She handed one to May.

"Yeah, but you love it."

She laughed. "I do, girl. And you know what?"

"What?"

"I'm not looking forward to it being over. I mean, I am, but"—
Ruth shrugged—"then what?"

"I don't know, Ruth. What?"

"I don't know either. School starts next week. I guess I'll be up to
my eyeballs in homework."

May frowned. "I don't envy you. I always hated school."

"Honestly. So did I."

"But it's all for a good cause. A college degree will make a big
difference. You'll see."

"I know. But shit, May. I'll be damn near forty years old by the
time I'm finished. A forty-year-old college graduate in desperate need

of a real job doesn't sound all that exciting. I'd hoped by the time I was that age I'd be in charge, or doing something important."

"You will be doin' somethin' important, Ruth. You'll have a degree."

"In what?"

"You got plenty of time to figure that out. Fo', maybe five years," May teased.

"Sounds like forever."

"In dog years, it is." May smiled. "Seriously, girl. It won't seem like that long. You'll be so busy with term papers, final exams, and writin' that thesis, time is jus' goin' to fly by."

"Sounds exciting. Doesn't it?" Ruth wrinkled her nose. "Kind of."

"To somebody, I s'pose."

"You ever thought about doing your own thing?"

"My own thing?"

"Owning your own business?"

May stopped stretching and stared back at Ruth. "Now where on earth did that come from?"

"I don't know. Where?" Ruth asked, playfully looking around the room.

"You been thinkin' 'bout that, Ruth?"

"No. Not really. No. Well, every now and then. But no."

"Yes, you have." She smiled. "Ruth Johnson, you have been thinkin' 'bout it, haven't you?"

Ruth felt embarrassed for even bringing it up, but lately she had been thinking a lot about it. "It's just . . . well, with planning the fund-raiser and all . . . May I've enjoyed helping put this together. I really have," she said enthusiastically. "I've loved every minute of it, all the planning and organizing and even the headaches and . . . I never thought I'd be able to do anything like this."

"Never?"

"No. And it's cool, you know. Working my ass off, putting the pieces together and watching them fall into place. It's been incredible."

"It's incredible 'cause it's important to you."

"It is very important to me and because of that I haven't minded all the hard work needed to bring it to light. We've gotten together to set up this whole agenda and all of us has worked hard to see it through and it's lovely. It feels good, calling the shots and making deals. But you know what's most incredible about this whole thing?"

"What, Ruth?" May stared at Ruth, admiring the genuine excitement emanating from this woman eyes. There was life behind them now. There hadn't always been.

"I had faith that Bernie could do it. Bernie can do anything she sets her hard head to. I had faith that Sharon could do her part and come up with a mean menu. That woman can cook, girl. Do you hear me? I knew Clara would hang in there and do whatever it took to see this thing through because that's her house we're trying to save. But I wasn't so sure about me."

"Ruth—"

"No, I'm serious, May. I've never stood up for anything in my whole life and I've never worked this hard for anything. I'm surprised at what I've managed to do, my role in this. And you know what? I'm proud."

"Ain't nothin' wrong with bein' proud, girl. Shoot. You got a lot to be proud of."

"I think I do, May. I finally think I do."

"So you seriously considerin' startin' your own business?"

"The thought's crossed my mind. Sharon loves being her own boss and she's good at it too. Even if I do go to school and get my degree, I'm still going to end up working for somebody else. Don't you get tired of working for somebody else, May?"

"Well . . . no. But that's 'cause I like my job, Ruth. I wanted to be a buyer and that's what I do best. But I see yo' point."

"I want to love what I do too. I want to wake up every morning and look forward to going to work. I have no idea what that's like."

"So what kind of business you thinkin' 'bout startin'?"

"I don't have a clue." Ruth laughed. "I haven't even thought that far ahead. I don't know."

"Well, let's see. You like planning things like this fund-raiser. Maybe you could do it professionally. A professional . . . Events Planner? I think that's what they call it. How 'bout that? Plannin' events?"

"May, we live in Jacksonville, Florida. I don't think they have that many fund-raisers here and I don't know how many people would pay me to plan their events. Besides, planning parties is Bernie's forte. Not mine."

"I read somewhere that if you wantin' to start up yo' own business, you need to figure out what it is you like doin'. So, what do you like doin'?"

"I like walking with you. But I don't think anybody's going to pay me to be a professional walker."

"No. Probably not."

"I like jazz."

"You play?"

"No. I like Adrian."

May sucked her teeth. "Ruth, ain't nobody goin' pay you to do nothin' with Adrian."

"Adrian might." Ruth winked.

"Why buy the milk when you can—"

"All right. All right. You've made your point." Ruth thought for a moment. "I like reading. I love reading."

"What about bein' a . . . publisher? Or an agent! Agents make good money."

"I wouldn't know. I wonder what an agent does?"

"Beats me. A publisher might be nice."

"Yeah . . . maybe. Or a bookstore?"

"A bookstore?"

"Sure. Bookstores are nice. I don't know how much money they make, but—"

"But, you could look into it." May said, finishing Ruth's train of thought.

"Of course I can. See how much money I can make, what I'd need to do to get started."

"What about a black bookstore? With books just about us and by us. You think that would be a good idea?"

"Girl, yes. And I could have authors come in and sign their books. Terry, E. Lynn, Toni. May, I'm getting excited."

"Me too, and this ain't even my dream. But it sounds excitin', Ruth. Real excitin'."

"It does, doesn't it?"

"You got a computer?"

"At work."

"Girl, you don't have one here? You don't have Internet?"

"No. Do I need it?"

"Ruth, you have got to catch up with the times, girl. Everybody's got Internet access. Where you been?"

"Here."

"And obviously out of touch."

"Not that out of touch, May."

"Get yo' shoes on. We goin' to my house."

"Right now?"

"Yes. Now."

Of course, it didn't sound like a bad idea and Ruth figured that, at this point, it was just a thought and there was nothing wrong with thinking. May and Ruth spent the rest of the morning researching bookstores, especially African American book stores, and what they discovered was discouraging at best. There wasn't a lot of money being made by bookstore owners specializing in books by and about African Americans. The money was out there, billions of dollars as a matter of fact, but folks weren't buying their books from these stores. They were buying them from the larger chain stores and surprisingly, on-line.

"You ever buy anything off the Internet, May?"

"Girl, yes. CDs, art, books."

"You buy your books on-line?"

"Yeah, it's usually more convenient for me, and it's easy."

"How convenient and how easy?" May took Ruth through the ordering process, showing her Web sites of the more prominent on-line bookstores and Ruth even bought a book. The whole notion made her a little paranoid, but May assured her that she'd have the book in a few days and that her credit card wouldn't be any worse for the wear.

"Do they have any sites just for African Americans?"

"I've seen a few. But most of them all link back to one of these folks, or they're jus' not real impressive."

She and May looked at each other and smiled. "I'm just thinking. That's all, May."

"I know. Jus' lookin' into it."

"Yeah, just looking into it, that's all. You think . . . Never mind."

"What?"

"How much you think it would cost to start up something like this?"

"Girl, I don't know. I guess it's cheaper than buying an actual store. Can't be much overhead involved."

"How do you suppose they get their inventory?"

"They buy direct from publishers, I think. Publishers. Distributors maybe."

"I'm just thinking about it."

May smiled. "You said that already."

"Do you think—"

"Yes. I think you'd be very good at it, Ruth."

"Thank you, May. But I'm only—"

"I know. Thinkin' 'bout it."

Ruth drove home with a million questions running through her mind. What in the world would she look like trying to run a business? And what in the world did she know about selling stuff over the Internet? And what in the world did she know about operating a bookstore? She had to admit, the prospect did sound exciting, though, owning her own business. Something like that was definitely easier said than done. But, if a woman were interested in starting up a business like that, how would she go about it? How would she process credit cards? How would she put up a Web site and who could she get to create one? How much would it cost? How much money could she make?

Wow! That much?

Star Light

⁊

RUTH AND BERNIE STOOD SIDE BY SIDE, ADMIRING THE GUESTS as they filtered into the dining hall. Local politicians, business owners, heads of corporations all showed up in support of Higgin's House. Time had helped erase memories of the scandal from their minds and Bernie had written very convincing letters and called in a few favors courtesy of her boss, Mitch. From the looks of it, all their efforts had paid off.

Bernie's eyes grew wide at the sight of Adrian walking into the room, looking like he'd just stepped out of a fashion magazine, wearing an Armani tux better than Armani ever could. "Damn, Ruth! Is that him?"

"Yep, that's Adrian," Ruth announced confidently. "Isn't he gorgeous, Bernie?"

Bernie stared at Ruth. "Gorgeous ain't the word, girlfriend. If I had a penis, it would be rock hard right about now."

Ruth frowned and suddenly started to worry. "You haven't slept with him, have you Bernie?"

"Ruth, believe me. If I'd slept with that fine bastard, you'd have heard about it," Bernie said, never taking her eyes off the man as he scanned the room for Ruth.

Adrian swaggered over in their direction. Ruth watched the expression on Bernie's face, and recognized that hungry look in her eye. Bernie was sizing him up and licking her lips like he was going to be the entrée.

"He's mine, Bernie," Ruth said possessively.

"I know, Ruth. I know."

Adrian smiled and leaned down to kiss her. "You look beautiful, baby. Absolutely beautiful."

"Damn!" Bernie muttered. Ruth pretended not to hear her.

"So do you. Adrian, this is my best friend, Bernie Watson. Bernie . . . Adrian."

"Nice to finally meet you, Adrian." Bernie gave Adrian a limp-wristed handshake, and held on a little too long, as far as Ruth was concerned. "Now I see why she's been keeping you all to herself," she said, eyeing him up and down. "I can't say that I blame her."

Adrian glanced at Ruth and smiled, then slowly brought Bernie's hand to his lips and kissed it. "I've been looking forward to meeting you too. Ruth told me you were beautiful, but—"

Bernie interrupted him, grinning slyly. "Don't start, Adrian. This woman's like my sister and that's all that's keeping me from wearing you like a second skin and rocking your world hard enough to make you seasick."

"Bernie!" Ruth exclaimed, but she knew better than to expect anything else from Bernie.

"You two have a lovely evening."

Okay, Adrian thought, watching Bernie saunter off. That one scared him and he made a mental note to avoid being alone in a room with the woman at all costs. He turned his attention back to Ruth standing there looking delicious in a gold sequined evening gown, draped low in the front and even lower in back. Adrian took both her hands in his and pulled her close.

"Did I tell you how gorgeous you look tonight?"

Ruth smiled. "Yes, you did and you look pretty gorgeous yourself."

Adrian twisted his neck and tugged at his tie. "Yeah . . . well. I hate monkey suits."

"Well, they love you." Ruth playfully swatted his hand away from his tie and readjusted it for him.

"That dress is loving you pretty damn good too," he said coyly. "You wearing panties?"

"No," she said simply.

"I didn't think so."

Ruth looked surprised. "You can tell?"

Adrian covertly eased one hand down her waist to her hip, then discreetly slipped it behind her and cupped her bottom. He smiled. "Yeah. I can tell."

Eventually she managed to get his hand off her behind, showed Adrian to their table, and went back to the business of greeting guests. A few minutes later, May and Jeff arrived looking like they'd been born to be together.

"That her?" Bernie asked, turning up her nose. She sniffed disdainfully. "I thought you said she was cute."

"Bernice!" Clara snapped.

Ruth instinctively felt obligated to defend her friend against the likes of Bernie's mean ass. "She is, Bernie. She's very pretty."

"Girl, you need your eyes checked," Bernie said smartly.

Ruth was starting to get annoyed. "Why do you have to be like that?"

"Like what? That is not a pretty woman, Ruth."

"Somebody sounds jealous to me," Clara said.

Bernie's neck swung around and she stared at both Ruth and Clara looking absolutely appalled. "Jealous? Of what? Her?"

"She's been like that ever since I first mentioned May's name, Clara. I think it's childish and petty. Yeah, she's jealous."

Bernie's lips tightened and she glared at her through narrow slits where her eyes used to be. "Ruth, if you didn't have to give that speech tonight, I'd take you out back and whoop you up good."

"Bernie!" Clara gasped.

"Bernie nothing! Don't you ever accuse me of being jealous of any female, Miss Johnson. You either, Clara!"

"Ain't nobody scared of you," Clara mumbled, then rolled her eyes.

"You're serious?" Serious or not, Ruth was hurt that she'd even gone there.

"Damn right I am!" Bernie snapped. "Love you like a sister. But I'll put a whoopin' on you—"

"I'm sorry! Dang!" Sarcasm laced that apology and if Bernie was paying attention, which Ruth knew she was, she'd heard it.

"Ya'll crazy," Clara said shaking her head, walking away.

Jeff and May spotted Ruth and made their way through the crowd to where she was standing. "Ruth?" May smiled, then hugged her. Jeff leaned in and kissed her cheek.

"May . . . Jeff, I'm so glad you both came." She beamed.

"We wouldn't have missed it for the world," Jeff said sincerely.

May quickly scanned the room and recognized some very notable faces. "This is so impressive, girl. I mean . . . I expected it to be nice, but this is incredible. You have done such a wonderful job."

Meanwhile, Bernie stood off to the side, sizing up this woman, and her good-looking, vertically challenged husband.

"May . . . Jeff." Ruth turned to Bernie. "This is Bernice Watson," Ruth said proudly. "And if it weren't for her, none of this would've happened. She also happens to be my best friend."

Bernie's insides turned to shit, but fortunately, from years of experience, she'd become an expert at hiding shitty innards.

"Hello." Bernie smiled, shaking each of their hands. "Ruth's told me so much about you, and it's wonderful to finally meet you." Bernie struggled to maintain the sincerity in her voice and smile.

"Oh, and I've been lookin' forward to meetin' you too," May exclaimed excitedly. "She talks about you all the time and well . . . you've done a fantastic job here tonight."

"I think you said that already." Bernie quickly masked her snide comment with a radiant smile, followed by a hearty chuckle.

Something about the expression behind Bernie's smile made May feel uncomfortable. She couldn't quite put her finger on it, but it was definitely familiar. Contempt, perhaps, that women sometimes feel toward other women for no real good reason. Whatever the case, this wasn't the place to confront it, but May filed it away in the back of her mind, and when the opportunity presented itself again . . .

Jeff instinctively came to the rescue. "Well, we'd better find our table before someone else takes our seats," he said jokingly.

Ruth hugged May again. "I'll see you after the show?"

"Most definitely." May smiled. "Again, it was a pleasure meeting you, Ms. Watson."

Bernie nodded as they walked away. "Same."

Ruth wasn't sure who was sulking harder. She or Bernie. Sometimes she just didn't understand how their friendship had lasted as long as it had. The two were totally different kinds of people with nothing in common, and honestly, there had been moments when Ruth didn't think she liked Bernie. She decided that after tonight, she'd never call the woman again.

"Your speech ready?" Bernie asked nonchalantly. Ruth knew better. Bernie really didn't give a damn, so why was she bothering to ask?

"Yes," she mumbled.

"You nervous?"

What's it to you? Ruth started to say, but opted for, "A little."

"You know," Bernie said softly, "I really do think you're da bomb." Bernie smiled.

"I know," Ruth said, smiling back.

"Give me a hug."

" 'Kay." Ruth was glad that was over. She always hated it when they argued.

She didn't think anybody noticed, but Ruth did. Most of the night Clara stood off in the shadows somewhere, alone, with her arms wrapped around herself, occasionally smiling, overwhelmed by the magnitude of the evening. They had believed in the cause and they had believed in her, and that had been the fuel behind this event.

Ruth almost hated invading her solitary celebration, but it was time to get started. She slipped up beside Clara and put her arm around her shoulder.

"Who'da thunk?" Ruth joked, looking out into the crowd of more than three hundred guests.

"Not me. That's for sure." Clara patted Ruth's hand, and fought diligently to keep the tears from falling, but Ruth knew she might end up losing the battle. "You did good, baby."

"No, Clara. We all did good," Ruth corrected her, then looked lovingly into Clara's eyes. "I love you. I love you more than you'll ever know."

Clara chuckled. "Back atcha, Baby Ruth."

Clara Robins had mothered Ruth from the first day they met, two years ago. She'd done it without trying and probably without even knowing, which made it all the better to Ruth.

She'd convinced Ruth to speak tonight because all Ruth had planned on doing was fading into the darkness next to Adrian and enjoying the show like everybody else.

"You got to tell them, darlin'," she'd said. "You got to tell them your story."

"What story, Clara? So my husband beat my ass. What's the story in that?"

"The story's not in what he did, Ruth. It's in how you overcame it and survived."

Had she overcome it? Maybe she had. Finally. Somewhere in the last two years, Ruth had peeled off her old self, and put on a new self that before now had been nothing more than a figment of her imagination. Ruth had no idea what she'd say, but she knew she'd have to say something and the truth seemed like a pretty good place to start.

She stood uneasily behind the podium staring out into the audience. Never in a million years had she ever expected to end up here. Ruth had spent so much energy trying to erase her past and suddenly she would bring it to light in front of a room full of strangers . . . and friends.

"I've never been a resident of Higgin's House, but I could've been." Ruth nervously cleared her throat. "My name is Ruth Johnson, and for fourteen years I lived in an abusive marriage. People are quick to pass judgment sometimes, and often demand explanations to questions you don't know the answers to. *Why? Why'd you let him do that to you? Why'd you stay so long?* The truth is"—Ruth shrugged—"I don't know. For years I held on to the hope that one day it would simply stop, the beatings, the name-calling. It would all stop and my marriage would be the kind of marriage I'd always dreamed of because I'd finally learn to stop pissing him off, and he'd finally remember that my name was Ruth and not Bitch. I could've waited forever, but that day was never going to come. He would never stop, so I had to. I stopped accepting that that kind of life was the best I deserved. I stopped being afraid of him and I realized I had nothing in the world to lose. You can't fall off the bottom. Right?" Ruth smiled sheepishly. "I mean, what did I have? Nothing, not even my life was worth a damn to me or to him. Especially to him. I simply didn't matter and we all need to matter, at least to ourselves. I'm learning that." She concluded quietly, "It's still not easy, but I'm learning and I know I will never go back and I won't accept anything less than respect." Ruth stared into Adrian's face.

She took a deep breath and continued, "The women at Higgin's House . . . some will go back, but many of them won't. Not as long as they have a haven, a safe place to think, to heal, to plan, and to clearly see that they have choices not to live under the threat of lies or fists. For a short time . . . enough time, Higgin's House is a home where nurturing and guidance are the foundation for lives that desperately need rebuilding. Higgin's House is a resting place and sometimes . . . a little rest is all any of us needs." Ruth wiped away tears and smiled at Clara. Speaking in front of all those people hadn't been so hard after all, and instantly, she felt exonerated. "Now . . . we've got some incredible entertainment lined up for you tonight. So, sit back, relax, and enjoy. Peace."

The audience rose to their feet and applauded as she made her way to her seat. More than anything, Ruth hoped they got something out of what she'd said. Something that didn't look a thing like pity or shame. But she wanted them to understand that people were pretty much the same. They all made choices in their lives, some right, some wrong, and they all deserved the opportunity to take advantage of their God given right to a second chance. As she made her way toward her seat, Adrian welcomed her into his arms, held her close, and whispered in her ear, "I love you."

Ruth smiled radiantly up at him and mouthed back. "I love you too, Adrian." She loved him more than she ever thought she could love any man, and no matter what else happened in her life, this night would be in her heart forever, because he loved her. Ruth Renee Johnson.

In the end, they raised nearly $200,000, which was way more than any of them ever expected. Not only that, but a private donor gave Higgin's House a trust fund and for the next ten years Clara Robins could count on getting $75,000 a year to keep the house open.

Love's Holiday

AFTER THE BANQUET, ADRIAN SURPRISED HER WITH THE ROOM he'd reserved for the two of them in the hotel. Ruth and Adrian lay naked next to each other, holding hands, breathless from making love.

"Not all men are like your ex-husband, Ruth. I'm not like him and . . . I'd never hurt you like that," Adrian explained.

"I know," she whispered.

"I mean . . . any man who'd hit a woman isn't a man."

"No, he isn't."

"But the last thing I want you to do is think that I'm going to trip like that. You know what I'm saying?"

Ruth sighed groggily. "I think so."

"I've got a temper. Hell, we all get mad, but I'm not down for shit like that. And you need to know this and you need to trust me."

"I know." She smiled.

"Because a relationship is built on trust, baby. Ours is no different."

"It isn't."

"And communication, Ruth. Don't be afraid to open up and talk to me. You've got something on your mind . . . no matter what it is, you need to speak up. Because how can I fix it if I don't know it's broken?" Adrian reasoned.

"I understand," she muttered, turning over and resting her head on his shoulder.

"I mean, I honestly don't understand what would make a man act like that and I might never fully understand why you did stay, but it'll never be like that between us. You know what I'm saying?"

"Yes."

"I've been in and out of relationships and I've been in love before, but not like this, Ruth. This . . . what we're building here . . . this is what I've hoped for my whole life and we don't need tension between us. You don't ever need to be afraid of expressing yourself, or being yourself, or telling my ass where to get off if I'm being a son-of-a-bitch. And I can be a son-of-a-bitch, Ruth."

"Sure."

"Not all the time," he quickly explained. "But my job is stressful and sometimes I might bring that shit home with me. Sometimes I might . . . and this isn't all the time, because most of the time, I'm pretty easygoing, but sometimes, I might even lose my temper and say some shit that I really don't mean, but that doesn't mean I don't love you, or want you in my life, and I'll never disrespect you. You understand what I'm saying?"

Ruth planted a soft kiss on his chin. "Yes, baby. I understand everything you're saying and I love you for saying it."

"I can't imagine there'd be anything you could do to make me want to—"

"Then don't imagine it, Adrian. Just make love to me one more time before I fall asleep."

He did.

After Taste

THERE WERE TIMES LIKE THIS SHE WISHED SHE'D NEVER QUIT smoking. Smoking had always given her something to do with her hands, especially after sex, while she waited for a lover to get dressed and leave. A cigarette would be nice now and Bernie wished she had one, even just to hold between her fingers, and put between her lips until he left.

Bruce emerged from the bathroom, buttoning his shirt, then sat down at the foot of the bed and slipped on his socks and shoes. Bernie had called him earlier and after glossing over some small talk, and catching up on missed time, she'd invited him over. Both of them knew the deal. There was no pretense between them, and there never had been. Bruce was a male version of Bernie. He'd been married, but after his divorce he had sworn off the institution for the rest of his life, and clung possessively to his bachelor status, ready to run like hell, screaming, in the opposite direction if any women even mentioned the word "marriage." Sex was all they'd ever had between them, and it had been the kind of crazy, uninhibited sex that true connoisseurs could appreciate; no-holds-barred, no reticence, very few limits. And when it was over, it was over, and one of them would get up and leave before the sun rose.

"That's never happened to me before," he stated, slipping into his socks. Bruce sat and reflected for a moment. "No. That has never happened."

Bernie lay in bed behind him, on her side, facing the wall. "There's a first time for everything . . . I suppose."

Bruce chuckled. "I suppose . . . you're right."

How could she have let that happen? Bernie questioned silently. It didn't make any sense whatsoever no matter how many times she'd gone over it in her mind.

Bruce walked over to the nightstand on her side of the bed, picked up his watch and slipped it on his wrist. "You going to be all right?"

Bernie rolled over and stared up at him. What kind of question was that? Was she going to be all right? Hell no, she thought. She was not all right, because something in her had slipped and she'd had no idea how she'd let that happen.

"Lock the door on your way out," she said quietly.

Bruce smiled, then leaned down and kissed her softly on her head. "If you ever snap out of it," he said, walking toward the door, "you got my number."

She heard him close the door behind him, and for the first time all evening, Bernie finally felt herself take a deep breath. Bruce had come over looking handsome and fine as usual, gathered her up in his arms, pushed her down on the floor right there in the living room. He'd raised her nightgown slowly above her waist, then expertly undid his pants, slid into a condom in less than five seconds, and slipped himself inside her before she'd even had a chance to say "hello." It hadn't taken him long to come because he'd missed the hell out of her ass. But Bernie knew better than to be pissed. Bruce always took care of the preliminaries before getting down to business, and the business of the night always included hours of foreplay, games, and fucking every way imaginable.

Eventually, they moved their efforts into the bedroom, and Bernie sat straddled above him, riding him the way they both loved; slow, deep, hard.

Bruce held her by her waist, and raised his head to watch Bernie's slippery, wet pussy slide slowly up and down his hard shaft.

"That's the way I like it, baby," he whispered. "Oh yeah! Give it to me, Bernie. Give me all that shit."

Bernie had thrown her head back and closed her eyes. "Mmmm . . . damn! Damn! Damn, baby!"

Bruce cupped her breasts, then pulled her forward and took her nipples, one at a time, into his warm, inviting mouth, nibbling gently on them with his teeth.

"Awww!" Bernie exclaimed, pushing herself farther down on him. "Baby," she squealed. "Baby, don't stop. Please don't . . . stop." Beads of sweat slid down her back, and Bruce reached one hand around her ass, aiding her in her efforts.

"Some good pussy!" he whispered. "Some damn good . . . That's it. That's—"

Bruce couldn't take it anymore, and raised his hips in the air to meet hers. The two slapped together, hard and furiously, caught up in the frenzy of their sexual escapade.

"I'm cumming!" Bernie screamed. "I'm cumming, Miles! Oh . . . baby! I'm cumming!"

Soon Bernie collapsed in a heap on top of Bruce, then rolled off and lay exhausted next to him. Neither of them said a word for a while, but it was Bruce who finally broke the silence.

"So . . . who's Miles?"

"What?" Bernie asked, shocked at the mention of his name, especially at a time like this.

Bruce chuckled. "You called me 'Miles.' "

"I did not!" Bernie exclaimed.

Bruce looked at her. "Oh, so I'm lying?"

Bernie was speechless for a moment. Had she called out Miles's name? No. No, she would never let herself slip like that, and besides, Miles was the farthest thing from her mind. She hadn't given his ass two seconds of her attention since the last time she'd seen him in the restaurant, weeks before.

"You in love with that dude?" Bruce asked. "Or is his dick just better than mine?"

"I think you need to go."

Bruce shrugged. "I know I need to," he said, getting up out of bed and heading into the bedroom. "Three people in a bed is one too many, baby—unless it's two of you and one of me," he said teasingly.

––––––––

After Bruce left, Bernie showered and went into the kitchen and poured herself a glass of wine.

"What the hell is my problem?" she asked out loud. Bernie took a long sip from her glass.

Bruce's words repeated themselves in her mind. *"You in love with this dude?"* She knew the answer to that question. It was an emphatic no. She was not in love with Miles. Calling out his name had been a Freudian slip, a subconscious error on her part and nothing more. Loving Miles or anybody else for that matter wasn't an option, because that's not what she wanted for her life. At least, not now. She used to think it was because she was bitter over her failed marriage with Monty, but now, Bernie knew better. For a time, maybe that had been the reason. The truth of the matter was, Bernie loved her freedom. She loved not being anchored to anybody unless she chose to make it that way, and if she remembered correctly, she hadn't chosen that.

Miles was a special man. He tried harder with her than any of the others had. Sometimes, she appreciated that. Other times, it got on her damn nerves. A man who put forth that kind of effort usually ended up expecting it in return, if not in the beginning, then later on. And that was the obligation Bernie wanted to avoid. Miles had proved her point before they'd stopped seeing each other. He'd come up with the brilliant notion that she should be his woman, and that they should commit to each other. He'd set her up, that's all. Miles had come at her feigning devotion, when all along, he'd had his own agenda of trying to bind a sistah in something called a "relationship." Sure, she missed him, sometimes. But that's as much as she'd admit to. Even to herself. Bernie finished her glass of wine and eventually went to bed.

High Hopes

"SO, TELL ME MORE ABOUT THIS IDEA YOU'VE BEEN WORKING SO hard on," Bernie said dryly. "Whatever it is, it's got you more excited than an ex-con in a whorehouse."

Ruth grimaced at her crude analogy. "Well, I'm considering starting my own business. A bookstore specializing in books by and about people of color." Ruth waited impatiently for Bernie's response, but the best she could come back with was a blank stare. "Did you hear me?"

Bernie shrugged indifferently. "I heard you."

"Well? What do you think?"

"Where are you going to get the money?"

"Well, I've saved up a little money over the years," Ruth explained. "Thirty-four hundred dollars. Not to mention, I still have some money left over from the sale of the house, and I've got an appointment to meet with a counselor at the SBA next week to find out what I'd have to do to get a loan."

Bernie leaned back in her chair and sighed. "That's the most ridiculous idea I've ever heard."

Naturally, Ruth was offended. "What? Why would you say that?"

"Black bookstores don't make money, Ruth, and if you'd done your homework, you'd know this. Why you want to waste your savings on some mess like that? Starting a business is one thing, but at least start one where you can make some money."

"I have done my homework, Bernice, and I know that black bookstore owners are struggling."

"So what the hell are you thinking?"

"I'm thinking . . . Internet!" The look of excitement on Ruth's face was blinding. "E-commerce, baby. It's all the rage."

"What do you know about e-commerce, Ruth?"

"A lot. I've been researching it for weeks. There are these big bookstores doing business on-line, selling everybody's books for as much as forty percent off what you'd pay in the stores. How can they do that, you may ask?"

"I'm asking," she said nonchalantly.

"There's no overhead, at least not like the overhead of owning an actual store. I save money . . . my customers save money."

"So if everybody else is already doing it—"

"They're doing it for everybody's books, Bernie. I'm going to offer books specific to people of color. Meaning customers won't have to wade through hundreds of thousands of books to find what they're looking for."

Bernie's expression softened and Ruth caught a glimmer of optimism sparkling in her eyes. "So, how much money do you think you can make from this and where are you going to run this business from?"

"Home." She smiled. "And I think I can make some damn good money if I market it right. The publishing industry generates millions, Bernie, and I only need a tiny piece of that pot to make me happy."

"When do you plan on getting started?"

"I kind of already have. I've got a business plan, sent out letters to distributors, gotten quotes on the cost of building and hosting a Web site—"

"Wait a minute . . . hold up. You're moving a little fast, honey," Bernie said calmly. Ruth was bouncing on her ass over this whole notion and Bernie knew she needed to be the voice of reason before she bounced her ass right into a mess. "Don't you think you need to take your time on something like this? I mean, we're talking a major undertaking, Ruth, and you don't want to get in over your head."

"I'm just looking into it, Bernie, and so far it looks like it could be a good opportunity."

"Sounds like you're doing more than looking into it, Ruth. People are always getting excited starting up these new businesses, only they end up filing bankruptcy because they thought they had it all figured out too."

"But I know a lot about this business, Bernie. I read any and everything I can get my hands on. There's nothing better to me than a good book. I've got a whole room full of them and I've been doing the research and—"

"So you love books, sweetie. That doesn't qualify you to run a business like this."

"No, it doesn't. But I'm an intelligent woman, and I'm not going to just dive into this thing without looking."

"I hope not."

"But the more I do look into it, the more excited I get about the idea, and if you'd take a look at my business plan, you'd see why."

"I'm just not convinced that running a business off the Internet is a smart thing to do, Ruth. You've got all kinds of crooks and con artists—"

"But it can be safe, Bernie. As long as you take all the right precautions. And crooks and con artists are everywhere. Running a business off the Internet is like running a business anywhere. You've got to be smart and careful about it and I'm perfectly capable of watching my back, Bernie."

Bernie sat quietly for a moment, taking in everything Ruth had told her. The idea did have potential. Bernie knew enough about dot coms to know that much, but only if Ruth ran it with her head and not her heart. Obviously, she thought looking into Ruth's eyes, the woman needed guidance.

"You're really serious about this?"

"I'm serious about looking into it. How's that? And if what I find out gives me some warm fuzzies, then yes, I'm serious about doing it."

"And what if it doesn't work out?"

"And what if it does?"

"You could lose a lot of money."

"I could make a lot of money."

"You could lose a lot of money, Ruth."

"And so what if I do, Bernie? I don't have anybody but me to take care of. So, I might lose some money. So what? Beats not trying and never knowing. I know you think I'm being hasty, Bernie, but I'm not. Right now, I'm just checking it out. That's all. But if I do decide to pursue this, I'm willing to take my chances."

"Sounds to me like you're determined to do this."

"I'm not too old to still be something when I grow up, Bernice. I want to do things and go places and meet people. If I mess up, then I mess up. But I know one thing, Bernie. I know how to get up. Not too many people know how to get back up after they've been down, the way I know how to get back up. I've been patient and I've been careful. Now I want to be an entrepreneur."

Bernie conceded that Ruth was definitely serious, so the only other thing to do was to get down to business. "You mind if I take a look at that business plan of yours?"

Ruth smiled. "I was hoping you'd say that." She went into her bedroom and came back with her business plan in less than a minute.

Bernie smiled as she read the name of Ruth's company on the cover sheet. " 'Pages.' I like it."

"Me too."

Figments

Lord, she must be in love! Ruth surmised, waiting at the meat counter while the butcher wrapped her order. What other explanation could there be for spending her whole paycheck on T-bone steaks for dinner with Adrian? Spring was definitely in the air, which probably accounted for all the slobbering she'd been doing over Adrian in recent weeks. He wasn't complaining, though, and that was the best part. She'd been scrambling around all day running errands and preparing for a quiet, romantic evening alone with him. Ruth walked slowly up and down the aisles, making sure she had everything for the dinner she'd promised to make him. Of course feeding Adrian wasn't hard. He liked the basics, meat and potatoes. The salad portion of the meal was her idea, along with the dessert. That sweet tooth of hers was definitely her Achilles heel.

"Thought that was you." That voice of his instantly sent chills down her spine. Without warning, he put his hand on her arm, and his touch seemed to burn into her skin like acid. Instinctively, she backed away from him.

Ruth stared up into his pale, green eyes. "Eric," she said simply.

He laughed. "Hey, baby. Whatchu been up to besides lookin' like a million dollars?" Eric's eyes slowly scanned down Ruth's figure. "I almost didn't recognize you, but then I said that's her. That's my Ruthie."

She was repulsed. *His Ruthie?* Not anymore. Not in years.

"Now don't give me that look, girl. How you been, baby?"

What should she have said? That she'd been healing and happy and cleaning out her spirit of all the trash he'd left behind? She'd cried and laughed and danced and pissed out nightmares and memories of him spitting in her face, calling her "bitch", slapping her, punching her, kicking her?

"Fine," was all she said.

"Yeah? You uh . . . lookin' good, baby girl. Lookin' damn good. Finally got rid of some of that weight, I see," he said, sounding almost anxious to Ruth.

Watch him, Ruth. Pay close attention. Eric was still Eric. She could tell. She could smell it on him. The stench that came from being evil was unmistakable and made her nauseous because she hadn't smelled it in ages. "Still workin' for that lawyer? What's his name?"

Ruth turned and started to walk away. "I'm still at the law firm."

Eric followed. "They give you a raise yet? I told you, baby. You work too hard for they asses down there. You need to go in one day and tell them they need to give you a raise. You got it comin'."

Ruth turned down another aisle and hurried toward the front of the store to the check out counter. "Yeah, well . . . I'm kind of in a hurry, Eric," she said earnestly. "I've really got to be going and—" Suddenly, she dropped her basket and everything in it. *Shit! Leave it, Ruth!* she scolded herself. *Just leave it!*

Eric knelt down at her feet and picked up her things. She wanted to run and never stop. To hell with the mushrooms and the expensive steaks. Her mind ran, but her feet stood firmly planted to the linoleum floor.

"You clumsy as ever I see," he said, rising to his feet and holding out her basket of groceries to her.

No. No, she wasn't clumsy. She'd never been clumsy, except when he was around. "These some nice steaks you got here, baby." He smiled. "Two of 'em? One of these for yo' man?"

"No I . . ." *Stop it!* She didn't owe him an explanation. Not anymore.

"He's one lucky son-of-a-bitch, whoever he is," Eric said, burning a hole in her with his gaze. "You a good woman, Ruthie. Always was a damn good woman." Ruth took her basket and walked away.

"Take care, Eric," she said over her shoulder, then hurried to the check out counter. Was he coming? she wondered, glancing quickly behind her. Eric hadn't moved and watched her watch him. Would he follow her? Panic set in, but she refused to give in to it. Of course, the idea of him following her was ridiculous. Wasn't it? After all this time to think he would still be playing those tired games was ludicrous. They'd been divorced for over two years and Eric had moved on with his life like she'd moved on with hers. When would she finally learn, and more important, accept that that chapter in her life had been closed a long time ago and it would stay closed.

Out of the corner of her eye, Ruth saw Eric walking in her direction. He stopped, then stood next to her and held out an onion. "You dropped this too." It wasn't a question.

Ruth shook her head and looked into her basket knowing there had never been an onion in it. "No. I don't think—"

"Look again, sweetheart," he said, his tone hard. "You sure you didn't drop this, Ruthie?"

She was sure. She was positive. Ruth reached out and took the onion from his hand. "I suppose I did. Thank you, Eric."

"No problem, baby. You take care of yo'self." He winked and left the store.

She hadn't dropped that onion. Ruth had plenty of onions at home so there'd been no need to buy more. Why'd she tell him it belonged to her? He knew it hadn't. She knew it hadn't. Why did she say it did?

"Excuse me? Miss? Miss, I can ring you up now," the cashier said impatiently. "Miss?"

Ruth emptied her basket onto the conveyer belt. *Dear God*, she said to herself. *What have I just done?*

Ruth hadn't said much all evening. She kept telling him that she'd had a long day, but something in her expression told him there was more to it than that. Adrian decided not to push it, though. He'd learned from experience that patience was a virtue with this woman and if he left well enough alone, maybe eventually she'd get whatever was bothering her off her chest.

Ruth finished up the dishes in the kitchen, while Adrian poured his full self down into the sofa. "Dinner was delicious, baby," he called out to her.

"Thank you," she said absently.

"You keep it up you're going to make a brotha fat."

Ruth glanced in his direction. "You'll never be fat, Adrian."

"You haven't seen my baby pictures."

Ruth feigned a smile and loaded the last of the dishes into the dishwasher. She hadn't been able to get the encounter with Eric off her mind. It wasn't running into him that bothered her. It was her reaction to him. All of a sudden, she'd been catapulted back in time to a dark place she thought she'd escaped long ago, and it was so familiar, it had been like she'd never left. After all this time, she'd convinced herself that she wasn't the same woman she'd been back then. But after what happened this afternoon, she wasn't so sure anymore.

Ruth turned off the light in the kitchen, then came and curled up next to Adrian. "You've been quiet all evening. You sure you're okay?"

"I'm okay." She smiled.

"No, you're not." He picked up the remote and turned off the television. "What's on your mind? Tell Dr. Carter all your problems," he teased, knowing full well that he was probably wasting his time, but hell, virtue or not, patience wasn't always his strong suit, and sometimes a man needed to take matters into his own hands to remedy the situation. It sounded good in theory, anyway. "I'm listening."

She'd been thinking about telling him all night, but what would that accomplish? What would it do but give power to Eric, who wasn't even in the room, and ruin their evening together? He didn't warrant their attention, she'd concluded. And Ruth decided that she wouldn't waste another second thinking about him. Ruth softly placed one of her fingers to his lips, then rested her head against his chest. "Shhhhh. You're going to make me miss one."

"One what?"

"One heartbeat," Ruth whispered, closing her eyes and listening to the gentle rhythm inside him.

He sighed. "That mean you don't want to talk about it?"

"It's just been a long day, Adrian."

"There's more to it than that, Ruth. I know something's bothering you, baby. C'mon now"—He lifted her face to his—"what's up?"

"Adrian, I just had a bad day, that's all. I don't want to talk about it."

He sighed again. "Just a bad day, huh?"

"That's all."

But Adrian knew better. "One of these days, Ruth . . . one of these days, you're going to trust the hell out of my ass and beg me to listen to your problems," he teased. "But I probably won't have time then. You need to hit a brotha up now, while you got me sitting here."

Ruth laughed. "I trust you now," she assured him. "But I don't want to spend the rest of this night bitching and complaining about nothing important." Eric wasn't important. Not now.

She squeezed him, and buried her face in the crook of his neck. Adrian raised her mouth to his, kissed her passionately and made love to her, filling her with unspoken promises until eventually, they both fell asleep in each other's arms, and Ruth felt safe.

See No Evil

THE FOLLOWING WEEKEND, ADRIAN PICKED RUTH UP EARLY AND they spent the day shopping for new computers. Ruth was getting more serious about starting her business and it was time to seriously move forward with her idea. Getting a new computer would be her first real investment in bringing her goal to light.

"What about this one, Adrian? It's got a fifty-gigabyte hard drive?"

"Ruth, you really think you need a fifty-gigabyte hard drive?" he asked, examining another system at the end of the aisle.

"I don't know. Do I?"

"No, baby."

"Maybe not now, but later on I might need it."

"With what you're planning? I doubt it."

Ruth moved over to the next unit on display. "What about this one? It's got a fifty-six-K modem. That sounds good."

Adrian smiled. "DSL is better, or better yet, cable. Check this out." He motioned to her. "Now this is exactly what you need. Memory, one hundred and twenty-eight megs, a twenty-gig drive, zip drive, speakers, seventeen-inch monitor and a printer. Twelve hundred dollars."

"That's all?"

"That's it."

"Is that enough? I mean, won't I need some more RAM or ROM or something?"

Adrian smiled. "This has got all the RAM and ROM you need."

"Okay. Well, you're the expert." She shrugged. "I'll take it."

Out of the corner of her eye, Ruth caught a glimpse of an apparition. Tall and slender, the light-skinned frame turned the corner before she was able to confirm her nightmare. Was that Eric?

"Ruth? You hear me?"

"What?"

"I said, you've got a rebate coming back to you when you buy this. Damn, I need to get me one of these. You all right, baby?"

"Yeah. I just thought I saw someone I knew," she said, trying not to sound shaken. "I guess I was wrong."

"C'mon. Let's find somebody to get your new computer."

Was her mind playing tricks on her? Was that Eric? It couldn't have been. What on earth would he be doing in an office supply store? she questioned in her mind. Ever since that encounter at the grocery store, she'd had Eric on her brain constantly, and everywhere she turned she kept expecting to run into him again.

Ruth paid for her new $1,200 toy and Adrian loaded the boxes into the back of his car. She happened to look up in time to see a silver Pontiac slowly drive out of the parking lot. That couldn't have been him. Could it?

Later that evening, Ruth watched in awe as Adrian effortlessly assembled her computer.

"You think it's a dumb idea?" Ruth asked, watching him work.

"What? The business?"

"Yeah."

"What do you think?"

"I asked you first."

"No, I don't think it's dumb. New Internet businesses pop up every day and a lot of them are making bank."

"I'm still not sure I'm going to do it. I mean, well . . . I'm just thinking about trying it and seeing how it works out."

"That's all you can do, baby."

"I've been calling around to see how much it would cost to get a Web site designed. It's really expensive."

"Yeah, it can be. But don't worry that. I've already talked to a friend of mine. He'll hook you up. Just let me know when you're ready."

"Really? I could pay him, not a lot, but I could give him something."

"You could, but you won't have to. He owes me. Come here." Adrian reached out his hand and pulled Ruth onto his lap. "You do know how to work this?"

"I know how to work the word processor and the spreadsheet. And I know a lot about databases. The only thing I'm not so sure about is the Internet."

"What don't you know about the Internet?"

"Everything and nothing." She laughed. Adrian didn't. "No, seriously. I've seen May run through it, but she knows what she's doing and she pretty much lost me."

"I see," he said absentmindedly.

"You probably think I've lost my damn mind starting a business on the Internet when my stupid ass has no idea how to use the stupid thing."

"Your ass ain't stupid, baby. As a matter of fact, next to your lips, your eyes, your titties, your pussy, and your feet, it's my favorite part of your body."

Ruth laughed. "You're crazy."

"I might be, but right now, I'm your teacher and we're about to start school, Internet one-oh-one. Everything and anything you ever wanted to know about the Internet, you're going to learn this afternoon. Pay attention. There's going to be a test afterwards."

Adrian took his time, patiently showing Ruth the ins and outs of Web surfing, explaining links, search engines, channels, and even scrutinizing Web pages of her would-be competitors. And he was right. There was a test afterward, but it had nothing to do with the Internet.

Adrian slept soundly next to Ruth, but she was wide awake. She nuzzled herself against his back and draped her arm across him. Even in his sleep, he seemed to know she was there and he pulled her closer to him. She knew there was nothing she wouldn't do for him.

All he'd ever have to do was ask. It had been as if her life started over from scratch the moment she laid eyes on him and he was her second chance.

She'd always hated the thought of forever with Eric. Had that been him she'd seen earlier? She was almost positive it was. And if that were the case, what did it mean? Did it mean he was simply shopping for office supplies too? Maybe he'd needed pens, or pads of paper, or envelopes. Or, maybe he was looking for her, but of course, that wouldn't make sense because they were divorced, so that was a ridiculous thought. And it couldn't have been him because Eric didn't buy pens, or pads of paper, or envelopes.

Adrian turned to face her. "What's up, baby? Can't sleep?" he mumbled sleepily.

She rested her head against his chest. "No."

"Excited about that new PC you got?"

"Yes," Ruth whispered.

"We'll play some more tomorrow," he said, then kissed her head. "Go back to sleep, honey. Goodnight."

Adrian moaned, then cocooned her inside him and the last thing she remembered before falling asleep was how much she loved him.

What's Love?

Then it's bitter
Making me smack my lips
Bringing tears to my eyes
It's hard to tell
The difference between the two
Sometimes
But . . . I don't care

"I UM. . . . I HAPPENED TO HAVE BEEN IN THE NEIGHBORHOOD," Bernie said jokingly.

Miles stood in the doorway of his home with an expression on his face that said he wasn't buying it.

Bernie decided to try the indignant approach. Some men found that attractive. "You going to make me stand out here all day?"

Miles casually stepped aside to let her in, then walked past her and called out to the kids in the living room. Every other weekend, the kids were with him, but he'd always been careful in the past to schedule his time with her around them.

"It's my turn, worm brain!" the little girl whined at her older brother playing the video game. "Daddy!" she called out to Miles when she saw him. "MJ won't let me play."

The boy was oblivious to the chaos around him, and Bernie got a warm feeling in her heart from watching him. Boys. There was nothing on the planet more beautiful than an indifferent little boy. Especially one with the uncanny ability to ignore some whining little girl, running to her daddy to rescue her from him.

"MJ."

"Yeah, Dad." The boy's eyes never left the television and his fingers never stopped flipping buttons on that control pad.

"Let your sister have a turn."

"Sure, Dad."

Miles walked off, but Bernie lingered behind, knowing full well that the boy would never turn over that controller to his sister. She was right.

Bernie followed Miles toward the back of the house into his home office. He sat down behind his desk and stared at her. Bernie had on a long, floral, rayon dress, split up the side, and strappy sandals. Her long hair was pulled back into a ponytail, showing off her exotic features, and Miles thought he'd bust right out of his pants if the woman so much as breathed on him. Damn! She was gorgeous and he'd missed the hell out of her mean ass. But he'd go to his grave before telling her. She didn't deserve him. It was just that simple.

Bernie closed the door behind her, and sat down in a chair across from his desk. She was a mass of jelly inside, and it was all she could do to keep from passing out. After all, history was being made here today. Bernice Watson was here, and she was here for him. Not that she'd ever intended on ever seeing Miles again. But somewhere between leaving the mall and going to the convenience store for a cherry slushie, her body had been possessed by a demon that had taken control of her mind, and forced her to drive over to Miles's house. First thing Sunday morning, she was dragging her ass out of bed and going to church to get baptized again. That was for damn sure.

"To what do I owe this visit?" Miles said resentfully.

Bernie's smile quivered slightly. "I take it from your tone of voice that you're not all that happy to see me?"

"Not at all."

And that was all it took, Miles sitting across from her, looking every bit like some pompous asshole sitting on a throne in the imaginary kingdom of his little mind, glaring down his nose at her. Bernie quickly realized she didn't care for him after all. She could almost see that little love demon leaving her body, and flowing out through the window in a puff of smoke.

"Well, I just stopped by to say hello," she said with attitude. "And to see how you were, but I see you don't need me to check on you."

Miles recognized the tone in her voice and fire in her eyes instantly. At some point, he'd hit a nerve and the idea made him smile.

"You miss me, Bernie?"

Bernie's face turned to stone and she resented his assumption. "You wish I'd miss you."

Miles's expression softened. Going head to head with this woman was not how he'd planned on starting his weekend, and he'd learned from experience when to be the yang to Bernie's ying. That's how they'd managed to get along for so long. Miles knew the art of compromise and how to make it work better than most people, definitely better than Bernie. That's the thing he'd always liked best about their relationship. From day one, he'd had the upper hand, and he'd been slick enough about it not to make it obvious.

"I do, baby," he said, simply. "I wish with all my heart that you missed me."

What the hell was she supposed to do with that? "Goddamnit, Miles!" Bernie spat. "What's that supposed to mean?"

He laughed, then sat back in his chair. "Exactly what I said, Bernie. What? You don't know how to handle that?"

Bernie also leaned back in her chair, and crossed her legs, revealing a scrumptious amount of thigh that made him lick his lips. Sex was Bernie's comeback. It always had been, and Miles had known it all along. It would've been easy to mistake the woman for shallow because of that, but he'd known better. There was depth to Bernice Watson, but she was particular about revealing it. He suspected she probably knew it would mess up her game if she came across as more than ass. Or if she came clean and admitted that there was more she wanted from a man than ass. That's why she was here. He knew it, even if she wouldn't admit it.

"So," she said, casually. "How's your little girlfriend?"

Miles looked confused. "My girlfriend?"

"The woman I saw you in the restaurant? The one with the fake boobs."

Miles grinned. "I assure you, Bernie, they're not fake," he said smugly. Of course, he was just guessing. Miles hadn't even been intimate with the woman, who happened to have been on her period every time they had a date. Either she had some serious female problems, or she'd had no intention of sleeping with him. He had a feeling it hadn't been a grave loss.

"Those titties were as fake as three-dollar bills, Miles. Trust me," she said, leaning forward. "Another woman knows fake titties when she sees them."

"Well, maybe, but fake or not . . . I enjoyed the hell out of them," he said, smacking his lips.

Bernie was just about to say "Fuck you" when his daughter came into the room.

"Daddy?" she said, walking over to Miles and sitting on his lap. She eyed Bernie suspiciously, and Bernie suspected that the little girl had come in to check out the prospect. Bernie smiled, but the child turned away.

"Um . . . can I have some ice cream?"

"Not before dinner," he said tenderly.

Bernie had never seen him in this light before. Miles as Daddy. He looked different with that child sitting on his lap. Bernie couldn't quite put her finger on it, but whatever it was, it was turning her on in a big way. Suddenly, his shoulders seemed broader and his voice deeper. His hands seemed larger and she felt the urge to climb up into his lap too. *Bernie Watson!* she yelled in her head. *Child, get a hold of yourself! It's only Miles; young, goofy Miles who tells stale jokes, sucks at Monopoly, and loses his mind over Freddy Kruger flicks. Miles, who drives down the street playing rap music so loud his car bounces on its axles. Miles, who doesn't know the difference between a filet mignon and a cheeseburger. For crying out loud, girl! Get a hold of yourself.*

Bernie stood up to leave. "I've got to be going now, Miles," she said icily. "But it was good seeing you."

The little girl crawled out of his lap. "You're welcome to stay for dinner, Bernie," he said, hating to see her go. "I'm going to put some burgers and hot dogs on the grill."

"No thank you," she said, leaving his office and heading toward the front door.

Before leaving, she turned to him and smiled. "We had some good times, baby boy. Some damn good times."

Sadness washed over his face. "We did. Too bad things didn't work out."

Bernie shrugged. "They worked out the way they should've. You take care of yourself."

He was, after all, only Miles, Bernie thought driving home. The Miles who knew how to make her laugh even when she was PMSing. The Miles who made the best peanut-butter-and-banana sandwiches in the world. The Miles who made love to her, even when she'd convinced herself it was just sex. The Miles who kissed her like he wanted to share his soul with her, even when she didn't think she wanted it. A tear escaped down her cheek. "You are so fucked up sometimes, Bernie," she cried. *Damn!* She missed him.

Serendipity

RUTH SAT UP IN BED AND RUBBED THE SLEEP FROM HER EYES AT the sound of his voice over the phone. As usual it was late. Adrian always seemed to call late at night whenever he was in California. Not that she minded. He'd call and that's all she cared about. "Hey, you back?"

"No, I'm still in San Francisco," he said wearily.

For the last two months, Adrian had been flying back and forth to California more frequently. He'd warned her some time ago that he'd be spending more time out of town, but he promised that it would only last until the final phase of the project was completed in June. It had been difficult not being able to spend more time with him, but Ruth didn't complain. At least, not to him. June was still a month away, but keeping busy had definitely helped her to pass the time. Between her job, classes, and working on getting Pages' Web site up and running, Ruth had just enough free time to sleep and that was it. "Still?"

"Yeah. We ran into a few glitches so I'll be here a few more days."

"So, you won't be back in time for Bernie's dinner party?" she asked disappointedly.

"I'm sorry, sweetheart."

"Well, you know, I could come out there for the weekend," she said, trying to hide her regret. "We could overdose on sourdough and sex. Sound like a good idea?"

"Sounds like a wonderful idea, but it's not happening. I'm in meetings and conferences all the damn time and I wouldn't be able to spend any time with you."

"So? Who says you need to spend time with me?" she asked jokingly. "Maybe I just need a vacation and want to spend it in San Francisco. Doesn't mean I have to spend time with you, chasing you up and down the beach and fucking you like a wild animal when you're weak with exhaustion. I might just want to do something else."

"Damn." He laughed. "I hope not."

"So, can I come?"

"Nope."

"Adrian," Ruth whined.

"Honey, I've got too much to do here and you'll just be a distraction. I'll be home in a few days and we'll spend some time together then."

"Promise?" she asked pouting.

"I promise," he reassured her.

Adrian had flown in late that afternoon and Ruth had taken the liberty of inviting herself over to his place under the premises of *"I'm not staying long, baby. I've just been missing you like crazy and I'd like to see you."* She'd packed an extra pair of panties in her purse, just in case her plan worked and he invited her to spend the night. Adrian was lying on the couch, with his head in her lap, and a soft melody played on the stereo. He'd been quiet all evening, trying to hide a solemn demeanor behind forced smiles and conversations, pretending to listen to her, nodding on cue. But Ruth knew that he was only going through the motions, watching her lips move and not listening to a word she was saying. But even that wasn't enough to shut her up. Ruth continued talking and laughing at her own jokes, hoping that something she'd say would snap him out of whatever mood he was in. She'd never seen this side of him, brooding. It made her uncomfortable because she had no idea where it was coming from, or where it was headed. He said it was his job and she prayed that was all it was. They were working him too hard, always flying him off to California, then back here just long enough to change his underwear. Meanwhile, Ruth had to catch up with him when and where she could just to get a glimpse, a whiff, a taste of him. Bernie teased her and constantly called her whipped. Hell, Ruth couldn't argue with that.

"You've been quiet all evening, honey. You okay?" she asked, running the tip of her thumb softly over his forehead.

He'd taken off into orbit until the sound of her voice reminded him it was time to come home. "Yeah. I'm just tired." He sighed. "This trip really took a lot out of me. The project's almost finished and we go live in a few weeks. Everybody's tripping and worrying that we won't be ready."

"Will you be ready?"

"Damn right we will be," he suddenly snapped. "I've worked my ass off to make sure of that."

"Well, I've got faith, if it's any consolation. I know you can do it." Ruth smiled.

"I have done it, Ruth. Bottom line. And I've done it in less than two months." The edginess in his voice was obvious. Ruth tried not to take it personally, but it wasn't easy.

"That's wonderful, Adrian, it is, and now I understand why you've been so tired." Ruth was starting to sound condescending and it was getting on his nerves.

Why'd she have to show up tonight? he wondered. More important, why'd he bother telling her he'd be back in town today? Adrian sat up abruptly and gulped down his glass of wine. "No. You have no idea."

"Okay, so maybe I don't," she said cautiously. "But I'm trying to. You've been under a lot of pressure lately and I do understand that. But it'll be over soon and we can take that trip together like we've been talking about."

"We'll see."

"We'll see? I thought—"

"I said, we'll see, Ruth," he said, not bothering to hide his annoyance. "I'm not sure what's going to happen after this project is completed. I might be assigned to another one real soon."

"But you can take a vacation, Adrian. Surely, your boss can understand that."

Adrian rubbed his eyes, signaling that he was tired and didn't want to talk about this. "It's getting late. I'm going to turn in." Adrian got up and put their glasses in the kitchen.

"You want me to stay?" she asked uneasily.

"That's up to you, Ruth." Adrian went into the bedroom, and left her sitting alone on the sofa.

Ruth was dumbfounded. Was that an argument? she wondered. And had that been an invitation?

Reluctantly, she followed him into the bedroom, unsure of whether or not she was welcome. "Have I done something . . . or said something? Are you mad at me?"

Adrian hung his head then let out an audible sigh. "No . . . Ruth. I told you, I'm tired, baby, that's all." He turned to her and tried to smile. As far as she was concerned, that was all the invitation she needed. An attempt at a smile was better than no smile at all and was enough encouragement for Ruth to interpret it into yes, he wanted her to spend the night.

While Adrian undressed, she snuck up behind him and wrapped her arms around his waist, then kissed that sensitive spot between his shoulder blades she knew drove him crazy and laughed when he squirmed. "Well, why don't you let me give you one of my famous massages? I'll run you a hot bath, wash your back, suck on your . . . the body part of your choosing, and rub you down with something that smells good. How's that sound?"

"Sounds wonderful. But you know you're going to put me right to sleep with all that."

"That's the idea, baby. You need some rest," she said soothingly.

He kept his promise and Adrian fell asleep as soon as that warm oil touched his back, but she didn't mind. She'd had a pretty rough week too and getting a good night's sleep wasn't a bad idea. She always slept like a baby with him, and had gotten used to it because when he was in town, they slept together almost every night.

Early the next morning, Ruth woke up in time to see Adrian getting dressed. "What time is it, Adrian?"

"Hey, baby." He leaned down and kissed her. "I didn't mean to wake you."

"You didn't, but it's early. Where are you going? I thought we would have breakfast together."

"I've got to go into the office for a few hours and finish up some things. I've got a meeting in the morning, so—"

"Can't you finish it here? I can make breakfast, then leave right after and I won't bother you. Promise."

"You know better than that. I can't get any work done with you around, Ruth." He smiled.

"But I won't bother you, Adrian, and I'll go home right after breakfast. I've missed you. C'mon, baby," she pleaded. "We've hardly seen each other at all. Don't you miss me too?"

"Every second we're not together, love." She was flattered, but still disappointed that he was leaving.

"Can't you stay for coffee? It wouldn't take long for me to—"

"Nope." He picked up his keys and headed out the bedroom door. "Lock up when you leave."

Ruth quickly jumped out of bed and hurried after him. "Will you call me later?"

"You know I will." Adrian kissed her and left.

Ruth waited all day, but he never called. So the next day, she called him, several times, but he never answered or returned any of her messages.

Life had a way of rushing at a man like a tidal wave sometimes. Adrian sat alone in his apartment, in the dark, drinking a beer. His stereo was playing something he'd hoped would soothe the beast raging inside him. Hell yes, he was angry because he hadn't been more careful, because he hadn't known, because he had no idea what to do next. Or maybe, he did know what to do, but the option definitely didn't sit well with him. He stared at the phone, listening to it ring the way it had been ringing all evening, and without answering, he knew who it was. It was Ruth. The last person he wanted to talk to right now.

His mind was flooded with the events of his last trip, and nothing else mattered except what he'd been told. The woman had left a message on his cell phone, asking him to call her. It was important.

Lana. Voluptuous Lana, half black and half Korean, exotic. He'd met her the first time his company had sent him to California, in a bar at the hotel where he was staying. He couldn't take his eyes off her, and eventually it was pretty hard to keep his hands off her too. But it had always been casual between them; after all, he lived on one coast, and she on the other. Neither of them had a problem with the nature of their relationship. They hooked up sometimes when he was in town. Nothing more, nothing less. But he hadn't seen her at all since he and Ruth had gotten serious. Her message to call her had definitely stirred his curiosity.

In less than an hour after returning her call, she was standing in the doorway of his hotel room, still beautiful and very pregnant. She sat on the couch, watching him pace back and forth, grilling her for answers that made some kind of sense. How did she know it was his? How could he be sure?

"It's been eight months, Lana. You couldn't have told me about this before now?"

"I hadn't planned on telling you at all," she said quietly. "But that wouldn't have been fair. Especially not to my baby."

Adrian had insisted on a paternity test and in an instant, his life had been turned upside down. He'd been careful to plan and control every aspect of his life. It was a design that he'd lived by for thirty-six years. Looking at Lana, feeling his child moving in her stomach, Adrian realized just how much this baby would impact his life.

"We have to do something about this," he'd said to Lana.

"Well, I think we're both adult enough to work out visitation, support," she reasoned.

"That's not enough," Adrian said firmly.

Lana folded her arms defensively across her chest, bracing herself for where she suspected he was taking this conversation. "What is enough, Adrian? What are you telling me?"

Fathers—good ones—raised their children. They provided for them, taught them, guided them, and he'd be damned if he'd do that every other holiday and summer vacations.

"I'm telling you that I need a bigger role in this."

"You're the father, Adrian. I'd say that's a pretty big role."

Adrian thought for a moment before blurting out his idea. "I could relocate."

Lana stared at him in disbelief. She was speechless that he'd even suggest such a thing. Adrian couldn't believe he'd suggested it either.

"You'd move here?"

He shrugged. "That's my kid, Lana. I've got to help raise it too, and I can't do that all the way from Florida."

The subject of marriage even came up during the conversation. Lana was the voice of reason on that topic.

"We're not in love, Adrian."

"I'm just saying, we should consider it."

"I won't rush into anything like that."

"We don't have to rush, Lana. Let's just see."

"No promises?"

"Not yet."

Adrian's phone rang again, interrupting his memories. He heard Ruth's voice over his answering machine.

"Adrian? I'm worried about you, baby. I tried your cell phone, but . . . Will you just call me and let me know you're all right? Please? I love you."

She did love him. He loved her too, and Adrian knew somebody's heart would end up broken. Hers. And his. Some things were bigger than love, though. Responsibility to his kid, that was a priority now. As much as he wanted to go back and pick up the pieces of his life where he'd left them before finding out, Adrian knew better. Men didn't run from their responsibilities, they ran *to* them. He'd been careless making a baby with a woman he didn't love, but his child wouldn't pay for that mistake. He'd see to that.

Fleeting Thoughts

MAY HAD SAID SHE WANTED SOME COMPANY, BUT FROM THE WAY she was acting, Ruth wasn't so sure that coming over had been a good idea. May spent all afternoon screaming at the kids, slamming pots and pans around the kitchen and clenching her jaws tight enough to grind her teeth into powder.

"What's wrong, May?" Ruth asked, watching her slam a hot cup of tea down in front of her.

"Nothing," she grumbled back. Ruth must've asked her that half a dozen times since she'd arrived and had gotten the same response every time.

"Allan!" May screamed to the boy in the other room. "Get yo' ass in here and take out that trash like I told you, boy!"

Allan walked into the kitchen, mumbled something under his breath and gathered up his prize to take to the Dumpster.

"How many times I got to repeat myself before I get you to do something?" she snapped, watching him drag the trash out the back door. "And clean that room when you finish!"

"Momma?" Shannon asked holding out a book for her mother. "Momma I can't—"

May impatiently swished her out of the room. "Can't you see Momma's tryin' to talk, baby? I ain't got time for that right now." Ruth watched the little girl's eyes fill with disappointment. May collapsed in the chair next to Ruth, only Ruth wasn't sure that she was in the mood to talk to May anymore.

"Girl, those kids are gettin' on my last nerve. I swear they are."

"Your period coming?"

May's eyes narrowed. "No, Ruth. My period ain't comin'." May sipped on her tea and neither of them said anything for several minutes.

"How's Adrian?" May asked shortly, giving Ruth the impression that she really didn't give a damn, but had only brought him up to make conversation.

"Not sure." Ruth shrugged. "I haven't seen much of him lately. He's been busy with work and some new project he's working on."

"He still flyin' back and forth to California?"

"All the time. I don't know, May. His job keeps him busy, it always has, but he's always found time to spend with me. I hope he's not losing interest in me . . . us."

"Is it that bad?"

Ruth smiled. "Probably not. I'm probably making a big deal out of nothing. But I'd be the first to admit, I'm paranoid. Especially when it comes to him. I miss him."

"You think he got somebody else?"

Ruth could practically see the wheels turning in May's head and no, she didn't appreciate what the woman was implying one bit. "No, I don't think that. I just said he's busy. I don't see him as much as I used to and I miss him." May took another sip of her tea. "I keep wondering if maybe I've said or done something—"

"He ain't said nothin'?"

She shook her head. "No. Just that when things settle down at work, we'll spend some time together. We've been together almost seven months now. Doesn't seem that long. I don't know what I'd do if he wasn't in my life. I hate not seeing him, but I'm trying not to smother him. Adrian's like those potato chips. Can't eat just one. Gotta eat the whole damn bag." Ruth laughed. "If he were food, I'd be big as a house." She paused. "You think it would be crazy if I proposed?"

May didn't say a word. She just stared off into nothingness trying hard to hold her tongue. Some women were too quick to close their eyes to the obvious. May couldn't help but feel annoyed at Ruth for her idealistic view of Adrian. He was a man, wasn't he? A man flying in and out of town doing only God knew what with God knew who back in California. Of course, there was another woman. Only Ruth was too damn blind to see it. Of all people, she should've known better. Men knew how to betray better than any other animal on the planet. Ruth should've learned that from her first husband.

"What's wrong, May? And don't tell me nothing."

May waited for Allan to finish lining the trash can with a new bag and leave the room before finally answering her question. "You wanna know what's wrong?"

"I wouldn't have spent all day asking if I didn't."

May slumped back in her chair and looked as if she were about to cry. Ruth looked concerned. "May? Honey, what's wrong?"

Tears filled the brim of her eyes. "That son-of-a-bitch!" May hissed, biting down on her bottom lip.

"Who? Who, May?"

"Jefferson."

"Jeff?" Ruth looked surprised. "What's going on? Has he done something to you?"

"He's out of town on business too. Only—"

"Only . . . what?"

"I ain't as sure of him as you are of Adrian. I think he might have somebody." May choked back the urge to completely break down in front of Ruth.

"Oh . . . no, May," Ruth said, trying to reassure her. "No, he wouldn't do that. You know how much he loves you. Why would he do something like that?"

May stared back at Ruth in disbelief. Because that's what men do. May had grown up with it. She'd seen it her whole life and watched the women in her family turn their backs to it like it wasn't happening. She'd had to do it too, with Frank.

"*Long as he payin' the bills, May, and takin' care of his chil'ren, you shouldn't fuss at him like you do. Frank is a good man, but he jus' a man, nonetheless. He love you and them kids. That's what matters.*"

Ruth continued to try and reassure May. "Jeff loves you, sweetie. He'd never cheat on you. He's not like other men."

"Will you listen to yo'self, Ruth? My God, you can't be that naive, not after all the things you been through."

May had a distant look in her eyes, and Ruth was starting to feel uncomfortable. She had no idea where this woman was coming from all of a sudden.

"May, I just think that you're overreacting. That's all. I'm sure that it's just a business trip and—"

"And I ain't blind, even if you are."

Ruth resented May's assumptions. "You don't have to go there."

"No . . . no I don't," May said apologetically. "I'm sorry."

Ruth wasn't convinced that she really meant it.

"May. Jeff loves you and the kids more than anything. Of course he's not with another woman. You know he's not."

May sat quietly for a moment. Ruth must've thought she looked like a fool, ranting and raving over what probably appeared to be nothing to her. Sometimes, May felt foolish too. Sometimes, she felt like she was being torn in half. Either her mind was playing tricks on her, and she was truly paranoid, or all her suspicions were correct and her husband was being unfaithful. She wrestled between these two dynamics more and more as time went on, hoping neither of them would ever be proven true.

"I can't help how I feel, Ruth," she said quietly.

"Well, do you have proof that he's been cheating?"

May shook her head. "Suspicions"—her voice quivered—"but that's all."

"And you're willing to let suspicions ruin your marriage?" Ruth asked gravely.

"That's not what I'm trying to do!" May said angrily. "I don't want to lose my husband, Ruth! You don't think I know how easy it would be to push him out the door by actin' like this? If he saw me trippin' like this . . . Why do you think I keep my mouth shut?" She started to cry.

Ruth couldn't believe it. May was having her own little private breakdown in front of everybody, but nobody knew because she was having it inside herself.

"Honey," Ruth said calmly. "I really do think you're overreacting. Maybe you need to talk to someone, a counselor or—"

"Fuck you, Ruth," May said icily, storming away from the table, and pacing the kitchen floor like a lion in a cage. "You ain't got room to tell me I'm overreactin', Ruth. Lord knows what Adrian's doin' out there in San Francisco all this time."

Ruth had had enough and picked up her purse to leave. "You know, I think I'd better—"

"How the hell you know he ain't fuckin' some bitch while he out there? He ain't been fuckin' you has he? Well? Has he?"

Just then the phone rang, and May sprinted across the kitchen to answer it. "Hello? Jeff? Jeff . . . baby. I been waitin' on you to call. How come you didn't call me earlier?" she said, in her softest, sweetest, honey-dipped voice. She was so wrapped up in her conversation with him, she didn't even notice Ruth leave. On her way out, Ruth saw the kids sitting in the living room. The television was on, but neither of them were watching it. Shannon sat quietly at one end of the coffee table, coloring and lost in a world that didn't include three dimensional characters or emotionally unbalanced mothers, while Allan slumped down in the leather sofa, thumping his fingers against the basketball he held in his lap, his eyes fixed on a spot on the wall he'd probably hurl it at, if he knew he could get away with it. She wondered if they went through this kind of drama every time Jeff went away on business. If so, she felt sorry for them.

Just because May wasn't in the mood for company didn't mean Ruth wasn't. Bernie answered the door still wearing her nightgown. "You still asleep? Girl, it's one o'clock in the afternoon," Ruth teased.

Bernie grunted a vague hello, then left Ruth standing in the open door while she poured herself a cup of coffee. Ruth knew that if Bernie was just getting out of bed, then someone had spent the night here. She quickly scanned the house, on guard in case she saw someone run through the place naked.

"He's gone," Bernie said, blowing on her cup of coffee. "You want a cup?"

"No, thank you. Who was he?"

Bernie didn't bother answering. It really didn't matter who he'd been. "Where you on your way to this early?"

"It's not early, Bernie, and I've just come from May's."

"How is Miss Queen of Florida and her big, new house?"

"There you go again."

"You know I'm just kidding."

"She's . . . flipping out."

Bernie's eyes lit up like Christmas lights. "Really? Like how?"

"I think she just misses Jefferson. He's been out of town on business a lot lately and it's getting to her."

"I'm not surprised. She acts like the type that needs a man around all the time."

"Bernie, you need a man around all the time too."

"For fuckin', Ruth. I like to fuck. Love to fuck, and yes, I need a man in order to do that the way I like it done."

"So, you need one for fucking and May loves Jefferson. You're no different than she is. Than most of us, as a matter of fact."

"Us? Wasn't that long ago when you didn't need a man. Perfectly happy without one if I remember correctly."

"That was a long time ago, before I knew what it was to be with a real man like Adrian." Ruth grinned.

"Here we go," Bernie said, rolling her eyes. "Good to the very last drop?" She raised her cup in a toast.

"I know that's right."

"Does he eat it, Ruth?" Bernie asked, leaning forward and looking devilish. " 'Cause if a man don't go downtown, he might as well put back on his clothes and get the hell out."

Ruth laughed. "You are so—"

"Right?"

"Yes. Absolutely, and he's great at downtown."

"Make your eyes roll up in your head?"

"Stop."

"Does he?"

"Yes."

"Keep him."

Baby Mine

LATELY, HER NERVES HAD BEEN ON EDGE AND THERE WAS AN uneasiness flowing through her veins. She'd been trying to ignore her feelings, but it was becoming harder to do. Ruth sensed a shift occurring in her small universe. Adrian seemed to be pulling away from her and she had no idea why. He wouldn't talk to her except to say that he was tired, or busy, promising that they'd talk later, but later never came. Most of the time she'd sit at home waiting for the phone to ring, hoping it was him and hoping things would be back to normal again. When that didn't happen, she'd go to bed and try not to think about losing him. But today he surprised her. Today he rang her doorbell and Ruth knew that their relationship had to be back on track.

"I should've called first," he said apologetically. "But I came straight from the airport." Adrian scooped her up into his arms. "Damn! I've missed you, baby." He took hold of her hands, pressed them against his face and kissed each of her palms. "I know I haven't been spending much time with you lately. So much has been going on and I've had a lot on my mind," he whispered. "Work's been kicking my ass."

"Oh . . . baby. I know you've been busy. I understand," she lied. "Whatever's on your mind you can talk to me about it, Adrian. You can always talk to me."

He shook his head. "Right now you're all that's on my mind, Ruth." She saw in his face that he was genuinely happy to see her.

She heard in his voice that he had missed her, but there was something in his eyes, something about his vibe that kept her from being completely convinced.

"We'll talk later, Ruth. Right now I just want to—"

Adrian undressed her, then himself, and laid her down on the floor. He kissed her tenderly on her face, neck, breasts, and then gently spread her legs and buried his handsome face between them, making love to her with his tongue. Adrian didn't hurry and she knew how much he enjoyed the taste of her as much as she enjoyed the sensation of him. Juices flowed from her like a flood and he lapped them up like he was dying of thirst. Adrian held her thighs in his hands and she held his head in hers. "Oooooo . . . Adrian. That's feels so good, baby," she whispered. "Don't stop, Adrian. Please . . . make me cum. Make me cum all over you."

"Mmmmmm," he moaned. How long had it been? Too long. He'd missed her so much, but Adrian had let his problems create a gap between them. He hadn't planned on stopping by. Keeping his distance had been critical to his sanity and to hers, even if she didn't realize it. But he just hadn't been able to stay away any longer.

"Adrian!" she screamed.

Adrian hovered over her, smiling. "Damn! You are sweet, Ruth. Taste it, baby." He leaned down to kiss her. "Taste how sweet you are." She inhaled her own scent on his lips as he eased himself inside her and then laid perfectly still, savoring their connection. Adrian kissed her, caressed her, and stared deeply into her eyes, reaffirming his love for her and easing any doubts she might've had that something had been terribly out of place between them.

"I love you, Adrian," Ruth whispered. "I love you so . . . so much." Could he feel it? Oh, he had to be able to feel it emanating from her pores, seeping out all over him. She held him as close to her as she could, wrapping her legs around him, pleading silently to God not to take him from her. Losing him wasn't an option. Whatever had been bothering him, whatever problems he had been having, she wanted to be there for him. She wanted to be his woman and help him work through them. No matter how difficult or impossible things might've appeared to him. Ruth would and could do anything for Adrian Carter. He had to know that.

Afterward, Ruth made him a drink and they curled up on the couch next to each other. "I don't know, Ruth. If I don't get some time off soon—" he said, sounding drained.

But it was more than just his job. Adrian had the weight of his problems on his mind and that's what was wearing him out. He and Lana had been going back and forth on whether or not he should move to the West Coast, until finally, he made the decision for both of them. And sooner rather than later, he'd have to tell Ruth he was leaving. But not tonight, he thought gazing into those big, beautiful eyes of hers. Tonight he'd pushed all his other issues aside and the only thing that mattered was the two of them. Adrian was what he was. A selfish son-of-a-bitch and he knew it. He'd always known it. Coming here hadn't been about her. Adrian swallowed hard at that silent confession. As much as he loved her, he knew that he'd hurt her by distancing himself, and he knew that very soon, he'd have to hurt her again. But for now, he needed her. He also knew that this would be the last time they'd be together like this.

Pandora's Box

❧

IT WAS LATE AND RUTH WAS EXHAUSTED. AS USUAL, SHE WAS the last one to leave the office and yes, late nights at the firm were definitely getting old. It had gotten to the point that she felt guilty if she left work before seven, which was a damn shame. She'd even put off becoming a full-time student for another semester. Ruth still wanted to get her degree, but it hadn't been that easy walking away from a full-time salaried job into the unknown.

Adrian had called earlier and asked if he could stop by later that evening. Of course she said yes, then wondered why he'd even bothered asking. It wasn't like she'd ever told him no. Ruth decided to stop by the market on the way home to pick up some catfish. Adrian loved her fried catfish.

The parking lot wasn't completely empty but damn near. As she approached her car, she noticed something on the hood. It was a package. Daisies.

"Heh . . . heh . . . heh." Ruth turned in time to see Eric getting out of his car. "Hey, Ruthie. I thought you'd get a kick out of this." He walked over to her and a chill ran down her spine freezing her where she stood. He hadn't been able to think about anything else since he'd seen her at the store that day. Ruth looked good. Damn good, and he'd remembered how much of a good woman she'd been to him. After she'd sold the house, she hadn't given him a new address. Not that he'd needed one. It had taken just one phone call to confirm what he'd suspected was true.

"Yeah, I'd like to speak to Ruth Ash . . . I mean, Johnson. Ruth Johnson."

"She just left for lunch. Would you like to leave a message on her voicemail?"

"Yes." He smiled. "Yes, I would." Before he finished listening to her greeting, Eric hung up.

"You remember the first time I gave you daisies? Damn!" He rubbed his chin. "You were fresh outta school back then. Weren't you? Fine as I don't know what. Just like now." Eric stared her up and down, then licked his lips.

All of a sudden, Ruth understood the uneasiness she'd been feeling flowing through her veins these past few weeks. She'd told herself that she was being ridiculous, and that her mind was playing tricks on her, giving her glimpses of a ghost she'd exorcised years ago. That meeting in the store . . . had it really been just a coincidence? Or, had he known where she was all along? Had he been following her all this time?

Ruth could tell by the expression on his face that Eric believed it really was this easy for him. Had it always been? Yes. He'd never had to work hard to get her and his confidence screamed that to the world. He wouldn't be here if he thought it would be hard. Daisies, a smile, and a compliment. Mix those ingredients with the desperate need she had for somebody to love her and the perfect love potion was created: deception. "You lookin' a little tired, baby. Like you been workin' too hard again. How many times I got to tell you all that ain't necessary?" Eric made himself comfortable, leaning his back against her car.

Ruth swallowed hard. She hadn't seen him in months and had convinced herself that God had answered her prayer and dropped him off the side of the earth. "What do you want, Eric?"

"What do I want?" Eric smiled. "What the hell kinda question is that, Ruthie? What do I want? What do you think I want?" His gaze burned into her like the butt of a cigarette. She'd never been able to fully understand Eric, but over the years she'd learned to anticipate him. His words never matched his actions. He'd say something nice to her, but then do something horrible and in the end she would be left confused but obedient.

"I have no idea."

"I jus' wanted to drop you off them flowers, Ruthie. Anything wrong with that? A pretty woman got to have pretty flowers." He picked them up and held them out to her, but Ruth didn't dare take them.

"I don't want your flowers, Eric. It's getting late and I've really got to be going."

Eric stared into her eyes. "I got these for you, baby. I ain't leavin' till I give 'em to you."

Reluctantly, she took them from him.

Ruth unlocked the door to her car, but Eric didn't budge. He stood there, looking offended. "Man, can't I even get a 'thank you'?" he asked leaning close to her putting his ear next to her mouth. "I can't hear you, Ruthie."

"Thank you, Eric," she said stiffly.

He laughed. "You very welcome, Ruthie. You know . . . we should hook up sometime. Jus' to talk, that's all. I mean, I know you got yo'self a new man these days. Don't you?" Of course he knew she was seeing someone. Eric always knew everything. "Fancy mothafucka' too. Damn! What kind of car is that he drivin'? A Benz? Always sportin' 'round in them expensive ass suits. He ain't cheap, that's for damn sure." He laughed again. "He treatin' you right? Better be. You a good woman and he better 'preciate it. You was always a good woman, Ruthie. I always thought so." He looked sad for a moment. "But . . . my dumb ass didn't 'preciate it at the time. I know I was wrong 'bout a lot of things, Ruthie. What they say 'bout hindsight? It's twenty-twenty." He chuckled. "That shit's clear as day now, baby. Believe that. I ain't the man I used to be, baby girl. That's for damn sure. Losin' you . . . hell! Like somebody cut off my arm, Ruth. My world ain't been worth a damn without you in it. So. He good to you?"

Tears rested inside her eyelids threatening to fall at any second. Wouldn't this merry-go-round ever stop? Standing there listening to this bullshit, she was reminded of how many times she'd heard it all before and how many times it had lured her back into that marriage. *Oh, Ruth. What a sad fool you've been and the worst thing is, he sees the fool in you too.*

"He's very good to me," she said softly. *Now, let me have this, Eric,* she pleaded with her eyes. *If you have one thread of sincerity inside you, leave me alone and let this be enough for you to disappear out of my life forever.*

"I could be good to you, Ruthie. I know I could, girl." He gazed into her eyes like he always did just before he told another lie. "I mean it, Ruthie. Things would be different this time, baby."

"Eric—"

"No, baby. Listen to me, Ruthie. Jus' listen to me for one minute."

"I've got to get home, Eric," she said, opening her car door. Eric leaned up against it and closed it.

"I know, baby. But look, we got a lot of years between us, Ruthie," he said earnestly. "Now, it wasn't good all the time, baby, and that's my fault. I know this now. I know what I did wrong and I know how to fix it. All I'm askin' for is a chance."

"No."

"A chance to show you how good I can be to you, Ruth. That's all. I've changed, baby. I'm not the same man I used to be back then and I can prove it to you, if you jus' give me another chance. Jus' one more—"

"To do what? Kick my ass again?" Ruth blurted out.

"How many times I got to say I'm sorry for that?" Frustration rose up in his voice.

"You never meant those apologies, Eric! Not once did you ever say I'm sorry, Ruth and mean it! Not once," she said.

"So? I'm fo' real this time, Ruthie. I'm sorry, baby. I'm sorry 'bout all that." Eric was desperate. Desperate to convince her that he'd changed and things would be different between them, but she was desperate too. Desperate to get as far away from him as possible.

"What kind of fool do you think I am? You've said that a million times before, Eric and—"

"And this time I mean it, Ruthie. I lost the most important thing I ever had when I lost you, girl. Lord knows I did. A man can't help but change when he lose the only thing in his life that ever meant a damn to him." Before Ruth realized what was happening, Eric pulled her to him and pressed his lips against hers. Disgust surged through her body like lightning and she yanked away from him, and slapped him across his face and shoulders with his damn daisies.

"Don't you ever touch me again!" she screamed. "Don't put your hands on me, Eric! Don't you—"

"Bitch!" Eric growled and pushed her away from him. "You lost yo' mothafuckin' mind, Ruth?" He balled his hand into a fist and Ruth hurried to get inside her car. In the distance she could hear voices. He heard them too. A group of men were coming out of the building into the parking lot. Eric dropped his fist to his side and glared back at her with an expression that was all too familiar. It was filled with contempt and hate and promises. He hurried back to his car and sped out of the parking lot.

It wasn't over. This wasn't the last she'd see of him. Realizing this, Ruth slumped into the front seat of her car, too shaken to move, and sat there until she finally stopped crying and drove home.

Twenty minutes after she arrived at her apartment, Adrian knocked on the door. The moment she laid eyes on him, Ruth wrapped her arms around him and held on to him with all her strength.

"I'm glad to see you too, baby," he said holding her.

"I've missed you."

"Obviously." He smiled.

Adrian's arms around her were all she needed to feel secure again. Of course she had to tell him about Eric, and of course he'd hate hearing it because Adrian despised drama. But she couldn't ignore what had happened today and Ruth was afraid to think of what he'd do next. Adrian had to be prepared, like she'd have to be prepared. Eric knew too much about him. He knew what kind of car he drove, how he looked, and Ruth had to warn him of what Eric was capable of.

"I've got something important to talk to you about, baby." His tone was serious and a solemn expression washed over his face.

"And there are some things I have to tell you too, Adrian," Ruth said nervously.

Adrian took her hand and led her to the sofa. His expression was serious and as anxious as she was to tell him about her encounter with Eric, she was more anxious for him to open up to her and finally tell her what had really been bothering him.

"What's going on, Adrian? Talk to me."

He sighed deeply. "A lot's been going on lately, Ruth."

"With work. I know."

"And other things."

"What other things, Adrian?"

Adrian leaned forward and rested his elbows on his thighs. He stared straight ahead and Ruth could see how tired he really was. "You know about the California project and how hard I've been working to get the system up and running?"

"You said it's almost finished, though."

"It is, but—" He sat back and draped his arm over the back of the sofa.

"But what, baby?"

"I've been asked to relocate, Ruth."

"Relocate?" she asked, caught off guard. "To San Francisco?"

"Yes. The company figures that since I'm the one who designed and set up the system, it only makes sense that I should be the one managing it, and I think they're right. It's been my project from the beginning and I'm not ready to hand it over to somebody else. Not yet."

The knots in her stomach were turning into boulders and to say this had been a bad day would be the understatement of the year. "When would they want you to move?"

He hesitated. "Soon. Within the next couple of weeks."

"Do you want to go?"

He shrugged. "There's a big bonus attached to it and like I said, I'm not ready to give it up. It's a huge project and I'd be heading up a whole department, at least on the technology side of the house."

"It's a promotion?"

"A huge promotion. Director of IS." He smiled.

Was that what had been bothering him all this time? Ruth wanted to laugh, not at him, but at herself. All this time she'd been afraid that she might be losing this man and this was it? This was nothing. Relocating, moving could be the answer for both of them. He'd get his promotion and she'd be away from Eric once and for all. More important, they'd be together.

"Are you worried about our relationship being long distance? Because if you are, I love San Francisco and I could pack up and move—"

His expression was serious. "No, Ruth. I can't ask you to do that."

"You're not asking. I'm volunteering, Adrian. If that's all this is about, moving, I mean, that's nothing, baby. That's no big deal for me. I just want us to be together and—"

Adrian put his finger to her lips. "Let me finish, Ruth." The tone in his voice was grave, and the relief she'd felt a moment ago was gone.

"Finish? There's more?"

He stood up and walked to the other side of the room, burying his hands deep in his pockets. What else could there be? Ruth didn't like the look on his face. Whatever else he was going to say wasn't good news. "On one of the first trips I took to San Francisco, I met someone." Someone? That wasn't so bad. She was sure he'd met lots of "someones." So, why did he look as if he were about to break her heart?

"It wasn't serious, but we spent some time together off and on for a few months." He glanced quickly at Ruth, then turned away.

Suddenly she felt like she'd been kicked in the stomach and Ruth asked the next logical question, knowing that his answer could crush her. "You're in love with her?"

"I didn't say that," he said calmly.

"So . . . what are you saying? Why are you telling me this?" Her heart beat like bongos in her chest and she prayed for him to say something, anything to set her at ease and reassure her that she was the only woman in the world that he could be happy with.

"We stopped seeing each other not long after you and I met, but recently I found out that . . . she's pregnant, Ruth. Almost eight months." Adrian stared at Ruth. "Before you even ask, yes . . . it's mine."

"Pregnant?" Ruth was stunned.

"I found out about the baby a month ago. She called the office and left a message for me to call her back. She said it was important, so I called her and that's when she told me. The baby's due soon and I have to be there. Hell, I want to be there, Ruth."

As soon as he said that the truth stood naked right in front of her eyes. "Did you ask to relocate, Adrian?" He didn't answer, but it was painfully obvious to her now. "I need to know. Are you in love with this woman?"

"No . . . I'm not. But I'm in love with this baby. I'm nearly forty years old, Ruth, and honestly, I was beginning to think—"

"That you wouldn't have children?" That was what this was about, wasn't it? Children. Adrian was like most people, feeling the need to perpetuate his own existence outside of a computer program and a boast that he'd live forever in a miniature version of himself. Ruth understood how he felt. "But I can give you children," she said desperately. "If you wanted a baby, all you had to do was tell me and I can give you a child, Adrian. I'll push out a whole football team for you if that's what you want."

He shook his head and looked at her with sympathy in his eyes. He'd sworn never to hurt her, but that was exactly what he was doing, and it was breaking his heart. "Baby, don't do this."

"Do what? Break down because my man is leaving me for another woman? Because she's pregnant?"

"It's not her I'm leaving for, Ruth. Right or wrong, she's not the reason," he tried to explain.

"Then, you are moving?" Her voice quivered.

"I'm doing what I feel I have to do, Ruth. I don't want to be a voice over the telephone. I can't live like that. I was raised in a family and I want to raise my children that way. With both parents in the picture."

"And what about me, Adrian? What about us? Exactly what does this mean for you and me?"

"Put it together, Ruth. What do you think it means?" he asked matter-of-factly.

It meant the end of everything she'd held dear to her heart since she'd first laid eyes on him. Hope. Love. Possibilities.

"I never meant for you to get hurt in all this, Ruth. You've got to believe that," Adrian said sincerely, hoping to convince her that he meant it. Hoping that it would somehow help ease her pain.

The weight of the day was heavy and Ruth felt drained. All she wanted to do was close her eyes and turn back the clock to the last time he'd held her, made love to her. And that was where she'd stop time. At that moment.

"Doesn't matter what I believe, does it? You've made up your mind about what you want to do. What the fuck does it matter what I believe, Adrian?"

"What do you expect me to do, Ruth? Send a check every month and visit on weekends?"

"And you and I are over, just like that? Nice and neat all wrapped up in a little box? 'Sorry Ruth, but I've got me somebody else' and that's all there is to it?"

"That's not all there is to it, Ruth. You ought to know me better than that. I've been wrestling with this for weeks now and it's been tearing me up inside! You know what you mean to me. You know how much I love you."

"Then don't do this to me, Adrian! Please. Don't do this. Not now." Because her maniac was back and he was after her again, and with Adrian gone who could she run to? Who could she hide behind? Who would protect her? And finally, who could she give herself to simply because she wanted to?

"There's nothing else I can do, Ruth. Believe me, honey. If I felt there was another way—"

"There are other ways, Adrian. Lots of other options, and together, we can come up with some, but we can't if you walk away from me like this. Don't walk away from us, Adrian. Please," Ruth begged.

"Ruth, I've already made up my mind," he said soberly. Adrian took a deep breath, and then held it, before slowly releasing it from between his lips. He'd always been guilty of over emphasizing the absolute, especially when it came to making decisions. He'd learned that from his father.

"When a man makes a decision, he needs to know that it's final. Right or wrong, good or bad. And everybody else around him needs to know, it's not up for discussion."

Fair or not, he'd made up his mind, and his decision hurt him as much as he knew it hurt her. But indecision on this matter wasn't an option. There was too much at stake, and cutting his losses, his love, was the sacrifice he knew he had to make, in order to do what he felt was best. Adrian sat down next to Ruth, took her hand and held it between his. He raised it to his mouth, and held it there for a moment.

"I'm not here to discuss my options," he explained, quietly. "I really don't see that I have any, baby."

"Of course you do," Ruth said, desperate to try and reason with him.

He stared into her eyes. "None that I can live with."

Ruth swallowed hard, and pulled back her hand. "Meaning me? You can't live with me? Are you going to marry this woman?" He looked away. "Adrian?"

"After the baby is born—"

"After the baby is born . . . what?"

"Yes, we're planning on it."

Blessings were like fragile pieces of handblown glass. If you squeezed too hard, they shattered into a million, tiny pieces. "You son-of-a— We made love right here not more than a week ago, Adrian! How could you make love to me knowing you were going to leave? Knowing all the time, you were planning to marry somebody else? What the hell is that?"

"This has been the hardest thing I've ever had to do in my life, Ruth! I love you and God knows I want you."

"You can have me!" she said, pressing her palms to her chest.

"But I can't walk away from this. This is my responsibility, and as a man, I've got to take care of it."

"Then take care of it! But don't let us go in the process! You don't have to do that! It doesn't have to go this far."

"It has gone this far, Ruth. I've got a kid that's going to be here in a month. It's gone that far already. I've got to be there. I can't do anything else." Adrian walked to the front door. "I'm only doing what I feel is right, which isn't always easy. You can believe me, or you don't have to, but I'll love you forever, baby. That's all there is to that."

He closed the door and left Ruth behind to fall apart.

———

Adrian sat in his car outside her apartment for several minutes before he realized he'd left something in her apartment. He turned the key in the ignition and slowly pulled out onto the road knowing it wouldn't do any good to go back and get it; after all, it belonged to her anyway, and he'd left it sitting right there in her lap. His heart.

One More Time

❧

BERNIE LAY NEXT TO MILES, STARING UP AT THE CEILING OF HER
bedroom. He'd come by earlier, without calling, without warning,
gathered her up in his arms and carried her to bed, then made love
to her. That's what it had been, lovemaking. And she'd let him. The
room was dark, but she could tell that he wasn't asleep either.

Bernie broke the silence. "It was just sex, Miles," she said softly.

"That's a lie and you know it."

"I haven't changed. You know where I stand. I'm not looking to
settle down with anybody, including you. Especially you."

Miles tenderly took her hand in his, raised it to his lips, and kissed
it. He sighed.

"Is your chicken ass still too scared to admit it, Bernie?"

"Admit what?" Bernie asked, turning to him.

"That you love me, or, at least, you could if you let yourself."

"You really are full of yourself, aren't you?"

"No," he whispered. "I'm full of you. So full in fact, that I drove
my ass over here straight from work, and knocked on your door,
halfway expecting you to slam it in my face."

"And that's what I don't get. I've gone out of my way to treat you
like shit, baby. What? You like being abused?"

Miles laughed. "When are you going to realize that I'm not scared of
you, woman? You might have all those other mothafuckas shaking in
their shorts, but you're full of shit, Bernie, and I know it. You know it too."

Bernie couldn't help but laugh. "I'm mean as an alley cat, Miles. You better watch it."

"And I'm a junkyard dog, baby. I got your alley cat."

"Oh please. You're a pushover, and all I ever have to do is say jump Miles, and your ass will be asking how high."

"If I jump, it's because I care about you. If I didn't, I'd tell your ass where to get off. You're on my good side, Bernie. You'd better count your blessings."

"Ooooh. I'm shaking in my panties."

"You should be. I ain't no pussy."

"You're too young for me."

"That's bullshit too." Miles turned to face her. "We're not perfect, Bernie, neither one of us. But we're perfect together, and that's all I know."

"You want us to be a couple, Miles, and that's not something I can do. Not now."

"Why not?"

Bernie was speechless. Before he'd come by, she'd had a host of reasons for not wanting to settle down with one man. Now, looking into his handsome face, she couldn't think of one. It had to be the testosterone, she concluded. Miles's was more potent than most, and as soon as it wore off she'd be back to her senses in no time.

"I'm not asking you to marry me, baby." He grinned. "Not yet, anyway. All I'm asking is that you give us a chance, Bernie. Throw away your little black book and I'll throw away mine."

"You don't have one."

Miles chuckled. "Yeah, right. But all I'm saying is let's get rid of all the outside influences, and concentrate on each other. It's not that hard."

"Maybe not to you."

"And not to you either. It's not fun anymore, Bernie. Maybe in the beginning, variety was the spice of life, but speaking for myself, I miss the familiar, baby. I miss having someone to call mine. Don't you?"

Bernie was quiet. She missed something, only she'd never given much thought to trying to figure out what that was. It was good having him here. And in retrospect, it had always been good. That's what she knew.

"I'm not making any promises."

"Then I don't need to be here," he said coolly.

"I'm just saying, we need to take this slow."

"Hell, I ain't in no hurry, Bernie."

"Me either."

Bernie kissed him softly on the lips. "Let me give you a sound piece of advice."

Miles smiled. "I'm listening."

"Once I commit myself to a man, I'm like a pit bull. I don't let go. But if I ever find out you're fucking up"—Bernie smiled—"I'll cut off your mothafuckin' dick."

Miles rolled over on his back and closed his eyes. "I wouldn't expect anything less from you, baby."

All I Know

CLARA'S HOME WAS AS COMFORTABLE AS HER PERSONALITY. She'd lived in her house for nearly twenty-five years, having shared it with husbands two and three and her daughter Carolyn, who was now married and living in D.C. with her husband and their two children who absolutely adored their "Nana." Ruth definitely couldn't blame them.

The two women sat on Clara's patio sipping on wine coolers, looking out into her garden filled with tulips and lilies, while watching evening blanket the sky. Ruth had come over hoping that Clara would have the answers she needed, or maybe the answers she wanted to hear. The kind that reassured her that Adrian was her soul mate and he had gone temporarily insane, but he would soon come back to his senses. Or the kind convincing her that it was as impossible for him to live without her as it was for her to live without him. All Ruth knew was that the last thing she wanted to hear was that she should just get over it because shit happened and that was the way life was. If she'd wanted to hear that, she'd have gone to Bernie's house instead of Clara's.

"Do you have any idea how much I love him, Clara?" Ruth asked, sorrow filling her voice.

"About as much as a woman can love a man, I suppose."

"This baby's important to him like all babies should be important. But I don't understand how he can let us go so easily."

"You know this wasn't easy for him. He put a lot of thought into this, Ruth. He told you that."

"He told me a lot of things, Clara. None of which mean a damn right now."

"You're hurt and there's nothing anybody can tell you that's going to make one bit of difference, Ruth. You're going to believe what you want to believe."

"Why couldn't he have come to me in the beginning? This whole thing isn't just about him; it's about me too, and I think he owed me that. He could've talked to me before making his decision. Adrian made up his mind for all our lives, me, him, that woman. How much you want to bet he talked to her about it? He left my ass in the dark while the two of them decided what my fate would be. You know that shit ain't fair."

"Now, you know you too old for that." Clara looked disapprovingly at Ruth. "Whoever told you life was fair?"

"Okay, but all I'm saying is, we could've come up with another solution. Maybe joint custody, or liberal visitation. He says he doesn't even love this woman. What kind of sense does that make? It's impossible to make a decent life with someone you don't love. I know because I tried and it can't be done," she reasoned. "Am I that wrong? Do you think I'm being selfish?"

"Sure you are, but I don't know a woman who wouldn't be."

"He's all I wanted, Clara. Adrian is literally the best thing to ever happen to me. He makes my life worth living. What am I supposed to do now?"

Clara frowned. "Making your life worth living was never his job, Ruth. Nobody deserves that kind of responsibility. That's something you're supposed to do for yourself."

"Maybe it's not his job, but that's how it is. Before he came along, I was content with nothing because it was better than being miserable with Eric. He made me feel like I was all that every time he looked at me."

"So, now that he's gone, you ain't all that?"

Ruth shrank down in her seat and shook her head. "You don't understand," she said, dismally.

"Oh, I understand all right. I understand you need to feel sorry for yourself now and that's fine. We all have to do that from time to time."

"I love him, Clara."

"How many ways are you going to tell me that? Loving him isn't going to change what's happened. Adrian's made a decision that unfortunately affects you and there's nothing you can do about it. The only thing you got any control over is you. You have to get on with your life, Ruth. Without him, baby."

"It's not that easy," she said, sadly.

"No. It isn't. But what else can you do?"

"That's like starting over from scratch. From where I left off with Eric."

"No, it's not, Ruth. You've come a long way from being the woman you were then and not just because of Adrian."

"He had a lot to do with it. More than he'll ever know."

"Why the hell does it have to fall on somebody else?" Clara said, exasperated. "Why do you always have to blame every problem you have on a man? First Eric and now Adrian. When are you going to learn, child? Men don't define who you are. *You're* supposed to do that."

"I don't know how to do that, Clara! It's either been all good or all bad. With Adrian it was all good and with Eric . . . my life sucked! So you tell me how I'm supposed to define myself? I wouldn't even know where to start."

"You need to get it in that hard head of yours, Ruth," she said sternly, pressing the tip of her finger against Ruth's forehead. "Everything you need to make it in this world is right here. Been here all along and nobody, not Eric, not Adrian got the power to take that away from you unless you let them."

"I'm not talking about—"

"I know what you're talking about, and yes, that bastard broke your heart," Clara said firmly. "Doesn't matter why he did it. He did it. But you're not any less of a woman without him, Ruth. Are you listening to me?"

"Yes, I'm listening." She sighed. "Basically, you're saying I need to get over it."

"Basically, that's all you can do. It won't be easy and it ain't going to happen tomorrow, but you can either get over it or be miserable for the rest of your life. That's up to you." Clara finished her wine cooler in one big, long gulp, then wiped her mouth with the back of her hand and belched.

"I always thought that if I ever fell in love, my whole world would suddenly fall into place. My man and I would do what we were supposed to do. Get married, have children, live happily ever after. The end."

"Most folks make the mistake of thinking that love fits nice and neat inside a jar, but it doesn't. It's big, sloppy, messy. Most of the time it doesn't even look like what we think love's supposed to look like. Most of the time, it can be downright ugly."

"Adrian used to tell me he loved me all the time," Ruth said reflectively.

"Adrian does love you, but he loves his child, and in his mind, he had to make a choice and he made it. May not be fair, but like I said, very few things in life are fair, which is why nobody is ever promised it will be."

Ruth smirked. "Well, somebody should promise something."

"Nobody can, because everybody's different with different aspirations, different needs. Everybody's got their own goddamned agenda, which means—"

"There are no guarantees with love."

"There are no guarantees . . . period."

Everything Clara had said made sense. Ruth could accept that. Maybe in time, she'd even be able to live it, but for now, all she knew was that she hurt all over. "I'd have walked on hot coals for him. All he ever had to do was ask. I'd have done anything for that man without hesitation or question. It was that good between us. How am I supposed to pretend it never happened?"

Clara placed her hand on Ruth's. "You're not supposed to erase it, Ruth."

"I wish I could. Be a whole lot easier," she said, wiping the tears from her face. "Here I go again feeling sorry for myself. You'd think I'd be tired of it by now." Ruth laughed.

"Child, ain't nothing wrong with feeling sorry for yourself. If you don't do it, who else will? Feel sorry for yourself right now, baby.

Everybody's supposed to mourn their losses. The hard part is knowing when it's time to stop mourning and get on with things."

"How will I know when it's time to stop?"

"Don't worry, dear, when everybody starts telling you they're sick and tired of hearing about it, that's a good sign that it's time for you to move on."

Funnel Cloud

HE WAS LOOKING FOR AN OPPORTUNITY, ANY OPPORTUNITY TO beat her ass. Ruth had tried telling herself that she'd been imagining things.

No, Ruth. That isn't Eric's car parked outside your apartment again. It just looks like it. Girl, you crazy? Of course he's not sitting across the street from your office building watching you hurry across the parking lot and into your car to speed home. And no, Ruth. That's not him you see in your rearview mirror.

Now she knew better. Ruth nervously fumbled around in her apartment, flipping channels on the television hoping to find something to watch that would take her mind off him. She dusted, cleaned out the refrigerator, refolded the towels in the linen closet, and from time to time, glanced out the window in her living room to see Eric's car parked outside her building, waiting. She hadn't felt this way in years; afraid, vulnerable, helpless.

Why was she so important to Eric? She'd asked herself that question a thousand times and could not come up with an answer that made any sense. He'd been with other women while they were married and while they weren't, but for some unknown reason, he'd always managed to migrate back to her. His first wife had put him out, and the woman he'd left Ruth for had walked out on him. Did he do this to them? she wondered. Did he beg them to forgive him and take him back? Did he threaten to kill them if they didn't? No, she concluded. Because neither of them played his game the way she did. When he'd hit Ruth, she seldom hit back. She never threw things or screamed at him. She never called the police. Instead, she'd taken her whoopings and tucked them away someplace safe where only he could get to them. Eric's mouth had always held the key. *"Bitch! Get yo' black ass in here! Yo' dumb ass must want my foot up yo' mothafuckin' pussy! Sorry ass, mothafuckin' ho!"*

She couldn't do this anymore. Ruth couldn't go back to living like that, ducking and hiding from Eric. But Eric was the one calling the shots, and it wasn't like he was going to get tired and go away. This was what he did better than anybody—make her life a living hell— and he wouldn't stop. Not until he'd gotten what he wanted, which was Ruth crawling around on the floor pleading with him to stop.

Ruth turned off all the lights, and sat quietly in the dark living room. Eric was still outside. She had some money saved up, and lately she'd been giving a lot of thought to leaving Jacksonville, and maybe even moving back home to Denver. She should've moved away a long time ago, and not just across town. Jacksonville was too small for the both of them. If she were going to move then she needed to do it right and get out of Florida altogether. That was the only way she would ever feel safe again. It was a good idea and Ruth decided on the spot to start making preparations as soon as possible.

She desperately needed to hear his voice and this time Ruth let the phone ring long enough for him to answer. "Adrian? It's me. Are you busy?"

Adrian hesitated before responding. "I was just on my way out. How've you been, Ruth?" *Call me 'baby,'* she begged in her mind. *Call me 'sweetheart,' like you used to, like you miss me, like you're happy to hear it's me on the other end of the phone.*

"I've . . . I miss you," she said apprehensively. "I've been trying not to call, but . . . I miss you."

"I've been trying not to call too." Adrian sounded regretful.

"Really? So, you thought about it? Calling me?" Ruth listened, straining to hear a hint of some sign that he'd changed his mind about moving away, or that he'd regretted ever telling her it was over, anything, to give her hope. "It's okay to call me, Adrian. I mean, if you want to talk, we always were able to—"

"Ruth, I was just on my way out. Can I call you later?"

"Will you call me later? I think that's the question."

"I've been very busy lately, running around trying to get ready to do this move, so . . . It might not be today."

"How about I make you dinner one night before you leave?"

"Ruth."

"I'll make your favorite. Fried catfish? We can just eat and talk . . ."

Adrian sighed. "You know that's not a good idea, Ruth. Not now."

"Oh, c'mon, Adrian. What's a little fried catfish between friends? Don't tell me we have to give that up too. Just dinner, that's all."

"I'll think about it." But they both knew he wouldn't.

"Or maybe we can go out. If you feel more comfortable, we can go someplace."

"I said I'll think about it."

"Can I call you back? I know you're busy and you might forget, but I can call you."

"That's up to you, but I don't have time to talk right now. Like I said, I was on my way out the door." The irritation in his voice rose and Ruth sensed she'd worn out her welcome, but it didn't matter. At this point, nothing mattered.

"There's a lot to discuss, Adrian. I'm having a hard time with this. I'm having a hard time without you," she said uneasily.

"I know this is hard for you; it's hard for me too and that's why I haven't called."

"I just miss you so much. I don't know how to let go, Adrian."

"You just do," he said simply.

"And that's what you've done? Just like that?"

"I don't know what else to tell you."

Tell me you love me. Tell me you need me too. Tell me you'll die without me. That's all.

"My priorities have changed, Ruth. I've got a baby coming that I need to focus on and that comes before me . . . and you. Like I said, I never meant to hurt you, but life can change on a dime and when it does, sometimes there's nothing you can do about it but change with it."

"I still think there are other options, Adrian. You just haven't looked at them because you decided all on your own without discussing it with me, without considering that there might be something else you can—"

"Discuss what with you?" Adrian snapped. "How I'm going to raise my kid? What the hell does that have to do with you, Ruth? What?"

She was hurt that he'd even ask the question when the answer was obvious. "You said you loved me, Adrian. That has plenty to do with me."

"I made the only decision I could under the circumstances. You might not understand it, but it's not for you to understand. I'm the one who's got to take care of this, Ruth. Not you."

"I'm not trying to take anything away from your child, Adrian. Believe me, I'm not. And I do understand your obligations, but—"

"I've got to go, Ruth. I'll try and call you back when I get a chance." Adrian abruptly hung up the phone without even saying goodbye.

It was after midnight and Eric's car was still parked outside her building. Ruth crawled into bed, but she knew she wouldn't sleep.

Sprinting

IT WAS ONLY A MATTER OF TIME BEFORE SHE CAUGHT UP WITH her. Bernie made herself comfortable in the seat beside Ruth's desk, crossed her legs, and cradled her cup of coffee between her hands, blowing on it every now and then to help cool it off. She took a couple of sips before saying anything, which was her way of making the statement that she wasn't the least bit happy about being dissed.

"You can't call a sistah? You can't visit a sistah's cubicle? You can't return a sistah's messages?"

"Adrian left me," Ruth blurted out.

Bernie stared sympathetically at Ruth. "I know. Clara told me. Question is, why didn't *you* tell me?" Ruth didn't answer. "When's he leaving?"

"I think he's gone," she said quietly. "His phone's been disconnected."

"You going to be all right?"

"No." Ruth swallowed.

Bernie sighed. "I hate it when shit like this happens. Feels like the end of the world, doesn't it?" Ruth nodded. "Wish I could say something to make you feel better." She smiled.

"I wish you could to." Ruth's voice cracked and she cleared her throat.

Sincerity washed over Bernie's face. "Might not seem like it, but you're going to be fine, sweetie."

"It was like I'd won the prize, you know? Like Adrian was my reward for putting up with Eric's ass all those years."

"Well, maybe for a while, he was."

"I wanted forever, Bernie."

"I know."

"Guess that was asking too much, huh?"

Bernie patted her hand. "There are plenty of other prizes out there, Ruth. He's not the only one."

"Eric's back, Bernie," Ruth stated simply.

Bernie's warm sympathetic expression immediately vanished. "Back? What do you mean, he's back?"

"Hang out here with me until I go home and you'll see him . . . sitting in the parking lot. Stop by tonight after work and you'll see him parked outside my apartment. Everywhere I go, there he is. Watching me. Always watching me."

"You call the police?"

She shrugged. "He hasn't done anything, Bernie. There's no law against sitting in a parked car."

"How long's this been going on?"

"Few weeks," Ruth whispered.

"Why haven't you said anything, Ruth?"

"For what? And who am I going to say anything to, Bernie? Eric does what he wants to do. Always has."

"You can at least get another restraining order."

"Like that's going to do any good. I know how he is. This time, that won't work. He's back, Bernie."

"And what the hell are you going to do about it, Ruth? Sit around and wait for that fool to try and kill you next time?"

"Of course not."

"Then what?"

Ruth opened her purse and laid an airline itinerary on the desk in front of Bernie. "One-way. From here to Denver, leaving on Saturday. I can't stay here, Bernie. Not as long as Eric's got breath left in his mean ass."

"Just like that? You're going to pack up and leave, just like that?"

"What choice do I have?"

Bernie stared at her searching for another answer, but she knew there wasn't one. "What are you going to do about your things?"

"I'm taking Friday off from work. I've got movers coming in to pack up and ship everything. It should all be there a few days after I arrive. I'll just stick it in storage or something until I find a place."

"McGreggor know you're leaving?"

"Not unless you tell him. Personally, I don't think it's any of his business."

"You want to stay with me for a few days?"

"It's bad enough he's running me out of town, Bernie. The least I can do is try and stand my ground for a few more days. Besides, I've got a lot of packing to do. But thanks for the offer."

"You still got the gun?"

"Gun?" Ruth had forgotten about the gun, which was probably buried under a mound of dust in the back of the nightstand. She stared wide-eyed at Bernie. "I doubt it'll come to that."

"Do you still have it, Ruth?" Bernie asked firmly.

"Yes, I have it." A tear escaped down Ruth's cheek. Was this what it had come down to, Ruth and Eric, with a gun between them?

"Good. Make sure it's loaded when you get home."

"Bernie—"

"Promise me, Ruth. Please."

"I promise."

Hell If I Know

❧

RUTH'S FACE WAS NUZZLED IN THE CROOK OF HIS NECK AND HE was so real that she could smell him. Adrian's body was a cocoon around her and they laid in each other's arms, naked. He whispered over and over again, "I love you, baby. I'll never let you go."

"But you left me, Adrian," she said. "Why did you leave?"

He squeezed her tighter and tighter, until she couldn't breathe. Ruth couldn't breathe. She couldn't . . . Her eyes opened to the sound of a knock at the door. She was gasping for air and the apartment was dark. But it had to be him knocking. She was convinced that it was Adrian knocking on her door. He'd come back just like she knew he would. Just like she'd prayed he would. She stumbled through the darkness, hurrying as fast as she could to get to him and answer the door before he changed his mind and decided to leave. Quickly, she unlocked it. Unchained it. Unbolted it. Her heart raced in anticipation of seeing him and holding him. But when she opened the door, it wasn't Adrian standing behind it. It was Eric and Eric's fist.

Ruth didn't remember falling, but she remembered hearing the door close behind him. Eric loomed ominously over her, then reached down and grabbed her by the front of her gown, pulling her roughly to her feet. *Whap! Whap!* Was she still dreaming? Had it turned into this, a nightmare? Was she in bed, asleep?

Eric pulled back her head and growled into her face. "Who the fuck you think yo' sorry ass messin' with, bitch?"

"Eric . . . please," Ruth heard herself beg. "Don't . . . don't do—"

"Fuck you, Ruthie! Yo' black ass think you all that! I'm goin' show yo' ass who the fuck you are! Who you always been! My bitch! Mine! Not his!"

He dragged her over to the sofa, then bent her over the back of it and forced himself inside her from behind. The sensation of him burned into her like hot iron and nausea welled up in her stomach. But before she could vomit he roughly drew her head back and swore into her ear, "I told you this is my ass, bitch! Didn't I tell you that?" He grunted and growled like an animal. "You miss me, bitch? Huh? You miss me, Ruthie? Tell me how much you missed my big black dick up yo' ass, bitch!" Ruth's mouth moved, but the words wouldn't come. "I can't hear you." He grunted, ramming himself inside her as far as he could go, torturing her from the inside out and the outside in.

"I missed you," she whispered.

Eric pounded furiously against her, but wouldn't come. Not yet. He was too angry to come. He pulled out, then dragged Ruth into the bedroom and threw her on the bed. His hard dick stared back at her, angry for release. "Suck it!" he demanded, standing over her. Then he pulled back her head and forced his dick inside her mouth. "I said . . . suck it, bitch!" He wasn't expecting pleasure. He was punishing her for living without him all these years, defying him, and refusing to let him back into her life. This was for refusing his daisies.

Eric pushed Ruth down on her back, climbed on top of her and pushed himself inside her. "Who's yo' fuckin' daddy, bitch? Who the hell am I?"

"Daddy," she said despondently, staring up at the ceiling, willing herself awake and away from him.

"That's right," he said, triumphantly, pushing deep thrusts inside her, forcing groans from her body until finally, Eric lost himself to the sensation of this catastrophe. His eyes rolled back in their sockets and he threw back his head.

"Fuck! Fuck you . . . Ruthie! Oh damn! Shiiii—!"

Eric's orgasm exploded and when it did, he relaxed, just for a second, and that was all she needed. Ruth reached over to the night-stand and grabbed the sculpture that Adrian thought was so ugly.

With all the strength she had, Ruth slammed it into the side of his head.

"Oh . . . motha . . . shit! Ruthie!" Eric rolled off her clutching his head trying to stop the blood from flowing down his face. Ruth pushed him off her, crawled out of bed. All she could think about was running.

Run, Ruth. Run as fast, and as far as you can. Don't stop. Don't look back. Don't pass go. Don't collect two hundred dollars.

"Bitch! I'm goin' to . . . kill your black ass . . . Ruth!" She could hear him calling behind her as she stumbled through the living room heading toward the door. "Don't let me find yo' ass, Ruth! Don't let me—"

Kill your black ass. Kill your black ass. Eric would. He'd kill her black ass. As long as he knew she was alive, he wouldn't stop until he'd killed her black ass. That's when she remembered the gun Bernie had given her. Ruth let go of the doorknob.

It was time to stop running. It was time to stop letting him rule her life. She walked slowly back into the bedroom and saw Eric rolling around on the bed, clutching at the gaping gash on his head. Then she reached into the drawer of the nightstand and pulled out the gun. It was time to stop running because, goddamn it, she was tired! This maniac had forced himself on her for the last mothafuckin' time and running away wasn't an option anymore. This time, she'd die before she'd run. Or better yet, she'd kill him.

"Ruth! You fuckin' bitch! You fuckin'—" Eric wiped the blood from his eyes and stared into the barrel of the gun she pointed at him. "What the—" He started to get out of the bed.

"Don't you move, Eric!" Tears ran down her cheeks into her mouth. "Don't . . . if you move . . . I'm going to kill you!" Gradually, she moved closer to the bed, the gun aimed at his head. Blood streamed down his face and he raised his hand to wipe it away. "I said, don't move, mothafucka!"

Her hands were shaking uncontrollably, but Ruth wasn't afraid. For the first time since she'd known this man, she was not afraid of him, because she knew that tonight someone in the room would die and this would all be over soon. The irony was incredible and Ruth marveled at the fact that this time, she was in control. She had the power, and she began to laugh. Ruth laughed so hard, she was afraid that she might not be able to stop. And she didn't want to stop, because if she did, she'd break. He'd been trying to break her since she was eighteen years old and he'd almost done it, but she'd held herself together. Ruth was stronger than he was, and suddenly it dawned on her, that she always had been. She'd put up with, survived, and overcame all of Eric's bullshit. He'd hit her, kicked her, cussed her, but she was still standing. A mothafuckin' gun was about to go off in his face and it might as well have been him pulling the trigger because it had been him who'd driven her to this and she was the maniac now.

"You . . . will . . . never put your fuckin' hands on me again!" she said, through clenched teeth. Eric didn't say a word. "Did you hear me? You will never put your fuckin' hands on me again!"

Fear filled his eyes and Ruth fell in love with that fear. The way Eric had fallen in love with hers for all those years. "Ruth . . . I'll leave, baby . . . just . . . put the gun . . . put the gun—"

She crawled onto the bed next to him and sat close enough to see beads of sweat form on his forehead. Eric raised his hand with his palm facing her, only this time it wasn't to slap her face. It was to protect himself from *her*. "I told you . . . I didn't want you, Eric. I've never wanted you, but you never cared about me, or what I wanted. You forced yourself into my life, my pussy, my peace because . . . why? Why, Eric? Why me? What the fuck did I ever do to you?"

"I can leave, Ruthie. You jus' . . . put that gun away, or . . . jus' let me get up out of here and you won't see me . . . jus' let me get up out of here Ruthie and I promise—"

"You promise?" The taste of blood pooled in her mouth and this time, she spat it in his face. "That's what your promise means to me, Eric." She laughed. "How many promises have you given me before? How many have you kept?" The gun felt so good in her hand, warm, like it was a natural extension of who she was.

She hated him with every ounce of herself and she knew now that it had always been her destiny to rid the world of his filthy ass.

"You wanna shoot me, Ruthie? Huh? You wanna shoot my ass? So shoot! Shoot me, bitch!" Eric yelled, trying to intimidate her.

Ruth pressed the barrel of the gun hard on his face, between his eyes. "Shooting you isn't an issue, Eric. The only issue I have is where I want to put the fuckin' bullet."

Eric raised his hands in surrender, afraid that he'd finally pushed her too far, and he had. Ruth was seconds away from doing what she'd dreamed of doing for a long time.

"Ruth."

"Right between your fuckin' eyes . . . yeah," she said, licking the blood and tears from her lips. "This would be a perfect place to put a bullet. Get rid of all those silly ass ideas you got floating around up there in that empty space where your brain should be. You're a stupid man, Eric . . . and stupid men give birth to stupid ideas. Like hitting women."

"You don't want to pull that trigger, Ruthie . . . I know—"

"You don't know shit, Eric! You don't know shit! You don't know me! You never did!" She slowly moved the barrel of the gun down to his chest. "Maybe this is where I should shoot your dumb ass. Maybe this would be good, because . . . but no . . . this wouldn't work. A heart's supposed to be there and we both know . . . ain't shit there! Bullet would just go right through you, huh?" Eric tried to laugh. "What's funny, Eric?" She ground the gun hard into his chest. He grimaced. "You think this is funny? What you've just done to me . . . is that funny? What about what I'm going to do to you?" Then she slid the gun down to his groin and pressed and pressed it against that pathetic lump of dark flesh he'd just attacked her with; his lethal weapon. "Is it still funny? Answer me. Is this shit funny now, Eric?"

Eric's eyes grew wide like saucers. "Oh shit! Ruth . . . no! Please . . . please . . . don't . . . not—!"

Her smile was sadistic. Ruth felt high and out of this world. Now she knew what it had been like to be Eric. Domination was the best high in the world. Ruling someone. Overpowering someone. Terrorizing someone. Her heart raced in her chest, and she never wanted to come down from this. Never.

"Now this . . . this would be the best place of all. I shoot this off and what would you have left? Hmmm . . . ain't this your world, Eric? I never liked fuckin' you. Did you know that? Did you know I hated every minute you stuck that piece of shit inside my body? You're the one who's always been all wrapped up in that. Not me." She shrugged. "And I for one wouldn't miss it."

It wasn't until she looked at Eric's bleeding, terrified face that she suddenly realized where she wanted to plant her bullet. Ruth raised the gun to his mouth, and rested it against his chin. "Open your mouth, Eric."

Eric shook his head from side to side. "You need to stop . . . Ruth! You need to jus' let me get my ass up out of here and—"

"I said open your fuckin' mouth!" Before she knew it, Ruth rammed Eric in the mouth with the butt of the gun.

"Aww!" he screamed, burying his face in one of the pillows, twisting in agony from the pain. Ruth stared blankly at him remembering all the times he'd put his fist in her mouth and all the nights they stayed up late until she'd learned her lesson, and all that was left was a bruised, bloody mess. Had this been his lesson? Watching him she also realized that she'd finally lost her damn mind. Ruth started laughing again, because along with everything else he'd taken from her over the years, he'd taken that too. She reached for the phone and dialed 911.

"Hello . . . you have to come and get him," she said absently. "You have to come and get him now . . . or I'm afraid I'll have to kill him." Ruth let the phone fall to the side of the bed and watched Eric writhe around in pain, screaming obscenities mixed with her name. "You touch me again Eric and I'll kill you."

By the time the police and ambulance arrived, Eric was lying groaning on the bed and Ruth had curled up in the corner of the room on the floor across from him with the gun pointed at him, daring him to leave.

She didn't remember giving up the gun, or the ride to the hospital. But Clara was there and as soon as Ruth saw her she felt safe enough to collapse in her arms.

"Shhhh . . . baby girl," she whispered. "It's all right now. It's over. It's finally over, baby."

She was examined for evidence of the rape then taken to the

police station to make a formal statement. Eric had been charged with assault, battery, and rape. Clara called Bernie who rushed right over to the station to take Ruth home with her. Clara and Bernie waited patiently for Ruth to shower, then tucked her into bed like she was a child. Did she ever wake up from that dream? Or was she still sleeping? It was so hard to tell. Maybe everything else in her life had been a dream. Maybe she'd only dreamed about Adrian, and of starting her own business. Maybe she and May never really did go for long walks in the mornings. And maybe this had always been her reality all along, and she was just now waking up.

Karen would've brought her a cup of hot tea. She would've sat down on the bed next to Ruth and rubbed her hair from her face. Then, she'd have kissed her cheek and whispered, *"You go on and cry now, Baby Ruth. A little cryin' never hurt a thing."* But it wasn't Karen. It was Clara. She slipped off her shoes and crawled into bed next to Ruth, then draped her arm over her. Clara didn't have hot tea, or comforting words, but she had a delicious tune that she hummed sweetly into her ear, until she finally lulled her to sleep.

Scattered

RUTH HAD TAKEN UP SHELTER IN BERNIE'S SPARE BEDROOM. HER life had unraveled in her hands once again, and she felt scattered and misplaced with no real direction in sight, no real remedy for piecing herself back together. Her body ached, her heart was broken, and her spirit . . . it was empty. She wasn't afraid anymore and every other emotion she could possibly succumb to—disappointment, sadness, anger—all merged together into one. Numbness.

Ruth sat for hours on end, staring out the window, at what she didn't know. Thinking, always thinking, about absolutely nothing. She could hear, but she wasn't listening. She ate, but nothing had flavor. She drank, but could never seem to quench her thirst.

Bernie didn't say much. She just walked around on pins and needles, void of answers to questions she didn't even understand. Every now and then she'd smile and put her arm around Ruth from time to time, letting her know that she was here, and for Ruth, that was plenty.

Sharon stopped by, and took one look at Ruth then broke down crying. Ruth wanted to ask, *Do I look that bad?* But Ruth let her cry until she couldn't anymore. For a moment she'd even thought about crying with her, but the tears just wouldn't fall. She promised Sharon she'd cry later.

The last time she'd seen May the woman was saved in the nick of time from having a nervous breakdown by a phone call from Jefferson. May came into the room, and sat down on the bed patting the spot next to her that she'd saved for Ruth. May hugged her and gave her a gentle squeeze.

"You doin' okay, sweetie?"

"No. No, I don't think I am," Ruth whispered.

May stared into her eyes from behind the tears glistening in her own. "You know what my momma used to tell me when I was a little girl? She used to tell me that the hardest part 'bout bein' wounded is the healin'." She laughed. "I had no idea what that woman was talkin' 'bout, 'cause Momma's elevator was usually stuck in the basement most of the time, if you know what I mean, so I never put too much stock in too many things she said. But when I grew up, I understood what she meant."

"Adrian's gone."

"I know, baby." She pressed her hand against Ruth's cheek.

"I miss him."

She smiled. "Bernie says you're leavin'? Goin' back to Denver?"

"I'm going home. That's where I grew up. I can't stay here. I can't stand it anymore, May. As big as this place is, I feel like it's closing in on me."

"You know anybody back there?"

"Not a soul."

"You sure leavin' is a good idea?" May asked, concerned. " 'Specially now?"

"I'm suffocating here."

"But all yo' friends are here, Ruth. And we all love you."

"I know and I love you too. But I can't stay."

"Whatchu goin' to do up there all by yo'self?"

"I haven't even thought about it," Ruth said unenthusiastically.

"You got a place to stay?"

"I'll find one."

"You got money?"

"Some."

May held Ruth's hand between hers. "If you need more . . . you call me. I still got money left over from Frank's insurance policy. Told Jeff I was savin' it for a rainy day. Gotta be rainin' some damn where." She laughed. "Whatever you need, baby. You call me."

"I will."

May hadn't said much all evening. After her visit with Ruth, she drove around for a while before coming home. That woman had been turned any which way but loose, but as wounded as she was, May couldn't help to admire her strength. She wondered if Ruth would eventually give in and break down, but then she figured she'd already done that with Eric, coming just short of pulling the trigger. Any other woman might have shot him, but Ruth hadn't for some reason. Maybe, nobody would ever know that reason but Ruth . . . and Eric.

Jeff was lying in bed watching the basketball game when she stepped out of the shower. "You all right, baby?"

May sat down on the side of the bed, and began rubbing lotion onto her hands. "Ruth told me that Adrian moved to California." She turned and looked at Jeff. "Did you know he was leavin'?"

"I'd heard rumors." He shrugged. "I knew they were relocating some people in our San Francisco division, but . . . I just figured, if he was going, she'd be going with him."

"No. He's seein' someone else," May said sadly. "You'd think he'd planned this whole thing with Eric, the way it worked out. I feel so sorry for her."

"That's too bad," Jeff said sincerely. "She's been through a lot."

"An awful lot."

Just then, May broke down crying. Jeff quickly sat up and gathered her in his arms. "Her face was all swollen, and—" May sobbed. "She wouldn't cry or anythin', Jeff. It's like, she's not even in the same world as the rest of us."

"She's strong, though, baby. Ruth has been through some things in her life, and she's always managed to pull herself up out of them—"

"But this time is different." May sat up, drying her eyes. "This time, I'm not so sure she will pull out of it. She's so . . . detached. It wasn't just Eric who hurt her, but Adrian too. I mean, what the hell was that bastard thinkin'? Comin' into her life like that, actin' like he was God's gift and then walkin' out on her the way he did. What kind of man does that?"

"Adrian's not a bad man, baby. Now I don't know what the circumstances are, but he's good people, and I'm sure—"

"There is no excuse, Jefferson." May glared at her husband. "If a man can't commit to a woman, then he shouldn't pretend he can. If he can't be faithful, then he needs to be man enough to admit it, long before a woman's heart is at stake."

Jeff sensed the hidden message there directed at him. May had been hinting around for months, without coming out and saying she thought he was cheating on her. He hadn't been deaf to her subliminal accusations. He'd just thought it best to ignore them, and hope she'd come to her senses and realize her overzealous imagination had gotten the best of her.

"I agree," he said genuinely. "A man who can't be faithful doesn't belong in a serious, committed relationship."

"Are you committed, Jeff?" May asked earnestly. She'd been driving herself crazy looking for the answer to that question, always expecting to find the answer she dreaded most. Always expecting him to be like every other man she'd known in her life. Her suspicions had been born of past experiences. Nothing more. Most of the time she knew this, and hated herself for being so insecure. Other times, suspicions were enough to override reason. May had a hard time distinguishing the line between the two, and that's what threatened to tear her apart.

Jeff looked surprised.

"How long have you been questioning that, May?"

"A while," she said quietly.

Jeff stared at her, hurt that she'd question his devotion to her when he'd gone out of his way to prove himself. "Tonight will be the last night this subject comes up, sweetheart."

May swallowed, then nodded her head. "I need to know."

"I have never been unfaithful to you, May, and as long as we're married, there will never be another woman for me. And if you doubt me, then our marriage is over. Is that clear?"

There was her ultimatum. Either believe in her marriage, or leave it. May didn't want to lose her husband, but if she weren't careful, her suspicions would drive him right out the door. Perhaps that's what she'd needed all along. An ultimatum. Now, she had a choice to make. No more straddling the fence between her fears and her fantasies. She had to choose. But could she?

"I don't want to lose you," she whispered with tears in her eyes.

"Then don't lose me, baby." Jeff raised her mouth to his and pressed his lips to hers.

Three weeks after the attack Ruth stood on the balcony of her hotel room, gazing out across a city that was like a foreign country. Denver, Colorado, might as well have been Paris, France, because as it turned out, Ruth didn't know a thing about either one of them. Too much time had passed and change had reconstructed her little home into something she no longer recognized. Ruth couldn't help but to feel overwhelmed, but she refused to run from it.

"I miss you already, girl," Bernie said sadly over the phone. Ruth had promised to call her as soon as the plane landed, but she didn't get a chance because Bernie called first. "Is it like you remember?"

"So far? Not at all."

"Well, if you get homesick for your best friend, you know you always got a home here."

"I know, Bernie. And thank you."

Ruth had spent the first fourteen years of her life in this place, but the home she knew as Denver had been a small ghetto neighborhood called the Five Points near downtown. She remembered spending her summers swimming at the pool in Curtis Park and Welton Street had been her playground. Old Mr. Tony used to sell pig ear sandwiches out of a phone booth on Welton. Ruth smiled at the memory. She'd never had one, but they must've been really good because he always had a line outside his store and the only thing he sold were pig ear sandwiches, hot peppers, and Dr Pepper. She and Karen would take the city bus to downtown and spend hours looking around in stores they could never afford to shop in, but Ruth had promised her that one day she'd make thousands of dollars and buy her anything she wanted. That day never came, she reflected sadly. Nothing was familiar anymore except the Rocky Mountains, which were as eternal as time, and Ruth at least found comfort in that.

Another Day in Paradise

RUTH MADE IT A POINT TO CONTACT A REALTOR THE MINUTE she arrived in town and within a few days he'd found her a place and offered her the deal of a lifetime. An elderly couple had a summer home in Estes Park that they were looking to rent out during the times they weren't using it, which, according to the realtor, was pretty much all the time. Well, Ruth fell in love with the place and rented it as soon as she saw it. It was convenient enough to the highway. That way she could make a quick getaway in the event of an avalanche or a ferocious, woman-eating bear. And it was secluded enough that she never even had to see a traffic jam. Best of all, it was cheap because the couple bought the place back in the Middle Ages and had no idea what the property values were in Colorado.

Ruth drove around town, amazed by how much Denver had grown over the years. Even the Five Points was going through some kind of weird metamorphosis caught some place between being the hood to what many considered to be prime, up-and-coming, downtown real estate. There was Lo-Do, Lower Downtown, which was where a yuppie who was any yuppie with pride in their yuppie-dom hung out. Shit, she never even knew there was a Lower Downtown, but somebody sure found one and it was obviously huge, because they'd had enough room for a baseball stadium, an amusement park, and a big aquarium. Go figure.

Time passed and that was all she needed. Ruth moved into her new home and quickly settled in. There was no agenda, at the moment, except for healing . . . again. And for that, she didn't need a clock or calendar, because there was no way to measure how long a full recovery would take this time, and honestly, she didn't want the added pressure of measuring it.

Her favorite time of the day had always been mornings and mornings in a home in Estes Park, Colorado, were breathtaking. The months had passed quickly and fall was settling in, paving the way for winter. Life moved slower up there than it did in Denver. Slow enough for her to watch the leaves change from green to red, orange, yellow. Real exciting stuff, but every morning she'd make herself a cup of coffee, wrap up in her long johns and thermal socks, and sit on her porch to watch the rays of old Mr. Sun dance through the leaves and come up to kiss her dead on the lips. She didn't mind the impending cold, or the long drives to the grocery store. She didn't even mind the lack of neighbors or social interaction. Solitude was the best company Ruth could possibly have. He didn't say too much and he was a great listener too. Didn't have opinions at all and she definitely appreciated him for that.

"Why the hell you gotta live in the mountains?" Bernie asked over the phone.

Ruth chuckled. "I like the mountains, Bernie."

"Only white folks live in the mountains, Ruth. Crazy white folks, who shave their heads and dream of starting race wars."

"You're so funny. Sharon said she'd love to live in the mountains."

"She would," she said smartly. "So, when you coming home? I miss your little ass."

"I miss you too. I'll be home next month."

"You said that last month."

"Did I? Well, I meant next month."

"You ain't never coming back, are you?"

"Don't be silly. Of course I'll be back. Next month."

"You coming back for the sentencing?"

Ruth hesitated before answering. "Probably not."

"C'mon, girl. At least go to see the look on his face when they tell him how long he's going to be locked up."

"I'd rather watch the grass grow, Bernie."

"You different from me, 'cause I'd be there with popcorn, some three-D glasses and twenty of my closest friends."

"I'm sorry that I can't muster up that same level of enthusiasm. Besides, he pled guilty and with time served, everybody knows he won't get more than a few years."

"Better than nothing, right?"

"Somehow, I just don't see the justice. I should've shot him." There was no emotion in her tone of voice. Pulling the trigger and blowing his head off would've been fair. A few years in prison just didn't compare. But she'd missed the opportunity, so Ruth had chosen not to dwell on it. These days, she'd made it a point not to dwell on too much of anything.

"Guess what I'm looking at right now?" Bernie asked excitedly.

"What?"

"Pages's Web site. It's beautiful, girl."

Ruth smiled. "Thank you."

"I guess you been taking advantage of all that free time you got, huh?"

"Girl, I can design Web sites with the best of them."

"Business picking up?"

"Yep. A little more every month. I'm not getting rich, by any means, but I'm enjoying it."

"So how do I buy a book?"

"Point, double-click, and put in your credit card number," Ruth said matter-of-factly.

"What about my discount?"

Ruth rolled her eyes and sighed. "What about it?"

"How much is it?"

"Ten percent."

"Ten percent? I'm your best friend in the whole wide world and the best you can give me is ten percent?"

"Okay . . . fifteen."

"Ruth?"

"Bernie. I'm trying to make a living here."

"Fifteen percent and free shipping."

"Your ass is cheap," Ruth said purposely sounding irritated.

"You just now realizing that?"

Pages had been in business for almost three months and it had become her baby. The thing was, Ruth hadn't started it because she believed she'd finally gotten her head together and was ready to take on the world, or because she wanted to be a pioneer and her determination had been so strong, her drive such a force, that it was her destiny to run this business. On the contrary. She'd started Pages because she didn't have the stamina to look for a regular job, and had no desire to be around a bunch of people, asking too many questions, forcing smiles that weren't genuine. She needed something to do, and this idea had been burned into her for months. That was her reason for starting Pages.

Nearly six months had passed and it was still too soon to say she'd gotten herself together. Honestly, Ruth couldn't ever see that happening because she wasn't sure anymore of what that meant. Had she put her past behind her? No, because like it or not, it was a part of her forever and it had molded her into who she'd become. So ignoring it, erasing it, would have been betraying herself. And Ruth couldn't bring herself to do that any longer. Had she exorcized her demons? Not even close, but she was learning not to be afraid of them anymore, and to look them in the face instead of running off screaming in the opposite direction. They'd always belong to her, and she'd come to terms with that.

She still thought a lot about Adrian and she missed him, terribly sometimes. She'd made the mistake of putting all the responsibility for her happiness on him, and that hadn't been fair to either one of them. Adrian was human. And that's all. He lived his life the best he knew how, and holding him accountable for hers seemed to be a waste of energy, and especially time. But like everything else, even that was getting easier to deal with. That was the one thing about living in this place. There was more time than anything else, so whenever she needed some, all she had to do was stick her head out the door and inhale. It was the only thing she knew of that was free and the supply was endless.

Cotton Blossom

❧

IT HAD TAKEN SHARON'S WEDDING TO BRING RUTH BACK TO Jacksonville and that heffa had the nerve to make Ruth the maid of honor and without bothering to tell her until the wedding. Yes, it pissed her off! But seeing how happy Sharon was and how beautiful she looked it was hard for Ruth to stay mad at her.

Nearly a year had passed since she'd moved away. Ruth had missed everybody, especially Clara, who, as soon as she spotted Ruth, smiled and planted one of her sweet kisses on her cheek. "How you doing, baby?"

"I'm fine," Ruth said, grinning. "I've missed you, though. When are you coming to visit me in Colorado? It's a beautiful place. I know you'd love it."

Clara just shook her head. "Child, you know I don't fly and I don't like too much driving either."

Ruth folded her arms across her chest. "That mean you're not coming?"

"That means you're welcome in my home anytime, my love." Clara laughed.

"Thanks Clara," she said dryly and smiled.

Clara looped her arm with Ruth's and the two strolled together on the grounds of the mansion where Sharon's wedding was being held. Sharon had been shacked up at this mansion for the last three months with her fiancé Wayne, whom she'd met at the vegetable stand. As it turned out, the man was loaded. He was also surprisingly sweet, and Ruth wished nothing but the best for them both.

"How long you staying?" Clara asked.

"Not long. Just a few days. I've got to get back and run a business."

"That all you doing these days? Running businesses?"

"That's all I want to do."

Clara stopped and looked Ruth right in the eye. "You're a young woman, Ruth. Don't grow old before your time, baby."

"I'm cool, Clara. Really. Stimulation is not something I'm ready for right now."

"A little stimulation never hurt anybody." She winked. "I need me some every now and then myself."

"Clara!" Ruth gasped.

"What? Even women my age need to get their groove on from time to time, baby. I ain't dead, you know. As a matter of fact, I got me a new boyfriend." Clara smiled slyly. "It's not serious, but he's fun. Before you leave, I want you to meet him."

"Before I leave, I plan on meeting him and giving him the once over too."

"No need. I've already done that and everything is exactly where it's supposed to be and is in fine, working condition."

Ruth shook her head and laughed. Leave it to Clara to throw a curveball at her.

Sharon looked beautiful and Megan, Ruth's own personal doll baby, made a beautiful flower girl.

"Hello, Miss Ruth!" Megan screamed, jumping up into her arms.

"Hello, Megan, sweetie." Ruth tried hard not to squeeze the life out of the child, but boy was she glad to see her.

Megan gave her a big, wet kiss, then ran her little hand over Ruth's hair. "You let your hair grow."

Ruth's once tamed, tailored, cropped 'do had grown wildly out of control and spread like a Colorado wildfire. Ruth had been cooped up in the wilderness for so long, she'd hardly even noticed it happening. Then one day, she caught a glimpse of Angie Stone on television and noticed that they had the same hairstyle. Her first thought was to find a barber and have her head shaved, but looking at Angie,

Ruth decided she rather liked the new millennium 'fro she was sporting and decided to keep it.

"I couldn't help it. It just kinda grew on its own."

"I like it." The little girl smiled. "You don't look like a boy anymore." The child was young enough for Ruth to let that comment pass without incident. But her momma definitely needed to teach her some manners.

Ruth gasped. "Megan! What happened to your tooth?"

"The tooth fairy took it," she said indifferently, as if Ruth should've known. "And she gave me a quarter for it."

"A whole quarter?"

"I wanted a dollar," she said, disappointed.

Cheap ass tooth fairy. Ruth would have to talk to her after the wedding.

Sharon came up behind Ruth and put her hand on her shoulder. "I'm glad you're here, Ruth. I don't know what I would've done if you hadn't come."

Ruth put Megan back on the ground and watched the little girl hurry away before laying into her mother. "You know I'm mad at you, Sharon. You could've warned me before I got here that I was the maid of honor. I would've worn a nicer dress," she fussed.

"Oh . . . you look beautiful and you could've worn jeans for all I care. I was not going to stand up here and marry this man without my best friend by my side."

"Better not let Bernie hear you talk about that best friend stuff. She thinks she's got dibs on me."

"I'm not scared of Bernie and today is my wedding day. If I want you to be my best friend, then she doesn't have a thing to say about it."

"Then I'm your best friend, honey, and let's forget all about that old Bernie." Ruth smiled.

"I heard that!" Bernie shouted, coming out of the house.

The wedding was beautiful, but then, what did she expect? Ruth had to admit, standing there watching Sharon and Wayne exchange vows, she couldn't help but to think of Adrian. How many times had she squashed fantasies of the two of them standing at the altar, reciting vows to each other? Too many. Maybe that had been the problem. Instead of squashing those fantasies, maybe she should've held on to them. Then maybe he would never have left her, and she'd have been Mrs. Adrian Carter. Then again, maybe the altitude in Colorado was toxic and filled with microscopic bacteria that sucked a woman's good sense bone dry.

Bernie and Ruth sat back and watched their friend and her new husband dance together. They'd both eaten too much cake and downed too much champagne to stand for more than sixty seconds on their own without toppling over, so they decided to be on the safe side, stay in their chairs until they either passed out, or made fools of themselves and one of Wayne's staff had to escort them off the premises.

"She's looks so happy," Ruth slurred.

Bernie nodded. "Yeah, she does."

"Don't you think she looks like a young Elizabeth Taylor?"

"You're right," Bernie said, as if seeing the resemblance for the first time.

"You think you'll ever get married again, Bernie?"

"I'm thinking about it," she said casually.

Ruth looked shocked that the woman would even admit such a thing. "Really? You and Miles? Since when?"

"Since . . . since . . . hell I don't know. Since today. And yes, me and Miles. Who else is going to put up with my ornery ass?"

"He's pretty good at it."

"Damn right he is. But don't you dare mention this conversation to anybody, Ruth Johnson or I'll push you down."

Ruth ignored the threat. "You love him, Bernie?"

Bernie sighed. "Hell yes."

Ruth laughed. "You're drunk."

"Hell yes."

Ruth reflected quietly for a moment, then took another sip of champagne. "I think I like being single. Don't have to answer to anybody, or be responsible to anybody."

"This is true," Bernie agreed.

"I can come and go as I please and nobody can say a damn thing about it."

"That's for damn sure."

"I'm thinking about getting . . . a dog." Bernie and Ruth looked at each other and laughed hysterically.

All of a sudden Bernie's expression turned serious. She'd been looking for an opportunity all day to bring this up, and now that both of them were drunk on their asses, this seemed to be as good a time as any. "I've got something to tell you."

Ruth frowned. "Don't do that, Bernie," she fussed. "We're having a good time. Don't get serious on my ass all of a sudden."

"I wasn't going to tell you because I didn't know how you'd take it."

"Then don't tell me."

"And I definitely didn't want to tell you before you got here because I knew if I told you, you wouldn't come."

"What is it, Bernie?" Ruth asked impatiently.

"And if you didn't show up that would've broken poor Sharon's heart and ruined her wedding day. You know that heffa thinks you're her best friend? If it wasn't her wedding day, I'd—"

"Bernie? Would you just say whatever it is you've got to say?"

So Bernie blurted it out. "Adrian's back."

Numbed by the effects of all that champagne, Ruth just sat there trying to make sense out of what she had just told her. "Adrian's back? What the hell does that mean?"

"It means . . . he's back. Moved back from San Francisco because apparently things didn't work out with his baby's momma so . . . he's back."

Ruth gulped down what was left in her glass and shrugged. "So he's back. Who cares?"

"He called me."

"For what?"

"Looking for you."

"What did you tell him?"

"The truth. That you don't live here anymore."

"Good. Good answer." Ruth poured the last of their bottle of champagne into her glass.

"And that Eric assaulted you."

Ruth couldn't believe her ears, and accidentally knocked over her glass at Bernie's confession. "Oh, no you didn't!"

Bernie continued, undaunted by Ruth's anger. "And that he was a sorry ass bastard for leaving you like he did for that other woman even if she was pregnant with his baby, because you loved him more than you'd ever loved any man, and he had no right to break your heart the way he did, and how could he have the nerve to call me up looking for you after what he did?"

Ruth was appalled. "You did not tell him all that. Tell me you didn't."

"If I told you I didn't, I'd be lying, Ruth."

"Why would you—"

"Because his pretty ass needed to hear it! That's why. Actually, the version I just gave you was the PG-thirteen version. It got ugly, Ruth. You know me, girl. I shrank that six-foot frame down to about two feet before he could get a word in edgewise. The lame ass motha—"

"Bernie Watson!"

"Bernie Watson nothing! If his sorry ass would've been here, maybe Eric wouldn't have come at you that night."

"If Eric wanted to get to me bad enough, Bernie, he was going to do it. But you had no right to tell him all that—"

"Damn if I didn't! He called my house, Ruth. That was an invitation to sit and listen to every mothafuckin' word I had to say and he did too. He sat there and let me say my piece. Just like his punk ass should've done. Me cussing him out was like you cussing him out. Might as well have been you, Ruth. And he sat there and took it. Which was exactly what he was supposed to do."

"And then what?" Ruth asked smartly. "After you said your little piece about all my business—"

"He admitted he was wrong and he said he was worried about you and wanted your number so he could check on you."

"You didn't give it to him? Because I'm over him, Bernie. I really am and I like being over him."

"You're not over him."

"I am over him. Maybe not completely, but—"

"I know you aren't over him."

"You had no right, Bernie. None."

"I know, girlfriend."

"So you didn't give him my number . . . did you?"

"Hell no!"

Ruth slumped back, relieved that at least she'd kept her mouth shut about that. "Good."

"I just told him you'd be in town this week."

"I don't believe this!" Ruth said wearily, rubbing her temples.

"At least talk to the man, Ruth."

"What?" she asked, shocked at the suggestion, especially from Bernie.

"He was so sweet about that cussing out I gave him, Ruth. He really thought he was doing the right thing with that woman and he was really upset that he couldn't be there to raise his son. But he realized that raising that boy in a house with two people who couldn't stand each other wasn't fair to the child and he knows that you're the only woman for him and if he can ever make it up to you . . . even though he knows you might not trust him right away, he'll do it. Whatever it takes."

"Whose side are you on?"

"Yours."

"No, that's not how it sounds to me," Ruth said gravely.

"Ruth, you know you love that man."

"Yes. I love him, Bernie. And that was the problem. I loved him and he left me."

"He was only trying to do what was right."

"Fine. He tried. Obviously he failed. I'm sorry that things didn't work out for him, but I'm not disposable. He said we were finished. We're finished."

"Fine. Then be finished. But just talk to the man, sweetie."

"What on earth for?"

"Let him tell you himself, how sorry he is. Just give him the opportunity and yourself the satisfaction of hearing him admit he fucked up."

"I don't need to hear him admit a damn thing."

"Yes you do," Bernie said intently.

"No, Bernie. I don't. I don't need anything from Adrian. Not his admissions, or apologies, or excuses."

Bernie sat quietly for a moment. She'd had a feeling this conversation wouldn't go well, but she'd promised Adrian she'd try. Well, she'd tried.

"Think about it? Please. For me?"

Ruth picked up her purse to leave. "This has nothing to do with you and you know it." She gave Bernie a quick hug. "I'm going to say goodbye to Sharon and Clara, and then I'm leaving. Good night, Bernie."

Ruth rode in the back of the limo Sharon had insisted she take to her hotel room. Bernie had had a lot of nerve coming at her like that. She'd come dangerously close to crossing the friendship line and if Ruth hadn't left when she did, she'd have crossed that line too and they would've ended up never speaking to each other again. It wasn't that she held a grudge against Adrian, but she'd moved on. Time had a way of dulling the pain and had helped her to get over him, and she'd needed big doses of the stuff. She was sorry things hadn't worked out the way he'd hoped. In retrospect, Ruth admired him for even wanting to make a life with his child. But the fact that it hadn't worked for him wasn't her problem. It was his.

Prime Time

MAY AND RUTH LAUGHED AS SOON AS THEY LAID EYES ON EACH other. "Girl, people are goin' to accuse us of readin' each other's mind. You let yours grow back too?" May's short style had morphed into a well-manicured afro a few inches shorter than Ruth's.

"I had to, girl. Gets cold up there in those mountains and I need all the insulation I can get."

They were having fish for dinner and this time May had insisted that Ruth help out with the cooking.

"How are things between you and Jeff?" Ruth asked, remembering May's strange behavior the last time she'd visited her home.

"Child, please," May said, sucking her teeth. "We're fine. I jus' need to stop bein' so insecure all the time. He ain't travelin' as much as he used to. I guess it was hard on him too, bein' away from us all the time."

"The kids okay?"

Just then Jeff walked in and answered the question before May had a chance to. "The kids are great." He walked over to Ruth and gave her a warm hug. "How you doing, Ruth?"

"I'm fine, Jefferson. How are you?" Ruth beamed.

He glanced at his wife. "Better than ever." Then walked over to her and gave her a long wet kiss, right there in front of Ruth. "Hey, baby."

"Jefferson Edwards now you know you can't be gettin' nothin' started now. We got company." She blushed.

He whispered loud enough for Ruth to hear, "Then I'll start something later."

"Mmmm . . . promise me?" she purred.

"Maybe I should leave?" Ruth suggested, feeling a little queasy by their blatant show of affection. But then, what else did she expect?

"Don't you dare leave, girl. See what you did, Jeff? You made her uncomfortable," May scolded.

"I'm so sorry," he said genuinely, and then smiled mischievously. "Please forgive me, Ruth. The last thing I intended to do was make you uncomfortable."

"I'll live," she said playfully.

May and Jeff locked eyes before he left the room. Didn't those two ever get enough of each other? Ruth wondered. "Now," May said, composing herself, "what 'bout you?"

"What about me?" Ruth grinned.

May's expression became serious and concern welled up into her eyes. "How you doin'? I mean, really?"

"I'm fine," Ruth reassured her, but May looked skeptical. "I am, May."

"You seein' anyone?"

"Not you too," Ruth said, exasperated. "I swear, if one more person asks me that question I'm going to throw up. No, I'm not seeing anyone, May."

"I'm just curious. You know how I am, always thinkin' love's what makes the world go round. Can't help it. I'm a romantic."

"Then be romantic. Lord knows with the way Jeff is always sucking on you, you have reason to be," Ruth teased.

She laughed. "You don't miss havin' somebody suckin' on you?"

"Nope. Not at all."

"So you ain't seein' nobody? Don't they got black men in Colorado?"

Ruth rolled her eyes. "A few."

May couldn't hold it in any longer. From the time Ruth had walked in the door, she'd wanted to blurt it out, but knew that if she had, the woman would've gotten into her rental car and driven all the way back to Colorado and disappeared into those mountains forever. But if May didn't say what she had to say, and say it now, she would bust wide open. So she made her announcement without hesitation.

"Adrian's here."

"Yeah, Bernie told me he was back," Ruth said, cutting up vegetables for the salad.

"No, Ruth." May carefully removed the knife from Ruth's hand and placed it in the sink. "Adrian's . . . here."

It took a few minutes for her statement to register, but when it did, all the oxygen in the room seemed to disappear, and Ruth was afraid she might pass out. She'd dreamed a million times of being in his arms, only to wake up to the truth that somebody else had that privilege. Ruth had been addicted to Adrian Carter like he was a drug. His kisses intoxicated her, his touch invigorated her, and purging him from her system had been like going through detox, to say the least. There were moments when she'd still cry over what she'd had with him and over what she'd lost, but those were moments that would quickly pass. The fact that Adrian was somewhere in that house meant that he was entirely too close to her, and Ruth knew that seeing him again could set her back a lifetime, and she wasn't going back. Fuck Adrian.

Suddenly, she'd lost her appetite and had lost her interest in reminiscing anymore with May. Ruth hurried out of May's kitchen, searching for her purse.

May followed. "Ruth," she called after her. The woman's house was huge and it wouldn't have been hard to hide a six-foot tall gorgeous black man if it was absolutely necessary. But Ruth wasn't looking for one. "Ruth," she said, grabbing hold of her arm. "He jus' wants to talk to you, that's all."

Ruth glared at May, and snatched away from her. "What about what I want, May? Which is not to talk to him."

"Baby, I think this is important. I think you need to hear what he has to say," May pleaded.

"He said everything he needed to say to me before he left, May. He's said all I ever want to hear," she said coldly.

"But—"

Ruth turned and hurried toward the door. *Damn! Was this some kind of conspiracy? First Bernie, now May?* "I'm flying out tomorrow. Tell Jeff I said goodbye. You still coming out next spring?"

"Ruth."

Ruth stopped dead in her tracks. There was no mistaking his voice. It stirred all those damn butterflies hibernating in her stomach and turned her legs into limp noodles. Jeff hurried and took May by the hand, and led her out of the room.

Ruth squeezed her eyes shut, and couldn't bring herself to turn around and face him. She didn't want to see Adrian, or to listen to anything he had to say. She heard him walking toward her. Suddenly, Ruth realized that she could still feel him. She could smell him and, oh God, she still tasted him. He stood close behind her, and Ruth shuddered uncontrollably.

"You look beautiful," he said, tenderly taking her by the arm and turning her to him.

Ruth yanked away. "I . . . have to go, Adrian. I have an early flight tomorrow," she explained nervously.

"Don't go. May's making a dinner Jeff swears is the bomb. Can't you at least stay through dinner?" he asked, nearly pleading.

Ruth shook her head. "I'd rather not." Ruth quickly turned away and hurried to the door. "I'm sorry. Tell May I'm sorry." She hurried out to her car, Adrian not far behind her.

Lord, not this. Not tonight. Ruth just wanted to go home, back to her Colorado home. She missed her mountains and her high altitude, her dry skin, her solitude.

Adrian reached out to her again. "Let's go somewhere where we can talk. I'll buy you a cup of coffee."

Ruth stopped abruptly and stared him square in the eyes. "What is there to talk about, Adrian?"

Her bluntness caught him off guard and Adrian hesitated before answering. Instinct warned him that now wasn't the time to bring up the conversation, but Adrian was desperate.

"Bernie told me what happened. How you doing?"

"That's none of your damn business!" she snapped. "Now, I'd say this conversation was over."

Adrian looked hurt, but as far as Ruth was concerned, that was his problem, not hers.

"I've missed the hell out of you, baby." His eyes glistened with tears, but he quickly blinked them away. "I've fucked up all the way around. Things didn't work out in San Francisco. Shit!" He smiled, nervously. "Turned out that we couldn't stand each other."

"I'm sorry for you, Adrian," Ruth said unemotionally.

"Are you?"

"Yes, Adrian. I know how much you wanted to be there for your child. And I'm sorry that didn't happen. And yes. You did fuck up all the way around." Once again, Ruth was amazed at how easy it was to hurt someone. What was even more amazing was how much she relished doing it.

Adrian gazed off into the distance and then back at her. No one deserved this more than he did. He'd hoped for a miracle, that Ruth would forgive him on the spot and he'd have her back again in his arms before the night was over. But Ruth wasn't giving him his miracle.

"I just wanted to do the right thing, Ruth."

"So what do you want from me?"

"You. Like I've always wanted you. I hurt you and I know that. I wasn't there for you and I know that too. But you can't honestly stand there and tell me you don't still love me, because I know I still love you." Sincerity poured through those words, but that wasn't enough for her anymore. Adrian could see it in her eyes. "It was deep, Ruth. What we had was real deep."

"It was and that's what hurt so much." Ruth felt her own tears pooling in her eyes. "You were my soul mate, Adrian. And when you left, you took a part of my soul with you."

He smiled sadly. "Don't you want it back?"

"I've learned to live without it."

It took every ounce of will power he had not to give in to temptation and scoop her up in his arms. Maybe then she'd soften, he reasoned. Maybe she'd be more willing to listen and to give him just one more chance to prove himself to her. But more than likely, she'd knee him in the groin and call him all sorts of creative names.

"You don't mean that, Ruth. How can you just—"

"Just let us go? How could you?" He didn't answer. Not that she expected him to. These days, Ruth tried not to expect too much of anything from anybody. Life just sort of happened, running its own course, doing its own thing, and expectations always seemed to hinder progress. "Goodbye, Adrian." There was no regret or remorse in her tone, or in her eyes, and all he could do was stand by and watch, brokenhearted, as she climbed into her car and drove away.

Make It All Right

Winter in the rocky mountains was no joke. Ruth had no idea as to what she'd been thinking. Somehow she'd managed to minimize this whole snow thing in her mind, convincing herself that yes, she was a native Coloradan and she could handle snow with the best of them. Right? Absolutely not. Her first winter there had been unusually mild and had tricked her into believing winter was all talk and no action. Ruth had gotten some selective amnesia along the way too, having forgotten what real winters were like back when she was a kid, attributing what little she did remember to the overactive imagination of a child. She'd forgotten how cold it could really get, and how quickly a good set of toes could freeze up if she didn't put on enough socks. She'd taken for granted how much of a necessity a hat, scarf, and gloves were, not to mention hot chocolate, firewood, four-wheel drive and . . . hell! Did anybody make extra-strength moisturizing lotion that worked? Her skin was so ashy that Ruth feared if she rubbed her legs together long enough, she'd start a forest fire.

Her little home didn't have central heat, so she relied heavily on her fireplace, electric heaters, and thousands of pairs of long johns. Ruth decided that she was definitely going to have to rethink the whole little log cabin in the mountains thing. When she'd first moved into the place she'd really given a lot of thought to possibly buying it, or someplace like it, but then again that had been in the month of June. As soon as her lease was up, she was going to find her a nice little place with lots of electrical this, central that, automatic who-sits, washer/dryer hookups, and reliable whatevers. Roughing it just wasn't in her nature.

Her fire was burning down and Ruth cringed at the thought of having to go back outside into that tundra to get some more wood. But what choice did she have? If she wanted to keep the feeling in her fingers and toes, none. She slipped into her boots, scarf, hat, gloves, and set out to brave the elements. Ruth quickly loaded up her wheelbarrow with firewood and rolled it back to the front of the house to unload. While she piled the wood onto the porch, a big black SUV pulled up into her driveway. Ruth stared at the truck straining to make out who was driving, but the windows were tinted and she couldn't see inside. She wasn't expecting anyone and didn't know anybody with a truck like that. Alarm started to set in. She'd survived fourteen years with Eric's ass and she'd be damned if she'd let some mountain man redneck take her out in the Colorado Rockies. Ruth eased her front door open, and readied herself to grab that rifle sitting idle and loaded just inside the doorway. The car opened and out stepped Adrian, looking like a spokesmodel for *Mountain Man* magazine, wearing a big black parka, plaid flannel shirt, way too expensive hiking boots, and a grin a mile wide.

Needless to say, Ruth was shocked, and that was putting it mildly. "What the hell are you doing here, Adrian?"

Damn, she was cute, he thought, staring at Ruth in her red long johns. Her hair was plaited and she looked like a little girl who'd just seen Santa Claus for the first time. Or maybe the boogie man, he thought, as he walked closer.

Adrian walked over to Ruth and kissed her smack dead on the lips. "Came to help you bring in this wood," he said, unloading the firewood, taking it into the cabin, and throwing some logs into the fireplace. He didn't say another word to Ruth until he'd finished. Meanwhile, Ruth was stunned and utterly speechless, standing there in the cold, freezing her booty off, watching him unload the wheelbarrow.

"Baby," he said standing in the doorway of her house. "You'd better get inside. It's freezing out there."

Of course she knew it was freezing out there. Ruth hurried inside and begged the question again. "What are you doing here?"

"We need to talk," Adrian said, taking off his coat and making himself right at home.

"You came all the way out here to talk?"

"Well, you wouldn't talk to me in Jacksonville." He blew breath into his hands, then held them up in front of the fire to help warm them.

"Because I had nothing to say to you in Jacksonville. Like I have nothing to say to you here," Ruth said belligerently.

"But I have things I need to say," Adrian responded calmly.

"You could've called me, Adrian."

"You would have hung up on me, Ruth. Which is why I'm here."

"This is crazy," Ruth muttered, plopping down into the chair. "You came all the way out here to say . . . what exactly?"

Adrian cleared his throat, then stared intently at Ruth who shifted uncomfortably in her seat. She wished he wouldn't look at her like that. It was a well-known fact that Adrian had laser vision that melted her like butter, and she didn't appreciate it one bit. "I was hard on you. Too hard and I'm sorry for that."

"Apology accepted," Ruth said quickly. "Is that it?"

"No." He smiled. "My pops used to say the only woman in the world worth having is the one you dream about when you're sleeping."

The expression on her face asked the question for her. "I don't really get it either." He laughed. "But all I know is that I dream about you all the time."

Ruth didn't give him the benefit of a response, and stared at him blankly, like he was the village idiot.

"Lana and I—"

"Lana?" He'd never told her the woman's name. Ruth felt strange hearing it. Hearing her name made her something else besides "the other woman."

"I wasn't fair to her either, Ruth. I kept looking for you in her and when I realized what I was doing I knew I couldn't live like that. Didn't take her long to realize it either."

Circumstances had bit him in the ass this time and had taught him some hard-earned lessons. Adrian had grown up believing that he'd had all the answers to every question life could possibly ever ask of him, and that any conclusion he'd reached was the only one that mattered. Never mind what anyone else thought, felt, wanted, because they had no fucking idea what they were doing. That had been his attitude with just about everything in his life, from his job, to his relationships, to everything in between. In this case, he'd believed he'd known what was best for all of them—himself, Lana, and Ruth—and Adrian had taken that ball and run with it without giving an ounce of consideration to what anyone else might've wanted. In a nutshell, the fact that he'd been a self-righteous, pompous asshole had been brought to his attention. Not that he'd ever openly admit that revelation to anybody, but it was now clear to him and he knew that that way of thinking had cost him dearly. At this point, it was about salvaging what he could and cutting his losses where he had no choice. This would be his last chance with Ruth. Adrian knew that, and on the drive up he'd prepared himself to dig in deep for the battle sitting there in front of him, wearing red pajamas and plaits in her hair.

"So what am I supposed to do about it, Adrian? Jump back in your arms like it never happened?"

"Sure," he said simply. "That would be cool."

"And impossible."

Adrian knelt down in front of her. "I love you, baby, and I still believe we can, and should, work this out."

Ruth shook her head in disbelief. "That's crazy, Adrian."

"Why is that so crazy?"

"Because I don't want to work this out."

"You don't love me anymore?"

Ruth shook her head. "I don't want to be with you," she said.

Adrian grinned. "So you do still love me?"

"You're—"

"Crazy. Yeah, I know. You already said that," he said playfully.

"How can you think—" Ruth took a deep breath in frustration. *What part of "no, go away" didn't he understand?* "Adrian, you dumped me. You broke my heart. How can you possibly believe I'd want to be with you again?"

"Because I'm admitting I was wrong, baby." Sincerity filled his voice. "I made a mistake. A big mistake at the expense of your feelings. And I love you, Ruth. I've always loved you and I always will."

"Since when is that enough?"

Adrian answered, quietly. "Then tell me what is enough and I'll do it."

"It's not that simple," she argued.

"It's not that hard. Not for me."

Ruth stared at him. "You're willing to do anything for me?"

"Damn right. Just name it."

"It wasn't that long ago when I was willing to do anything for you, Adrian," she said sadly.

"I know."

"Then you also know, it's not enough."

"Ruth—" Disappointment showed on his face, but again, that wasn't her problem.

Sadness filled her eyes. "I honestly don't know what to tell you. There isn't anything I want from you and there's nothing that's going to change the way I feel. Not now. Probably not ever."

"So, you're cool with this? Living by yourself, in the mountains, alone."

"It's not about that. It's about taking care of me, making sure I'm okay. I can't depend on you or anyone else to do that for me. I've got to do it."

"And being with me isn't taking care of you? That doesn't make you happy? I didn't make you happy?"

"For a while, you made me very happy, but I can't depend—"

"On me? Is that what you were about to say?"

"I shouldn't have to depend on you," she reasoned. Ruth realized, gazing into his face, that none of this was about him anymore. It hadn't been for a long time. Adrian was of no consequence in her life, and finally she knew; she accepted that she was indeed, over him.

Adrian sensed his opportunity slipping away from him, and he knew he'd better figure out something fast, or he'd be driving back down that mountain alone. He hadn't come all this way to leave empty-handed. That just wasn't an option. "That's fine. Then don't. But does that mean you have to deny yourself, Ruth?"

"I'm not denying myself. I'm learning to live with myself."

"And you're denying yourself, baby. Don't you see? It's not about having one or the other, Ruth. You don't have to choose between me or you. You can have me and you. All you have to do is take it. Take me."

But then that would mean losing herself in him again, and that was a bigger risk than she was willing to take.

"I'm human, baby. I made a decision and it was wrong. I hurt you and me. But I learned a valuable lesson. It was hard, but I learned that a man needs to go with his gut instinct and mine told me not to let you go," Adrian said, desperate to get through to her. "I opted to go with my head, lost the woman I love and ended up being the kind of father I didn't want to be in the first place. Long distance."

"Those are your consequences Adrian, not mine. If I've learned anything in life, it's that we all have to be held accountable for the decisions we make, good . . . bad—"

"Fine, then hold me accountable, but don't make me liable for the rest of my life," he said. "Would you want to be held liable, Ruth? All I'm trying to get here is a second chance and correct me if I'm wrong but didn't you once say we all deserve second chances?"

Sure, she'd said that. Back when she was blissfully happy, she'd said a whole lot of things in those days. Propaganda mostly. The past was not something she'd ever wanted to go back to. Not even a good past, because it had been left behind for a reason. He stared at her with deep, black eyes and all she could see was sincerity and honesty. Ruth wished he'd never come there.

"I'm not obligated to you for anything, Adrian. I don't owe you a damn thing."

"No, you don't. But you owe yourself."

"You're right. I do and that's all I'm trying to get you to understand. I'm taking care of me. I'm making me happy now."

"Who are you trying to fool, Ruth? You call hiding out up here in the middle of nowhere, taking care of yourself?"

"You don't have to believe me."

"And I don't. You ran away from home, baby. Away from every-body and everything that ever hurt you. Admit it."

"I do, and this is the way I want to live, Adrian. It's my decision to make and I've made it—"

"No—"

"Yes."

Frustration was building up inside him, and Adrian felt himself on the losing end of a battle. "No! You want what you had with me, Ruth. You want to be back in my arms, in my bed, in my life."

"I loved being with you! But you're the one who walked out on me, remember?"

"Hell, yeah, I remember! Every day you're not in my life, I fuckin' remember, Ruth, and that's why I'm here, baby. To fix what's broken for both of us. And don't stand there and try to tell me you're not broken because I know better."

"So?" *Brilliant comeback, girl. You tell him.*

Adrian smiled. "I'm wearing you down."

"No, you're not."

"I took two weeks off from work to come up here."

Ruth folded her arms defensively across her chest. "Well, you can't stay here."

"I'll chop your wood."

"It's chopped."

"I'll fix your plumbing." He winked.

"It's not broken." Ruth rolled her eyes.

Adrian stopped smiling and gazed lovingly into her eyes. "I'll make it up to you."

Ruth wished it could be so simple. She wished that she could forget and forgive and that everything between them could be the way it used to be. But how could it when she'd changed so much?

"It wouldn't work, Adrian," Ruth whispered, then reached out and pressed her palm to his face. Tears filled her eyes, and that was the opportunity he'd been looking for. Adrian pulled her close to him and pressed his lips to hers, filling them with every promise he had yet to make. She hadn't planned on succumbing to him, but instinc-tively she did, and they made slow, languid love in front of the fireplace.

Neither of them spoke when it was over. The sun had long since set for the night, and night filled the room lit only by the light from the fireplace. He was amazed at how quiet it was outside. No traffic or sirens. No wonder she didn't want to leave, he'd surmised. Adrian held her in his arms, and finally asked the question he'd been wanting to ask almost from the moment he first saw her. "Will you marry me?"

Of course he had no idea what he was asking, or even who he was asking. Ruth wasn't the same woman she'd been when they'd first met. She'd grown stronger and more committed to serving her own needs.

"I've changed, Adrian," she confessed quietly.

"I know," he told her.

"I'm not sure you do."

"After everything you've been through, baby, I'd be worried if you hadn't changed."

"You might not think it's for the better."

"Of course it is. It's gotten you through some painful moments and heartache," he said regretfully. "Can't be a bad thing, because it had been necessary. All I know is that you are still a beautiful woman to me, and I love you more now than ever."

Ruth was quiet for a moment. "How can you be so sure? How can I be sure?"

Adrian rolled over on top of her and smiled. "My ass would not have driven ten thousand feet above sea level in the dead of winter for a woman I didn't love. My ass would not get up in the middle of the night to get firewood for a woman I didn't love. My ass would not use up all my vacation time to spend it in the North Pole for a woman I didn't love."

Ruth laughed. He definitely had a point.

"Then I guess, I'm going to have to think about marrying you," she said with tears in her eyes. "But . . . we have to take it slow, Adrian. I want to be careful this time."

"We can take all the time you need, baby. I'll wait."

Discussion Questions for Reading Groups

1. Do you think the issue of spousal abuse is adequately addressed in the African American community? Why or why not?

2. Do you feel that Ruth could have chosen a different, less volatile way of confronting Eric and ending her union with him?

3. Ruth is trying hard to heal and move on with her life. In what ways do each of her friends help or hinder her?

4. Why do you think Eric continually pursues and seeks out Ruth, rather than any of the other women in his life?

5. Do you think it's possible that May will overcome her own insecurities? Why or why not?

6. Before their relationship ended, Ruth had a very idealized view of Adrian. Do you feel her opinion of him changed at the end of the book? If so, how?

7. Do you think Miles is the right man for Bernie? Do you think she deserves him? Why or why not?

8. Who was your favorite character in the book and why?

For more reading group suggestions visit www.stmartins.com

Get a **Griffin**

St. Martin's Griffin

Take a sneak peek at

J. D. Mason's

Upcoming Novel

One Day I Saw a Black King

Perpetual Motion

SEX WASN'T A THING TO BE RUSHED. IT WAS GOOD WITH TERRY Matthews, even missionary, because of the way she moved.

"Mmm . . ." she moaned in his ear. "That's it, John. Right there. Right . . ." He liked the way she wrapped her legs around him. The way she held him, and dug her nails into his back.

"Look at me, Terry," he whispered to her. "Look at me, baby."

She opened her eyes and pulled his face to hers to kiss. John knew she was on the verge of coming. Her tongue wrestled with his and he felt himself ready to explode inside her. The whole room smelled like sex. It was a smell that made his mouth water. A smell he sometimes wished he could put on and wear like a shirt.

"Aww . . . baby!" Terry Matthews raised her hips to meet him. Harder. Faster. "John?" she squealed. "John . . . I . . . I'm comin'! I'm comin', baby!"

He came too.

She wasted no time falling asleep after they'd finished. In the morning, he'd tease her about it like he always did, and she'd laugh then say, "But baby, you've got it goin' on like that." He'd wonder if he really did. Then shrug it off as another insignificant thing in the world. He'd never been the kind of man to beat on his chest and proclaim his dick as the best dick that ever was. It was all-relevant to John, anyway. Good pussy bred good dick in his opinion. Simple as that.

She slept curled up against him, which was cool, sometimes. Other times, he felt crowded and nudged her gently, encouraging her to move over. He wasn't used to having someone sleep up under him like that. At least, not every night. Terry Matthews was the kind of woman who never seemed to get tired of touching. She hugged, kissed, and squeezed on him so much it got on his nerves, and he'd find himself pulling away from her, or pushing her off him, careful not to hurt her feelings, but enough to let her know he needed his space.

Every day she asked how he was feeling and what was on his mind. Fishing. Prying? Trying to find out how long he was planning on staying, because that's something she'd wanted from the beginning. He'd like to stay, but he knew he couldn't. Terry Matthews was a fine woman, with the prettiest hips he'd ever seen. She was accommodating to a fault, desperate to leave him no excuse for being unsatisfied. She wasn't the reason he was leaving, so how could she be the reason he'd stay? If he told her she was too good for him, she'd argue and think he was full of it because he had to admit, that was a lame excuse even if it was true. If he told her he was too good for her, she'd just double up on the good sex, good food, and cater even more to his every whim, bending over backward, or any other way he wanted it, trying to anticipate needs he didn't even know he had.

She needed him and that was the problem. Some men don't need to be needed and he was one of them. He disappointed her all the time and she insisted on believing she was the problem. Whenever he told her otherwise, she'd accuse him of lying. So this was the nature of their relationship. He let her need him, while he'd enjoyed the fruits of her good sex, good food, good catering to all his damn needs, continued to prove himself irresponsible and did whatever the hell he wanted. Then, like clockwork, he'd stop by her apartment every Friday night to spend the weekends making sweet, slow love to her. That was more responsibility than he knew what to do with. But all in all, it hadn't been a bad trade-off.

She rolled over, and laid a warm hand on his chest. "Mmm . . . Can't you sleep, baby?" she purred. Terry Matthews pressed her warm lips against his shoulder and kissed him there.

"Yeah, I'm about to doze off. Night, baby."

He kissed her head, and knew he was going to miss her.

Her own slow, heavy breathing echoed in her ears. She'd been running so long. Too long. How far had she come down this road? The exhausted girl turned briefly, looking behind her. The road had disappeared into blackness. She couldn't see them, but knew that they weren't far behind. She stumbled, but managed to keep from falling. If she fell, she'd be too weak to get back up. The girl struggled to focus on the path ahead of her. It was too dark to see where it led, but she had no choice but to continue running.

The rocks beneath her bare feet were sharp and cut into her soles like pieces of glass, but she kept running. Sweat poured into her eyes and mixed with tears streaming down her face, pooling in the corners of her mouth. She wanted desperately to stop and rest, but the voices behind her were getting closer.

They'd been chasing her for miles. Their voices were closing in on her, laughing and mocking her. "We gon' get you, gal! We comin' after you!" The girl's white dress was torn and dirty. The soft curls that once covered her head and framed her face had become matted and nappy. She was exhausted to the point of collapsing, but she couldn't stop because if she did, they'd catch her. And if they caught her, they'd tear her apart. That's what they always did. Pulled at her, tore at her flesh like she was meat, until she screamed and died . . . then . . . it started over again. It never ended. They never stopped chasing her and she'd run until she couldn't run anymore.

Rocks dug into her knees when she finally fell to the ground. The voices were even closer now. "We comin' for you! We gon' get you, gal!"

"Noooo!" she cried, clutching her hair. "Noooo! I can't do this! He killin' meee! He killin' . . . ."

Her legs felt like lead, too heavy to move even if she could manage to pull herself up on. The girl raised her hands to her face and saw that they were covered in blood. Blood so red it looked black. Dark faces of laughing men snarled down on her. It was too late. They'd caught her—again. "We got you now, gal! We got you now!" they laughed.

"Aaagh!" she screamed in agony and terror. Heat tore through her body and she felt the warmth of blood pooling around her. It was finished. The faces that had loomed above her disappeared, and the girl slowly rose to

her feet. She held the child in her hands. He was black, covered in blood,
screaming like a man would scream. He fought to get away from her,
squirming in her small hands until she could no longer hold him. Moonlight
broke through the darkness and she raised her face to where it shone.
Slowly, the girl's face began to transform and Mattie's face became Agnes's
as she looked up at the dark sky that opened up into blue and screamed,
"I can't do this no more!" Agnes dropped the boy, then raised her arms
towards the sky. "I can't do this no more!" The baby fell, crying, kicking,
anticipating hitting the ground and feeling the razor sharp rocks cutting
into his back, but just before he did, John woke up.

He blinked, wondering if his eyes were opened or closed, looking
for her, scared to death he'd see her. Who? Mattie or Agnes? Eventually, John's eyes adjusted to the darkness and he stared at the ceiling fan whirring above him. Terry Matthews was sleeping soundly
beside him. John sat up on the side of the bed, then rubbed his hand
over his head, which felt like somebody had slammed a sledgehammer into it. The room was cool, but he was covered in sweat and
had to pee.

"You okay, John?" she called from the bed.

John finished using the bathroom, shook off his penis, flushed the
toilet, and then splashed cold water on his face before answering.
"I'm fine. Go back to sleep."

He stared at himself in the mirror, wondering how he'd managed
to lose track of time. Complacency had managed to set in again.
How'd that happen? A decent job, warm home, food on the table,
and a body to curl up next to at night . . . he'd made the mistake of
getting comfortable. Comfort fooled him into thinking it was all
good, when it wasn't. Damn nightmares had a way of reminding him
of that. John's nightmares were like alarm clocks that woke him up
and told him to move on. Nightmares of a woman he hadn't seen
in years pushed him out the door every time he'd made up his mind
to settle down. This was the third one he'd had this month, urging
him to pack up once and for all and forget about Terry Matthews
and Birmingham, Alabama.

He was thirty-seven years old and John couldn't remember what
he'd been running from, or to. He'd forgotten why. All he knew was

that this place, like all the other places, wasn't his place. Moving was his place. Living on the road was his place. Motels were his place. Fast food and sleeping with nameless, faceless women was his place. As tired as he was of living like that, that kind of life held him prisoner.

No sense waking her up to say goodbye. He wasn't down for the drama of all that and dressed quickly, packing his things in a duffel bag quietly enough to keep from waking up Terry Matthews. She'd been patient with him. Sweet. Generous. She'd forgiven him for things she had no idea he'd done, all for the pleasure of his temperamental company. Terry Matthews was lonely and like other lonely women, he'd taken advantage of her too. He opened his wallet and put two hundred dollars on the nightstand. He knew she needed the money. All that she'd been to him and all that she'd done hadn't been enough to exorcise his demons. He peeled her key off his key chain, then slipped out of the house for the last time.

Women like Terry Matthews were better off without men like John. How come they couldn't see that? Because he was fine? That's what they told him. "John, you a fine man." Silly women. Fine on a man could open up some women's doors, and legs, just by flashing some attention in their direction. Being fine was easy. Too easy and was one of those insignificant things in the world that in the end, didn't mean a damn thing. Fine withered like flowers and faded into old age like everything else.

He tossed his bag into the backseat of his old El Dorado, started it up, and put in his favorite CD, which was anything by Marvin Gaye. Before dawn was always the best time to start traveling. Before coffeemakers and televisions came on. Before school buses and rush hour. He never minded driving. That was the only time he felt optimistic about things. Maybe because the road was home. It was where he belonged. Not shacked up with obliging women like Terry Matthews.

He pulled over the shoulder of the on-ramp just before turning onto the highway. "East or west?" he asked out loud, flipping a coin he caught in mid-air. John looked at the coin in his palm. "West." He pulled back onto the road, then headed towards the Rocky

Mountains. He'd never been that far West before, but he'd always planned on making his way out there someday. Today was as good as any. Marvin would be his best friend for the next two thousand or so miles. He turned up the volume, bobbed his head, and sang, "Let's get it on . . . Let's get it on . . ."